DEDICATION

To the DreamWeavers of the World

The Language of Love

by William Blyghton & Lorna Howarth

PANACEA

BOOKS THAT REIMAGINE THE WORLD

Published by Panacea Books, 2022
www.lornahowarth.com

ISBN 978-1-8382866-1-3

With our thanks to Beth Lewis for the book interior and cover design and to Lydia Duncan for the cover illustrations: @candyland_studios_gallery

ACKNOWLEDGEMENTS

With gratitude to our beta-readers:
Pauline Smith, Teri Martin, Ian Hobbs, Robin Swan,
Betty Howarth

CONTENTS

SOMETHING OF HIM REMAINED

Sometimes the memory of the day James died still overwhelmed Sarah and when that happened, she either took refuge in her cottage or she walked through the village and then down a steep lane that ran alongside the churchyard, its high stone banks vividly green with moss and ferns. Then she would cut through the woods and into the valley bordered by a fast-flowing river, eventually joining the well-trodden path that ran parallel to the sea – the sea that had received James's ashes and carried them away.

Sarah was struggling with grief and in the early hours of this particular morning, unable to sleep, she got up, put on her coat and boots and set out to walk in the pre-dawn light. The people of Elmsford were still asleep and only the village cats saw her go. She took her usual route and joined the rugged coastal path, the one that had become a route of pilgrimage for long-distance walkers whom she would occasionally meet, having set off from Minehead in Somerset bound for

Poole Harbour in Dorset, their rucksacks looking heavy and their legs weary.

She walked for half an hour towards the old lighthouse, the arduous terrain all but taking her breath away, and her thoughts too. Then, as she stopped to catch her breath on the brow of a hill, having climbed many wooden steps to reach the summit, the sun cleared the horizon in the east and she turned her face to the light, admiring the way the low rays caught the underbelly of the clouds, dusting them pink. Before she could deflect it, a memory of a similar early morning walk with James flooded her with grief and she began to cry. Being left behind was painful.

A cold wind came off the sea and she decided to make her way home. She had taken a circular route north, which meant she would not have to walk back past James's house. She had not taken the southerly path for almost a year now. Feeling the chill of the wind she quickened her pace, but by the time she reached her cottage she was cold to the bone. She took off her coat and muddy boots and climbed the staircase to her bathroom, where she drew herself a hot bath. Lying there in the steamy water, sponging her tired body and soothing it with lavender bath oil, she tried to wash away the memories of James's death. The hot water felt good, and she closed her eyes so that she could relax more deeply. Gradually her mind began to settle, and she felt she would be able to face the day.

Perhaps, she said to herself, *there will be a day when I can start again.*

She stood up, stepped out of the bath and taking a towel, began to dry herself. Walking into her bedroom, she caught a glimpse of herself in the mirror. She needed a haircut and her eyes were still puffy from her tears. She reached for her mascara, thinking that it might help, but then, as happened most days, she just couldn't see the point in making herself look presentable. There was no-one now who would notice.

She put on her watch, the one James had given to her. It was still only seven o'clock.

As Sarah was clearing away her breakfast dishes, the phone rang. It was Alice, James's beloved housekeeper and Sarah's closest friend.

"I've just been speaking to Julia," she said.

"How was she?"

"Her usual self, very direct. She hadn't exactly called for a chat. Anyway, I thought I should let you know that she and Mark have decided to let James's house. They're going to put it on Airbnb – you know, like B&B but without the breakfast."

Sarah put down the cup she was holding and felt a stiffness in the back of her neck. Only yesterday she'd read an article in a magazine about this new trend for Airbnb, that had apparently begun in the US and was now becoming popular throughout Europe.

"Oh, okay... Thanks for letting me know, Alice."

"Julia said that they're going to advertise it as 'The Sanctuary' because it's in such a peaceful setting."

"Well, it certainly was James's sanctuary," said

Sarah, at once feeling upset. For some time, she had been wondering what James's children would do with his house. She sighed.

"I know it's silly Alice, but I really dislike the idea of anyone else living there, in James's space. You know what a private man he was, and now the place will be open to all and sundry."

"I know," said Alice. "It bothers me a bit, too, but I suppose this Airbnb idea is better than the house being sold, isn't it?"

"You're right. If that happened, I'd feel as if every bit of James was lost forever."

"Me too," said Alice, hesitating before saying what she'd really rung up about. "The thing is, Julia said she wants me to help her manage the visitors and do the cleaning and laundry."

"Does she now?" Sarah had never found James's daughter particularly easy to get on with. She was rather sharp and abrupt. The opposite of her father. "What did you say? You've got a lot on yourself, what with the veg boxes and your gardening work."

Again, Alice hesitated.

"I said I'd do it. I could do with the extra money, to be honest, but the thing is… I don't want to go there on my own. I don't know why, but I can't face it. Will you come with me?"

Sarah was not expecting this, and it startled her.

"I know this is difficult for you," Alice continued, "but it is for me, too. We both loved James so much and we both love his house too, and I know that making it ready for other people will feel very strange, but I do feel I should try and help out – after all, Julia can't come down from Manchester every time someone makes a booking, can she?

"The thing is, I need you to be there with me, Sarah. At least to begin with, until I get used to being in the place without James. I've only been back a few times to check that everything is okay and to fill Willow's food dispenser up – not that she eats much now she mostly lives with you – but it's strange, so quiet and... I don't know, it's as if some part of James is still there. Do you know what I mean? It's as if he's not quite gone."

Sarah knew exactly what she meant though she hadn't mentioned it to anyone, this feeling that James had not entirely left the house, that something of him remained, and yet here was Alice feeling the same way.

"Yes, I do know what you mean, Alice. I feel it too. That's why I haven't been back at all since his funeral… I've avoided the place completely."

"Then maybe it's time we put all that behind us, don't you think? I'm not asking you to do the cleaning or change the beds or anything like that, but could you keep me company, just whilst I find my feet?"

Sarah thought she might say 'no', say it was too difficult for her. But then she thought that James would have wanted her to help Alice out – Alice who had been so kind to James after the death of his wife, all those years ago.

"Okay then," she said. "I'm not sure how this is going to feel, but I'll give it a go."

Alice sighed in relief.

"Thanks Sarah. I really don't think I could do this without you there to help me – just until we all get used to the idea of strangers being in James's house."

"The Sanctuary, you mean."

"Yes. I like the name, don't you?"

There was silence.

"Sarah, are you still there?"

"Yes, yes – sorry… I'm still here. I just had to sit down for a moment. I'm shaking like a leaf."

"Oh no, I hope I haven't upset you?"

"No, you haven't upset me. I just didn't sleep very well last night and I'm having a 'Missing James' day today. I seem to be always on the verge of tears. I feel so… so tender. Ever since James died, I've had to turn my back on his house, on the memories of what happened inside, because it's all so painful. I've had to stop myself imagining what it's like in there, without him. And now it's going to be opened-up, and strangers will be staying in his home…" Sarah began to sob. "I'm sorry Alice, it just hits me hard some days."

"I know, I know. He was such a wonderful man, wasn't he? His loss is hard to bear. But maybe some good will come of this, Sarah? Perhaps it will help us both to come to terms with his passing?"

"Yes, maybe…" Sarah sniffed. "It just all still feels so raw, and now things are beginning to change, so soon."

"I know, but the house has been empty for almost a year," Alice gently reminded her friend. "If it's left any longer, it will begin to deteriorate."

"You're right, I know you're right. I have to take this next step. I can't carry on like this forever…"

As much as she felt uneasy about returning to James's house, Sarah knew deep down that she needed to do it. Her grieving had been long and deep, but of late, she'd noticed something was shifting, and in the days that followed on from Alice's phone call, as Sarah began to come to terms with the house being let, she'd also come to accept that actually for things to change as she knew they needed to, she herself had to change. She couldn't go on in ever decreasing circles of grief and so she had to do something about it.

She'd loved James more than she had loved anyone else, and only wished they'd had longer together. There was never a day when she didn't think of him and some days the pain was unbearable; days when she had to shut herself away and just do her best to get through – until the next day. But slowly it was becoming clearer to her that she wanted to face up to his death, that it was time to accept it. Until recently, she just couldn't comprehend the sheer finality of it, that he was gone, that she would never see him again. Perhaps that was why she'd avoided his house – because she could still hope that he was there, instead of seeing beyond doubt that he was not.

James once told Sarah that his wife had spoken to him after she died, and Sarah had hoped fervently that James would come to her, speak to her, but he hadn't. Now, she knew she had to go to him – she had to go back to his house.

At that moment, James's cat, Willow, walked into the room and jumped up beside her. As with most cats, Willow had several places she called home. She still let herself through the cat-flap into James's house, but more often than not she now lived with Sarah, as if she knew her company was needed.

In less than a month, 'The Sanctuary' was listed on Airbnb, and Alice and her partner Rachel had driven over to Sarah's cottage from the neighbouring village to finalise plans before the first visitors arrived. Alice took her laptop to show Sarah the Airbnb listing. There were beautiful photos of the inside and outside of The Sanctuary, together with pictures of the local beach and the sea view from the garden, and one of what had once been Sarah's shop, taken in sunlight with its striped awning over boxes of fruit and vegetables. Sarah missed the shop.

"It all looks lovely," she sighed "but I don't think James would be very keen on any of this. He never much liked people visiting and now a bunch of strangers will be wandering in and out of his house. I don't think he'll like it very much."

"But then he's not living there anymore," said Rachel, ever the pragmatist, "so perhaps he won't mind at all."

This was typical of Rachel, who was unsentimental to a fault. Alice winced and moved the screen of her laptop back a little.

"I know that's true, Rachel," Sarah wiped a stray tear from her cheek with the back of her hand, "but I still think of him as being there and I still imagine him in his study, or sitting on his bench in the garden..."

"I'm sorry," Rachel smiled and put her hand on Sarah's arm to comfort her. "I didn't mean to upset you, but acceptance of what has happened is a huge part of recovering from grief."

Sarah smiled wanly at this young woman, wondering if she'd ever experienced loss and grief in her short life.

"Well, anyway," said Alice, deftly changing the subject, "the first couple have booked for a fortnight's time, so we need to get things ready."

"I suppose that means sheets and towels?" said Sarah.

"Yes, I'll sort that out, and Julia asked me to leave some basic provisions in the kitchen – tea, coffee, cereals, that sort of thing. Oh, and she wants me to give the house a deep clean and remove what's left of James's clothes. I hate to ask, Sarah but could you give me a hand with that?"

"I'd offer," said Rachel, "but I'm doing double-shifts at the hospital for the next couple of weeks to cover someone's sick leave."

For Sarah, the idea of James's clothes being thrown into black plastic sacks was awful; clothes that he had held her in, clothes she had watched him take off and put on. She took a deep breath, but a sob caught in her throat.

"I hadn't thought about that," she said regaining her composure, "but, yes, I suppose if the house is going to be let, his clothes will have to be removed."

"I'm afraid so. I thought maybe you'd like to have one or two of his things, you know, as keepsakes."

"Yes, perhaps... What day works for you?"

"Next Tuesday morning at, say, ten o'clock?"

"Alright. I'll meet you there."

After Alice and Rachel left, Sarah sat on the sofa and buried her head in her hands, wracked by her memories of James, by the loss of their love. She couldn't stop crying. After a while Willow jumped up beside Sarah, seeming to sense her distress and began to press her face into Sarah's arms, until she noticed the little creature and her sobbing came to an end.

"Poor me," she said, as she stroked Willow's head. "Poor old widowed me." For although they had never married, Sarah felt utterly widowed.

Gradually she began to feel calm, and her courage returned. In her heart she knew that the only way forward was for her to go to James's house and face up to him not being there anymore. Perhaps Tuesday would be the start of something new – the start of the next chapter… though quite how it would take shape, she simply could not imagine.

That evening, instead of walking down the lane as usual, Sarah took a deep breath and walked through the churchyard, and past the old fishermen's cottages until she came to the gates of what was now called The Sanctuary. She hesitated and then, for the first time in many months, she opened the gate and walked into the familiar garden, stopping and sitting for a while on the veranda steps. Then she gathered herself, stood up and turned the handle of the front door, but of course she had no key, and it would not open. Very slowly she let go of the handle and turned away from the house.

"In a few more days, I'll be back in your home, my dearest James," she said. "Will you be there for me?"

The following Tuesday, Sarah walked to James's house. Alice had just arrived and was unlocking the front door. Beside her was a box of cleaning cloths and sprays, and a roll of black plastic sacks. Sarah could feel her heart beating faster. Coming to the house a few days before had been a start, but now, being back in his house, her emotions intensified and the memories she'd worked so hard to dispel came flooding back.

James had not told her that he was ill; not until the day she had demanded to know what was going on. It was the only thing they'd ever had cross words about. For some time, she'd noticed that James had stopped inviting her to stay for supper and he made excuses for not coming over to her house to eat – that he wasn't hungry or that he wanted to meditate. And then he'd suggested that they didn't share a bed anymore, saying that he was struggling to sleep and didn't want to disturb her. But it was more than that, and she knew it. He was losing weight before her eyes and he had no energy, no interest in all that they'd previously shared.

On the day that she confronted him and asked him to be honest with her, her heart was already heavy, but when he told her that he had oesophageal cancer, the shock hit her like a tidal wave.

He'd known for quite some time; known that it was a secondary cancer that had spread from his liver and known that there was nothing that could be done for him – and he had chosen not to tell her. That was the part she couldn't bear.

"Why, James? Why didn't you tell me? I want to care for you, I want to look after you."

James sighed and looked out of his study window, down to the rocky cove in the far distance, a view that had soothed his soul on many occasions.

"I want you to remember me as I was, not as I will become."

"But I love you. Please let me help you."

"No, I don't want you to, Sarah. I don't want you to see me disintegrate."

"That's just so bloody… selfish!" she'd shouted and ran out of his house, slamming the door as hard as she could.

An hour later she walked back to his house, and they comforted each other as best they could.

"Please let me in, James. Please let me be here for you."

He had reluctantly agreed, but it was only a few days later that he took to his bed. Sarah knew it was time to ring his children, Mark and Julia, but neither of them made it from where they were living in time to be by his side.

Sarah had only gone home to put her washing out on the line, and then to collect a few bits and bobs from the village shop. It couldn't have been more than an hour from when he'd smiled up at her from his bed and held her hand a little bit longer than usual.

"I love you, Sarah," he'd said.

"And I love you. Now, shall I get the weekend papers? We can sit and do the crossword together."

"Perfect," he'd said. "Just perfect."

They were the last words he ever spoke to her.

And the thing is, she knew. As she was walking past the row of fishermen's cottages, every cell in her body knew he was leaving. She began to sob.

"I know you can't do it whilst I'm with you, James. I know you need me to leave you so that you can leave me. Go well, my dearest, go well."

When she returned from her errands he had gone, peacefully it seemed, and as was typical of James, with as little fuss as he could muster.

Now, standing at the door of his study again, she was unable to bear the memories of that day, her tears falling like rain. Alice came over and wrapped her arms around this woman she had grown to love.

"Oh Sarah…" she whispered, and the two of them clung to each other and wept until Alice eventually sniffed and wiped her nose on her sleeve. "Come on," she said. "This won't do, let's go and have a cup of tea." They turned away from the study and closed the door.

Sitting at the kitchen table, Sarah was still trembling. She had to hold her cup with both hands to stop the tea from spilling. She took a few sips, feeling the warm liquid running down her throat, soothing her as it always did.

"I feel so emotional," she said, tears welling in her eyes yet again. "This is so hard. But we both loved him, didn't we – and now here we are without him, and I don't know how to live, Alice. I don't know how to live without him. I miss him so much."

For a few moments they just sat at the kitchen table unable to find words of comfort for each other, both women lost in their memories of James; Alice recalling his generosity, always putting an extra ten-pound note in her pay packet, "for your petrol," he'd say – and Sarah remembering the feel of his arms around her, the way he would twist a lock of her hair in his fingers.

"Thank you for coming to help me today," Alice said eventually. "I really needed you to be here with me."

"I haven't done anything, I've just cried."

"Just having you here is enough."

Sarah smiled at her and took her hand.

"Well, I couldn't let you do all of this by yourself," she said. "Come on, let's go and sit on James's bench in the garden. I love the view from there."

They walked together through the beautiful garden that James and Alice had created together – a little overgrown now – and came to his bench, angled to make the most of the view down the sweeping vista of the wooded valley that led to the rocky shore. Although some way from the house, they could hear the crash of the waves and the drag of the pebbles as they were drawn back down the beach by the receding tide.

"Do you remember when we scattered his ashes down there?" Sarah asked.

"Yes, what a day that was."

"I'm never quite sure how you know that the box they give you actually contains the ashes of your beloved, but there it was, with James's name on it. Do you remember?"

"Yes, I do."

"And then, as the family were doing the scattering, a breeze came up from nowhere and blew the dust all over their legs. I'm sure I heard James chuckle."

Alice laughed, and linked arms with Sarah, snuggling into her, needing her familiarity, her warmth.

The two women took comfort in each other.

"And when it was all over, we walked back to this house for tea. A simple ceremony. It felt right; just what James would've wanted."

"Yes..." Sarah returned her hug, "and after everyone left, I stayed behind. All I wanted was to remain close to him. I didn't want to leave him."

For a while they just sat there, but then Alice stood up and stretched.

"I guess we'd better get going," she said. "We've got loads to do."

They walked back to the house and as Alice started to prepare the rooms for the guests, folding luxuriously thick white towels into neat piles on the end of each bed and ensuring the wastepaper bins were empty, Sarah began to collect James's clothes from his dressing room and put them into black sacks ready to go to a charity shop in Bideford. She found one of his woollen cardigans, his favourite one with the slightly frayed cuffs and collar, and she held it to her nose. In the way that only fragrance and music can evoke, a flood of memories assailed her. Memories of laughter, of being held, of being kissed. Memories of love.

"I think I'd like to keep this" she said, showing the cardigan to Alice, who had come in with a feather duster to flick behind the curtains.

"Yes, do," replied Alice.

It was in that moment, Sarah had a sense, dim at first, that something rather wonderful was happening.

"It's odd," she said, "but just now, touching his clothes, I have a sense that James is here. I feel he's with me – with us."

"I hope he is," Alice said, hugging Sarah's shoulders as she returned to the kitchen.

"Hello James… hello my darling." Sarah wrapped her arms about herself, holding his cardigan close. "Are you really here?" She sat on his bed, wanting to hold on to this feeling of being with him for as long as possible. Much to her surprise, for she had long avoided this moment, it felt good to be there. It was as if, sitting there and holding his cardigan close to her, some part of her grief was being taken away. She could hear Alice busy in the kitchen, but the sounds were muted, as if they were a long way away, in another place.

After a while, Alice came back in and sat beside her. She had finished her chores.

"I'm sorry I'm not being of much help," said Sarah, "but most unexpectedly, I think today is helping me."

"And me. It doesn't feel at all gloomy here, does it?"

"No. Quite the opposite. Perhaps the house is ready for new people to enjoy it after all?"

"I'd like to think so, and I'd like to think that James would approve of what we're doing."

"I think he would. He wasn't sentimental like me at all. I've just been remembering some of the things that happened here in those last years of James's life; how content we were. Do you remember? He seemed to have come to terms with life, with who he was, and he softened and began to slow down. A bit, anyway."

"Well, he had you with him, didn't he?"

"We had each other. And perhaps I was able to give him something he needed." Sarah smiled at her friend.

"You loved him. That's what you gave him."

"I did love him. I do love him…"

"I'm about finished here," said Alice. "What about you? Is there anything else that needs to be done?"

"I'll just go and check the study and make sure it's all clear in there."

Sarah walked through the living room and once more came to the study door, hesitating to open it. But then she remembered the smell of the cardigan and her courage returned.

Alice had already stripped James's campaign bed and made it up with cushions so that it now looked more like a sofa. Sarah was pleased as she didn't want strangers to think they could sleep in this room, sleep in his bed.

It was then that she thought she heard his voice, not just felt his presence, but heard him as if he were sitting there, watching her. She felt a sudden excitement.

"I'm glad you're here," the voice said.

She felt sure it was his voice, and her heart began to beat faster.

"I wondered if you would come," she said. "Are you really here?"

But there was no answer. She smiled to herself, comforted by the memory of his voice. In that moment, it was as if he really was with her once more. She let her fingers run over the surface of his desk and over the chair where he would sit and write.

And then she saw on his shelves two books they had shared, *The Gospel of Mary Magdalene* and *The Gospel of Thomas*. James had marked certain places in the books with slips of paper and underlined passages in pencil. The memory of him as he worked with his beloved books felt so good that she took the gospels and put them in her bag and laid the cardigan on top.

Alice called her.

"Are we all done?"

"I guess so," said Sarah and surprised herself by adding, "I could pop in again just before the guests arrive to check everything's okay."

"That would be good. I've got a spare key for you."

She locked the door and handed Sarah a large brass key with a label that said: 'The Sanctuary.'

Although she did not know it then, something inside Sarah had cracked open, and though it was painful, it laid bare a new path for her.

Later that day, after taking a long walk south along the coast path and coming back on the circular route past The Sanctuary, Sarah sat alone in her cottage, feeling for the first time in almost a year that she could relax – really relax. She took the cardigan and the gospels from her bag and put the cardigan on, wrapping it around herself and luxuriating in its softness, in his smell, and then she picked up the gospels, and placing *Thomas* on the table opened *The Gospel of Mary Magdalene.* How good it felt to be turning these pages, just as James and she had done when they had sat together in the evenings, James reading aloud to her. Somehow, she was connected to him once again.

Why did I leave it so long to do this? she asked herself. To her surprise, a voice in her head – or was it in the room? – said, *Trust that the timing is always perfect.*

"James?" she asked aloud. "Is that you?" But as before, there was no reply.

And then she found that on the first page James had written: 'For you, dear Sarah – a reminder of the times we spoke of Love.' And he had signed it, 'Your James' and marked the page with a kiss. He must have known she would one day find it.

Sarah began to read. She'd forgotten how wonderful the gospel was, quite unlike anything she had learnt as a child in school when she had sat through classes of Religious Studies, with endless stories about how sinful everyone was and how 'our Saviour' had died an excruciating death for us upon the cross. Yet here in these pages it was as if Sarah could hear the voice of Jesus himself; as if she were there sitting with his disciples, listening to him.

She was not an especially religious person, not much of a churchgoer, but she had been astonished when James first read these words to her, and now she was astonished again. She read the gospel right through. She especially liked the passage at the beginning:

All that is born,
All that is created
All the elements of Nature
Are interwoven and united with each other.
All that is composed shall be decomposed;
Everything returns to its roots;
Matter returns to the origins of matter.
Those who have ears, let them hear.

'Interwoven and united with each other.' She liked that. And a few lines later, she read the passage where Jesus had said, 'There is no sin.'

She put the book down. How many times had she listened to James talking about this sort of thing? Because she knew so little of religious texts herself, she had been content to let him tell her what he knew. After all, he had read widely, and had studied the writings of scholars who argued endlessly about these things. She also remembered how she'd once told him that he talked about things she didn't understand, and how he'd said that she just understood things in her own way.

Back then, she hadn't really been sure what he meant, but now, sitting in her cottage and reading the gospel again, she knew he was right. It was as if the teachings were familiar to her, as if she had always known of them. And reading them again felt liberating, as if darkness and light had come together and enveloped her, and she felt complete in a way she had not done since James died.

She laughed at the simplicity of it.

But perhaps that's how the truth is? she thought. *When we see it in the light, it is so clear that we laugh at our own struggling in the dark to find it; we laugh at how we have been taken up with all the other things we thought were important.*

As she held the gospel in her hand, she felt something growing in her. What was it? Comfort? Not quite. Strength? Something like that. She felt as if she was starting to become herself again. The painful memories had at last begun to give way to fond memories of James and the love they had shared.

In the silence, she let her thoughts begin to settle, wondering at what was happening to her, enjoying this feeling of release since she had taken her courage in both hands and returned to James's house.

ANGEL

Jeremiah Browne had an angel, whose name was Angel and on this unseasonably damp June morning they were standing at the window of Jeremiah's flat looking down at the street that runs alongside Spitalfields Market. Beneath them they could see men and women hurrying to work, the collars of their raincoats turned up, some hidden under umbrellas. Everyone had somewhere to go, but not Jeremiah. He had no work and nowhere to go and only Angel for company. The dreariness of the day echoed Jeremiah's mood.

Apart from doing some teaching after he'd first left university, Jeremiah only ever had one job. He'd sold Turkish carpets, the very best and most expensive Turkish carpets that money could buy. But a few months ago, Jeremiah's business partner, Stephen Porterhouse, had talked him into selling the business saying that he'd had enough of all the work and responsibility and that he wanted to retire with his wife so they could travel and enjoy life together. Jeremiah hadn't really thought about retirement – it certainly wasn't something he wanted to do – and he didn't have a wife either, but he understood that Stephen needed to stop, and so he'd agreed. Now here he was, with nothing to do, and nowhere else to be.

Standing there, watching London come to life, he was thinking back to how it all began.

Jeremiah never had many friends – he wasn't shy, though he was by nature a private person – but he met his dear friend Stephen when they were both at university. They were studying history at King's College, London. Or rather, Jeremiah was studying history and Stephen was trying to get by with as little actual studying as possible, so he took Jeremiah under his wing, not least because Jeremiah's class notes were detailed and thorough and Stephen did not always get to every lecture, especially the ones first thing in the morning after a party the night before. They could not have been more different, for Stephen was confident and sophisticated, or so he seemed to Jeremiah – after all, he had a car and flat in Pimlico.

Jeremiah smiled to himself as he remembered one particular party that Stephen had insisted that they should go to, though he had not been at all keen. That was where he'd first met Angela and it turned out to be a life-changing event, a moment in time that would bring great pleasure and as much pain.

Angela was the only person Jeremiah had ever spoken to about Angel, but she didn't take him seriously. Full of her own world, and knowing nothing of his, she had assumed he was speaking metaphorically, that he was imagining some kind of guardian angel, and because of that, Jeremiah felt it was better if he said no more about it.

Angel was now reclining on the sofa in Jeremiah's living room, having become rather bored with the scenes unfolding below the window. His beautiful wings could not be seen as they were tucked under his robe, except that is, for the small wings on his ankles. Angel never wore socks or shoes. He had no need to as his ankle wings allowed him to hover above the floor and, being an angel, his feet were never too cold.

Angel had first appeared when Jeremiah was seventeen and he could still remember the day vividly. He had just completed his mock A-level exam in History and was pleased with himself, because he had been able to select questions that reflected the topics he'd revised. He could hardly believe his luck, except, of course, it wasn't luck, because Jeremiah was always well prepared. As he put his pens back in his leather school satchel, together with the books he needed to revise for his English exam two days later, he was pretty sure he had done well. What a relief. He put on his school blazer and set off home, walking along the pavements of uneventful Ilford in suburban East London.

But all that was about to change.

When he opened the front door of his parents' semi-detached house in Duncan Way and walked into the hallway, he thought no-one was home; everything was silent. But then he heard the sound of someone crying. He walked into the front room to find his mother and two people he didn't recognise. His mother was holding a handkerchief to her face. He came close and between her sobs she whispered to him that his father had died.

Jeremiah dropped his satchel and sat beside his mother, not sure what to do. He couldn't bear to see her cry so he took her hands and held them, hoping that it would feel reassuring. He had never seen her cry before. His family weren't like that. Like their neighbours and their neighbours' neighbours in Duncan Way in 1957, they were not inclined to show their feelings.

His mother, whose name was Lucy, worked in the office of a local Building Society and it turned out that the two people Jeremiah didn't know were the manager of the Building Society and his secretary.

"This is Mr. Jenkins," said his mother, wiping her eyes, "and this is Sheila. They have been very kind."

"We're so sorry…" said Mr. Jenkins.

"I'll make some tea," said Sheila.

After they left, Jeremiah and his mother sat quietly together, not really knowing what to say to one another.

For some weeks Joshua Browne had been in hospital, gradually becoming weaker as the cancer in his lungs held fast and day by day took away his life, until in the last couple of days, he could hardly breathe at all. When pneumonia eventually set in, Joshua was too weak to fight it.

Lucy was at work when her manager discreetly took her to one side to tell her that the hospital had phoned and that her husband had died, and now she and Jeremiah were to go to the hospital to view his body and arrange for him to be taken away by the local undertaker. Lucy's sister and her husband were on their way in their car to take them both to the hospital. Lucy had never learned to drive.

Jeremiah was an only child and at the cremation he sat in the front row beside his mother. His aunt and uncle and their children were on the bench behind. Much to Jeremiah's surprise, as they sat there waiting for the service to begin, his uncle leant forward and patted his shoulder in a gesture of comfort. Jeremiah didn't turn around. He knew that if he did his uncle would feel embarrassed.

Sitting there, not listening to the Methodist minister his mother had chosen to take the service, Jeremiah tried to think kindly of his father; tried to bring him back to life in his memory – but the only thing that came to him was that his father, who had been a heavy smoker and only 57 when he died, suffered from chronic headaches. He had this vision of his father lying on the sofa of their sitting room, his head propped up with cushions, the curtains drawn to keep out the light. But he hadn't died of headaches.

Jeremiah wanted to remember something else, but he couldn't. He wanted to think well of his father, but he couldn't. Then he remembered how much his father hated his work. He had been a clerk in an insurance company and although he often said he was going to, "do something about it," he never did. Perhaps he couldn't. Jeremiah wished fervently that this strange numbness he felt in his heart would go away.

As the organ music began to play and his father's coffin passed through the curtained hole in the wall, Jeremiah took his mother's hand and stood up. As he did so, he saw an angel standing in front of him, smiling and with outstretched wings. Jeremiah let go of his mother's hand and collapsed onto the floor.

Jeremiah could vaguely remember being bundled into his uncle's car and then sometime later he awoke and found himself lying fully clothed on his bed at home, a glass of water on his bedside table. He reached across and took a sip. Downstairs he could hear voices. Then there was a knock on the door. It was his mother. She came in and sat beside him on the bed.

"How are you feeling, love?"

"Fine, thank you Mum. What happened?"

"You fainted. I think the chapel was a bit stuffy."

And then he remembered what he had seen in the chapel and was about to ask his mother about the angel but thought better of it.

"Shall I bring you a cup of tea?"

"Yes, thanks Mum. Sorry about this."

"That's okay, it gives me an excuse to escape from downstairs." And she winked at him, touched his arm in a comforting sort of way and went to get his tea.

Jeremiah got up from his bed and went to the bathroom for a pee. When he came back, he undressed and put on his pyjamas. Then, as he turned around, the angel he'd seen in the chapel was standing there, looking at him. Hesitantly, Jeremiah pulled back the covers and got into bed. He felt his head swirl and closed his eyes, but when he opened them again, the angel was still there. Jeremiah looked away, but curiosity got the better of him. He turned towards the resplendent being in his bedroom who was smiling at him, and who was not in the least bit scary.

Jeremiah looked more closely. The beautiful wings he'd seen before seemed no longer to be there, though he was aware that the angel, who was not obviously a man nor a woman was levitating slightly off the ground.

"I know what you're thinking," said the angel, "but it's up to you. Do you want me to be a man or a woman, or shall I be neither?"

Jeremiah sat bolt upright, and for a moment he did not know what to say. He was having great difficulty with the very idea of speaking to an angel let alone having to decide whether it was male or female.

"I… I'm not sure," he said.

"Well, for the moment I'll be neither," said the angel. "You can always change your mind later, if you want to. You can just call me Angel."

And with that, the door opened, and Jeremiah's mother walked in with a mug of tea and a slice of fruit cake. Angel had disappeared from view.

"Oh, good," she said, "you're ready for bed. Drink some of your tea – it will make you feel better."

Jeremiah took the tea and the cake, unable to stop his hands from trembling.

"Thank you, Mum."

"Are you alright, love?" she asked, touching his arm in that reassuring way of hers. "You look a bit pale."

Trying to shake off the image of the angel, Jeremiah looked at his mother and smiled.

"Yes, I'm fine. We'll be okay, Mum," he said.

She took his hand and squeezed it and then left him to rest while she said goodbye to her family and friends and then cleared away the plates and cups, taking some consolation from the quietness that had settled upon the house.

Later, there was another knock on Jeremiah's door.

"Come in."

"I thought I'd just pop in and say goodnight, love. What a day it's been."

"Yes, what a day," said Jeremiah, although his mother could not have known quite what a day it had been for him.

"Get some sleep, now," she said. "We'll take it easy for a day or two."

"Okay, Mum," he said. "See you in the morning."

She closed Jeremiah's door and went to her own room, where she sat for a while on her bed, crying quietly. She didn't want Jeremiah to hear her.

Jeremiah picked up the book he was studying, but he could not concentrate, and as he closed it and put it down on his bedside table, he saw the angel again.

This time, Jeremiah felt able to talk.

"You're back then?"

"I'm always here," replied Angel. "It's just that sometimes you don't see me. It's you, not me, who calls forth my appearance."

Jeremiah watched, mesmerised, as Angel sat on the end of his bed. "What do you mean, 'always'?"

"Ever since you were born."

"But I've never seen you before."

"That is true, but perhaps you have never needed me

before now?" Angel's wings rustled and then settled.

"This is really weird."

"Don't worry, you'll get used to it."

Jeremiah suddenly realised how tired he was.

"I really have to sleep now," he said. "It's been a difficult day. Perhaps I'll see you in the morning?"

"Perhaps you will."

As Jeremiah closed his eyes, a cloud of light, white and yellow and gold, gathered Angel in.

Back in Spitalfields, Jeremiah shook himself out of his reverie and turned to the angel who had been living with him for all these years, the angel who had become his confidant and his bedrock, and who was, in Jeremiah's eyes, most definitely a male angel.

"Do you remember how awful my last years at school were?"

"Yes, of course," said Angel. "What makes you ask?"

"I'm just reminiscing. I have so much time to do that now I'm retired," replied Jeremiah as he walked into his kitchen to make tea and toast.

Carrying his plate and mug back into the living room, he chose an armchair opposite Angel.

"I don't think I could have got through it all without you."

Jeremiah had always felt like he didn't fit in and it was a feeling he'd carried with him all his life. Although in those last years at school he had friends, both boys and girls, he discovered that he wasn't quite like them and this became a problem to him. The other boys were always talking about sex, boasting about what they'd done with their girlfriends, or at least what they were going to do. And although Jeremiah sometimes thought that talking about it seemed more important than actually doing it, he also knew that even if only half of what they said was true, it was a world that was utterly unfamiliar to him. He liked the company of his friends, he liked going with them to the cinema or the local café, but that was it. He just didn't feel what his friends were telling him they felt. He wasn't aroused in the ways they said they were, he didn't feel 'sexy' in the ways they said they did. Not at all. And when they boasted about their experiences, it left Jeremiah feeling that there must be something wrong with him.

He didn't so much feel that he was missing out on something the others were doing, he felt that something was actually missing in him. And he had no-one he could talk to about it. Certainly not his friends, who he knew would just think he was weird and certainly not his mother – and for some reason in those early years, not Angel either.

So, as the months and years passed by, being with Angel had become more and more important to him. And the best thing about this was that there seemed to be no price to be paid for his friendship and support. It was unconditional. Jeremiah didn't have to be smart or good and he certainly didn't have to go and sit in church, begging for his sins to be forgiven, in order to see Angel. No, Angel was always just there. When Jeremiah was hunched up in his room studying for his exams, Angel would quietly sit there with him, keeping him company.

Sensing what Jeremiah wanted or needed, Angel mostly appeared in brown robes – that Jeremiah thought made him look rather monk-like – with his wings tucked away. At these times he seemed solid and of this world. But sometimes, when he appeared with his wings opened wide in a shimmering white gown, Angel was beautiful, ethereal and clearly not of this world at all. Whenever Jeremiah looked for Angel, Angel was there beside him. He was no longer surprised by any of this, but he never spoke to anyone about it.

Just before Jeremiah sat his A-level exams and was at home, sitting up in bed, revising, Angel, appeared and asked Jeremiah if he was okay.

"You seem very serious," he said, "always studying, not going out much."

"I suppose so," said Jeremiah. "Does it matter?"

"Not really," said Angel. "Some of my angel friends are very serious, too. They tend to hover quite a lot and sing religious songs. I'm not like that at all. I like to get to know people. I like it when they share their lives with me. Most of all I like it when they are in love, so I'm hoping you'll fall in love someday."

"Love?" Jeremiah put down his book and turned to Angel. "Why would you be interested in love?"

"We've never really talked about this, have we?"

"About what?" Jeremiah sensed and didn't much like the direction the conversation was taking.

"About love, and, more especially, about your own feelings. Don't look so surprised. I know how you feel, or rather, don't feel. I know all there is to know about you. But you have never talked to me about it."

Jeremiah was in a quandary. This was the very thing that he kept most hidden, that he felt he could never talk about or share with anyone. But now it appeared that Angel knew all about it anyway.

"It's a bit scary to think that you know everything about me."

Angel smiled. "I need to know, otherwise how can I take care of you? I want to help you to be who you are."

"Thank you, Angel."

"So, tell me," said Angel, unfurling his wings which Jeremiah noticed he tended to do when speaking of things he deemed important, "who do you think you are?"

Jeremiah hesitated before replying, not at all certain how to respond to this question.

"Well, I'm not really sure," he said, wondering whether speaking about this at all was such a good idea. "I appear to be something of an oddity… I just don't seem to have the same feelings towards girls as other boys do. I'm not… oh, what's the word? I'm not turned-on by all that stuff my friends show me in magazines. I don't feel anything, Angel. And I have no interest in the constant stories they tell me about their sexual exploits. It just doesn't interest me and to be honest, I think they make most of it up to look cool."

"That makes you different, but not odd."

"Well, I feel odd. When my friends talk about being in love, it seems to me that what they really mean is having sex."

Angel laughed. "Yes," he said, "people often mistake one for the other, especially teenagers."

"I just don't get it," said Jeremiah.

"There is something rather absurd about all that

fumbling and gasping isn't there," laughed Angel.

Jeremiah laughed too. "I'm glad you agree. I just don't seem to fit in to their world."

"Well," said Angel, sitting on the bed and folding back his wings, "angels are especially important to people who don't fit in. We think of them as family."

"But I want to fit in, Angel. I want to be normal."

"You fit in to other worlds, with other people Jeremiah. You fit in with the angelic realm. After all, how many people these days believe in angels, let alone see their angels? Hardly anyone. So that makes you special, but not odd. And in some ways, you're quite like us because we don't do sex either. Ecstasy, wonderment, rapture, yes, but not orgasm, and certainly not fumbling and gasping."

Jeremiah laughed again and then he stretched and yawned. He was pleased that he could share his feelings with Angel. It felt good, and he was comforted by what Angel said.

"I've never thought of myself as being special," he said, "but I still don't understand this – you and me. Can other people see you?"

"It depends. There are people who only see their own angel, but some people can see their own angel and someone else's angel. And a very few people see angels everywhere. It's all about belief."

"Well, I think I'll just stick with seeing you. That's enough for now."

"In a way," said Angel, "this is true of every part of your life. You only see what you believe is there, what you've been told is there. You were lucky to have parents who never told you not to believe in angels."

"Actually, they never talked about such things one way or the other," said Jeremiah.

"Exactly, and that has worked well for you. And perhaps other people who can see angels choose not to talk about it, in case people think they are odd too?"

"Well that's possible I suppose. I never have."

"There you are then. Think about how many other people there might be out there who aren't talking about their angels either."

"Perhaps one day I will meet someone who can see you."

"Almost certainly."

But now Jeremiah felt sleep coming upon him.

"I'm going to sleep now," he said, and he pulled his bedcover up to his chin, switched off his bedside light, turned onto his side and closed his eyes.

Within moments he fell into a dream.

He found himself in the most beautiful countryside. It was early morning and he was walking through pastures and woodland that ran down to the bank of a river, which sparkled with sunlight and swirled over large round stones. From the reeds at the edge of the river a beautiful moorhen swam out, a red mark on its beak with a yellow tip, its dark eye set in even darker blue-black plumage. Jeremiah sat on the bank and felt the warmth of the sun on his face. Then, as if from nowhere, on the other side of the bank, a host of angels gathered together as a choir and sang most beautifully.

When he woke the next morning Jeremiah felt… what was it? Peaceful? Yes, that was it, he felt peaceful. And Angel was standing at the end of his bed in full angelic form, wings spread wide, a light shining all about him.

"I hope you liked the singing," said Angel.

"How do you know about it?"

"I was there. I thought it was wonderful."

"You were in my dreams?"

"Of course."

"Oh…" Jeremiah was not at all sure he wanted Angel to be part of his dreamworld too. "Well, I certainly feel peaceful this morning."

"That's good. Remember that feeling – you may need to rediscover it sometime. And you should know that angels see no difference between dream time and waking time. It's all one time to us, just different realms of being."

That was all a long while ago and yet here was Angel, still sitting beside him.

"Do you remember the day the letter came from King's College?"

"I do. You were very excited."

"And do you remember what my mother said when I told her?"

"Yes, she asked you where King's College was and when you said it was in London, she said, 'Good, that means you can stay here and live with me'."

Jeremiah smiled at the memory.

"I think she knew that I was about to leave the nest, and after father died she needed me more than I needed her."

"But that wasn't to be."

"No, it wasn't to be."

Jeremiah took his empty mug and plate back into the kitchen and washed them up, and Angel disappeared from view.

MAKING ROOM FOR OTHERS

Summer came to Elmsford, and something was shifting for Sarah. Life in the village was much the same as it always had been and she continued her long meanders along the coast path, but now she often walked home past The Sanctuary, feeling a connection with it that was no longer painful. Sometimes, when there were no visitors, she would open the gate and sit on the veranda as if she were waiting for James, or she would go into the house just to see if she could catch that essence of him that somehow still remained.

She was keeping in touch.

July and August brought more Airbnb visitors, and Willow and Sarah watched them come and go.

"You know, Willow," said Sarah, as she placed a bowl of dry cat food on her kitchen floor, "I don't really mind the visitors that come to James's house. When it was empty it felt as if the house had died too. Now at least life has returned, and I think James would be pleased that those who come to stay seem to love the house – they always say so in the Visitors' Book. He knew people needed peace and quiet and if they find it in his house, in his sanctuary, then that's a good thing, isn't it?"

The cat did not reply.

Whenever Sarah went to the house, she talked to James. The conversations were rather one-sided, but Sarah enjoyed them.

Talking to James was part of who she was becoming.

Once a week on a Friday morning Sarah caught the bus from Elmsford to a little village about three miles away where Rachel and Alice rented a tiny and rather damp old cottage. A year ago, Alice had taken the leasehold on a market garden that had fallen into disrepair on the edge of a large country estate which owned many farms and cottages in the vicinity, and since then she had worked her fingers to the bone, bringing the garden back into productivity. For the last few months, in fact not long after James passed away, Sarah had joined her for a day a week, helping with whatever needed doing.

Sarah absolutely loved her Fridays at the market garden with Alice. It was wonderful to be with her beloved friend, but more than that, she enjoyed the feel of the sun on her skin as she turned the compost heaps, or waded through the rows of broad beans, bending to find the ripe pods and smelling the sweet aroma of the last few flowers that were yet to be pollinated.

Alice had started a veg-box scheme and had about 25 customers who came to the garden gate on a Friday afternoon to collect their vegetables and grumble about how difficult their week had been. Between them Sarah and Alice filled each box with whatever was in season, sometimes adding a bunch of sweet williams or some extra strawberries to cheer their customers up. On this particular early September morning, as the corn on the cob was ripening, and the onions were drying in the sunshine, Sarah and Alice were deep in conversation as they weighed out the potatoes and placed them in brown paper bags in each of the boxes.

"Is it getting any easier, going to The Sanctuary?" Alice asked, as she expertly twisted the corners of the paper bags so the potatoes couldn't escape.

"By degrees, yes, it is. I still talk to James, as if he can hear me and sometimes I think I hear his voice, but it is only the wind in the trees or the flutter of birds' wings. But I don't feel quite so… devastated. And funnily enough, that's down to Julia and Mark deciding to Airbnb the house. You know how hurt I was by their decision, but now I realise that it was just the next step for them, and because of it, I was able to take the next step too. Does that make sense?"

"It does. I know it's been tough for you. I felt awful that day when Rachel said that James wasn't there anymore – I could feel how hard that hit you. We had a bit of a row about it, actually."

"Did you?"

"Well, Rachel can sometimes be a bit insensitive, don't you think? She doesn't mean to be, but she's just so damn logical. She doesn't really have an empathy mode. She's very supportive and she's very kind, but she doesn't do 'feelings' so well. I often think she's in the perfect job, because if she did do feelings, she'd get too involved with her patients and would be unable to help them in the ways she does."

"But how does Rachel not doing feelings affect you? It must be hard if you're emotional about something and can't share it."

"I just share it anyway. But Rachel focuses on the practical resolution – she thinks tears and tantrums are a total waste of energy. Actually, a few years ago, we split-up for about six months because of this. I moved from Tavistock where we lived at the time and found a little winter-let in Elmsford. That's when I met James."

"Yes, of course. I remember when you moved into Rose Cottage up on Old Cuddy Lane and you helped James design and plant his garden – you transformed it. You caused a bit of a stir in the village, you know."

"Really? Why's that then?"

"Well, I remember Felicity coming into the shop and asking me if I knew who the woman in pink wellies and shorts with her nose pierced was."

"Well, I suppose Felicity would be a bit shocked by that."

Sarah now lived next door to Felicity and her sister Linda and on the whole, they were good, if sometimes disapproving neighbours.

"So how did you resolve this dilemma then?"

"Well… I suppose because we'd hit rock bottom, we had to either sort it out once and for all or call it a day. But we knew that we loved each other, that wasn't in doubt, and when I was able to work out that it was her emotional distance that affected me, she opened up a bit and was able to tell me why she reacted that way."

"And why was that, if you don't mind me asking?"

"Well… it's very deeply rooted, but I'm sure Rachel won't mind me sharing this with you. She was the youngest child of four and her brothers and sister were a lot older than her and left home quite early. So, she was the only child left at home and her father who was a vet worked long hours, and was often absent in her life. Rachel told me that her mum would work herself into a state of heightened anxiety at the merest thing: if her husband didn't come home when he said he would, or if the dog had escaped – you know, normal family stuff. Her mother would get hysterical and start blaming and accusing Rachel or her father, and Rachel became very withdrawn and anxious herself.

"But one day, in a flash of awareness, Rachel realised that her mother was using these emotional outbursts to control her husband and daughter. That actually, she could cope perfectly well but chose not to; that she was – now, what did Rachel call it…? – she was acting like a 'damsel in distress' because she always wanted to be rescued. In the rescuing, her mother found the emotional connection and the control that she craved."

"Wow, that's so interesting…"

"Yes. I think Rachel's psychology degree helped her work that one out. So anyway, she vowed to herself that she would never be swayed by the emotions of another. Instead, she would always try to find a solution to whatever was causing the emotional outburst. She became so good at it that she even approached our relationship the same way."

"But you're still together, so you must've been able to come to a compromise?"

Alice went into the shed and brought out a basket of the early apples from the ancient, espaliered trees on the south-facing wall of the garden.

"Taste this!" and she tossed an apple to Sarah, who only just caught it. "Yes, we found a way through. Once Rachel explained all this to me, I gradually became less focused on her lack of emotional response and more aware of her amazing ability to be calm in a crisis, which, believe me is an incredible skill. And over the years, she has really opened up to my need for affection and affirmation – so together, slowly but surely, we've found a middle way. We'll have been together for ten years, all told, at Christmas. Isn't that amazing?"

"It's wonderful. I do so admire the two of you. Do you think it's because you're both women that you were able to work it out like that? I know if I ever approached my husband about my feelings, he would shut down immediately and refuse to speak to me, sometimes for days at a time. In the end, I learned to keep my feelings to myself."

"I know how hard that is."

"Yes, and I think it affected our son, Nicholas. He was such a lovely little boy, but as he got older, he became quite withdrawn and I think he was constantly striving to 'be a man' in his father's eyes. I always felt his dad was hard on him, but I was accused of being too soft. I wish I'd done things differently, but I didn't..."

"My mum once said to me that guilt is the default setting for parents. Guilt that they should have done things differently or paid more attention to their children or been a better role model, but my mum was 19 when she had me and still growing up herself. In a way, we grew up together. And no, to answer your question, I don't think a gay relationship is any easier than a straight one to be honest, Sarah. It can all get a bit messy."

The two women laughed and then spontaneously hugged each other.

"Oh, I do love coming here," said Sarah. "I love being with you."

"Fridays are my favourite day of the week," said Alice, returning to counting out the apples, "because I know you're coming."

On a beautifully sunny early autumn morning a few weeks later, Alice called by to see Sarah on her way to one of her gardening jobs in the village. She wanted to let her know that Julia had rung to say that her son Tom and his girlfriend Katharine were going to stay at The Sanctuary for the weekend. They were planning to arrive at about four o'clock on Friday afternoon.

"I remember Tom so well, from when he came to visit James," said Sarah, "but Katharine I only met fleetingly. It will be good to see them both again."

"The thing is, Rachel and I have plans to meet friends in Exeter on Friday," Alice said, "and I just wondered if you could welcome them instead of me?"

Of course, Sarah said yes.

Tom and Katharine arrived as planned and Sarah was at The Sanctuary to let them in and help them to get settled. Unexpectedly, Tom hugged Sarah and thanked her for welcoming them, and just the feel of his arms around her brought memories of his grandfather flooding back. They were so alike; they had the same lithe build, the same jawline, and interestingly the same smell, an almost imperceptible sweet musk that could've just been their choice of aftershave. Nonetheless, it evoked memories of James in a way that was visceral, unsettling.

Without waiting to unpack, Tom asked Katharine to walk with him to his grandfather's bench at the bottom of the garden to see the view and get a breath of fresh air.

"Would you like a cup of tea?" Sarah asked.

"Oh, yes please. We're a bit parched after the long journey. Thank you. We won't be long."

They returned before the kettle had time to boil, Tom looking forlorn, agitated. He sat down in what had always been his grandfather's armchair, stretching out his long legs and holding on to the arms as if for support. Katharine came and sat on the floor beside him.

"It's so strange being here without Grandpa. I thought it would be alright, but it feels empty, and his garden is missing him. He was my mentor you know," said Tom.

And he was my lover, thought Sarah to herself, but she didn't say it aloud. She wasn't sure if Tom and Katharine knew about their relationship. It wasn't that she and James had hidden their love for each other, it was just that when Tom visited, their discussions had always been about other things: his university studies or later on, his scientific research. Tom worked for a company that designed instruments for detecting levels of atmospheric and marine pollution. He had recently been promoted and had a responsible job for one so young, heading up a team of scientists. But it was also true that James and Sarah had felt that their lovemaking was an intensely private affair. That's how they liked it to be. Their secret. Of course, Alice and Rachel knew, but no-one else really.

Or so Sarah thought.

Tom was still talking about his grandfather.

"Grandpa was the one who encouraged me in everything. Unlike my parents, he approved of me being a scientist – I don't think mum and dad thought science was a proper job. I wish I could talk to him now. I wish I could tell him about my work…"

Tom's grief was palpable.

"He would have loved that, Tom," smiled Sarah. "He was so proud of you. Look, why don't you put your bags in the bedroom, and I'll bring your tea through to the veranda. I seem to remember that you both like it black?"

"That would be lovely. Thank you," said Katharine.

While the two of them began to settle in, Sarah put two cups of tea and a plate of sandwiches she had cut for them on a tray and took it through to the veranda, placing it on a low table between the wicker chairs.

When they came back, Tom was wearing a pair of his grandfather's Kilim slippers. "I found these," he said, "and I know they're meant for me."

Just seeing him wearing them made Sarah smile. "Well, they really suit you," she said. "Where did you find them?"

"They were beside the bed in the dressing room."

"What? Well, that's very strange," Sarah replied, clearly surprised, "because Alice and I cleared out all your Grandpa's belongings from the house quite some time ago – or at least we thought we did..."

"Or maybe Grandpa hid these especially for me?"

"Perhaps he did," Sarah smiled. "Perhaps your grandfather wanted you to find them."

Sarah was about to leave but Katharine asked her to join them for a cup of tea.

"That's kind of you, but I don't want to intrude on your holiday – I'm sure you'd rather be alone."

"Please do stay," said Tom. "You're my connection to Grandpa now."

"Bless you both and thank you Tom – that means so much to me." She went back to the kitchen to get herself a cup.

"Come and sit between us," said Katharine, moving the chairs.

Sarah was touched by Katharine's kindness. *So, this is who she is*, Sarah thought to herself. *The one who makes room for others.*

The three of them sat together on the veranda and Tom and Katharine told Sarah about their lives and their work. As they talked, Sarah observed them. In the year or so since she had last seen them, they both seemed to have changed, at least from how she remembered them. Tom was tall and raggedly handsome and had his hair cut short at the sides but left longer on top. He had a stubbly beard and was wearing ripped jeans and a thick blue woollen jumper. Katharine was also tall, with long wavy auburn hair and she was wearing a flowing skirt in blues and greens down to her ankles and a cream woollen cardigan, and much to Sarah's delight, she was barefooted.

As a girl, Sarah had never liked having to wear shoes all the time but there had been no question about it – she had to. Her mother always wanted her to be what she called, 'presentable'.

Well, it's never too late, thought Sarah and as Tom and Katharine spoke, so earnest and serious, she undid the buckles on her summer sandals and slipped them off, her feet resting on the rattan rug that adorned the bare wooden floorboards of the veranda.

Katharine was talking about education and how she was about to go back to university to do a part-time PGCE so she could become a secondary school teacher. She already had a job teaching English to overseas students via Skype which she really enjoyed and though it was only a dozen or so hours a week, it helped to pay the bills, and through it, she'd realised how much she enjoyed teaching. So, she had applied to a number of colleges one of which was in Truro, across the border in Cornwall.

"Well, Truro is a lovely place to be," said Sarah, "and it's not so very far from here so perhaps you could come and stay sometimes? The two of you."

"But won't there be guests here?" Katharine asked.

"Well, if there are," said Sarah, without really thinking about what she was saying, "you can always stay with me." She wasn't sure what had made her say that – perhaps it was their mutual love of James – but more than that, there was something about Katharine that made her feel protective, motherly, almost. Perhaps it was her bare feet.

Katharine looked at her for a moment and smiled. "That's so kind of you, Sarah. Thank you. We'd like that," she said, and she pulled Tom close to her. "That's if I get the place in Truro and if I can get Tom to come and see me. He's so busy all the time."

"Me?" he tugged her hair playfully. "You're always the one who can't ever come to the pub because you've got to do your lesson planning."

They laughed and hugged and Sarah was touched by their obvious love for one another. Willow appeared and came and sat beside Sarah, and when she left for home, the cat followed her.

Sarah didn't see Tom and Katharine for the rest of the weekend, intuitively aware that their time together was precious, a snatched moment. But in the beautiful golden light of late summer where everything shimmered and the burnished leaves slowly drifted from the trees, Sarah busied herself in her garden. She was aware of the timelessness she always felt as the wheel of the year turned, and the tendrils of autumn took hold. It was a time when she often felt overwhelmed with nostalgia. Was it the quality of the light, or perhaps the smell of the plants as they set seed and their stems dried to a husk, or the plaintive call of the robin as he cheep-cheeped in the hedge that wove a tapestry of memories connecting her right back to her childhood?

As she gently worked through her borders weeding

out the odd wildflower but leaving most of them in place, for in truth she loved wildflowers best of all, Sarah was lost in reminiscence.

She was laying under the apple tree in the back garden of her parents' house, a red brick mid-terrace on the outskirts of Exeter, with a long and unkempt back garden full of weeds and butterflies. She had drifted away as she watched the swallows and house martins darting in the sky above her, her mind for a moment as carefree as the birds. And then something tugged her back down to earth. It was her mother standing over her, hands on hips, blocking out the sun.

"What are you doing, Sarah Louise? I've been calling you for ten minutes."

"Oh, sorry Mum, I was just…"

"You're a daydreamer, that's your trouble, and lazy with it. Now get up and come and peel the potatoes for dinner. Your father will be home soon, and you know what he's like if his food is late to the table."

Sarah tried to picture her parents' faces – she couldn't, but she could hear their voices as plain as day, and more often than not, those voices were scolding, grumbling. Sarah wondered if her parents had been happy. She thought not.

On Sunday, Tom and Katharine called in to see Sarah before they left for home, to give her the brass key for The Sanctuary. To her delight, both of them gave her a big hug. Sarah didn't realise how much she had missed being hugged.

"It was so good to be back in Grandpa's house, even if it was a bit strange at first," said Tom.

"You must miss him too, Sarah?" Katharine held Sarah's eyes in her gaze.

"I do, very much."

By the way she looked at her, Sarah realised that Katharine knew she and James had been lovers. And when Katharine hugged her, it felt as if she too needed to be comforted. There was an intensity to her, almost a longing.

Then, as they got into their car Katharine, who was driving, opened the window, as if she'd just remembered something important.

"It's been lovely being here and especially reconnecting with you, Sarah. I'd like to take you up on your offer to come again at some point."

"Well, that would be lovely," said Sarah, and she meant it.

Sarah watched their car disappear up the street and out of the village, and as she did so, she wrapped her arms about herself, mirroring the hugs she'd just been given. Then she picked up the key to James's house and walked down the street and took the shortcut through the churchyard. She took off her sandals and enjoyed the feel of the warm, short-mown grass under her feet.

At The Sanctuary she found everything had been left clean and tidy. They had washed up all the dishes and cutlery, puffed the cushions on the armchairs and stripped the bed in the guest room, folding the linen ready to be laundered. Alice would pick it up later.

Then Sarah found a sunny spot on the veranda and sat for a while just sharing her day with James.

"Your grandson is like you in so many ways," she said. "He's passionate and intense, and before he's finished telling me whatever it is he's telling me, he's already deep in thought about something else. I have to concentrate to keep up with him. Just like I did with you. And he misses you, you know. So that's something he and I share."

Sarah pulled back a lock of hair from her forehead and tucked it behind her ear as Willow appeared from the side of the house and came and sat beside her.

"I'm just talking to James," said Sarah.

Willow said nothing.

She stroked the cat's head and after a while she walked home, carrying her sandals and followed by Willow.

Sarah wondered if Tom and Katharine would come and stay again. She hoped so.

ANGELA

As summer drifted away and the days began to shorten, Jeremiah felt somewhat imprisoned in his flat, and so he started to take long walks, whatever the weather, to break his boredom – for that is how he often felt now he had no work: bored. He walked, sometimes for hours on end, and he found it did help to lift his spirits. He walked south towards Whitechapel and then cut through the streets past Aldgate and then to Tower Bridge. All his life he had been drawn to the river – he loved to be near water – and it struck him on his walks that London had a certain beauty to it as the trees began to take on their autumnal hues.

Jeremiah often found himself lost in thought as he walked, and this morning was no different. He was recalling how he had gone to King's College and found it unexpectedly liberating. He was able to focus entirely on his chosen subject, Medieval History. Religious conflict and the power of the church fascinated him. He was serious about his studies and he worked hard. In the evenings, he would take the tube back to Ilford, walk home from the station, have supper with his mother and then go to his room and work, writing up his notes and reading additional texts.

The History Department loved him. It was not all that common to find a student with this kind of dedication, and they asked him to join the College's History Society, which was an honour, as membership was only by invitation. Although Jeremiah enjoyed the meetings of the Society, he continued to keep himself to himself, never joining the others in the pub afterwards, but always making his solitary way home.

Angel remained his constant friend and mentor, sometimes adding bits of theology to the stories of kings and emperors. Often the two of them would sit in Jeremiah's bedroom in the evening, his mother watching her television programmes downstairs – Dixon of Dock Green and, of course, This is Your Life and Twenty Questions. This was 1960 and, literally in black and white, there was still a certainty about what was good and what was bad.

Jeremiah loved his studies, but he was still finding that he didn't fit in with the lives of other students, many of whom seemed to live from one party to the next, drinking more than he could imagine and certainly having sex. Or that's what the men said, boasting nervously in the college bar; 'nervously' because this was a time before the contraceptive pill became widely available, when both young men and women were fearful of the girl becoming pregnant, dreading those tense days before her next period came, or didn't. And so, it seemed that 'having sex' was often little more than the fondling of breasts or hands caressing otherwise secret parts.

But even this was not something that Jeremiah wanted, and again he wondered why. He wasn't homosexual – he knew that – and although he suspected that one or two of his male friends were, this was not something that men admitted to in the early 1960s; and he had certainly never met a woman who was a lesbian, or at least, not one who said she was.

Working hard was an escape for Jeremiah. Sitting alone with Angel in his bedroom, none of these questions troubled him, or only occasionally. And, for a while at least, it seemed that life in Duncan Way would remain the same forever. But change is inevitable, and it came to Jeremiah sooner than he expected.

As Jeremiah unlocked the door to his flat, he could hear the phone ringing in the living room. It was Stephen.

"I was just wondering how you're doing in your retirement?" he chuckled. "My guess is you're stressed."

"Well, more bored, I'd say," said Jeremiah. "Actually, I was just thinking about you and our time together at university. You must have picked up on my thoughts."

"Well, all I can say is thank God for all your notes, otherwise I'd never have got through," and they both laughed. "Do you remember that first party you came to with me, when you met Jenny and Angela? You were so reluctant to go, but I knew Angela would take care of you. By the way, Jenny sends her love and wants you to come over for supper."

The party had been at Jenny and Angela's shared flat, close to where Stephen lived. They were both at the Chelsea Art School, where Jenny was studying Graphic Design and Angela was studying History of Art. Like Jeremiah, Angela took her studies seriously.

Jeremiah had dreaded going to the party, but much to his surprise it turned out to be a great success. There was a lot of drinking and the rooms were full of cigarette smoke, but although the flat was small, he found a quiet corner where he was able to relax and observe. He was soon joined by Angela, who asked him who he was and what he was doing. When he explained he was studying Medieval History, she seemed genuinely interested.

"That's so fascinating," she said. "I'm studying History of Art, and I'm particularly interested in the paintings and sculpture of the Middle Ages. Have you ever been to Florence?"

"No," said Jeremiah. "Have you?"

"Yes, I have, and you should definitely go. And Venice too – you should go to Venice."

"Tell me what you've seen there," said Jeremiah.

He couldn't have said anything more likely to endear Angela to him. Most people she talked to, especially most of the young men who were studying Physics or Law, seemed to think that being interested in the art of the Middle Ages was a 'girl thing'. And it was evidently something they had no interest in hearing about. But here was Jeremiah, tall and tousled-haired, who wanted to know what she had seen.

That evening, Jeremiah and Angela just talked and talked about what they loved – history and art – and although Stephen came by a couple of times to top up their glasses and to make sure Jeremiah was okay, it was clear that he was. Both he and Stephen stayed to the very end and helped Jenny and Angela clear away the bottles and glasses. When Stephen told him he was going to stay the night with Jenny, Jeremiah wasn't sure what to do. He didn't want to walk all the way from Pimlico to Ilford.

"I think it's too late for me to get home," he said.

"Well, this sofa's quite comfortable," said Angela, puffing up the cushions and bringing him a blanket.

When he woke in the morning, Jeremiah saw Stephen appear from what was evidently Jenny's bedroom, yawning, stretching and scratching his head. It was just after ten o'clock.

"I guess we'd better be off," he said.

As they drove along the embankment of the Thames, Stephen asked Jeremiah what his plans were for the Easter weekend. Jeremiah replied that he had nothing planned, although he did want to complete an essay that had to be handed in after the Easter break.

"Okay," said Stephen, "put the essay on hold and come to Aldermaston with me."

"Why Aldermaston?"

Stephen sighed.

"Sometimes, Jeremiah," he said, I wonder whether you and I are living in the same universe. Aldermaston is the home of the Atomic Weapons Establishment, and this Easter weekend is when the Campaign for Nuclear Disarmament – you know, CND – carry out their protest march from Aldermaston to London. We, my friend, are going to join the march. Have you got a sleeping bag?"

"Yes, I've got one somewhere."

"Well, dig it out. And pack a rucksack with some warm clothes and food. We'll take the train to Aldermaston on Thursday evening and then we'll join the march on Friday morning. You'll love it. Lots of people chanting 'Ban the Bomb, Ban the Bomb!' You may not be able to speak for a week afterwards. Jenny's going to be there, too, and so is Angela."

Although he did not know it at the time, Jeremiah's life was about to change. For Stephen was going to become his closest friend, and his life would be forever entangled with him, and with Jenny and Angela.

"Are you still there, Jerry?" From the beginning of their friendship, Stephen had made it clear that the name Jeremiah, was a bit too biblical for him, hence 'Jerry', which at first, Jeremiah tolerated, but later came to rather like. He liked the intimacy of it, the fact that at first, only Stephen used that name.

Jeremiah shook his head as if to clear his mind.

"Sorry," he said, "I was remembering that CND march we went on?"

"Well, from what I can recall, you only came because I said Angela would be there."

"Happy days," said Jeremiah, remembering the nights he spent cuddled up with Angela in the rooms and village halls provided by supporters of the CND march. "And do you remember all those people in duffle coats? I think I've still got mine somewhere. I've even got the copy of Jack Kerouac's *On the Road,* that one of those hippy-looking guys gave me. I remember he said I could have it, 'as a gesture of brotherhood and disregard for bourgeoise possessions.'"

"He's probably a stock-broker now, with a huge mortgage and school fees."

"Yes," said Jeremiah, "but there was something special about it for me. I don't know whether you remember, but it was after the march that I left home and came to live in your flat."

"Yes, of course, the beginning of your downfall."

"It was the beginning of my life, Stephen. You, Jenny and Angela – you rescued me from Ilford."

"That's all well and good, mate, but what are you going to do with your life now? Jenny and I want to go back to Turkey. Our old friend Ahmet has passed his business to his nephews, but he's still in touch with the carpet makers that we used to buy from – or rather, with their sons and daughters. We'd like to go and see them all again. And then Jenny has plans for us to go into Afghanistan. Are you sure you wouldn't like to come with us?"

Jeremiah could not think of anything he would like to do less.

"As you can imagine," he said, "I do not want to go with you. Not at all."

"I thought you'd say that, but Jenny wanted me to ask you. Well, anyway, come to supper on Saturday. Jen has promised to make your favourite vegetable lasagne, and I shall open several bottles of red wine."

"Sounds perfect. I'll be there."

When Stephen rang off, Angel appeared.

"He's been a good friend to you."

"More than that," said Jeremiah. "Without Stephen I would probably still be teaching bored teenagers who hated school. God, I detested that job, but when I graduated it was all I could think of doing. Back then, a degree in History didn't seem to open any other doors, and unlike Stephen, I had no sense of adventure."

"But when he came up with his business idea, you were brave enough to throw in your job and join him."

"I was quite unable to refuse him. And I was so innocent in those days. I would never have thought of starting a business myself, but I trusted Stephen completely, recklessly really, and I just loved the energy and colour he brought into my life."

Suddenly Jeremiah wished that Angela was there with him. He remembered how much she had encouraged him in the early years of the business. And he recalled how much he had loved her.

In those first few months of getting to know each other, Jeremiah could not believe that this wonderful young woman could love him. And they had loved each other – in their own way.

At first, Jeremiah had thought that the flat Angela lived in belonged to Jenny, but he soon discovered that it was the other way around. The flat was Angela's and Jenny shared it with her in just the same way that he shared Stephen's flat. Apparently, Angela's father was wealthy and she was his adored daughter, his only child.

Anyway, one evening, the two of them were in Angela's flat, tucked up together on the sofa eating baked beans on toast.

"Do you mind coming over here?" asked Angela. "Is it a nuisance for you to keep having to leave Stephen's flat so he and Jen can be alone?

"Not at all, I love it here. It's quiet, and you know how much I like being with you."

"Don't you ever wonder why Stephen and Jenny want to be alone?"

Jeremiah hesitated. "Not really. I know they like to listen to music, and I guess they know I can't work when they do that."

Angela chuckled.

"Are you really that innocent?"

"What do you mean?"

"Well, do you really think that's all they're doing?"

"I guess not," he said.

"Well…?"

Jeremiah felt his anxiety rising. He had known that this conversation would have to happen, even if he hoped it wouldn't. He stood up and went into the kitchen to get a glass of water. When he came back, Angela had moved to sit in one of the armchairs, facing him, her legs tucked beneath her.

"I do know what you mean," said Jeremiah.

"Then tell me about it," said Angela. "There's nothing to be afraid of."

Jeremiah sat on the sofa opposite Angela, holding his head in his hands. Then he sat back and began to speak, softly, as if someone else might hear.

"I know you must think it's odd that I haven't tried to, you know, be with you sexually," he said. "I don't know how else to say that, but I guess that's what you want to know about?"

"Sort of," said Angela.

"Well… you must know I'm very fond of you, and I have never felt so much at ease with a woman before. You're the best, Angela."

"But – there's a 'but' isn't there?" Angela's, voice was gentle, as if she wanted him to know that he could share his confidence with her.

Jeremiah drank from his glass of water. It gave him time to consider what he wanted to say next. And then he sighed and said it.

"You see, for as long as I can remember, I have never felt aroused, sexually aroused. I know it sounds impossible, but it's true. It just doesn't seem to happen to me. And so far, you seem to have accepted it, which has been great for me."

He looked into Angela's wide blue eyes.

"But perhaps it's not so great for you?"

Angela came over and cuddled up to him, resting her head on his shoulder.

"It's not what I had expected you to say," she said, "but I had begun to wonder. And it's okay. Actually, it's fine. I've always felt safe with you, and perhaps that's partly because you've always been as you are – I mean, well, you want nothing more from me. And now that you have told me why, I can understand it. Well, a bit. It doesn't stop us being close, does it? I love having you as my friend. We share so much, and that's worth a lot."

If Jeremiah had not been so relieved to have shared his story with Angela, he might have wondered more about what it was that she was really saying. But he didn't. Not then.

They sat there for a while, and Jeremiah put his arm

around Angela, hoping she wouldn't push him aside. And she didn't.

"Has it always been like this?" she asked.

"For as long as I can remember."

"And do you know why?"

"No, I don't. I suppose I may have been born like it, or maybe something that was meant to happen to me just hasn't. I don't know."

"Poor you."

"Well, I guess poor me, but it doesn't seem quite so important now that I've met you."

"You know, for a while, I wondered if you were in love with Stephen." Angela picked at the sleeve of her sweater. "Sorry, I shouldn't have said that."

"No, it's okay," said Jeremiah. "I suppose, in a way, I do love him. After all, who wouldn't? And he is my best friend, a true friend. I think I just admire him, and I certainly like being with him. But I don't feel for him the way I feel for you. I think what I feel for you is much closer to love."

That night, Angela and Jeremiah slept together, holding each other close. They talked until after midnight, for the first time saying all the things they felt for each other. Jeremiah had 'confessed' to Angela and she had received his confession with a kind and loving heart. In the end they had agreed that even if they were not going to be lovers, they would always remain friends.

ENTANGLED LIVES

Katharine phoned Sarah. She had received notification from the University of Cornwall's Truro College offering her a place on their teacher training course starting in October. She had accepted and had caught a train down to Truro and found a flat to rent on the first floor of an Edwardian house near the college, overlooking the often-muddy creek of the Truro River which eventually ran out to the sea at Falmouth. Katharine was elated, and somewhat to Sarah's surprise, she wanted to tell her all about it.

"You won't believe how lovely the flat is," she said, and told Sarah about her landlady who lived upstairs, about the sash windows with wooden blinds, the bare floorboards covered with rugs and the river views. She was breathless and giddy with excitement.

"It sounds lovely," said Sarah. "Please send me a photo. I've learnt how to open them on my new phone, you know."

"Good for you. Okay then, I will. This place is just right for me, Sarah."

A pause. A pregnant one.

"And for Tom?" Sarah asked.

"Well, of course he's really pleased for me and says he'll come to stay when he can, but it now looks as if it won't be that often."

"Oh... Why's that?"

"It's his work, Sarah. He's got such a lot on."

Sarah thought she heard a sadness in Katharine's voice, and she felt a pang of tenderness.

"Are you okay Katharine?"

"Yes, I'm fine." She hesitated momentarily. "Sarah, you know I said I would like to come to Elmsford again, and you said I could always stay with you?"

"Yes, I remember."

"Well, I was just wondering whether I could come and visit you this weekend?"

This was unexpected, but Sarah didn't have to think about it.

"Yes, of course you can," she said.

"Thank you. I'll be on my own though. Tom's going to a conference in Glasgow. Is that still okay?"

"Yes, absolutely. It'll be lovely," said Sarah. She had sensed a hesitancy in Katharine's voice, as if she felt uneasy about asking for something for herself. Sarah recognised this. That was how she had been as a young woman, too. She knew what that felt like and she knew that Katharine needed to be welcomed and comforted. "I have a very nice spare room," she said, "and Willow and I could do with some company."

Sarah put down the phone and turned to the cat who was washing her face with her paw.

"Good news," she said, stroking the cat's ear affectionately. "Katharine's coming to stay with us this weekend. I want her to feel at home here, so you must be nice to her, okay?"

Willow took no notice.

Katharine arrived late on Friday afternoon, her small and rather battered car noticeable as it came along the village street for being bright yellow. She parked outside the cottage and Sarah welcomed her in.

Katharine hugged Sarah. "It's so good to see you."

"It's good to see you too. Let me show you your room, then you can unpack and settle in."

She led Katharine up the stairs, and Willow, who had been sitting in the living room, followed them. Sarah's spare room was small, but it had a double bed a wardrobe, and a chest of drawers beside the bed with a lamp made from driftwood on it. The bed was covered with a patchwork quilt that Sarah had bought years ago from Par Market and had always loved. And there was a window looking down onto Sarah's pretty garden at the rear of the cottage where Katharine could see the bird feeders, an apple tree, a whirly washing line and a garden bench.

"There's a towel here on the chair," said Sarah, "and the bathroom is next door. You settle in and I'll make some tea. Take your time."

"Okay, thanks Sarah. This is a lovely room."

Sarah heard Katharine opening draws and moving around in the room upstairs, and then there was silence.

Maybe she had lain down on the bed? The mattress was soft, really soft, and it was very comfortable and inviting. Sarah noticed that the cat had stayed upstairs with Katharine. She smiled to herself. *So, you were listening to me.*

When Katharine and Willow came downstairs, Sarah had prepared a tray of tea, with her best teapot and most colourful mugs, and a plate of buttered banana bread. She put the tray down on the low table between the sofa and the armchairs. Katharine chose the sofa.

"I'm glad you like your tea black," said Sarah. "I do, too. Before I met Tom's grandfather, I hadn't tried it, but that was the way he drank his tea and I got to like it. So now I always have it black. Like my clothes," she added.

They smiled at each other.

"You look lovely in black," said Katharine, "especially with your red toenails."

Sarah had now got into the habit of not wearing her shoes whenever possible and had painted her nails as an extra mark of defiance against her rather puritanical childhood. She had now built up quite a collection of nail varnishes.

She poured a mug of tea and Katharine took it in her hands, warming herself.

"So, how are you getting on in Truro?"

"Well, it's really early days, but I'm loving it so far – you could come and visit me one weekend, if you have time. We're quite a small group on the course, which I like, and we come from varied backgrounds. There are twelve of us, all in our early twenties, both male and female, which gives a good balance to the group. And the course lecturers I've met so far have been excellent and all of them have experience of working in big comprehensives, so what they're teaching us is totally based in the reality of school life."

Katharine took a sip of her tea and ate her slice of banana bread with obvious relish.

"It's good to be here, though," she said, and once again Sarah sensed her hesitancy, as if she wasn't quite sure it really was okay for her to be there.

"Well, it's good for me to have someone here to look after."

"Apart from Willow."

"Yes, apart from Willow. And I'd love to come and see you in Truro some time – it's been years since I visited, and the cathedral is wonderful."

The two women began to relax, Katharine settling back into the cushions and tucking her legs up under her, looking around the room as if she wanted to take it all in, make it part of her.

They talked for a while, Sarah asking more questions about Katharine's life in Truro, and Katharine wanting to know how Sarah was feeling, what was happening in the village, what sort of people were renting James's old house, and whether Julia or her brother had been in touch, which they hadn't.

"Do you fancy a short walk before the light goes?" asked Sarah, gathering up the tea things and taking them into the kitchen. "We can wander down to Kingfisher Bridge and then have supper when we get back. I've made a vegetable lasagne, so all we have to do is heat it up. Does that sound okay?"

"That's absolutely lovely – I adore veggie lasagne."

Sarah and Katharine put on coats and boots and walked along the village street, turning down the steep lane that was beginning to darken as dusk fell. Bats darted overhead, and they heard the call of an owl in the distance.

"Do you know, I've just realised something," said Sarah. "I do most of my walking at dawn or dusk. It's not a conscious decision, but it seems to be when I most feel the need to walk. I do love the quality of the light though, and how white flowers seem almost luminous – look at this meadowsweet." Sarah caressed the blossom of a tall cream-coloured plant with a reddish stem, and Katherine could smell its faint honeyed scent.

"Oh yes… I've never noticed that before."

They came to an ancient bridge spanning a shallow river strewn with large rocks, that flowed along the valley to the sea, dubbed 'Kingfisher Bridge' by Sarah because she saw one there so often. They stopped to lean over the parapet and gaze into the water below.

Without thinking, Sarah had brought Katharine to a place that was filled with memories of her beloved James; a place they once came to regularly, where they would linger and take in the incredible views along the watermeadows towards the sea, the valley flanked either side with sessile oak and beech woodland, alive with the song of blackbirds, thrushes and wrens, and the thrum of woodpeckers – and always the distant sound of the sea as it turned on the pebbled beach in the far distance. At that moment, Sarah felt the pain of her loss sharply, and it caught her off-guard. She took a handkerchief from her pocket and wiped her eyes, not sure if Katharine had noticed this touch of sadness.

"What's that bobbing up and down?" Katharine whispered, pointing upstream.

Sarah had to crane her neck to see the little bird in the semi-darkness. "It's a dipper. There's a pair of them who patrol this part of the river. They feed on insects underwater and they often chase the kingfisher away if he's trying to fish from one of the overhead branches. I love to watch them."

"A dipper… I've not seen one before. I suppose I'm a bit of a towny really. But I do love the countryside. I want to learn all about it. You can teach me, Sarah."

Sarah wandered to the other side of the bridge to look at what was happening upstream, and Katharine followed. It was so peaceful, just the sounds of the wildlife settling down for the night and the soft trickling of water over stones.

"Do you believe in fate?" Katharine asked, speaking softly. "I mean that things happen for a reason?"

"I don't know… I think I do," said Sarah. "Why do you ask?"

"Well, I wasn't going to come to stay at The Sanctuary with Tom. I was feeling a bit low, actually. I hadn't heard from any of the courses I'd applied to, and my best friend had just moved to Italy and I was missing her. But Tom was desperate for a break from work, so in the end, I decided to come with him and then… I don't know. When I saw you again, you felt so familiar to me – you were so warm and friendly that I felt like… Oh, I don't know, it sounds a bit silly, but I felt like I'd come home. And I felt it again today, in your house – like I'd been there before. Does that sound weird?"

"No, not at all," said Sarah. "I'm glad you felt that way."

"Maybe I was your daughter in a past life?" Katharine nudged Sarah's arm playfully.

"Well, I've always wanted a daughter!" The words had come to Sarah without a thought, but as she said them, she felt as if her heart opened up a little. It was a physical sensation, connected to grief, perhaps an easing of it, which Sarah welcomed.

Katharine pushed her hands deep into the pockets of her coat.

"I miss home. My mother and father divorced a few years ago, and afterwards I… I kind of lost touch with them. I had no idea they were going to break up and so it was a shock for me, and then within a year, my father had remarried. Since then, he's been completely taken up with his new life and we have hardly spoken. It's like he doesn't really have time for me anymore, or that's how it feels, anyway."

"Goodness. That must have been hard for you."

"It was… it still is. It was the same year I went to university, and once I'd gone, my mother decided to move to Aberdeen to live with her cousin, so I don't even have a family home to return to now, you know, for Christmas or holidays. That feels so strange. I feel uprooted somehow. It's ironic really, because my family home wasn't all that happy, but at least I had one.

"And although me and Mum occasionally speak on the phone, I feel this distance growing between us. And it's not just because she lives so far away, but it's like she's never got anything to say to me. I don't know, maybe I'm being oversensitive…?"

As this story of Katharine's family unravelled, Sarah thought back to the time when her own son, Nicholas, had insisted on leaving school at sixteen so that he could go to work at the same brewery where Alan, his father, worked. She had wanted Nick to have the advantages she'd not had; to go on to take his A-levels and apply for university. But neither he nor his father would have any of it. Alan had said that if it was good enough for him it was good enough for his son; "Make a man of him," he'd said. Nick seemed totally in awe of his father, and always wanted his approval, so much so that he was prepared to model his own life on his father's values. And now she wondered why she hadn't put up more of a fight, but she hadn't. Both her husband and son were determined that he would leave school and start work straightaway. And so inevitably, that's what happened.

"Have you spoken to your mother about how you feel?" Sarah asked.

"That's the thing," Katharine sighed. "I can't find a way to broach the subject. She's like a closed book, one I can't open. She doesn't want to talk about the marriage breakdown, or the fact that me and Dad have lost touch."

Katharine frowned and picked at the moss on the stony parapet.

"Actually, looking back," she said, "I think my mother has always found it a bit difficult to show me affection. I've sometimes wondered if she loves me at all… I think the difficulties between her and my dad made her withdraw into herself and put up barriers, you know? She always seems so wrapped up in herself; she doesn't really want to know what's going on for me. But there's something else..."

She hesitated again, and Sarah's heart went out to this vulnerable young woman who had been all-but abandoned by her parents.

"Resentment," Katharine said. "Yes, that's it. I think my mother resented me going off to university. She married my father when she was very young, and she's had no life of her own to speak of. I think she felt trapped in her marriage and trapped being a mother, and she became jealous of my freedom."

"I felt the opposite," Sarah said. "When my son was sixteen, he left school and started work. I wanted him to go to college, to have fun and be free. I wanted him to have the opportunities I didn't – but that was not what he wanted. Like his father, he wanted certainty, security and a wage packet. He didn't even want to leave home."

"Well, he no doubt had a lovely home," Katharine smiled at Sarah, "but I couldn't wait to leave, and when I left, I didn't want to go back again, not at first, anyway. I loved my freedom. And, of course, I met Tom at university, and we had a great group of friends. Our lives became entangled, and we didn't seem to need anyone else."

As Katharine said this, she turned away from Sarah, as if she was not quite sure what she meant. In that moment, Sarah caught a glimpse of something missing.

"And do you still feel the same?" she asked. "That you don't need anyone else?"

"Not really... Not now. At the time, it felt like Tom and my friends were enough, that they were my new family. For a while it seemed that they would always be there for me when I needed someone to turn to. But then we all left university and went our separate ways, and now I know that life's a lot more complicated than that."

"Perhaps your parents just picked up on the fact that you were relishing your new-found freedom at University? Perhaps they didn't want to worry you with their problems?"

"Maybe at first," Katharine sighed, "but it's been years now, Sarah, and they've never once invited me to stay with them, and they rarely ring me. I always have to be the one to make the effort to connect. It hurts, it really hurts..." Katharine began to cry, and Sarah instinctively embraced her and held her until her tears subsided, giving her a clean tissue from the packet she always kept in her pocket.

"That's tough, Katharine. I really feel for you, but all I can say is, us parents get it wrong all the time. I'm not defending your mum and dad's behaviour, but parents are not infallible. Mostly, we make it up as we go along, whilst struggling to understand our own feelings." Sarah was thinking of her rather strained relationship with her own son. She had often wondered why things were no longer easy with him.

Katharine sighed deeply. She looked at Sarah. "You're right – perhaps I just need to chill out about it all. It's not like we were a close family anyway, so perhaps it's natural that we've all gone our separate ways. Maybe I just have to accept that and make a new family. With Tom. And with you."

Sarah wasn't expecting that last comment. Again,

she was caught off-guard, but hadn't she just said she'd always wanted a daughter?

"Sometimes things just work themselves out without you having to do too much, Katharine. Your parents may be grieving the loss of their marriage in their own ways, and believe me, grief takes as long as it takes."

Katharine blew her nose. "Oh, Sarah, it feels so good talking about this with you."

Sarah reached for Katharine's hand and gave her a reassuring squeeze. "I find that talking about things always helps. It's as if, in uttering the words, you begin to have a new understanding of the situation. That's what happens when I go over and help Alice in her market garden on Fridays. We just pick the vegetables, and we talk. And eventually, we begin to make sense of things. Anyway, we should turn back before it gets too dark and put that lasagne in the oven."

Although she couldn't be sure, Sarah sensed that being comforted was a rare experience for Katharine, and that she appreciated it.

For good measure, Sarah said, "I'm happy to be someone you can talk to, Katharine. Any time."

"Thanks Sarah. That means a lot to me. It's just what I need."

"Me too," said Sarah. "Me too."

"Really?" Katharine raised her eyebrow, quizzically.

"Yes, really. I've been immersed in grief for long enough. It's good to speak of other things."

Sarah's response was genuine. Although she had felt Katharine's need for comfort, she also recognised that need in herself, and she did find it comforting to have another human being around, another person milling about in her cottage. James had been the one who comforted her in times of need, and after his death, there had been no-one apart from Alice who she could share her feelings with. Sarah had been taken aback by the depth of her own loneliness, the overwhelming emptiness of her grief. But now she was coming to see that it was all a necessary process and that perhaps grief had simply opened her heart?

And yet, she also wondered whether something difficult was unfolding between Katharine and Tom, and whether Katharine was unable to say what she was really frightened of. Sarah thought she'd wait until Katharine felt ready to tell her about it.

They walked through the woods and back uphill, in the field that ran parallel to James's house. A skylark was suspended in the air above, singing its heart out despite the deepening gloam, an unusual sound so late in the year and one that gladdened Sarah's heart.

There were visitors staying at The Sanctuary; the lights were on and the sound of conversation and jazz music drifted out of an open window.

Later that evening, when Sarah was getting undressed and ready for bed, she caught a glimpse of herself in her bathroom mirror. Who was this person staring back at her? She saw a mature woman in her late-sixties, grey showing in her golden hair, and laughter lines around her eyes. How did she get so old? Sometimes Sarah didn't recognise herself.

When Katharine woke at half past eight the next day, the sun was casting its golden rays across the garden. It really was a beautiful autumnal morning. Sarah, who was already downstairs, heard her pulling back the curtains. She appeared in the kitchen wearing a cardigan over her long nightdress.

"Good morning," said Sarah. "How did you sleep?"

"Well, it took me a while to drift off, but that bed is so comfy it was hard to get out of it just now."

"Help yourself to breakfast – there's muesli and yogurt and some late raspberries from the garden. And tea and toast."

"Wonderful. A feast!"

Sarah brought the teapot to the table and they sat together as the low sun shone into the cottage. Katharine pulled her cardigan round her body, seemingly deep in thought.

"Tom rang me last night," she said.

"How is he?"

"He's good, but..." and Sarah knew that Katharine was about to share what had been troubling her since the day she first came to The Sanctuary. "Well, a little while ago, Tom was assigned to a new project at work, and now he's been told that they want him to go to the US to join their team in Washington DC. He'll be leaving at the end of November and it's on a six-month rolling contract."

"Oh... that's good, isn't it? I mean, it's good for his career, at least."

"Yes, it is. It's been on the cards for a while, and we've both been dreading being apart. But now it's definitely going to happen. He's accepted the offer."

"How do you feel about that?"

Katharine didn't answer, at first.

"Numb… I think. It feels like another blow to my sense of security."

"I can understand that. Will he be away for Christmas, then?"

"I think so… He'll have only just got to the US by then, so I doubt he'll want to fly back again so soon."

Instinctively, and because she didn't want Katharine to have to ask, Sarah said, "You can always come here for Christmas."

"Can I?"

"You can come and stay here whenever you like, darling," the word 'darling' slipping out before she'd thought about it.

Katharine's relief was palpable. "Oh, Sarah – thank you. Thank you so much – that means so much to me. I'd really like that."

"I think it would be lovely, for both of us."

As she said it, Sarah realised how much she wanted to have someone else in her life again.

"Can I come back next weekend, then?" Katharine asked with a cheeky grin.

"Of course you can."

"Thank you, Sarah. It's so good to know I have a home here."

Sarah looked at this young woman who seemed to want to be with her. *Is this what having a daughter would have been like?* she wondered. *A daughter I could have cared for…* And then she thought that somewhere out there was another woman, the mother who was unable to fully love her child.

Katharine stood up and hugged Sarah as she sat at the table, kissing the top of her head, then disappeared upstairs for a bath. Tears came to Sarah's eyes, and she brushed them away with the back of her hand. She contemplated the conversation that had just taken place. Was it okay, to let her heart speak so freely, to let Katherine into her life like that? But as she'd been doing more often of late, she decided not to let her mind interfere with what felt right in her heart. She wanted to just let it be, to become whatever it was going to become.

And so it was that Katharine took refuge with Sarah, and Sarah took comfort from her. The receiving and the giving of love. For most of her life Sarah had thought love was a duty, but her love for James had been quite different, for with him, the giving and receiving seemed effortless, natural. And now, here she was, willingly giving her love to a young woman who received it and returned it with increasing ease.

Sarah told James about it, and although he didn't reply, or at least she didn't hear his voice, she felt he was close, that he was happy for her.

As it turned out, throughout the rest of that term, Katharine came to stay most weekends with Sarah, except for the one time that Sarah caught the bus to Bude and then changed for Truro and stayed with Katharine in her flat. Sarah couldn't quite believe how much she enjoyed the change of scene, visiting the cathedral and wandering around Lemon Quay, and then on Sunday morning at high tide, getting a little ferry to a pub called the Heron Inn for lunch. And they were at ease together; they laughed a lot. When Katharine visited Elmsford, Sarah cooked the foods that she knew Katharine would enjoy; lots of soups, vegetable lasagnes and macaroni cheeses. And Katharine liked cooking too, so she sometimes made them supper.

Then came the Christmas holidays and Katharine was with Sarah all the time. She had lots of work to do for her course and lesson planning for her job, and during the day she took over the living room. Sarah moved the furniture around so that Katharine had a table for her laptop, and she seemed happy as tuppence. And so was Sarah.

Sometimes when Katharine was studying, Sarah would sit quietly beside her reading passages from some of the books she had strewn across the table. Katharine had chosen to take an additional evening class on 'Feminism and Women's Issues,' and one of the books was on domestic abuse and the rights of women in the home. Sarah wished she'd known about this when she was Katharine's age. She might have stood up for herself a bit more, instead of always giving way to her husband to avoid an argument.

She could remember time and time again wanting to challenge what he was saying, but she hadn't been brought up to do that, and Alan didn't invite discussion. He just sat there rolling himself a cigarette and saying what he thought, assuming that was how it was going to be. And she had assumed that, too. She'd kept quiet. That was what everyone had called it back then: 'keeping quiet'. It had been expected of women in those days. Sarah didn't think Katharine was going to do that. *And*, she thought to herself, *perhaps I won't keep quiet now, either.*

Katharine also spent time with Alice and Rachel, who were nearer her age and welcomed her to their home. She would drive over to see them in her little yellow car, and Sarah loved the fact that she was making friendships in the area, that she was becoming rooted.

One evening, Katharine looked up from her studies and said to Sarah, "I sometimes wonder what you are thinking? You're such a good listener but you don't tell me much about your life, only bits and pieces. You must have lots of stories from when you ran your shop."

Sarah smiled. "Well, that's true, and in those days I knew everything that was happening in the village. I sometimes thought that people came into the shop just to let off a bit of steam."

Sarah laid the book she was reading to one side.

"And then?"

"Well, after I retired and sold the shop, I became taken up with my beloved James, and I suppose, a bit like how you felt at university, I didn't need to be with anyone else. It was such a wonderful time."

"Were you lovers?" asked Katharine.

At first, Sarah was a bit taken aback by such a direct question, but then she realised she was pleased Katharine had asked, that she felt she could ask and that she wanted to know.

"Yes, we were," she said, and smiled at the thought, a shared confidence.

Katharine smiled too. "I'm glad you had that special time with James. It was so sad when he died, wasn't it? He seemed… too young, somehow."

"Yes, it was sad, though he was in his late seventies, you know. He didn't seem old though, at least not to me. We'd just discovered each other – we only had five years together – and then he died, and I was bereft. I took a knock and I'm still recovering."

"He was lucky to be loved by you. "As I am."

"Loving you is very easy," Sarah said.

"I wish my mother felt the same." Katharine sighed and looked wistfully out of the window.

"Perhaps one day your mother will be able to express her love for you. Until then, try to hold her tenderly in your heart Katharine, and remember that her own path is probably not easy." Sarah paused, wondering whether she could now say to this young woman what she really wanted to say. She looked at Katharine and closed the book she was reading. The gusty wind of earlier in the day had dropped and the house had become very quiet. She decided she would try. "There is something else I want to tell you."

Katharine closed the lid of her laptop and came over to sit beside Sarah.

"What is it?"

"Well, just recently, in the last few months or so, I've felt a new closeness to James. Ever since The Sanctuary was let out for visitors, things have changed. For a year after he died, I couldn't visit the place, I couldn't face it. I couldn't face knowing he wouldn't be there. But I did face it, with Alice, and ever since then I feel so different; it's like I have let go of him in my head – I know he's no longer here – but he has come back to me in my heart.

"And sometimes, I imagine James is talking to me. He's not, of course, or at least not in the sense that I can hear him, but sometimes I can feel him. Like he's with me. It's as if he's standing close by and I can sense his presence. Do you think that's silly?"

"No Sarah, I don't think that's silly," Katharine said. "Not at all. I don't know much about this sort of thing, but perhaps it's all part of your grieving process; perhaps it's how you are letting go and moving on? I guess you just can't explain everything you experience in grief…"

"No, that's right, you can't. And sometimes I still cry and cry into the night. I'm not in the same place of grief that I was a year ago, but I feel at times that I'm still struggling. Sometimes I go to bed early, in the hope that sleep will carry me away, and occasionally it does. But often it doesn't, and then, after being asleep for an hour or two, I am wide awake, and I just feel so desperately alone."

"That happens to me, too," said Katharine. "It's awful, isn't it? I wake at three o'clock in the morning and my mind is racing and everything seems much worse than it really is. I know that what I'm coping with is nothing like what you're coping with. For me it's usually only about an essay I haven't written, or some test I have to do, or it might be what Tom said on the phone, you know. But in those early morning hours, I feel that my life is just too overwhelming and that I can't cope. I'll get up and make myself a cup of camomile tea, or I'll read for an hour or so and then fall asleep again."

"I do that," said Sarah. "Good old camomile. But Katharine, darling, don't you think you might be grieving, too? You've lost a connection to your parents and to your home, and even though it was never easy, it's a loss. And now Tom has also left, and although it is just for a short while, it's still a loss, of sorts. Perhaps we can both help each other to come to terms with our losses?"

"I hadn't thought of it like that..." said Katharine her thoughts drifting and then turning to Tom. It did feel akin to grief, this emptiness in the pit of her stomach at just the very thought of him. Tears welled in her eyes.

"Sometimes at night," said Sarah, "I get up and go to the window and look down along the street, where everything is dark – except sometimes there is a light reflecting from Linda's bedroom window next door. She has difficulty sleeping too, and I know she often stays up into the early hours of the morning reading in bed. It's funny really, but there's a sort of comfort in seeing her light on. Then I go back to bed and hope that James will appear before me – I long to see him, just one final time – but he doesn't, of course. Not really... but now I feel this closeness to him in my heart. At least I have that.

"And there's something else," Sarah continued. "In the last few weeks, I've noticed a shift in me. And you are part of it, Katharine. Despite the fact that I miss James so much, I am finding I can still give love; I can love you and Alice, and my little Willow," she added, stroking the cat's head, "and I find it helps my grieving so much."

"Well, it certainly helps me," said Katharine.

Sarah smiled. "Thank you for listening to me," she said.

After not quite knowing what they would do on Christmas Day, Sarah and Katharine decided to accept an invitation from Alice and Rachel to spend the day with them, where, in addition to the turkey, there was a nut roast for Katharine. There were also, of course, roast potatoes, parsnips, Brussels sprouts, and bread sauce, which Sarah adored. She had made a Christmas pudding and mince pies, and Rachel had bought some very fancy crackers, which they pulled with crossed arms and then wore the paper hats. They didn't sit down for lunch until two o'clock, and had only just finished by four.

And then in the diminishing light, they decided to go for a walk, to aid digestion, and ended up out on the coast path headed towards a local landmark known as Angel's Wings – a charming wooden seat with a 360 degree views of Bideford Bay and the surrounding countryside, with a carving on the lintel depicting an angel with wings outspread. It was one of those mild, muggy Christmas Days, where the footpaths were muddy and slippery and the going was tough.

Well before they got to the shelter of Angel's Wings, the heavens opened and it began to pour with rain. They ran back to the cottage as fast as they could, but were soaked to the skin by the time they got there, Sarah's wellington boots sloshing with water that had dripped into them from the hem of her raincoat.

They dried themselves off by the Rayburn, full of laughter, piling their wet things on the towel rail, and Rachel poured them each a small glass of brandy "for medicinal purposes." But Sarah was beginning to feel tired, and so before long, Katherine bundled her into the little yellow car and they set off for home.

Sarah went to bed quite early that night, replete and happy to have spent time with her lively young friends, whilst Katharine stayed up to call Tom in Washington.

It had been a memorable Christmas.

A WOMAN WHO LOVES WOMEN

Stephen and Jenny had invited Jeremiah to join them for Christmas, but he'd declined. He wasn't in the mood. He joined them most years and they had always been happy times. Jeremiah made a fuss of his godchildren, Johnny and Olivia, buying them special presents and enjoying how they always brought an exuberance to Christmas that he otherwise would not have felt. But this year, Johnny and Olivia, being grown-up now and with lives of their own, would not be there, and somehow Jeremiah just couldn't conjure any energy for the festivities.

Instead, he stayed in his flat with Angel for company, the solitary life he had made for himself both comforting and lonely in equal measure. Once again, he found himself deep in reminiscence, as if by living his life backwards, he might find the meaning in it all.

It was the summer of 1962 and Jeremiah, Stephen, Jenny and Angela had graduated. Jenny and Angela were still living together, Jenny going to work in a design studio just off the Fulham Road, while Angela went on to the Courtauld Institute to fulfil her dream of studying the paintings of the Italian Early Renaissance, especially the fresco paintings of Fra Filippo Lippi and Fra Angelico. This was grand stuff and quite unlike Jeremiah's life, which became even more ordinary than before. Partly because he needed the money and partly because he didn't know what else to do, he'd taken a job in a comprehensive school in West London, teaching History to reluctant teenagers, which meant moving to a small flat in an inexpensive part of Hammersmith – with Angel, of course.

It was only Stephen who seemed uncertain as to what he would do. In the Sixties, the world was undergoing a kind of revolution. The contraceptive pill and the women's liberation movement were freeing young women from what many of them regarded as a kind of subservience. And young men and women began to travel, including Stephen, who set off to experience the wonders of Greece and Turkey.

During this time, Jeremiah received an occasional postcard from Stephen recounting tales of his travels, but he also saw less of Angela and Jenny. They all seemed to be going their separate ways and work and travel commitments meant the four friends weren't always able to keep in touch. One postcard from Stephen mentioned that Jenny had joined him for a holiday in Turkey, and that they had gone south to explore the beaches of Antalya.

As often as they could, Jeremiah and Angela got together for a drink or supper. It was always good to see each other and when they did, they felt a special closeness, but their lives had diverged and sometimes they were unable to meet up for weeks on end. As part of her studies, Angela was travelling regularly to Florence and Rome, and when she did, she sent Jeremiah a postcard, with a picture of the frescos she was studying. As always, she was very absorbed in her work and, of course, she had entered a different world at the Courtauld and was making new friends.

Jeremiah remained in Hammersmith, though he now had quite a collection of postcards of far-away places. He was taken up with his teaching, which was very demanding, and at weekends he would visit his mother. She had not been well and had decided to retire from her job at the Building Society, which meant that more than ever, she looked forward to Jeremiah coming to see her.

Then one day, eighteen months later, Stephen returned to London with an idea that would change everything.

"Hi stranger, it's me, Stephen," he said when Jeremiah answered the phone. "I'm back – can we meet up?"

They agreed to have dinner in a small Italian bistro in Pimlico that had been one of their favourite places to eat.

Jeremiah arrived early, something for which he was famous amongst his friends. He just hated being late. Then Stephen walked in with his usual swagger, his black hair even longer than it had been at university, his skin nut-brown and he had grown a beard. They embraced, holding each other like long lost brothers, which in a way they were.

Stephen ordered a bottle of the bistro's house red, and once they had chosen their food, he and Jeremiah began to ask each other questions about what had been happening over the last year and a half. As they ate Jeremiah talked about his teaching job, admitting that he wasn't enjoying it very much, what with the endless repetition of tasks, the dreary staffroom and the reluctant and resentful faces staring at him in the classroom.

That seemed to be exactly what Stephen had been waiting to hear.

"I knew you wouldn't like it," he said, "but you seemed so keen when you started that I didn't say anything."

Jeremiah smiled. "Thanks for not telling me."

"But anyway," said Stephen, "don't worry because I am going to rescue you."

"What on earth do you mean?"

"Just that, I'm going to liberate you from a lifetime of endless disappointment."

"You're barmy."

"Yes, I am, but at least listen to my story."

"Okay."

Stephen took a gulp of his wine and wiped his mouth with the back of his hand. Then, leaning back in his chair, he told Jeremiah what it was he had come to say.

"Listen," he said, "during my travels, I met and stayed with a wealthy Turkish merchant in Istanbul, called Ahmet Sakalli, which means 'the bearded one'."

"As you now are."

"As I now am. Anyway, Ahmet specialises in buying and selling Turkish carpets and he and his wife, Verda – which means 'roses' by the way – well, they took a liking to me. They have no children of their own, and so when I arrived looking for somewhere to live, they took me in, and after a few months began treating me as if I were their son. More to the point, Ahmet began to teach me all about his business. I think I mentioned in my postcards that I took some Turkish language classes, and after a while, I began to travel with Ahmet and sit with him while he bought these beautiful carpets. Oh, mate – some of those carpets – you should see them, Jerry…

"Anyway, Ahmet only trades in the high-end, traditional, hand-made carpets, and I began to learn how to tell the good from the bad, and the excellent from the good – colour, pattern, the number of knots per square inch, all that sort of thing. Some of the best carpets, which are often bought for a particular customer, cost thousands and thousands of pounds."

"Really? It sounds like a fantastic experience."

"It certainly has been. But listen to this. One day after we'd had supper and Ahmet and I were sitting, smoking and drinking coffee, wonderful Turkish coffee, he told me that he thought that the market was about to boom. He said that as more and more people travelled to Turkey and saw these beautiful carpets, the prices would spiral. He thought that most tourists would just be buying the cheaper rugs, but, as they did so – and this is the point of my story – the international market for the best carpets would grow in value, too."

Stephen stopped to pour some more wine.

"Although I knew that Ahmet had grown fond of me, I wasn't expecting what came next. That evening he said that he wanted me to help him expand his business. He told me he wanted to set up a warehouse in London as a link between Turkey, Europe and the US, and that he needed someone he could trust who spoke English and Turkish. And that person, he said, was me."

"Wow. Extraordinary. But then, I'm not really surprised because you are extraordinary my dear Stephen. Who else would have such an adventure?"

"But this is where you come in, Jerry. This is how I am going to rescue you."

Jeremiah looked surprised, but knew he had to let Stephen go on.

"You see, just as Ahmet needs someone he can trust, so do I. If I'm going to do this, and if I'm going to spend time in Turkey with Ahmet buying stock and arranging for shipments to London, I need to know that everything will be okay here. I need to find someone I can trust, and whenever I think about that, I think of you. I don't know anyone I can trust more than you."

"Hang on a minute," said Jeremiah. "Are you saying you want me to give up my job and work for you?"

"No, not that. I don't want you to work for me. I want you to be my partner. I want us to go into business together. Porterhouse & Browne, Importers of Fine Carpets."

Jeremiah didn't know what to say. He hated sitting in his flat every evening marking papers and preparing lessons. He hated having to go to the school every working day, only waiting for the last lesson to end so that he could escape. But it paid him a regular salary, and he had his mother to think of, too. He was intrigued by Stephen's story, but unsure of his part in it.

And then he saw, Angel standing behind Stephen in full angel garb, wings and all, beaming at him. What was that supposed to mean?

The door of the bistro opened and in walked Jenny and Angela. The two men stood up to welcome them with warm hugs. Angela caught hold of Jeramiah's hands, and kissed him on both cheeks.

"Just in time for dessert," said Stephen and called the waiter over.

Jenny took a chair beside Stephen and Angela pulled up a chair close to Jeremiah, smiling at him and then taking his arm in hers.

"It's got to be the tiramisu," declared Stephen, evidently delighted to be amongst his dearest friends once more. "Don't anyone suggest anything else."

And so they sat and ate tiramisu and drank more wine, Jenny and Angela talking about what they were doing, and Stephen asking Angela about Florence and Rome.

They ordered coffees and the waiter bought a plate of amoretti biscuits, and then Stephen ordered glasses of grappa.

"I give you a toast," he said, now leaning back in his chair, his arm around Jenny. "To Porterhouse & Browne. We're going into business together."

"Hang on," said Jeremiah. "I haven't said I will yet."

"Not yet, but you will," said Stephen, with an enormous smile of certainty and satisfaction.

"What are you two talking about?" asked Jenny.

"I am rescuing our dear and most beloved friend," exclaimed Stephen.

"Most beloved," repeated Angela, quietly to herself.

And Stephen told them the story about Ahmet the bearded one and his carpets.

That night, Stephen and Jenny went back to his flat, and Jeremiah and Angela went back to hers. It was a Friday – there were no classes to attend to in the morning and Angela had no travel plans, so they could take their time and enjoy being with one another. It had been a while since Jeremiah and Angela had curled up in bed together, but it seemed like the most natural thing in the world. They talked and talked before they slept, waking in the morning in each other's arms.

Jeremiah had missed this.

So that is how it had all begun and now, many years later, Jeremiah recalled those days as being the happiest of his life. Back then he'd always had something to do. At school, at university, and from the very start of his partnership with Stephen, he'd always had something to do. Now, he had nothing to do, and he didn't know how to cope.

Jeremiah's flat was the top half of a large Georgian terraced house, at the edge of what was, when he first went there, the Spitalfields fruit and vegetable market. It was just around the corner from the carpet warehouse where he'd spent most of his life working as a partner in Porterhouse & Browne.

Jeremiah had rented the flat as soon as the company was established, but then, after his mother died, Jeremiah had sold the house in Duncan Way and bought the flat and not long after that, Angela sold her flat and moved in with him. It was perfect. Being close to the warehouse meant that Jeremiah could easily walk to work and keep watch on his precious carpets and rugs. And it was easy for Angela to get to the Courtauld Institute where she combined a part-time teaching job with her doctoral studies on images of the Annunciation.

Sometimes she smiled to herself at the irony of it all: here she was, studying a woman, Mary the mother of Jesus, who like her, had apparently never had sexual intercourse with the man she lived with. But they were happy in their unconventional and, at that time, unquestioning relationship.

It was shortly after they had begun to live together that Jeremiah told Angela about Angel.

"He has been my closest companion since I was seventeen, and he is always with me."

"Well, I've never seen him," said Angela, "which is surprising since I spend so much time looking at images of angels. But are you sure you really see him and that he is not just a figment of your imagination?"

"No, I really see him. We talk to each other."

"Do you now?" said Angela in a voice that obviously implied that she did not really believe what she was being told. "The only angels I've ever seen have been looking down at me from ceilings and domes of convents and churches. I'd never expect to see one sitting on a sofa in a flat in Spitalfields – which, I suppose, is why I haven't."

She looked across at this man she was living with. "But then, I'm not you, am I?" she said, "and there is something about you that is oddly angelic. I think it's something to do with innocence."

Jeremiah smiled. He was disappointed that Angela dismissed Angel so readily. For her, angels were make-believe, a religious relic that someone had once painted onto a wall or a ceiling. Angels were something to be studied, something to be admired, but not something to believe in.

Jeremiah decided to keep quiet on the subject of Angel for the time being, but as it turned out, he rarely mentioned Angel again. Instead, he said, "There's something I've been meaning to ask you."

"What is it?"

Jeremiah hesitated, not entirely sure he wanted to hear the answer. "Are you… are you content – being with me, I mean?"

"Very much," she replied without hesitation. "I love you completely."

"And I love you," Jeremiah said. "Completely."

Later that evening, Angela went to a lecture at the Courtauld Institute, leaving Jeremiah at home with Angel. She had left open on the table a book showing Fra' Angelico's fresco of Annunciation in the Convent of San Marco, in Florence, with the hands of both the angel and Mary folded across their breasts, their heads bowed.

Jeremiah was standing looking at the open page, and Angel came and stood beside him.

"What do you make of it?" Angel asked.

For a moment Jeremiah said nothing, he just looked at the painting and at the expression on the faces of the angel and the woman.

"Wonderment," he said eventually. "Wonderment."

Angel smiled. "That's just the word I would choose. Can you imagine what that moment must have been like, the moment when the Angel Gabriel appeared to Mary and told her that she was to conceive the Son of God?"

"If it were me, I'd probably have fainted," Jeremiah laughed, recalling the first time he'd seen his angel. Then he looked again at the image of Mary and the Angel Gabriel. "I just wonder if there might be something more to it, another meaning – something about grace, something about receiving the blessing of grace."

"God's grace?"

"Yes, that's it. I think she must have felt God's grace, surely, otherwise she would've been full of doubt and fear, don't you think?"

"Possibly."

"Do you think she actually saw Gabriel," asked Jeremiah, "or did she just feel some kind of angelic presence? After all, I suppose she would have been familiar with stories of angels."

"Well," said Angel, "you have seen me."

"But most people don't, do they? Not even Angela."

"No, but then most people don't expect to see angels. You see, even if they look at all those paintings and frescoes or read holy books, they will have been told that angels are far away, up there in some kind of distant Heaven, not here on Earth at all. You can't expect to see an angel if you think they are not here or, worse still, if you just don't believe in them."

Jeremiah went into the kitchen, coming back with a glass of wine. He and Angel sat together and for a moment or two neither spoke, then Jeremiah remembered something he'd been meaning to ask.

"Angel, I've often wondered – why have I never once seen you eat or drink?"

"We don't need to."

"Then how do you survive?"

"We are nourished by rays of light, the energy of the Cosmos."

"No queuing at the till in the corner shop, then?"

"No, and no washing up, either."

They laughed.

"Do you think Angela will ever see you?" Jeremiah asked hopefully, though he already knew the answer.

"It doesn't seem very likely, does it?

At that time Jeremiah and Angela were at peace. It seemed as if nothing would ever harm them, and for quite a long while, nothing did.

Years passed and while Jeremiah prospered in his work, Angela completed her PhD and took up a research and teaching post at the Courtauld Institute of Art.

But then, in 1971, at the age of thirty-one, Angela lost both her mother and her father within six months of each other. Her mother had been diagnosed with ovarian cancer, and her remission was short, just two years. After her mother's death, her father had seemed to be coping, but although he hid this from Angela, he became increasingly morose and depressed until one morning he took an overdose, leaving a message apologising but saying he just didn't want to go on. It was the most terrible and utterly unexpected shock, and Angela was devastated and angry.

For some months she would not leave the flat. Her mother and she had not been close, but her father had always been her protector, and now she felt dreadfully vulnerable. Jeremiah tried to bring comfort to her, but she would not, could not, accept his help – the wound was too raw, too deep.

And then as the months passed, finding it difficult to express her grief, she turned her frustration onto Jeremiah. Ever since her father died, she had become increasingly hostile to him. All their private ways that had been accepted for so long now became awkward. She resented him. She was often withdrawn and wanted to sleep alone, and she was taking unexpected trips to Florence without explaining why she was going or how long she would be away.

She began to talk about an Italian colleague called Francesca, a woman a little older than her with whom she was travelling to visit museums and galleries. At first, Jeremiah thought she was simply finding a place where she could grieve, somewhere away from London with all its memories of her father. But then he began to wonder whether there wasn't something else going on. He had asked about Francesca, but Angela was reluctant to talk about her, saying she was, "just a friend."

One morning while he was cleaning his teeth, he

decided that he needed to speak to Angel about it. As soon as the thought arose Angel was there, standing beside him.

"You're wondering about Angela," he said.

One part of Jeremiah wanted to speak about it, but another part didn't want to have to think about it at all.

"I suppose I am," he sighed, raking his hand through his hair. "She's gone away again and there is a distance growing between us – haven't you noticed it? When she's here she is distracted and moody, and when she is away, I don't hear from her for days on end. I have tried talking to her about it, but she just says I'm being over-sensitive. The other day she said I was like her father, always trying to control her."

"And are you?"

"No, of course not. Whatever else I might be, I have never wanted to control Angela's life. I can honestly say I've always enjoyed her sense of adventure; of being true to herself. And although I've never wanted to go to Florence with her, I've always enjoyed her stories about the Uffizi and about the churches and all the other places she goes to."

He walked back into his bedroom and sat down heavily on the bed, despair etched on his face.

"Perhaps the truth is, Angel, that although she does not say it, she can no longer put up with my lack of sexuality? Perhaps the truth is she wants something I cannot give her?"

"Have you asked her what she wants?"

He leant forward holding his head in his hands.

"Not exactly." His voice was muffled. "I've always thought that our life together was enough for her; that I brought her tenderness and comfort, that I was always there for her. She told me once that she loved me completely, but now it feels like she'd rather not be with me."

Jeremiah looked at his watch.

"I must go," he sighed. "We have a delivery at the warehouse this morning. I have to be there, though it's the last thing I want to do right now."

That evening while Jeremiah was busy in the kitchen cooking his supper, the doorbell rang making him jump, for he wasn't expecting any visitors. Jeremiah opened his front door to find Stephen standing there with a bottle of wine in hand and Jenny beside him. He welcomed them in.

"Sorry to arrive unannounced," said Jenny, "but we wanted to know if you're okay?"

"Yes, I'm okay," said Jeremiah, gesturing for them to come in. "Why do you ask?"

"It's just that we had a rather odd postcard from Angela this morning," said Jenny.

"Really? I haven't had a postcard from her. What did she say?"

"Maybe you should take a look," said Jenny, and passed the postcard to Jeremiah. The card showed a picture of the front of the Uffizi Gallery. He turned it over and read what Angela had written.

> Hello you two
>
> I'm having a wonderful time here with Francesca. We visited this gallery again today – it is such an incredible place. I feel so much better when I'm

here. I just wish I could stay forever. It feels like home to me now.

All my love, Angela

Jeremiah dropped the card onto the sofa, as if he could not bear to be holding it. Stephen who had walked into the kitchen to find glasses and a corkscrew, opened the bottle of wine and poured each of them a glass.

"What does she mean, 'It feels like home to me now'?" Jeremiah was aghast. "Has she said something to either of you?"

Jenny looked across to Stephen who nodded his head and then took a gulp of his wine.

"Do you know what this means, Stephen?" repeated Jeremiah, certain now that they had been talking to Angela.

Stephen sat down in one of the armchairs, opposite Jeremiah. He was clearly uncomfortable, his head down, his shoulders slumped.

"It's just one or two things she's said to Jenny, recently," he replied. "Personal things, you know… I didn't want to hear about it."

It transpired that soon after her father died, Angela had told Jenny all about her relationship with Jeremiah – about what seemed to be missing in him, and, most especially, about what she felt was now missing in her. Angela had told Jenny that she loved Jeremiah and that she had learned to live with him, but now – now that she had met Francesca – she had begun to resent him, resent their life together. And that resentment had turned to anger.

"I think she's wanted to get away from it all for quite some time," said Jenny.

"Get away from what? From me? Why didn't she say that to me?" Jeremiah felt an unbearable pain across his chest. He breathed deeply and stood up. He needed to let something go or he would break. He couldn't bear what was being said to him and he broke out in a cry of hurt and sorrow.

Stephen stood up and held Jeremiah close.

"It's okay mate," he said. "Hang on in there. We'll get you through this. Why don't you come and stay with us tonight?"

Jeremiah wiped his eyes and took another deep breath. He'd been momentarily lost in childhood memories and the shame of crying.

"No, no. That's kind of you," he said, "but I'll be okay. We'll talk in the morning. I just need to be alone now." He showed his friends to the door, unable to look them in the eye.

Later that night, Angel appeared.

"I can't tell you how much it hurts," whispered Jeremiah. "How can something that I've felt was always going to be there suddenly be gone? Just like that?"

Angel said nothing but held Jeremiah within the shelter of his luminous wings.

The next morning, Jeremiah was unable to get out of bed. When Stephen rang his doorbell, he refused to answer it at first, until his friend's insistent calls through the letterbox annoyed him so much, he got up in his pyjamas and opened the door.

"I've brought some croissants," said Stephen.

"I don't want bloody croissants."

Stephen ignored him and walked into the kitchen and put the kettle on. It gave him something to do, for in truth, he didn't know how to console his friend.

Jeremiah slumped in a chair, elbows on the dining table, head in hands, unable to think straight, a ball of anxiety twisting his stomach into knots.

Before long Stephen had made coffee and brought it through on a tray with the croissants.

"Come on mate," said Stephen, "eat some breakfast. We've got work to do – the Hendersons are coming in from New York today, to see those carpets we commissioned for them, remember?"

"I'm not going to the warehouse," mumbled Jeremiah. "You'll have to see to the Hendersons by yourself. Gerald will help you."

"But I want you to be there. It's always best when you're there."

"Not today," said Jeremiah, and walked back to his bedroom, got into bed and turned onto his side, pulling the covers around his neck, the lyrics of a Beatles song playing on a loop in his head:

The Hendersons will dance and sing
As Mr. Kite flies through the ring,
Don't be late.

It took two weeks of patient attention from Angel and tender friendship from Stephen and Jenny, to get Jeremiah back on his feet. Eventually, he returned to work, admitting that being alone in his office was better than being alone in his flat hoping that Angela would get in touch with him.

Then, one evening when he got home from work, there was a letter from her on the doormat.

> Dear Jeremiah
>
> Please forgive me for all of this and for not calling you. I am sorry. I have been trying to work out what to say to you and actually, I was scared to speak to you, scared to tell you the truth.
>
> I shall be coming home next week, and we have much to talk about. Everything in my life was in total chaos, but now I can see things a bit more clearly. I will explain everything when we are together again. I am hoping you will understand what I have to say to you.
>
> I will let you know the date and time of my flight, but don't meet me at the airport – I'll take a taxi.
>
> With love,
>
> Angela

Jeremiah put the letter on the table in the kitchen and sat down beside it. Angel sat opposite him.

"What do you make of this?" he said, pushing the letter across to Angel.

Without looking at the letter, Angel said, "You will have to listen carefully to her."

"I'm dreading it," said Jeremiah, and took the letter and put it into the table drawer.

Two days later, he received a postcard from Angela, telling him that she expected to be back at the flat at about eight-thirty on Friday evening.

That was all a long while ago, but recalling it now, it felt like only yesterday for Jeremiah. He roused himself from his memories and made himself a cup of tea.

Angel appeared beside Jeremiah as he sat at the kitchen table, staring into his cup.

"My head is in such a mess, Angel." Jeremiah raked his hands through his hair. "It's just memory upon memory crowding in on me. I can't seem to let it go..."

"It was all a long time ago, my friend."

"I know! I know I should be over it by now. For God's sake, all these years and I still feel the pain of it. But, I can't help wondering what I did wrong?"

Angel stood behind Jeremiah, gently enveloping him in his luminous wings.

"Would it help to talk through it with me?"

Jeremiah wasn't sure it would help. But he didn't know what else to do; he didn't know how to stop the memories from flooding him with sadness. Perhaps, now – now that he was where he was, having to think about making changes in his life – it would be good to face up to it once and for all; to let go of the pain, for pity's sake. He leaned forward.

"I remember that on the day Angela was coming home, I stayed at the warehouse for as long as I could, but then I closed my office, locked the warehouse doors and walked back to the flat. For some reason, I decided to cook supper, as if everything was going to return to normal. I suppose I was nervous, and it helped to settle me down a bit."

Jeremiah looked acrosss at Angel, who nodded in remembrance.

"Then I heard the front door opening and there was Angela. I wasn't sure how to greet her, but I needn't have worried because she threw open her arms and embraced me, holding me close. She said something like, 'It's good to be home,' and foolishly, I thought that everything was going to be okay.

"I poured us a glass of wine each, and we sat here in these armchairs. It was awkward, and for a moment neither of us spoke, but then Angela said, 'I'm sorry about all this, but…'. And for some reason that's when I knew that actually, it wasn't going to be okay. I asked her what had happened, and she said she would try and explain. You'd told me I would need to listen, so I let her say whatever it was she needed to say.

"I could tell she was nervous, but she had obviously been thinking about what she wanted to say, because she spoke without any hesitation, almost as if she was reading from a script. She asked me if I had ever wondered why she'd been happy to accept our relationship – you know, being lovers without sex – and then she said something that absolutely floored me. She said, 'You see, I didn't love you despite the lack of sex. I loved you because of it'.

"I had not expected that, but then, as she continued, I saw how naïve and stupid I'd been. She told me that although she had never been able to say it, she was like me. She told me that throughout her teenage years and her early twenties she couldn't feel sexy, well not with men, but she hadn't been able to admit it. Not even to me. And even when I told her about myself, she didn't feel able to say anything. I found that very hard to understand, because she knew how much courage it had taken me to be honest with her, and now I realised that she had been too afraid to be honest with me. Despite what I had told her about myself, she hadn't really been able to accept who she was. Do you remember? She said she just couldn't believe that she had been lucky enough to find a man she really liked, someone she came to love, who didn't want to have sex with her. For quite a while she'd thought that was that. But then she said that in the last year or two of our relationship, she'd begun to admit to herself who she really was: 'a woman who loves women'."

Jeremiah took off his glasses and wiped his eyes. He had long ago accepted that Angel knew everything there was to know about him and Angela, but speaking about it was hard. Even now, it was still hard.

"Did you not suspect that she may have had feelings for her friend, Francesca?"

"Not really. Angela sometimes mentioned her, and I knew she was part of the school Angela and her colleagues were setting up in Florence, but she mentioned other friends, too, especially a woman called Alison, who she'd told me was a feminist. Looking back, it seems so obvious, like it was staring me in the face, but I didn't suspect a thing. I couldn't see it… I couldn't see her. Perhaps I didn't want to.

"And the greatest irony of it all was that Angela's father was the one who knew about who she really was – not me, not her boyfriend. He'd always been the one she'd gone to for advice. Never her mother, always him. Apparently, when she first told him of her predilections, he was very calm about it. At first, she thought he understood her and was being supportive. He said she should stay with me. He said he knew I loved her and that staying with me would be for the best – for everyone, which, of course, meant him too. But eventually she realised it wasn't the best for her."

Jeremiah sighed, wrapping his arms around himself.

"And then, when her mum died and her dad killed himself, she was completely overwhelmed with anger and resentment."

On that dreadful day, after listening to Angela telling him about herself and her feelings for Francesca, Jeremiah had walked out of the flat in anger and stayed the night in his office in the warehouse, curled up in an armchair and covering himself in rugs to keep warm. The next morning, Angela had come to the warehouse carrying a thermos of tea. He'd let her in and without saying anything they'd gone up to his office. Angela poured two mugs of tea and he took one, drinking it down to warm himself. He was cold to the bone.

"I don't know what people do when this sort of thing happens," he said.

"Nor do I," said Angela, "but we're not 'people', we're you and me. Maybe no-one else is like us? Maybe no-one else would do what we'll do?"

"What will we do?" asked Jeremiah, his voice and everything within him subdued, broken.

Then Angela began to tell him what she wanted.

"After all these years," she said, "I cannot imagine you not being part of my life. We've shared too much. Loved too much. But I want to ask you to let some of this change."

"Go on," said Jeremiah, sullen.

"I'm going to live with Francesca in Italy. But I would like to be able to come to London sometimes and, if you agree, I'd like to stay with you at the flat. We have two bedrooms, and I could make the smaller one mine. We could still be together as friends. I could pay rent if you like?"

She stopped, hoping that Jeremiah would respond, but he didn't. He couldn't. He was having difficulty trying to make any sense of it at all. She'd clearly thought all of this through, even made a plan, but did she really think that their life could just be re-arranged like that, so that she could have what she wanted?

"So, when are you planning on going back?" he asked, eventually.

"Well, that rather depends on you and whether we can talk all this through."

Something inside Jeremiah cracked.

"I don't feel we can talk about it at all," he said sharply. "I can't make any sense of it, of you... And right now, I don't want to talk about it. I don't want to talk to you."

"But we have to talk, I came back so that we could talk."

"Well, you've had a wasted journey, then. I can't talk about this."

There was silence. Then Angela stood up and put the thermos back into her basket. Now she was angry.

"Then I shall go back on Monday," she said.

"Good. That would be best," said Jeremiah. "I have nothing more to say to you."

Angela left the warehouse, and Jeremiah lay back in his chair and closed his eyes. He had lost her. He was numb. He had nothing left. He pulled the rugs back over his body and lay there, neither asleep nor awake.

Later, he rang Stephen and told him what had happened. Stephen listened but said very little.

"I need somewhere to sleep this weekend," Jeremiah said.

"Yes, of course, Jerry. Come and stay here, mate. The kids can bunk up, and you can have Olivia's bedroom. I hope you don't mind purple?"

Jeremiah arrived at Stephen and Jenny's Edwardian terraced house in Hackney and took a shower. As it was a Saturday, the children were at home and delighted to see Uncle J, as they called him.

Once the children had gone to bed, Jenny came and sat beside Jeremiah, leaning towards him so that she could put her arms around him.

"I am so sorry to hear about what's happened," she said.

"Did she say anything to you?" asked Jeremiah.

"Yes, she did. She called me from Italy about a week ago and said she was planning to come home and try and talk to you about it."

"It?" queried Jeremiah.

"About her decision to live with Francesca. But she asked me not to speak to you until she had. I'm afraid I agreed. I'm sorry."

"That's okay. You were in a difficult position. But what scares me," said Jeremiah, "is how quickly something you feel you can depend on can fall apart in front of your eyes, or rather behind your back."

"Have you any idea what you're going to do?" asked Stephen, who had come into the room.

"Not really," said Jeremiah.

"Well, we've plenty coming up at the warehouse in the next few weeks. That new delivery we're expecting will be here in a couple of days. That'll keep you busy. There are some very special carpets this time."

Jeremiah smiled wanly at his friend. Even the delivery of some very special carpets could not cheer him up.

Angela returned to Florence, taking two extra bags of her clothes and some other bits and pieces with her. The flat seemed to fall into a state of brooding silence and Jeremiah spent more and more time at the warehouse, avoiding going home to the emptiness. Eventually, he wrote her a letter.

Angela

I had never expected that I would write this letter. If love is blind, then my love for you has been as blind as can be. You have been a blessing to me, that is for sure, but it is because of this, that I cannot see myself entering into the new kind of relationship you have asked for. It's not who I want to be – a part time lover, sharing you with someone else and waiting in the hope you might decide to come home. That is what it would feel like for me.

So here it is. If you are convinced that your life has changed in the way you say it has, if you have become a different person, then we should accept that and face up to what it means. It's up to you in a way. But if you decide that the change must be made, then I need to separate my life from yours. I dread it, but I can't manage it in any other way. Just let me know. One way or the other, I need certainty in my life. Then, and only then, can I move on.

Jeremiah

After he had finished it, Jeremiah read through the letter again, folded it into an envelope and wrote the address that Angela had left for him. He walked down the road to the Post Office, bought the stamps he needed, stuck them on the envelope and posted it in the post box. It was done.

Jeremiah suddenly felt cold and stood up and stamped his feet as if to get the circulation going, then went to his desk, taking out from one of the drawers, a letter in an envelope. He unfolded the letter and showed it to Angel.

"Do you remember this?" he said.

It was Angela's response to his letter, written to him after she had returned to Florence; after their bitter break-up. When he received it, although he had been expecting it, the letter had felt like a knife in his side.

Angel looked at the letter, though he knew what it contained.

> Dear Jeremiah
>
> I know you must be hurting and that saddens me, but I have been hurting too. I have been so full of anger. At first, I thought it was grief about the death of my parents and then our break-up, but then I realised how angry I was and everything just seemed to intensify.
>
> I now realise the truth about my father, and it has hurt me so much. When I thought he was protecting me, caring for me, he was actually protecting himself, and trying to control me and my decisions. When I confided in him about my relationship with Francesca, he didn't really want to hear it – I can see that now – and despite

appearing to be calm, he never accepted me for who I am. He just wanted me to 'set it all aside' and stay with you because that suited him; because then he didn't have to think about any of it anymore. And now, as I think back over my life, I realise that this has happened many, many times before. He always controlled me, and I couldn't see it.

Now that he is dead, I realise – feel more than realise – that because of this strange turn of events, I can be free. He has abandoned me without even saying goodbye, and I no longer need to do what pleases him. I can be myself.

I had been longing to tell you, dear Jeremiah, but I didn't know how without hurting you. And then when I came back to London and tried to explain everything, I did hurt you. I never wanted that to happen, please believe me. But now I have to say goodbye to you. Although I love you very much, I can't come back to you. I have to be true to myself.

I hope you can understand, and I hope you can forgive me?

Angela

Suddenly a wave of emotion crashed over Jeremiah.
"Why in God's name did it have to happen like that Angel?" Tears came to his eyes. "We were happy,

weren't we? We'd found a way to be together… I hate how this makes me feel."

Angel unfurled his wings and fluttered them. As he did so, his being became translucent and shimmered. Jeremiah recognised this as a sign that Angel was about to say something of great importance. Over the years he had discovered that it takes quite a lot of energy for angels to appear to humans; their light bodies have to become denser so they can be seen at all, and so when they choose to speak like this it is always profound.

"My dear friend," said Angel, looking straight into Jeremiah's eyes, "everything happens for a reason, though sometimes that reason is hard to decipher. In choosing to be true to herself, Angela had to leave you, but she did not choose to hurt you. By holding on to the pain, you are hurting yourself."

"But I don't know how to let it go, Angel. I don't know how to let go of the pain."

"Can you see it as love – great love? Can you see what you call 'pain' as the reverberations of the love you felt for each other?" Angel had levitated slightly off the ground, his luminous wings outstretched and magnificent. "There is a fine line between joy and despair. Sorrow can be sweet, and love can hurt. You need to transmute your feelings through forgiveness, my friend."

Jeremiah shifted in his chair and then unexpectedly and almost imperceptibly, something shifted in him.

"I think I have to forgive myself, first Angel. I think I have to forgive myself for being different from other people, and for wasting my life feeling sorry for myself. Angela was true to herself, but I haven't had the courage to be true to myself. I've hidden away, licking my wounds..."

Angel rustled his wings in approval.

"But you haven't wasted a moment of your life Jeremiah. That is not possible. All things have led to this point. What you do now is up to you."

Jeremiah watched as Angel gradually faded away.

WILD SWIMMING

Why did I say yes? Sarah thought to herself as she rummaged through her closet for her swimming costume, a garment she hadn't worn since Nick was a teenager. *What possessed me?*

She'd been down at The Wharf with Alice, Rachel and Katharine on New Year's Eve, and they'd all had a little too much prosecco, when Alice raised a toast.

"To us – the wild women of Elmsford!"

"To us," they all cheered in unison.

"But why 'wild'?" asked Rachel, after their chatter had died down.

"Well, we're all a bit crazy, aren't we?" Alice giggled.

"Speak for yourself," said Sarah feeling giddy and happy.

"I'm totally crazy," said Katharine. "I'm going in for a swim."

"No, no, don't do that." Rachel sounded alarmed. "We've all had too much to drink. But lots of people go in for a dip on New Year's Day – so why don't we all come down and do that tomorrow? We can take the plunge together."

"Are you mad?" Sarah had absolutely no intention of going for a swim in the frigid Atlantic ocean on New Year's Day, or any other day for that matter.

"Not mad, just wild," shouted Katharine. "I'm in!"

"I'm in," said Alice.

"And me." Rachel nudged Sarah. "Come on, what do you say? Let's all make a splash together."

"No way," Sarah laughed. "Absolutely not."

"You know Sarah, when I was doing my NLP training, one of the things they taught us was that what we often need the most is just beyond our comfort zone, and that the more we challenge ourselves, the freer we become." Rachel had suddenly become serious, as was her wont.

"I like my comfort zone just as it is," said Sarah.

"Oh, please Sarah, go on, just for me..." Alice embraced her friend. "Go on."

And then all three of them started chanting, "Sarah, Sarah, Sarah!"

"Oh, alright then. If it will shut you lot up, I'll come for a New Year dip, but I'm only going in up to my knees, okay?"

She found her costume in a crumpled ball right at the back of her knicker drawer, the elastic slightly rotten around the leg holes. She had forgotten it was a lurid shade of fuchsia pink.

"Are you ready?" Katharine shouted upstairs.

"I'll never be ready for this."

"They're here – come on Sarah, get a move on. I've made a flask of coffee. Don't forget your woolly hat."

Grumbling good-naturedly, Sarah climbed in the back of Rachel's car and they set off on the short drive to the harbour at the bottom of the steep cliffs, which the locals called The Wharf. Sarah couldn't believe how many cars there were in the car park and was even more surprised when about 50 people in various states of undress or conversely, dressed in silly costumes, were congregating by the harbour wall.

Sarah was astounded – there was Mrs Penny and her daughters and grandchildren. Mrs Penny was older than Sarah and she was ready and waiting in her swimming costume; and there was Clive Cannon, the architect with a woolly hat on his bald head the only thing he wore apart from a pair of skimpy trunks. Sarah averted her eyes. And no… surely not – there were the sisters, Felicity and Linda, her next-door neighbours, in matching Santa Claus costumes with their red trousers rolled up to the knee. Like Sarah, they'd obviously gone for the dip rather than the swim option.

"Isn't this great?" Katharine chuckled, taking off her jumper and jeans to reveal her bare torso in a bikini.

"Oh no… I can't do this." Sarah suddenly became nervous. The heaving grey sea and the bare pink bodies made her feel slightly nauseous.

"Yes you can," said Rachel, taking her hand. "Come on, let's go."

"That's alright for you to say in your wetsuit," Sarah grumbled, beginning to regret the third glass of prosecco she'd enjoyed the night before.

"Look, the secret is to dunk right down and get your shoulders under the water, but keep your head above water, then scream as loud as possible, take a few strokes and get out as fast as you can," said Alice. She hoped it would reassure Sarah, but it didn't.

All at once, as if a gun had been fired, everyone began to make their way to the water's edge. It was high tide, and the sea was lapping up the slipway. Sarah knew from past experience when she'd paddled here before that within a couple of steps it was possible to go from ankle-deep to thigh-deep. She was being jostled along by the sheer number of people intent on going for their New Year swim, but she was caught by their excitement too, carried by their sense of fun, of being in the moment.

And then something took her, something she'd never experienced in her life before – from deep within her, a feeling arose that was at once powerful and all-consuming; she felt fearless. She was going in. She plunged through the water, not stopping at her knees, allowing the intense cold to flow around her thighs and hips. It was exhilaratingly, gloriously painful. And then she was under, her shoulders below the water, gasping for air, laughing and alive. She felt so utterly alive. She swam a few strokes then turned to see Rachel, Katharine and Alice standing on the slipway just staring at her, mouths open, eyes wide.

"Come on in," she shouted at them, "the water's lovely!" The three young women looked at each other, held hands and plunged in to catch up with Sarah, who had by now swum out beyond the harbour wall, and so they occasionally lost sight of her head as she bobbed up and down in the swell.

They could only stand the cold for a minute or so, and all four of them made their way back to the slipway to don towelling robes and open the thermos of coffee, spiked with a little brandy for good measure.

"Oh my God – that was incredible," gasped Sarah. "That was amazing."

"YOU were amazing," said Alice giving her a wet hug.

"I feel… sensational. I'm tingling all over. I feel so… oh my goodness, I feel so alive."

"Isn't it wonderful?" Rachel also gave her a hug. "I knew you'd love it."

Katharine passed them each a small cup of coffee, and they all took a sip. Their teeth had begun to chatter, and their hair felt as if it were freezing solid in the wind.

"Put your hats on girls – it'll help to keep the warmth in," instructed Rachel, and they all did as they were told.

After a while, the crowds died away, but Sarah caught Mrs Penny looking towards her a couple of times. As the four women turned to walk up the hill to the car park, Mrs Penny called over to Sarah.

"Is that you Mrs Silver?"

"Yes, hello Mrs Penny. That was fun, wasn't it?"

"It was. I do it every year – it's a family tradition. Listen, I don't know if you're interested, but there's a group of women, all of us retired and a bit frayed around the edges, but we come here for a swim once a week for much of the year. Sometimes we can't swim for months on end because it's too rough or just too cold, but we usually start in late March and finish in October or sometimes even November, depending on the weather. You'd be welcome to join us if you like."

"Really? Thanks for inviting me, but I'm not sure…"

"We have a WhatsApp group called the Elmsford Elderberries and we just arrange the day of the swim according to high tide. If you let me have your mobile number I'll add you as a member, and you can just come along whenever you like."

"Do you know, I think I'd like that. Thank you."

"You're welcome. I've never seen anyone dive into the sea as fast as you did just then. You're a natural."

For the rest of the day, Sarah was on a high. She hadn't felt this good for years. It was a different feeling to being happy with James or content in Katharine's company, there was an energetic quality to it that was vibrant, that warmed her to the core. She felt so energised, and she couldn't stop smiling. That evening, she downloaded WhatsApp onto her phone. And that was how Sarah joined the Elmsford Elderberries.

As it turned out, from New Year until Easter, there was not a single high tide where the Elderberries could safely swim. A series of Atlantic gales blew in relentlessly from the north-west, creating heaving grey mountainous waves and sprays of spume that blew across The Wharf car park like snow. Then it turned bitterly cold as the wind swung to the east, and the Elderberries decided that it was not sensible to swim in those conditions. Some of the women drove to the sea pool in Bude, where many years ago, a swimming spot had been carved out of the cliffs on the edge of the vast beach, which was filled twice a day with fresh sea water – but Sarah didn't want to travel to Cornwall to swim in the sea pool, she wanted to swim at The Wharf, in the wild waters that had enlivened her spirit at New Year. And so she waited until the time was right.

And then on Good Friday, with the weather set fair and hardly a breeze to ruffle the daffodils, the message came through: Swimming today at 2.30. A thrill coursed through Sarah's body and she ran upstairs to put on her new swimsuit, which was black. She would put on her shorty wetsuit, which Alice recommended she should wear until the water warmed up, once she got to The Wharf. She packed her rucksack with a thermos of tea, some sandwiches, her wetsuit and beach towel, an extra jumper and a paperback novel she'd picked from the library van the last Wednesday. She was expecting Katharine to arrive later that evening, but before then she intended to spend the day by the sea.

She set off to walk to The Wharf, knowing it would take about half an hour. As she made her way past The Sanctuary, she waved, as if James could see her, and she told him what she was doing. She thought he might raise an eyebrow and call her intrepid. And she could see Willow curled up on the doorstep asleep in the sunshine. As she walked along the top footpath across a couple of fields before she got to the cliff path that descended to harbour, she could see the sea in the distance, a sapphire shade of blue, a few white crests showing on the waves indicating that there might be a bit of a swell to contend with.

Oh well, Sarah thought, *if it looks too choppy when I*

get there, I might sit this one out and just see how the other Elderberries do it.

But when she got there, the sea was quite calm because the bay was sheltered from the brisk easterly wind and the high tide seemed to fill the entire cove like a glass of water that was brimming over. Sarah found a spot in the sunshine where she could lean her back against the warm rocks, and she settled in to enjoy the view. She could hear a peregrine falcon overhead although she couldn't actually see it, and then she heard the shrill peep-peep of an oystercatcher as it flew across the bay. She loved the call of seabirds, especially the gulls which she delighted in watching as they flew past her cottage, chattering to each other as they made their way back to their night roosts on the cliffs, the setting sun turning their breasts pink. Not for the first time, Sarah felt blessed to live by the sea.

She ate her sandwiches and read a few pages of her novel, but she couldn't really concentrate for in truth, she was excited at the prospect of going for a wild swim. She was also slightly scared, for she knew the sea could be treacherous and that it had to be respected and studied for knowledge of its currents and rip tides, and yet it was her sense of anticipation that she noticed most, and it overruled the fear.

And then they came, Mrs Penny and Glenda Johns who lived at Ford Cross, and to her surprise Claire Cannon, the architect's wife, who she'd always thought was rather aloof and not one for community groups. Before long there were eight older women, including Sarah, chatting and getting undressed, leaving their clothes and shoes on the rocks or the sea wall, and then together they headed down the slipway. One or two of the women, in swim caps and without wetsuits immediately spearheaded the group and in strong crawl strokes headed in a diagonal line across the bay towards Gull Rock on the other side, where they would take a rest before the return journey, but the others with gentle breaststrokes headed north from the harbour, slowly wending their way towards Ship Rock, a huge flat-surfaced rock that was aptly named for its shape. Sarah was pleased to stay with this group, swimming slightly behind them, a little uncertain as to how far she wanted to go. The water was cold, but not frigidly so, and her wetsuit helped to keep her relatively warm and buoyant. And again, the feeling of euphoria engulfed her, and she couldn't help but grin from ear to ear.

About halfway towards Ship Rock, Sarah decided to turn back. She was a good swimmer, but she wasn't as fit as she once was, and she didn't want to push her luck. Instead, she swam leisurely back to the mouth of the harbour and floated on her back for a while, admiring how different the bay looked from sea level. Eventually, she headed into the shallows and walked up the slipway, surprised to find that the women who had swum to Gull Rock were already back and drying themselves, glimpses of breast and buttock unabashedly displayed as pants and socks were donned, conversation continuing where it had left off.

On her walk back home that afternoon, Sarah thought that joining the Elmsford Elderberries was one of the best things that had happened to her. Ever.

THE SHADOW OF FEAR

Jeremiah was half-heartedly busying himself sorting through documents and various correspondence – not throwing anything away, for he rarely did that – but it gave him something to do, nonetheless. Once again, he was contemplating the words Angel had spoken a few weeks ago which had remained with him since: 'You haven't wasted a moment of your life. All things have led to this point. What you do now is up to you.'

He took some comfort in the thought that his life had not been wasted, although he felt he hadn't done very much with it. And now he was perplexed by the future. He had no idea what he should do next, nor even what he wanted to do.

Jeremiah looked across the room at his steadfast friend from the angelic realms, who was standing by the window gazing out at London life below, dressed in his usual brown monk-like robes, the view out of the window seemingly always of interest to him, though Jeremiah couldn't think why.

"Angel, do you think I could've made more of my life?" asked Jeremiah. "After all, I did quite well at university – I could've gone on to become an academic, or at least put my history degree to good use, but I didn't, I sold carpets. So, was all that studying really worth it?"

"I think that regret is a pointless exercise, my friend." Angel was using his ankle wings which were often hidden by the hem of his robe, to hover a few inches above the floor – something that he knew amused Jeremiah.

"I'm not saying I regret my work with Stephen. Stephen rescued me, in a way. It was Stephen who introduced me to Angela and saved me from a fate worse than death teaching at that dreadful school. It was Stephen who invented Porterhouse & Browne. And then it was Stephen who talked me into selling the company. But what have I done? I've just followed on behind him as if he were the Pied Piper of Pimlico."

Jeremiah chuckled at this. It was the first time he'd smiled in a while and it lifted his spirits.

"But I've been thinking about what you said the other day, Angel – that none of it has been a waste of time, and all of it has led to this point, and it… well, it has comforted me."

"And it is true," said Angel. "Remember, everything happens for a reason – everything. When you ask me what I think of your life, I think it is blessed. I know you find it hard to believe, but you are blessed by the angels."

Jeremiah looked at Angel and, not for the first time, noted that he never seemed to age. He looked the same on this spring morning as he had done when Jeremiah had first seen him, at his father's funeral all those years ago. Angel was still neither young nor old.

"Well, I am certainly blessed to have you as my guardian angel, that I do know," said Jeremiah, "but I feel that I have been cursed in other ways. All those years while Stephen and Jenny were having 'great sex', all I did was get into bed with Angela and listen to her telling me about Fra Angelico."

"She didn't mind."

"No, she didn't – not for a while, anyway – and neither did I. And, of course, I eventually learnt that even if I'd been normal, whatever that means, Angela and I still would've parted, because she is a woman who loves women as she once described it. So, we were never really meant to be."

"But you were, Jeremiah. You were 'meant to be' – can't you see that? You had a relationship with Angela for many years, you loved each other, and you cared for each other, and though it came to an end, that doesn't mean it was a failure. All things come to an end; all things must pass."

Angel had levitated further off the ground and was now slowly rotating in small circles – something that gave him obvious pleasure. Jeremiah was always impressed at his ability to do so.

"Thank you for saying that," said Jeremiah. "You're right, of course. To have found love once in a lifetime is a gift. And you're right that I should count my blessings. After all, how many people can say that they are blessed by an angel?"

"Well, everyone actually, even though they may not know it. Can you imagine how different life would be if they did? Anyway, counting your blessings is a good plan."

And then the question that Angel had been expecting came; it was the one thing he knew Jeremiah had never been able to come to terms with, had never quite been able to accept about himself.

"But could I have done something about my sexuality, Angel? Could I have changed? They say a leopard can't change its spots, but is that true?"

"Well, you could've tried to find out."

"Yes, but I didn't. Why was that?"

"You know why it was."

"Yes, but I want you to tell me. I want to hear you telling me."

For a moment Angel said nothing, looking at Jeremiah with deep love in his eyes. Then he said it.

"You were frightened."

"Yes, I was frightened. Thank you." Jeremiah sighed. "I think that being different made me afraid – afraid of being caught-out, of being denounced, of being humiliated somehow – and then I was so hurt when Angela left me that I've lived my life in fear of what loving another person would require of me."

Jeremiah groaned and put his hands to his head, sweeping away the hair from his forehead and then rubbing the back of his neck with his fingers to ease the tension that always resided there.

"The cause is not out there, somewhere else, my friend. The cause is within; in who you are, who you always were. Accepting who you are will be your greatest lesson and your greatest liberation."

"But I don't like who I am Angel. I don't like being fearful, I don't like being different. How can accepting that be liberating?"

"Accepting who you are without judgement, but with loving compassion is the key to relinquishing all your fears. When you love yourself unconditionally, all your fears will disappear. Why not see what love can do, instead of bowing to fear?"

"I think fear has been who I am for so long I can hardly conceive of any other way of being; it's the reason I do things and the reason I don't do things. It's why I've hidden myself away in a carpet warehouse for years and it's why I've never ventured out into the big wide world like Stephen has. Unlike him, I always wanted to be safe at home rather than out there, making a name for myself and having adventures. I think it's why I hate travelling."

"You've been to Turkey and to France and Portugal."

"Yes, and all the time I just wished I could go home. I couldn't wait to get on the plane and fly back."

"And you've been to the westcountry."

"That's different. I loved the westcountry."

One summer, some years before the sale of the company, Stephen and Jenny had decided to take a holiday house in the Cornish seaside town of Bude. Olivia and Johnny were both at university, and so could only join them for part of the time. They had rented the house for three weeks, and had invited Jeremiah to join them for at least a week or ten days if he wanted to, although they rather doubted he would come at all.

At first Jeremiah, was not sure what he would do all day by the sea, but as usual Stephen was very persuasive and so he agreed to visit. Stephen and Jenny drove to Cornwall with their mountain bikes strapped to the roof of their car and three days later, Jeremiah took the train to Exeter station, where Stephen met him.

When they arrived in Bude and parked in the drive of the house, Jeremiah could not believe that the beach and the sea were so close by, just across the canal. The colour of the golden sand seemed to him so soothing, and he imagined himself just laying on it and resting, totally resting.

Then Stephen took him upstairs and showed him his room, an attic bedroom overlooking the sea. It was breathtaking. The room faced west and every evening it was washed crimson by the setting sun. It only rained on one day. Just the one day.

After unpacking, Jeremiah went downstairs to have tea on the patio which was adorned by lavender and thyme in tasteful pewter pots, and then he and Jenny decided to go for a walk across the canal bridge and out onto the sandy beach.

"Come on, I want to show you something," she said and grabbed his hand and started jogging across the golden expanse of sand.

"Hang on," Jeremiah said, and bent down to take off his shoes and socks. He felt the warm sand beneath his toes, felt his shoulders relax. "Oh, that's better." Then in a rare flash of joyfulness he caught Jenny's hand and they ran across the beach like two kids let loose from school, whooping and hollering.

"Look at this," Jenny said when they stopped. She

was out of breath and could hardly get the words out for it was a big beach, and they'd run quite a way.

"What is it?"

"It's a sea pool. Twice a day, the high tide washes it clean and fills it up again. Come on, up these steps."

And then Jeremiah knew what he would do on holiday. He would swim. He hadn't swum for years, but as a teenager, he loved to swim and he had frequented the local lido every day in the summer holidays.

"It's wonderful…" he said, admiring how the pool seemed to blend into the sea in an endless expanse of water.

"Isn't it. Stephen and I have been getting up early and coming for a swim before anyone else is around. It's quite cool, but absolutely magical."

"Well, I think I shall be coming along with you."

When eventually they got back to the house, Stephen asked Jeremiah if he would like to join them the next day for a drive out to meet some friends of theirs who were staying in a village about ten miles away, just across the county border, in Devon.

"They're called Edward and Rosie Davenport, and they're visiting Ed's father Bernard, who has very kindly invited us all to have lunch with him in his walled garden. I think you'll like them. Ed is a carpenter and Rosie is a musician. What do you think?"

Ordinarily, Jeremiah would have baulked at the idea, but the holiday spirit had relaxed him.

"That sounds good," he said, feeling happier than he could remember.

And so, the next morning, they set off north along the coast road, then turned right after about half an hour taking some narrow and twisting lanes before entering a pretty little village that had won a Britain in Bloom competition some years before, but still proudly boasted the fact on the village sign. They parked up and found the house, which from its size and proximity to the church must once have been a manse or vicarage, close to the centre of the village.

Rosie came to the door and welcomed them in and before long, they were all sitting around a wooden garden table under a large umbrella in the most quintessential cottage garden Jeremiah had ever seen. It was exquisite. Being a walled garden, it was sheltered and warm and it was filled with a profusion of foxgloves, roses, clematis and bees – ah, the bees...

"I feel like I've died and gone to heaven," Jeremiah said, kicking his sandals off and letting his feet sink into the lawn that was spotted with daisies and left to grow long in places.

"Lovely, isn't it?" said Rosie. "You can see why we like to visit Bernard as often as possible."

"Nothing to do with seeing me," Bernard chuckled. "It's the draw of this garden and the ripe peaches and fresh strawberries in the summer. Not many people can grow peaches in the UK, but here, I espalier them against the walls to give them warmth and protection, and they are wonderfully prolific. Here, have one." And Bernard proffered a bowl of peaches that exuded a fragrance so sweet and spicy, it made Jeremiah swoon.

He took one and bit into it and the warm juices ran down his bare arm. He wondered why he had never eaten a ripe peach plucked fresh from a tree before. It was surely one of life's greatest pleasures?

Jeremiah looked about him, marvelling that life could be this colourful, this relaxing. He knew that often on holiday, the contrast with everyday life is sharp and unnerving, but as the luncheon progressed, Jeremiah became keenly aware that his life – from flat to warehouse and back again – was grey in comparison to Bernard's vivid life in his walled garden.

He did not know it then, but a seed was sown that took many years to germinate.

Conversation was easy and intriguing, and Edward was talking about one of his passions – churches.

"The towers of Devon churches mark the landscape," Edward said, "in fact, there's a rather remarkable church near here, in a village called Elmsford. Its tower has eight spires which shows that Elmsford was once a rich farming area, because most parishes could only afford four spires on their churches when they were built. But what I love most about Elmsford's church are the stained glass windows – they are ancient and magnificent. You must call in on your way back to Bude – it's a little off the beaten track but worth the visit and the views from the village out towards Lundy Island in the Bristol Channel are just outstanding.

"Well, that sounds like a perfect little detour on our way home," said Stephen reaching across the table to help himself to a little more of the excellent Yarg cheese that Bernard mentioned was a westcountry speciality.

So, later that afternoon, having lingered over coffee after lunch, and having heard all about life in the village and beyond, Stephen, Jenny and Jeremiah left Bernard, Rosie and Ed and made their way to visit the remote village of Elmsford.

It was impossible to get lost, because for miles, the church tower with its eight spires was visible from the brow of every hill. All they had to do was point the car in the right direction. They drove through the village and round a sharp bend and came to the church, set within a well-kept churchyard, its old and lopsided gravestones telling their own stories. The church was huge and built of a dark local stone, with an impressive arched south entrance.

The afternoon was hot, the air still, the village quiet, and all three of them caught the feeling of the place – so ancient, almost brooding.

And when they went inside, the church was, as Ed had told them, very impressive. The stained glass windows were indeed remarkable, but what Jeremiah liked most were the ceiling panels, all carved intricately with flowers and leaves and the occasional angel too. The whole ceiling was a work of art.

While Stephen and Jenny walked around the church, Jeremiah sat on one of the pews and took in the place he had been brought to. But then he began to wonder if the delivery of new carpets had gone smoothly and whether the shippers had picked up the consignment bound for Japan.

Stephen, Jenny and Jeremiah spent the week taking early morning swims and walking the coastal paths both north and south of Bude. Unused to so much sunshine, Jeremiah's body caught the sun and turned golden brown, which made him look well. Or perhaps it was just that he had truly relaxed, had found himself a niche in the sand dunes and had lain there and slept whilst children made sandcastles and the ice-cream van that was parked by the river jingled its merry and enticing tune.

At the end of the week, Jeremiah left Cornwall with mixed feelings. He had enjoyed every moment of his holiday and part of him longed to stay, but he had also become anxious to get home, to check-out what was happening in the warehouse and to reassure himself that his foreman, Gerald, had coped in his absence.

Back at work he soon became busy once more with carpets and customers. He was a man of routine, so it felt reassuring to be home, but something of the softness of the westcountry, its slowness and its remoteness, and perhaps most of all, the peacefulness he felt as he walked and swam, had affected him and left a lasting impression.

THE LIFTING OF STONES

Even though it was still early summer and the schools were not yet on holiday, it was hot, unusually so. For several weeks a heat wave had settled over the westcountry. No-one in Elmsford could remember it being as hot, without even a sea breeze to cool things down a little.

Alice and Rachel were sitting in Sarah's garden, under a sunshade and Sarah had just brought out a jug of her homemade elderflower cordial, the ice cubes tinkling as they began to melt.

"When there's no breeze like this, the heat takes my breath away," said Sarah, "and my heart begins to pump at an alarming rate. The other day, when the tide was out and I couldn't go for a swim, I got so hot that I ran a cold bath and just sat in it."

Alice laughed.

"What's so funny?"

"Well, it is a bit amusing, you have to admit. I love the way you're coping with climate change."

"Apparently, they had to stop the trains from Plymouth to Penzance yesterday because some of the tracks had warped." Rachel took a long swig of her drink and smacked her lips. "Mmmm, lovely Sarah – not too sweet – just how I like it."

"Yes, and at Heathrow, some flights had to be cancelled altogether," added Alice, "because the tarmac was melting on the runways. Temperatures are breaking records all over the world."

"I wouldn't be surprised if we had thunderstorms later," said Sarah.

That afternoon, after checking with Alice that there were no Airbnb guests at The Sanctuary, Sarah felt the need to go and sit for a while on the veranda, where there was some welcome shade. For a few days, she had been experiencing a wave of grief. They came less often now and were not as intense, but nonetheless, she wanted to be in James's garden. She wanted to be in a place that he had loved.

The sun was still hot and there was only the faintest breeze coming off the sea, enough to rustle the papery seedheads of the honesty and tease the tall and graceful verbena bonariensis that had not quite come into flower. A damsel fly was flitting to and fro near the small pond that she had helped James to install a few years ago. They'd taken it in turns to dig the ground which was solid and stony, and found it hard to comprehend how such a huge pile of spoil could come from such a small hole. As she watched the damsel fly hover above a lavender bush, its iridescence complementing her favourite flower, Sarah's mind became lost in memories – but they were no longer painful. They were nostalgic and tinged with sadness, but they did not hurt her, they did not overwhelm her.

After a while, Sarah realised that Willow was sitting in front of her, looking at her inquisitively.

The following day, a blistering Friday afternoon where time seemed to stand still, Katharine arrived from Truro in her little yellow car. Sarah had been looking forward to her visit.

The two women hugged, and then unpacked the car. Katharine was not one to travel lightly. She took her bags up to her room whilst Sarah made some iced lemonade, and they sat in the cool of her living room to drink it, as it was just too hot to sit outside.

"How's life in Truro then?"

"It's fantastic – I love it, and there's so much in my course that I hadn't expected." Katharine took a long gulp of her drink, relishing the cool sharpness.

"What hadn't you expected?"

"Well, I'm used to studying, but this course is really challenging me; it's much more practical than I thought it would be, I think because it's so pupil-centred, so we have to think and respond in ways that students will relate to, you know? It's really interesting, and it's making me realise how lacking some of my teachers were. Anyway, I've got a lot of studying to do over the holidays. No slacking for me."

Sarah sat and listened. She delighted in this clever young woman, in all her excitement and enthusiasm and she loved how this unexpected friendship continued to deepen; how each time they met there seemed to be a new level of confidence between them. It reminded Sarah of when she had befriended a robin in her garden. At first, he was nervous and skittish; he wanted to come to her to take the suet treats from her hand, but he was uncertain, distrustful. But over days and weeks, she coaxed him and cooed at him and eventually he began to trust her, and he would perch on her fingers for a few seconds, pecking at the treats in her palm, feeling safe. It felt a bit like that with Katharine – as if the pain she had experienced in her estrangement from her parents was slowly being healed by the love and reassurance from Sarah.

Of course, Sarah knew her role was temporary – how could it not be, for this young woman had her whole life ahead of her – but just to be there for her and to share in her life was enough. For now.

"Do you fancy a swim before supper?" Sarah asked. "It's high tide in an hour and it'll cool us down a bit."

"God, yes!"

Just as they were about to leave for their swim, Sarah's mobile rang. It was Alice.

"Hi Sarah, we're going to the Quaker Meeting in Bideford on Sunday and we wondered whether you'd like to come with us again? We know you enjoyed it last time you came. And then if you like, you can stay and have lunch with us afterwards. What do you think?"

"I'd love to, but I have Katharine staying with me this weekend – could I invite her, too?"

"Oh yes, I forgot. Of course, please invite Katharine. That would be great – it's been ages since we saw her."

When Katharine came downstairs and into the

kitchen, a huge clap of thunder echoed overhead, and they both instinctively ducked their heads.

"Oh, thank goodness the weather has broken. I don't think I could stand much more of this heat," said Sarah. "I hardly slept a wink last night. You don't mind swimming in the rain, do you? It's rather special – it's a different experience altogether, and the sound of the rain on the sea is magical."

"Well, as long as we don't get struck by lightning when we're swimming..." Katharine sounded a little uncertain.

"Oh, no – we'll be fine. The storm is moving inland I think," and then after almost forgetting in her excitement to get down to the Wharf for her swim, Sarah told Katharine about the invitation from Alice.

"Lovely. Lunch with Alice and Ruth will be great – but I'm not so sure about the Quaker Meeting... I've never been to one and I'm not at all religious."

"Nor had I until Alice invited me to join them a couple of months after James died."

"But, I didn't think Alice or Ruth were particularly religious either?"

"Well, they're not, and neither am I really, but Quaker Meetings aren't necessarily about religion, they're more about… how can I put it – values. Quakers hold certain values as core to their life and practice, such as, now let me see, what did Rachel say they were... integrity, peace, stewardship of the Earth, and simplicity too. Isn't that rather lovely?"

"Yes, it is – far better than all that sinful stuff in Christianity."

"Well for me, Quaker meetings are mostly about the

quality of silence and about giving myself an hour to just sit and be and let go of my worries. I think it's a different experience for everyone, but I find the silence so comforting – I've never experienced anything like it before."

"Really? Well, I'm all for a new experience, so yes, let's do it."

And so, on Sunday morning in torrential rain, Katharine and Sarah drove over to Rachel and Alice's house which was on the way to Bideford, and they all shared a car to the Meeting House on the Quay, facing the wide river estuary that was sometimes a ribbon of mud and at others a glittering expanse of water. On the way, Alice explained to Katharine that a Quaker Meeting was held in silence, broken only if someone stood to speak, or 'give testimony'.

"Sometimes, no-one speaks at all for the entire hour of the meeting," said Alice.

"That can be the best of all," said Sarah.

They were greeted at the door by an elderly lady dressed as if it were the middle of winter, in a cardigan and a long woollen skirt and sensible shoes, who shook their hands and welcomed them in. Sarah had seen her before but had not been introduced to her. Her hair was drawn back in a loose bun and, somewhat unexpectedly, it seemed to Sarah, she was wearing long dangly earrings made of gold leaves and feathers.

The meeting room was large and high-ceilinged with tall windows, the sills set just above head height and the windows rising almost to the eaves. The room was plain with white walls and a wooden boarded floor, and just as they entered, the sun broke through the clouds and flooded the place with light. As usual, upright padded chairs were set in two circles, one within the other, around a simple square table on which there was a small bunch of flowers in a vase and a number of books, including a Bible, *Quaker Faith and Practice* and a slim volume called *Advices and Queries.*

When she had first come to the Meetings with Rachel and Alice, Sarah had been told that these were the only books of governance, or spiritual guidance that Quakers had, and even these were simply considered as suggested reading. On occasion someone might feel moved to read aloud from them.

Around the edges of the room were old wooden benches with padded cushions, and Sarah noticed that, as had always been the case when she was there, only one person chose to sit on them, an elderly man with a somewhat bent and crumpled look about him. Sarah wondered why he insisted on the discomfort, as he lent forward resting his hands on a walking stick. But, she thought, it was probably only a habit; that perhaps he just liked the fact that the benches had been there ever since the Meeting House was built.

They sat down in the outer circle of chairs, and by the time the clock on the wall had moved to ten-thirty there were twelve people sitting quietly together. The silence, which had already been in place when they came into the room, now deepened. Sarah could almost feel it entering and easing her body, and she looked across to Katharine and smiled. Katharine smiled back and then closed her eyes.

Of course, to begin with Sarah's mind was fizzing about, wondering who all these people were and whether Katharine was okay, but as the silence and the stillness took hold, so her mind began to still.

After a quarter of an hour, one of the elderly women in the inner circle who had come into the room walking difficultly with two sticks, leant across to the table and picked up the book of *Advices and Queries.*

Unable to stand, she remained seated opening the book and speaking with a clear voice.

"Advices and Queries, Number Two," she said. "'Bring the whole of your life under the ordering of the spirit of Christ. Are you open to the healing power of God's love? Cherish that of God within you, so that this love may grow in you and guide you. Let your worship and your daily life enrich each other. Treasure your experience of God, however it comes to you. Remember that Christianity is not a notion but a way.'"

She closed the book and the woman sitting beside her helped her to place it once more on the table.

The silence returned and Sarah thought about the words: 'So that this love may grow in you and guide you.' *Is that what's happening to me?* she pondered.

For about half an hour there was unbroken silence, but then, just as Sarah thought that perhaps no-one else would speak, an elderly man, somewhat shortened by age, stood with his hands clasped behind his back. For a moment he just stood in the silence, his eyes closed. Then he spoke. His voice was quiet, but clear.

"Friends," he said, "it is so difficult to speak of God these days. And religion has a bad name. Sometimes for good reason. But our Advices ask something else of us: to cherish 'that of God'; God's love within us, not for the sake of dogma, but as a way of life."

He paused, but remained standing, his eyes still closed. Then he continued.

"That may sound a difficult thing to do, but I find this love everywhere. All around me. In this room. At home. In the queue at the Co-op. This is not theology it is just what I find. What I call it is, I suppose, a private matter. What I do with it is a public matter."

Another pause.

"But something else is at work, too. Beyond me and within me I sense that there is a universal principle at work. Call it what you will: Love, Harmony, God. How should we know its name?"

He stopped speaking and again, for a moment, remained standing. Then he sat down, placed his hands in his lap and opened his eyes, letting his gaze rest upon the floor. The silence returned.

At eleven-thirty, a man and a woman sitting side by side in the inner circle shook hands to signify that the Meeting had come to an end, and then everyone shook hands with the people beside them. Sarah was sitting between Alice and Katharine and so she shook their hands. She felt as if she had been in a special place, and for a moment she wished she could remain there.

It felt as if she had lifted one of the stones mentioned in *The Gospel of Thomas,* that James had left for her, and found beneath it the presence of the Divine. It is not the stone that holds the answers, she thought to herself, but the lifting of it. She was beginning to understand the wisdom of the gospel, and, remembering him, she thanked James silently for bringing it to her.

There was something very moving about the

simplicity of the meeting room, with nothing required of her except that she should add her own silence and stillness to the silence and stillness of others. And she felt as if she had received something, although she was not sure what it was. She just felt that she had been in the presence of Love.

Katharine, too, was quiet and for a moment they both sat where they were, whilst everyone else, including Alice and Rachel, left the meeting room and went into an adjoining room which had a hatch opening into a kitchen where people were making tea and coffee and putting biscuits onto a plate. Then they, too, stood up and joined them.

Afterwards, they drove back to Alice and Rachel's cottage. For a while no-one spoke. It was as if they were still held by the silence of the Meeting. Then Alice asked what Katharine had thought about it.

"It was very strange," she said. "I have never before sat in such deep silence. It's not like being quiet on your own, is it? After a while, as we sat there, I felt as if I was being gathered in, and somehow, I couldn't resist it. And I loved what the old man said."

"Yes, that was Richard Bright," said Rachel. "He is what's known as a Birthright Quaker, which means that he was born into a Quaker family. What he spoke of will have been a part of his life from a child, as natural to him as breathing in and out. He often speaks aloud to us and I always love what he says."

"What he said really touched me, too," said Sarah. "It was exactly what I was thinking about – the meaning of love. It was as if he knew what I wanted to hear."

"When that happens," said Rachel, "Quakers say, 'he spoke to my condition,' and they say it's common to find that someone speaks about something that has been on your mind, or something you have been wondering about. It's quite strange, but it's certainly happened to me before."

They arrived back at the cottage and busied themselves with lunch. Alice had prepared a dish of vegetable lasagne, which she put into the oven to heat up, and there were the last of the broad beans and peas from her market garden, which she put on the hob to steam. Not for the first time, Sarah felt very happy in the company of these young women, her dear friends, and somewhat honoured too, that they should choose to include her in their lives.

Katharine asked Rachel about her work, and during lunch, she began to talk about what was happening at the district hospital where she was an occupational therapist. She often worked with elderly people, either visiting them at home, or in their hospital ward, or sometimes at the hospice. It was the part of her job she liked best.

"Many of the people I see are very ill," she said, "and for quite a number of them there is little or nothing that the hospital can do. They are dying. And they are frightened."

"What can you do for them?" asked Katharine.

"Not much, but I know it is important for them not to feel abandoned. So, I just sit with them. Sometimes I gently massage their hands. Or I listen to what they say. They ask me questions about my life, and I ask them the same. Sometimes they want to talk, but often they don't. And whilst some of them have family support, many have nobody to turn to. No-one at all. In a way, it is easier to help those with no support, because it's just being with them that matters. Where there are families, it can be quite difficult. Often, no-one seems to know what to do when someone is dying, so they either chatter away as if nothing is really the matter, or they fret or, worse, they complain. None of this helps."

"Rachel wants to try and do something about this," said Alice, collecting the plates.

"What can you do?" asked Katharine.

As usual, Rachel had thought it through.

"Well, I think there are two things that need to be done. Firstly, we need to educate people about dying, so that families are less frightened; and secondly, we need to find people who will volunteer to be with the dying, so that no-one dies alone. There's a growing trend in the US for this kind of care, and those who volunteer are called 'Doulas'. I had to look up what 'doula' means, but it's similar to a midwife, so just as we have midwives for the birth process, now there are midwives for those who are dying. I think that is so important, don't you?"

"Of course, there are no funds for this sort of thing," said Alice bringing in a pot of coffee and another of mint tea.

"So, we just have to get on and do it," said Rachel. "Isn't that what women do? We just have to get on with it. Make a start and see how it goes."

That evening the sunshine returned and bathed the garden in golden warmth tempered by a gentle westerly breeze. To make the most of the clement weather, under the shade of the apple tree Sarah laid out a blue and green checked and rubber-backed picnic blanket that was a freebie from The National Trust when she'd once joined as a member. Then she placed bowls of nuts and olives and a bottle of chilled white wine and two glasses on the little mosaic table that she bought from a junk shop in Bideford and she and Katharine leaned against the trunk of the apple tree, picking at the nibbles, and enjoying the peacefulness of the garden.

Katharine was looking over some course work that she was preparing for the following week, and Sarah was browsing through a travel magazine that her neighbour Linda had passed on to her. It featured holidays in Italy. It wasn't that she was planning a vacation. Not at all. In fact, the last holiday she'd taken was a bus tour of the Lake District when Alan was still alive. He'd gone reluctantly and had grumbled the whole time. But she did watch holiday programmes on the TV, and afterwards she often felt as if she had actually been there. Now, flicking through the magazine, she felt much the same – as if the photographs themselves transported her to these wonderful places. She liked the look of Tuscany, and showed the photos to Katharine.

"Look at these beautiful villages," she said. "I can feel the warmth of the sunshine, as if I was sitting there with a bowl of pasta and a glass of wine."

Katharine took the magazine from her and began to look through the pages. "Actually, I might go to Rome before the new term starts, just for a week," she said. "I have a friend from uni who lives there, and I'm thinking of asking Tom if he could take some time off work and come with me. That's if I can get all my course work done first."

"Well, that sounds good, and you deserve a break – both of you."

When she went to bed that night, Sarah longed to talk to James.

"If you were here," she said, "I'd ask you to take me to Italy. But you're not, so I can't."

The next morning at breakfast, Katharine seemed a bit dejected, and Sarah asked her if she was okay.

"I'm not really," she said. "After talking to you about Italy last night, I phoned Tom to see if he would be able to fit in a trip to Rome before the end of the summer, but he said that he couldn't. Actually, he said he thought it was unlikely he'd be able to take a break from Washington until later in the year." Katharine looked exasperated. "I think I mentioned to you that the company had got funding for their research? Well, Tom told me last night that he and his colleagues are having to redevelop their systems to justify the funding, and it's proving really difficult, so everyone in the team is working flat out. Apparently, a trip to Rome would look like he was letting the side down."

"Oh, poor Tom. That must be hard for you both. Maybe you could travel by yourself and stay with your friend?"

"Maybe, but I wanted to be there with Tom."

"Perhaps you could fly to Washington and see Tom?'

"I've mentioned that once or twice before, but I get

the feeling he doesn't want to be distracted by me. He's giving everything to that bloody job. Everything!"

Sarah felt her anguish. "It won't be forever, darling."

"No, it won't because I can't take this distance between us for much longer, Sarah. I really can't."

After breakfast, Katharine left and drove back to Truro, still seeming a little crestfallen. Watching her drive away, Sarah wondered whether Katharine and Tom would be able to survive this time apart.

"I do hope she's okay," said Sarah to Willow as they walked back into her cottage.

A week later, Katharine phoned.

"Hi Sarah, I just wanted to tell you that I've booked my ticket to Rome. I'm really looking forward to it, and my friend Abbie is excited about me coming. I'm going to stay with her in her flat right in the middle of the city, so we will be able to walk everywhere, which is great. And she knows all the best places to eat."

"Well, that sounds wonderful, darling. Make sure you send me a postcard."

"Of course. At least one."

"And what about Tom? I've been wondering how things are between you?"

"Okay, I suppose. I'm a bit pissed off with him to tell you the truth, but I'm hoping I'll feel better after my holiday."

"I'm sure you will. So, I won't see you for a while?"

"No, but I'll come and visit when I get back from Italy, if that's okay with you?"

"That will be lovely. Have a wonderful time Katharine. You really deserve this break."

"Thank you. Actually, I do feel it's just what I need."

AT ONE AND UNAFRAID

After his visit to Bude, Jeremiah did not take another holiday, but, once more, devoted himself to the care and sale of his beloved Turkish carpets. He was either in the warehouse or in his flat and that was his life. He didn't see his life as bleak or lonely because he genuinely loved the exquisite, handcrafted carpets Porterhouse & Browne imported, and he took great pride in ensuring their customers' satisfaction. Nonetheless, his life had undoubtedly narrowed over the years. Jeremiah hadn't thought of the colour and scent of Bernard's walled garden again, until now – because now the warehouse was gone, and he was set adrift.

At least he had begun to find some new interests – he'd started going to visit some of the museums in London and his old love of history was rekindled, and cooking had become something pleasurable rather than a chore to be done at the end of the day. Looking in his desk for a pen to write out his shopping list, Jeremiah came across a birthday card sent to him by Angela on his 50th birthday.

"What's this doing in here?" he wondered and showed

it to Angel who was practising hovering, his large, shimmering wings outstretched and his ankle wings fluttering rapidly

Angel looked at the card. On the front was Botticelli's 'Primavera', and inside Angela had written:

HAPPY 50th BIRTHDAY
To my dear Jeremiah
When are you coming to Florence?
You could see this!
With love from
Angela x

On the day he'd received the card, Jeremiah had set it on the mantlepiece in his living room, and then stood for a while looking at it until, because no-one could see him, he allowed the tears to come. Angel had appeared and comforted him.

Jeremiah, of course, would have done nothing to celebrate his birthday, but Jenny took over their favourite Italian restaurant for an evening, and invited thirty-odd guests to join them, mostly friends of hers and Stephen's, but also Gerald from the warehouse and his wife, Betty. It was the same restaurant that the four friends had been to 26 years before, when Stephen returned from Turkey and told Jeremiah that they were going into business together. This time, Angela was not at the party. Jenny had asked her if she would like to come, but she had declined. She'd said that she would have to bring Francesca with her, and she knew that would be too much for Jeremiah.

That same evening, in Florence, sitting alone in the

flat she now shared with Francesca, Angela had poured herself some Valpolicella and raised her glass to Jeremiah.

"I hope we will be friends again," she'd said.

Jeremiah turned back to his desk, still pondering the card.

"I wonder what it would have been like if I'd agreed to what she asked for."

"Yes, I wonder," replied Angel.

"I think it would have been better than this."

"Maybe."

"But I couldn't do it then. And never since. For some reason, I've been unable to find the strength to reach out to her."

Jeremiah and Angela had written to each other on occasion and sent birthday and Christmas cards – they'd even had a couple of lunches in London when Angela had returned for one reason or another, but the lunches were a little awkward and they were both relieved when they were over. As the years passed their separation became entrenched, and to Jeremiah it seemed impossible that things could be any other way.

"She has asked you to visit her."

"Yes, but… it's not just about the travelling, Angel, I've never really been sure how I would feel, you know, being with Angela and Francesca."

"That sounds like jealousy."

"Of course it is! I'm very jealous of Francesca, and with good reason. She has lived with Angela all these years and they have shared a life together. That's what I wanted, that is what I had until she took it from me."

Jeremiah swung round to face Angel, his eyes

ablaze, but then they softened, and he sighed.

"This is ridiculous – I sound like a petulant child, don't I?"

"It is not Angela or Francesca who created the circumstances of your life, my friend. It is entirely down to the choices you have made. Choices which have led to who you are now."

"I know... you're right. It's my fault that I'm lonely and miserable. It was my choice not to see Angela again. I shut her out of my life and I wouldn't let anyone else in. I did that. Me." Jeremiah slumped in his chair. "What's happening to me, Angel? Dear God, why can't I stop digging into my past? Ever since I retired, I've been living in the past – I've been watching my life unravel before my eyes like a film and I don't like what I'm seeing. I don't like who I've become."

Angel fluttered his wings. It was a sound that he knew comforted Jeremiah. "This is what you humans sometimes call 'a dark night of the soul', and it is difficult, but without looking deeply at yourself you're stuck, you can't move on. But then, unexpectedly, you find something that shifts you, and then you can really see, as if for the first time. And that leads to epiphany. Revelation." Angel stopped hovering and turned to face Jeremiah who had set his gaze out of the window. "And Jeremiah, hear this: the timing of epiphany is always perfect. Even though you don't know when it's coming, it always comes at just the right time."

Jeremiah huffed. "I honestly don't know what you're talking about," he grumbled as he put the card back in the drawer and found the pen he'd been looking for. Then his eye rested on the small painting hanging above his desk, the one he'd bought on a holiday he had grudgingly taken with Angela in France. It was a beautiful representation of an angel, though it looked nothing like his Angel.

"Don't you think it's rather odd, that after all these years of living with an angel, I have no spiritual practice, no religious beliefs, nothing that guides or shapes my life at all? I don't get on my knees and pray or chant or go to church, not even at Christmas. I don't even sit and meditate. Nothing. I have you, but you never ask anything of me. Wouldn't you think that something of you would have rubbed off on me; that I might at least have been more inquisitive of where you come from, who sent you to me?"

"Seeing your angel has nothing to do with being religious or going to church," replied Angel, "although many people throughout history must have thought it did, since there are so many pictures of angels painted in churches. It's not even about what is now called 'spirituality', which these days could mean anything at all. Actually, as it happens, I do quite like going to churches, especially when they're empty. There is often a stillness there that I like. And there is something about the quality of the light that nourishes me.

"But seeing your angel is about love – it is about my love for you and your love for me. And you know, Jeremiah, you are a kind and tender person. You have always helped others, without fail, selflessly and expecting nothing in return. There's something angelic in that. You are more like us than you know."

Jeremiah gazed at Angel, feeling the deep love Angel spoke of in his heart.

"Thank you," he whispered.

"The only person you are not so kind to is yourself, Jeremiah. Try not to berate yourself so. All is well and all things shall be well."

"Maybe one day I'll come to understand who I am, though it seems to be taking me forever."

"This moment is forever," said Angel. "It has always interested me how you humans have such a strange relationship with time, and it seems to be connected to your misunderstanding of death. You think death is the end, therefore you only have a limited time to achieve what you deem important in life. But, in fact, time is not like that, it's not linear, it's cyclical. And you may only come to understand things many years after the first impulse, the first intuition, comes to you. Time bends in on itself to respond to that impulse and comes full circle.

"And anyway, time has little meaning for us angels, so what seems to you to be a long time, to us is but a moment, and in terms of your evolution it is but a moment too. I neither fret about the past nor yearn for the future. I'm just here, now. You should try it."

Jeremiah suddenly had a flash-back to the Aldermaston March and something that the hippy-guy who'd given him the book had said: 'We need to be here now, man.' Back then, Jeremiah hadn't a clue what he was talking about, but now, it seemed, everything was coming to the surface and demanding to be dealt with, here and now.

"They say your life flashes before your eyes when you are about to die," said Jeremiah, "and it feels like that's happening to me. Am I going to die, Angel? Is that why my life keeps crashing in on me?"

"We all die every day and we are reborn in every moment," said Angel enigmatically. "And remember, Jeremiah, I wasn't sent to you by anyone. I am simply part of a dimension that you dwell in because you are you. Most people are never able to come here at all."

"As far as I remember, I didn't exactly come to you, you came to me."

"Not really. As I've told you before, I was here all the time, but you didn't see me. You came to me when you needed me, and in that moment, you believed what you saw. That was your gift: you didn't doubt or reject what you saw."

"But I did faint," said Jeremiah.

"Yes, you did faint."

There was silence, and once again Jeremiah found events in his life surfacing in his memory, unbidden.

"There was this one time," he said, "…I'm trying to remember when it was and how it happened… It was a day when I was on my own in the warehouse. I had just been examining a particularly beautiful and large carpet that had arrived in a shipment the day before. There was something about it that carried me to another place, and I remember that as I looked at it, I heard a voice asking me, 'What do you want, what do you really want?' and without thinking, I replied: 'I want to be at one, in awe and unafraid.'

"The words just came to me, like that, and I remember thinking they were the most beautiful words I had ever uttered. It felt almost as if they came through me, not from me: to be at one with all that is, Angel, and to surrender myself, in awe.

"And I remember one night when I was in France with Angela and we walked down to the beach and stood looking up at a sky full of stars. As we stood there, just feeling the wonder and magnificence of the night sky, I felt a sense of awe. Does that make sense?"

"Yes of course. You see, in that moment you were truly aligned; your mind, your heart and your spirit."

"How could I have forgotten those moments? Why didn't I pay attention to those feelings?"

Angel was now standing in front of Jeremiah, his hands folded across his chest, his wings stretched wide and shimmering.

Like time itself," said Angel, "a gift is there for you to discover when you are ready."

"Am I ready now?"

"Do you feel ready?

"Well, something has to change because the one thing I do know is that I can't go on like this. I can't spend the rest of my life regretting my choices."

"That's a good start. What about being 'unafraid'?"

"Well, I may not have managed that yet."

It was then that the realisation dawned on Jeremiah of what he had been doing ever since he was a teenager. He had deliberately shut himself away. Even in those happy days at university when he'd first met Stephen, Jenny and Angela, he had always kept part of himself closed-off, distanced. And he'd liked it that way. It had felt safe. Nobody asked anything of him. And so, when those words came to him – to be at one, in awe and unafraid – rather than act, he had quietly filed them away and forgotten about them, unable really to open himself to them. Once again, he had shut himself away, this time in the warehouse – and now he knew that he was in danger of shutting himself away again in his retirement, that he might become a grumpy old recluse who raged at the world.

"You know, Angel," he said after some time, "you're right. Those words were a gift, and perhaps it's time for me to begin to explore what they mean to me? And maybe the first thing I need to explore is what it is about me that stopped me from doing that in the first place; what stopped me from opening up to the world?"

"It is connected to who you are."

Jeremiah was frustrated. "But why am I who I am, for God's sake? Why am I not like other people?"

This had always been forbidden territory for Jeremiah who, for years after Angela left, had shut himself down and refused to explore his feelings. During this time, he had met and begun relationships with a number of women, but each time, however much he liked them, or was fond of them, because of his lack of sexual arousal the relationships had faltered and then failed. He liked the company and friendship of women, but he had never been able to find someone for whom he was enough; someone who found his tenderness and his kindness enough.

"Sometimes," he sighed, "I wonder if I am the only person who feels like I do."

"You are not alone Jeremiah," said Angel, softly, "and there is something I want to tell you."

Angel leaned forward, his demeanour now serious, full of intent. "There are people all over the world who are born to explore what we in the angelic realm call, divine tenderness. It's a different kind of loving. It's not what everyone looks for, but for some it's a kind of perfection, a special kind of love. And it can be a path of grace and ease. And remember, you are who you are because you have something to tell."

"Want on earth do you mean?"

"The time will come, my dear Jeremiah, when you will fulfil your name."

From somewhere deep in the recesses of his memory, Jeremiah recalled his mother telling him that he'd been named after his paternal grandfather, whom he never met, and that this man was devout and god-fearing. Jeremiah had never much liked his name, probably because he had been teased about it as a child.

"In what way?" Jeremiah asked, intrigued.

"In biblical times, Jeremiah was a prophet. He said things that people of the time did not always want to hear, but he spoke them nonetheless."

And with that, Angel slowly faded from view.

Sitting there in his flat in Spitalfields, Jeremiah could not take it all in – this conversation, his feelings, the changes that were arising all around him. He also felt an energy arising within him, something he didn't recognise, and it disturbed him.

The next day, Jeremiah got up early and opened his new laptop, a present he had given to himself after the company had been sold, as he could no longer use the computer in his warehouse office. After such a strange day in conversation with Angel, he'd struggled to sleep that night and had lain awake pondering all that Angel had said. And now, he felt a need to contact Angela, to reach out to her. He began to write an email:

Dear Angela

I hope you are well and that you are enjoying life in Florence.

It has been a long time since I was last in touch, for which I apologise. Much has happened since then, not least that Stephen and I have sold our business. Someone came along and offered us more than we had supposed it was worth, and so we decided to sell. I think Stephen was tired of travelling on his own, and, as usual, I was persuaded by him. He's very pleased and now he and Jenny are planning to travel together. Jenny wants to visit Afghanistan, which, as you can imagine, I think is madness.

So, here I am – all those years of being in the warehouse have come to an end. I suppose I too should be pleased, but actually I have been rather at a loss and I'm still not quite sure what to do with myself next. As you know, my life was my work, and now I seem to be missing it all.

He stopped typing. He didn't know what else to say. He saved the email as a draft, closed his laptop and walked through to the kitchen to put the kettle on the hob, standing beside it until it came to the boil. After making his tea and reading the newspaper for a while, he reopened his laptop and read what he had written to Angela. He looked at those last few words again. Was it a bit pathetic to admit to missing what some would see as a dreary job in a carpet warehouse? He thought that perhaps it was. He sighed deeply and continued to write.

> Anyway, I thought you would like to know that things are changing for me, and it leaves me wondering about my life and why you and I did not work out something better than we did. I think it was my fault, and I am sorry about it. I think I did not have the courage, or even perhaps the intelligence of the heart to know what to do or how to respond to you.
>
> Angela, if it's not too late to say it – and my angel tells me it is never too late – I'm sorry, I really am. I wish I had been a better friend to you.
>
> How is Francesca? And how is Alison? Please pass on my best regards to them.
>
> With love – Jeremiah

He read the email through, pondered for a moment and then pressed, 'Send'.

He walked into his kitchen and opened the fridge. It was almost empty, so he picked up his shopping basket and the list he'd made the day before, and went out to buy groceries, relieved to have this at least to do.

When he got back and after he had restocked his fridge and pantry, he opened his laptop. Much to his surprise, there in his in-box was an email from Angela. He was delighted that she had replied so soon.

Angel appeared beside him and Jeremiah opened the email and read it aloud.

> Dearest Jeremiah
>
> What exciting news, and although I understand how much you must miss your work, and how you may for a while feel at a loss, I hope you will soon find whatever it is that you will do next.
>
> I would ask you to visit me in Florence, but I know what you will say. I have never been able to tempt you to come and see me, but the invitation is always there. I did speak to Jenny on the phone the other day and she and Stephen seem well and, as you say, are making their travel plans.
>
> Some less good news. Francesca has been diagnosed with ovarian cancer, which as you can imagine brought back some difficult memories for me, as that is what my mother died of. It was such a shock for us both. It's been caught early, and we are hopeful, but it has not been an easy time for us.
>
> Jeremiah, like you, I don't really understand why we behaved as we did all those years ago and, just as importantly, why we never seemed able to recover our special friendship. But I want you to know that I have never blamed you for it – and I agree with your angel (I had forgotten about him) – that it is never too late.

> We were who we were, Jeremiah, but now, we are who we are. Let us make a good fist of it this time. I do hope we shall be able to meet up before very long.
>
> Sending my love to you.
>
> Angela

"That's very sad news about Francesca," said Jeremiah, closing his laptop. "What a worry for them both. Perhaps I should ring her?"

"Why not?"

"You mean now?"

"Yes, why not?"

Jeremiah opened a drawer in his desk knowing exactly where to find the slip of paper with Angela's telephone number on it. The paper was old and creased and had lain there for twenty years. Jeremiah had looked at it many times, wondering whether he should ring. He never had. But now he dialled the number.

At first there was no reply, then a woman whose voice he did not recognise replied in Italian.

"Hello there," said Jeremiah. "I wonder, do you speak English at all?"

"Yes, I do," said the voice.

"Ah, that's good – unfortunately, I don't speak Italian. My name is Jeremiah, and I'd like to speak to Angela if that is possible."

"Oh Jeremiah, of course you can. This is Alison. I'll get Angela for you."

Jeremiah could hear Alison calling her. Then there

was the sound of shoes on a wooden floor.

"Jeremiah! What a lovely surprise."

"Hello, Angela. I just wanted to let you know how sorry I am to hear about Francesca."

"Thank you, Jeremiah. Thank you, but actually she is managing very well, and we have been told that the treatment should be successful in keeping the cancer in check. She has had surgery and is recovering now."

"Will she have to have chemotherapy?"

"Yes, she will have to go back to the hospital for a series of treatments, but we are not sure when."

"Gosh, that's a lot to have to think about."

"We'll manage."

"Thank goodness you are there for her."

"Thank you, Jeremiah. It is kind of you to say that."

"I mean it. You must be a great support for her."

There was a silence.

"Would you mind letting me know how things go?" asked Jeremiah.

"Of course. Of course, I will."

"And give Francesca my very best wishes."

"Thank you, Jeremiah. Goodbye for now and thank you again for ringing."

Jeremiah put down his phone and looked at Angel.

"Why did I never do that before?"

"It was most kind of you to send best wishes to Francesca."

"Well, it is time for me to accept that they love one another."

Angel bowed deeply to his friend and disappeared.

SEEDS OF INDIFFERENCE

The week after Katharine called about her plans for Italy, Sarah received another phone call, this time from her son Nicholas, to say that he was planning to bring his two daughters, Bryony and Iris, for a short holiday to London and then on to Devon for a couple of days, before flying home from Bristol. He said he realised they couldn't all fit into her cottage, so he had arranged to stay in a B&B in Bude for a couple of nights.

The call was unexpected, and Sarah was delighted. Although they only lived in Dublin, a short flight away, she had not seen her son and his family for nearly four years and she was looking forward to seeing how her granddaughters, now teenagers, were growing up. She had invited them to visit many times before, but each time it seemed that it was difficult for Nicholas's wife, Chloe, to leave her elderly parents and Nicholas didn't want to travel without her. They had never once invited Sarah to Dublin.

Even on this occasion, Chloe didn't accompany them, but perhaps because the girls were older, Nicholas felt he could cope on his own. They would be arriving a week on Friday, going first to their B&B and then coming to Elmsford after lunch the following day.

As planned, at three o'clock on the Saturday afternoon, a car pulled up and there was Sarah's son and two girls she hardly recognised. The last time she'd seen them they were just kids. Now they were young women, or almost. Nicholas hugged her, as did his daughters, somewhat awkwardly.

"Come on in," she said. "How was London?"

Sarah felt a pang of anxiety, an odd feeling, for here was her son and here were her granddaughters and she was really pleased to see them, but as they came in she realised that they were like strangers to her and there was a stiffness in the girls, a mixture of forced familiarity and embarrassment. Nicholas looked around and said nice things about the cottage and the two girls agreed, but added nothing more, and Sarah felt uncertain of what she could say to them. She resorted to tea, and the girls seemed impressed with the Victoria sponge she had made with fresh cream and raspberries.

After tea she suggested a walk. Nicholas said yes, but Sarah sensed the two girls were a bit reluctant. They were both wearing new trainers that were clearly more suited to pavements than footpaths. She found them a pair of old wellies each, that she kept in the cupboard under the stairs, and it enabled her to make a bit of a fuss of them and give them a hug.

"I like your nail varnish, Gran," Bryony said.

They set off and walked down the village street, but instead of going into the woods, which even at the height of summer could be a bit muddy, she took the route through the churchyard and past James's house and along the footpath through fields where the grass was burnished by the sun, and then to the cliff edge overlooking the sea. The views south to Cornwall were stunning, but both girls' eyes were glued to the screens of their phones. Sarah thought they ought to look where they were going, but they were not in the least bit interested in the views, nor joining the conversation with their father and grandmother; they were preoccupied, taking photos of each other in various pouting poses with the sea as a backdrop.

Nicholas took his mother's arm and they walked further down the cliff to a grassy bank where they could sit and admire the views. Sarah asked Nicholas about his work at the Guinness Brewery in Dublin.

"Work's fine. You know, it's just work, but I like the guys I work with, and I don't want to work anywhere else. The company's pretty good to us."

"And Chloe's parents?"

"They're not well. Not at all. Actually, Chloe says she's worried they'll not survive the coming winter."

"Oh dear, poor Chloe. That's a lot for her to have to cope with," said Sarah, though she felt it was perhaps a little early to be worrying about the winter.

"Yes, it is. But what about you, Mum? Are you well?"

As Nicholas had never before shown much interest in her wellbeing, Sarah wondered if he thought that she too might not survive the winter.

"I'm well, thank you. I'm… enjoying my retirement. I've joined the Elmsford Elderberries, a group of us older women who meet up for a swim once a week, down there in the harbour."

"What on earth do you do that for? It doesn't look at all inviting – it just looks cold and grey and dirty."

Sarah had expected this reaction. Her son rarely saw the beauty in things.

"It makes me feel alive," she replied. "At my age, that's a good enough reason to do anything."

After a while, they walked back to Sarah's cottage, past The Sanctuary.

"A very dear friend of mine used to live there," Sarah ventured, pointing at the house, "but he passed away eighteen months ago."

Nicholas did not respond, and she wondered if he had even heard her. Sarah had never told her son about James, fearing his wrath, knowing that he would see it as a betrayal of his father. Nicholas had always seemed more concerned about protecting the feelings of his father than accepting those of his mother.

When they got back to Sarah's cottage, Nicholas began making ready to leave, saying he wanted to get back to the B&B before it was dark.

"But you'll stay for some supper, surely?" asked Sarah, feeling like she was being abandoned. "I've made a lovely quiche and some salad."

The girls looked at each other in alarm. They either hated salad, or they had plans for a night out in Bude.

"Ah, you know how it is Mum. I'd forgotten how dodgy these back lanes are, so I'd rather set off whilst it's still light." Nicholas ushered the girls out of the door. "Look Mum, tomorrow morning I'm taking the girls to St Austell to show them where I grew up, and we're going to visit Dad's grave. I've ordered a bouquet of flowers for him, and I want my daughters to know where their granddad is buried. So, we'll pop back here tomorrow afternoon to say goodbye, on our way to the airport. We won't be able to stay long."

After they'd left, Sarah felt exhausted, wrung-out. It would be at least another couple of hours before dusk and it only took 30 minutes to drive to Bude. It was obvious they didn't want to stay. And also, though she hated to admit it, she felt offended that Nick preferred to spend what little time they had in the UK tending the grave of his dead father rather than spending time with his mother, who was still very much alive. Was it uncharitable to wish that he'd bought flowers for her?

"That was hard work," she said to Willow, who had appeared from nowhere.

These people were her flesh and blood, her family and yet she felt so disconnected from them. They all seemed so distracted, so distant, in touch with another world that Sarah was not part of.

The following afternoon, they called by on their way to Bristol airport to catch an evening flight to Dublin. Again, Sarah felt the distance between them, and it saddened her. They didn't have much more to say to each other, and soon they made moves to leave.

Just as she was about to slam the passenger door shut, the older girl, Bryony, had second thoughts. She got out of the car and went back to where Sarah was standing. A little awkwardly, she put her arms around her grandmother's waist and gave her a hug.

"Thanks for my birthday present, Gran. It was just what I wanted," she said, and squeezed Sarah a little tighter. Then she hopped into the car and they were off.

Sarah watched them drive away, Bryony and Iris sitting hunched in the back seat looking at their phones. She stood and waved goodbye to them until the car was out of sight, but the girls didn't turn and wave to her. She walked back towards her cottage, wondering whether she would ever see them again. After all, why would they come? She doubted they felt anything very much for her, though Bryony's hug did cheer her up a bit. But what did Nick feel? A sense of duty? A touch of guilt, perhaps? It didn't feel like love. He was like his father when it came to love – silent.

This hurt Sarah, and it made her think of Katharine and what she had said about her relationship with her parents. Perhaps, just as she had, Katharine's mother had tried her best to be a good parent, but had it been good enough? Perhaps, as Alice had once told her, at some time or another, all parents think they should have done things differently?

She had loved Nick as a child, of that she was certain, but her husband Alan frowned on overt expressions of love. He thought it was 'soppy' and would 'make the boy soft'. So, she had allowed a distance to grow between them. Now she could see that without meaning to, she and Alan had sown the seeds of indifference in their son.

"Why didn't I stand up to Alan?" she asked Willow who was curled on the sofa in a pool of sunshine, preening herself. "Why did I just accept his word as law?" And then, because of the way she felt about

Katharine, "Do you think I would I have loved a daughter differently?"

Willow didn't answer of course, but Sarah thought that there were a lot of things she would do differently now, with age and hindsight. She certainly thought she had let her husband dictate their lives too much. Alan never wanted to talk about feelings – whether hers or his own. It embarrassed him, and if Sarah tried to express how she was feeling, he just walked out of the room. After a while, she'd stopped trying to discuss such things. That's just how it was. It made her sad, but she could see no way out. And it had left an emptiness in her, an emptiness that was always waiting to be filled.

Perhaps that's why she had loved James so much? They had known each other for such a short time, a few precious years, and yet love had emerged so easily between them and with almost no effort, or so it now seemed to Sarah. It made her wonder where love came from. She could only say she knew that James needed love. Recovering from the death of his wife, he had needed to receive love and to give it. And Sarah had liked that, because when she had seen it in him, she realised it was what she needed, too. And perhaps that was why she and Katharine had found each other. Isn't it the same thing really, the giving and receiving of love? Isn't that what we all need?

Sarah sighed. All she could do was hope that her son and grandchildren were happy, though she had seen little evidence of that during their visit.

"I wonder what you would tell me, my dear James?" she said aloud, and for a moment she imagined he was there. But she knew his presence was receding.

WHAT HAS TO HAPPEN

The days passed into weeks and then months and Jeremiah gradually became more accustomed to life without work. He had begun to read a great deal more than he had done when he was at work; one of the pleasures of being retired and not always feeling exhausted at the end of the day, he supposed. He'd taken to the habit of visiting Foyles Bookshop in Charing Cross Road just for the pleasure of looking through shelf after shelf of books in both the cookery and history sections, though of late he'd been branching out into contemporary literature too, on the advice of a friendly man who wore a badge saying, Store Manager, a role for which Jeremiah thought he looked far too young. They had struck up an acquaintance, and the young man seemed to enjoy setting aside books for him.

In fact, Jeremiah had to admit that he was beginning to enjoy his retirement. His constant questioning of life seemed to have subsided since his 'breakdown' – as he'd come to see it – after he retired. And of late, he had initiated a new regimen, allowing himself an extra half-hour or so in bed in the morning, to write in his journal (another new habit) and then to shower and take a leisurely breakfast. His norm whilst at work was to grab a coffee and croissant from the café near the warehouse, but now it was fruit and yoghurt, followed by toast and tea, or porridge and honey when the mornings were cold. He had also got into the habit of taking longer walks to far flung markets where he found unusual ingredients for his cookery experiments, and he'd even been to the theatre a couple of times, a treat he and Angela used to enjoy on occasion.

But what he relished most was the frequent exchange of emails he was having with Angela. Francesca, it seemed, was doing well and responding to her treatment, much to Angela's relief. And although they didn't mention their estrangement again, Jeremiah felt that there was some kind of unspoken acceptance between them, an understanding that what had happened, happened and that there was no blame or guilt to be felt about it.

And yet even though much had changed for the better, Jeremiah had a mounting sense that something was missing from his life, though quite what, he didn't know. He was happier in his new routine, certainly, but now he felt a restlessness too, and it was not a feeling he liked, at all. Restlessness had never once plagued him in life before retirement, but now he felt it as a kind of frisson throughout his body; a ball of anxiety in his stomach, and the bones of his legs often ached and felt uncomfortable, as if they did not know what to do with themselves. He looked up his symptoms on the internet and couldn't believe that there was actually a name for this: Restless Legs Syndrome.

The longer walks he was in the habit of taking helped to settle his legs a little, but at night when his legs ached most, all he could do was pace his flat and this very act reinforced his restlessness.

He wrote to Angela about it, and about something else that he was becoming acutely aware of.

> I have come to see that although I have always lived in London, and in Spitalfields for many years now, I hardly know anybody. I see familiar faces, yes – the woman who serves in the grocers, or the old chap I buy my newspaper from by the Tube station, but apart from the young man in Foyles and my beloved Angel, I hardly speak to a soul from one week to the next. All these millions of people in London and all the busyness and bustle that surrounds me, and yet I feel as if I am a stranger here.

And then something dreadful happened.

One warm evening in July, quite late, Jeremiah decided to go out for a stroll before going to bed, to try and settle his legs. On the way back to his flat it began to rain, and so he decided to take a shortcut through a narrow street only lit by a lamp post at the far end. He rounded the corner and was in sight of his own front door, when he noticed a group of four young men, hooded and wearing dark tracksuit bottoms, coming towards him. They seemed to be joking with each other and he thought they were just messing about, but as he walked towards them, he saw that they had formed a line across the street, and he realised that they were not going to let him pass.

Jeremiah slowed down, unsure of what was going on, and eventually stopped walking. They looked to see if anyone else was coming, but the street was empty and in the houses of Jeremiah's neighbours, the curtains had already been drawn. One of the lads stepped forward.

"Not your lucky night, mate," he said, and pulled a knife from his pocket.

Jeremiah froze. "What do you want?" he said, trying not to show his fear.

"Well, we'll start with your phone and your wallet."

The other young men hung back, and Jeremiah sensed that they were uneasy with what was happening, but the one wielding the knife took another menacing step towards him.

"I don't have my phone with me."

"He don't 'ave his phone," the lad sneered, turning to his friends. "What a surprise, granddad. Well, what do you 'ave? Let's see that watch."

Jeremiah took off his watch, a cheap Timex, and handed it to him, and then, as the young man – no more than a boy really – stood there smirking at him, he also handed over his wallet. It only had about thirty pounds of cash in it and no credit cards. Jeremiah didn't approve of them.

Stupidly, Jeremiah smiled at the boy and said, "Not really worth it, is it?"

The boy punched Jeremiah in the stomach and then kicked his legs, so that he fell to the ground and hit his head on the road. Then he continued to kick Jeremiah viciously in the ribs, one blow after another making him double-up in pain. The boy was yelling at him, swearing and calling him a useless piece of shit. Then he stood over Jeremiah, the knife pointing at his face and it looked to Jeremiah as if all the hate in the world was etched on that boy's face.

Time seemed to stand still and for a long moment Jeremiah thought that his life was about to end, but then one of the others pulled him away as a car turned into the street. They left Jeremiah and ran off, the boy with the knife throwing Jeremiah's watch back at him in disgust. As it hit the tarmac, the watch case cracked and then the car drove past and crushed it completely. Whoever was driving didn't stop to see if Jeremiah was alright. They obviously didn't want to get involved.

Slowly, Jeremiah picked himself up off the floor, each breath like hot knives in his ribs. He staggered along the pavement to his flat, blood running down his cheek from a cut to his eyebrow. His hands were shaking so much that he could not get his key in the lock. He slumped to the floor, the shock suddenly draining the energy from his legs and for some time he stayed there, dazed and confused in an agony of pain, his head throbbing, nausea rising in his throat.

Eventually he found his feet, got his key in the lock and opened the door. He didn't know what to do, so he did the only thing he could think of; he called Stephen.

"Stephen..."

"Jerry? What's up, mate?"

"I've… been attacked… can you… pop round? I feel… a bit rough."

Within ten minutes Stephen was there. Long ago the two men had given each other a spare key to their homes, just in case, but this was the first time one had been used. Stephen let himself in and found Jeremiah throwing up in the kitchen sink. He could not see that Jeremiah was being held in Angel's wings.

"Bloody hell," he said as he ran the tap and plunged a towel into a bowl of warm water. "What the hell happened?"

"Mugged," Jeremiah managed to whisper and then collapsed to the floor.

Stephen rang for an ambulance and put a dry towel under Jeremiah's head, dabbing at the deep cut over his eyebrow with the damp towel.

Jeremiah came round and groaned, still finding it hard to breathe.

"Shh, shh, don't speak. It's okay – we'll get you to A&E, and patch you up. I've called the police too. We'll get the bastards who did this."

"Kids… it was just kids."

"Jesus!"

Jeremiah had two broken ribs and mild concussion, but other than lots of cuts and bruises, he was okay. The police were worse than useless, inferring that if Jeremiah was stupid enough to go out walking late at night, what else could he expect but to be mugged?

Stephen insisted that Jeremiah convalesce with him and Jenny so that they could take care of him and cook his meals, and for that, Jeremiah was grateful, for even getting out of bed for a pee was painful.

Gradually, his ribs began to mend, and his bruises faded – but it wasn't the bruises on the outside that were the problem. Jeremiah had been bruised on the inside. Never before had he felt so afraid, so violated. He did not consider himself an old man, but he was certainly feeling his age after experiencing the fear and violence of the mugging.

Two weeks later, Jeremiah returned home. But it was a place that no longer felt safe to him. The feelings he was having before the mugging – of isolation and loneliness – seemed to intensify. He walked over to the window in his living room and looked down on the busy street below. Were any of these people the ones who attacked him? What were those boys doing hanging around by the bus stop? He was sure he recognised them. His heart began to beat faster and sweat formed on his brow.

Jeremiah couldn't comprehend how it could be possible to feel safe in his home again; how he could walk the streets, as was his wont, without being in fear for his life. He sighed and winced at the pain he still felt from his bruised ribs.

The morning after he arrived home, waking in his bed still feeling sore and frightened, Jeremiah began to formulate an idea.

Angel appeared.

"How are you feeling?"

"Not great. Not great. And Angel, I've been meaning to ask for some time; where were you on the night of the mugging?"

"I was with you, but as you know, I can do nothing to prevent what has to happen."

Jeremiah was wishing his head didn't ache so much.

"But why did it have to happen? I don't understand why you say that."

"Turning points often come in the wake of crisis."

Jeremiah pondered this response for some time.

"Actually, you might be right. I think I have reached a turning point. So much has happened Angel; first the business closing, then reconciling with Angela, and now... I feel sure it's time for another change."

Angel rustled his wings.

"What have you in mind?"

"I've decided to leave London – for good."

"That is quite a change."

"But do you approve?"

Angel looked at him and smiled.

"It is not for me to approve or disapprove. As you know, Jeremiah, only you can make these kinds of decisions, but perhaps something is being offered to you. The mugging was horrendous, but suppose it was necessary?"

"What do you mean?"

"Well, what if something like that needed to happen

to allow you to make a change? I think it might be telling you something."

Jeremiah thought for a moment.

"I think so, too. And I feel it Angel. I feel it is time to begin again, and to be somewhere else. I have been feeling so restless, but as soon as I am fully recovered, I am going to make some changes in my life. I'm going to make some big changes."

"So where will you start this adventure of yours?"

"Do you remember that holiday we had in Bude?"

SLIPPING AWAY

It was Saturday and Sarah was looking forward to Katharine returning from her holiday in Rome. She'd said she would arrive just before lunch, and so earlier that morning, Sarah had made a flan with feta and asparagus, Katharine's favourites, and a leafy green salad, most of which she'd picked from her garden. She set the dining table, with linen napkins and glasses for the white wine she had chilling in the fridge. She wanted it to be special, a little celebration.

Just before mid-day, Katharine's yellow car pulled up in front of her house and there she was, smiling and looking well, her skin slightly tanned and her long red hair piled loosely on her head in chic bun. Sarah went out and hugged her and helped her in with her bags.

"Oh, it's so lovely to be here," said Katharine, and flopped down onto the sofa beside Willow, who stood up and stretched and began to purr as Katharine stroked her.

As they sat together and ate their lunch, Sarah was surprised by quite how much she had missed Katharine, and how good it felt to have her back.

"This flan is delicious," said Katharine, reaching for her glass of wine.

"I knew you'd like it. So, tell me all about Rome."

"It was absolutely wonderful, Sarah – just what I needed. Abbie's flat is fabulous, right in the centre of the city so we could walk everywhere. We just walked and talked really. Abbie and her boyfriend aren't getting on too well, so we spent quite a lot of time talking about men. He's decided to go back to university to take a Masters in some kind of physics, which means he's going to be away in Milan. She is a bit upset by it all, and I know how she feels."

"You certainly do, darling."

"Yes, but we talked about how Tom and I are learning to cope with being apart, and I think she found that helpful. It's happening to a lot of our friends, you know. It seems to be part of the world we live in now. We can move about more easily than ever before, but that sometimes means we move apart, too."

Sarah thought how different this all sounded to her life. The kinds of difficulties she had had as a young woman were about feeling she couldn't escape rather than worrying about being apart.

"Anyway," said Katharine, "Abbie showed me all the things you have to see in Rome. You know, the Coliseum, the Trevi Fountain, the Pantheon, and the Sistine Chapel, which was my favourite. Then we drank a lot of wine and ate a lot of pasta. And talked and talked."

"Did you take photos?"

"Yes, lots. Look."

Katharine took her iPad from her bag and began to

show Sarah the sights of Rome, including a lot of pictures of young people drinking and laughing and making faces into the camera. She had obviously had a good time.

"So, how did you get on with Nick's visit?"

Sarah placed her knife and fork on one side of her plate.

"Well, alright I suppose, but I found it unsettling."

"Oh no. Why?"

"Well, it was good to see Nick and to know that he and Chloe are okay – although her parents are not at all well…"

"But?"

"But the girls were like strangers to me, really."

"What do you mean?"

"Well, I don't know what I was expecting – after all, they hardly know me – but I don't think they wanted to be here at all. They're just being teenagers, I suppose."

"Not known for being chatty."

"No, but they took endless pictures and selfies."

"But not of you?"

"No, not of me. But I did get a hug from Bryony just as they were leaving. She'll never know how much that meant to me."

Katharine stood up and put her arms around Sarah.

"I'll give you a hug," she said. "Would you like to go to Bude this afternoon? We could walk along the beach, and then have tea in that lovely new café by the canal."

That was exactly what Sarah needed.

They parked in the car park just behind the beach and walked across the golden sand to the sea's edge, where they stood looking out over the water, seagulls flying over their heads.

"I have to go back to Truro on Monday," said Katharine, "to get ready for the new term and do my lesson planning, and then I'm going to a conference in Exeter the following weekend, but I'll be back the weekend after that, if that's okay?"

"Of course." Sarah bent down and picked up a smooth black pebble, holding it in the palm of her hand. "What's your conference about?"

Katharine sounded excited. "It's about the role of women in education," she said. "I think it will be fascinating. There's one particular lecturer who's giving a talk called, 'The Suppressed Voices of Women' – how about that? She's called Professor Miriam Husk, and everyone says she's terrific."

"That sounds really interesting. I'm feeling a bit suppressed at the moment, so you'll have to tell me what she has to say."

"I'm sorry you're feeling like that, Sarah. Families can be so bloody tricky, can't they?"

"They certainly can."

Katharine walked away from her a little further down the beach and then turned in towards the dunes, finding a sunny spot and beckoning Sarah to join her. They sat together, not saying much, just enjoying being there.

Sarah was still somewhat preoccupied by her feelings of estrangement from her family. Had she wanted to be a mother-figure for Katharine because she was so disconnected from her own son? When Katharine first came to stay, Sarah often thought about her in terms of a surrogate daughter, but as time passed, Sarah felt more and more that they were meeting as equals, as two women who enjoyed a deep and loving friendship. And that felt right. It felt simple, it felt easy – not convoluted and awkward, as her feelings were for her son.

As they drove home, Sarah told Katharine something that she'd wanted to share with her for some time .

"You know I told you about how I was still talking to James?"

"Yes, I remember," said Katharine.

"Well, recently he seems to be slipping away from me. I know that might sound strange considering he passed away nearly two years ago, but I am wondering whether this is what happens when we lose someone we love? At first the memory is intense and raw, painful even, but in time, whilst the memory remains, it becomes more subtle, more dreamlike. Do you think that is what is happening to me? Do you think James is slipping away?"

Katharine was quiet for a moment and then she said, "Is it possible that love finds other ways to express itself and that then, an old love becomes a memory?"

Sarah did not reply, but Katharine had sown a seed that would grow and shoot forth.

Katharine arrived back in Elmsford a couple of weeks later, but Sarah was not there to meet her. She was at The Sanctuary with Alice, preparing for the guests who were to arrive that afternoon. Alice didn't really need Sarah's help anymore, but it was always a good excuse for the two friends to get together and have a cup of coffee and linger on James's veranda and catch up with all their news. And Alice had some exciting news to share with her.

"Guess what?"

"What?"

"Me and Rachel are going to buy a house!" Sarah's first thought was that they might move away from the area and her heart sunk, but then Alice added, "We found out last week that Rachel's Uncle Ian has left her some money in his Will. She was very close to him and he didn't have children of his own and he always told her she was his favourite niece. Anyway, it's not a huge amount, but it's enough for a deposit, so we've decided to look around this area and see what we can afford. We'd like to move into Elmsford if we can, but properties here are so expensive."

"It's because we're by the sea, apparently. Mrs Penny was telling me the other day when we were getting changed after our swim that if you buy a house that's on the other side of the Atlantic Highway – you know, inland – they're often about 25% cheaper than the sea side."

"No way…?" said Alice. "I must mention that to

Rachel when I get home. She'll probably start looking online straight away. She's really excited about all this. We both are actually."

"I think it's wonderful Alice – I hope you find a home that's perfect for you both."

To her delight, when Sarah got back to her own lovely little home, she found Katharine sitting on the sofa stroking Willow.

"Hello, hello – how lovely to see you."

Katharine beamed and got up to hug Sarah. "It's so good to be here. I've missed you."

"Let's get a cup of tea and you can tell me all about the conference."

They busied themselves in the kitchen, Sarah finding the packet of chocolate ginger biscuits she'd been saving for Katharine's return, and Katharine warming the pot ready for the tea.

"Well, how was it?"

"Oh, it was just great to be with so many other trainee teachers, and as I expected, the star speaker was Professor Husk – for me anyway. She spoke with a kind of quiet authority, which I guess comes from the depth of her own research. She seems to have read just about everything and has a lot to say about how women must learn to speak up for themselves. In fact, I've just ordered her book, *Women's Wisdom.*"

"You sound very taken by it all."

"I am, Sarah, and it has absolutely confirmed to me that what I want to do is teach."

"Well, that's grand."

They took their drinks into the sitting room and made themselves comfortable.

"Oh, by the way, there's something else I need to tell you. In one of the breaks, I got talking to Professor Husk, and she told me that she's in the middle of a research project and is looking for a place of solitude to complete her work. A refuge. Well, of course, I immediately thought of The Sanctuary, and showed her the pictures on the Airbnb website. She said it looked perfect. And then, when I said it belonged to my boyfriend's mother, she straightaway asked if I thought it would be possible for her to rent the house for the winter. What do you think? I said I'd speak to you about it."

"Well, I suppose it might be possible. The bookings are always a bit thin in the winter months. I think it would be best to speak with Julia about it. You know how she likes to feel in control of things."

"Yes, I do. Can I put a few things through the washing machine?"

"Yes, of course."

Katharine went up to her bedroom to sort out her clothes and Sarah wondered whether Professor Husk would really come to live at James's house.

Later that day, Katharine called Tom's mother and then reported back.

"She liked the idea of Professor Husk staying at The Sanctuary. She said it would save her lots of time fretting about whether or not the house would be occupied and reduce the cost of Alice preparing the house each time for new guests."

"That sounds just like Julia – ever the pragmatist."

"In the end she suggested that Professor Husk speaks to her directly. So, I'll send her an email."

All of that sounded straightforward, but there was something in Katharine's voice that worried Sarah. She seemed upset.

"Are you okay, darling?"

Katharine pushed a lock of her hair back behind her ear.

"Not really," she said, quietly. "The thing with The Sanctuary was fine, but then Julia asked me whether I knew when Tom was coming back, and I said I wasn't sure, and… I don't know, just talking about it stirred up all that's happening between Tom and me."

Sarah sat beside her and took her hand. Katharine was looking down into her lap, and a tear slowly trickled down her cheeks. She sniffed and wiped her eyes with the back of her sleeve.

"I'm getting used to being without him, Sarah. After all, it's nearly a year now. Mostly, I've got used to not wondering too much about what he's doing or who he's with – or if he's missing me like I'm missing him – but then, either he calls or sends a text or something like this happens, and it upsets me. I accept the distance between us and think I can cope, and then we're in touch, but not really in touch, and somehow that makes us seem further apart than ever. You'd think it would help being able to talk on the phone or Skype, but actually sometimes it makes things worse because I feel what I am missing so intensely, and there seems to be no end to it."

They sat for a while.

"What do you want to happen?" asked Sarah.

"I want him to come back. I know he has to do his work, of course, but I miss him. A lot."

"Does he talk about what his plans might be?"

"Sometimes, but it's all very uncertain at the moment. He loves his job, but he has a lot of responsibility and I think that weighs quite heavily on him. All he said the last time we spoke about it was that he hoped he would be back before the end of the year, but that's months away."

"Well, at least that gives you an idea of when he might be home, doesn't it? Isn't that something?"

"I suppose so. Actually, I've been thinking about going to see him when my course finishes, if finances allow."

"Well, that would be good. Does he know how you are feeling?"

"I'm not sure if he knows how upset I get."

"Well, you must tell him. He needs to know."

"The thing is, Sarah, I do support what Tom's doing one hundred per cent. He's so passionate about his work because he knows that it's important to find out how we're impacting the Earth's systems. And that's another thing – he won't just fly back for a week because he knows exactly what damage those carbon emissions do. I know that without people like Tom, we'd have a very uncertain future, so he's working for all of us in a way. My mind knows this, but my heart just misses being with him so much. It actually hurts."

"I know something of that pain, darling," she said. "I felt it so sharply after James died, and I still do. But I am coming to terms with it. Perhaps, eventually, you will feel it less keenly, especially as you know you'll see Tom again before too long, and that he's doing what he's doing for good reasons. And it would be great if you could visit him at some point. Anyway, you're going to be very busy over the next few months."

Katharine let out a deep sigh.

"Yes, I am," she said, "and that will help."

"We may even have your Professor Husk living in The Sanctuary."

Katharine smiled. "Well, that would be good – I think you'd like her, Sarah."

Sarah thought that James would approve of a scholarly woman working in his study.

FATE

It took six weeks after the mugging for the pain to lessen in Jeremiah's ribs, but having made a decision to leave London, he used his time wisely. First of all, he paid a decorator to come in and give the flat a lick of paint. He was rather embarrassed to admit that the last time the flat had been decorated was the summer Angela lived with him, before her father died. She'd chosen some colour schemes that would now be considered 'very 1970s' and he could see the decorator was rather startled by what he saw. He advised Jeremiah to go for neutral tones of stone and lichen to which Jeremiah agreed.

It turned out that because of the length of time that his flat had been left unattended, there were quite a lot of other jobs that needed to be done, such as sanding and staining the wooden window sills and all the floors too, filling holes in the plaster and replacing the cracked stained glass in the front door. Jeremiah had not noticed that any of these things needed repairing, or at least, they had not bothered him, but now he saw them as symbolic of his own decline: that he cared for his home about as much as he cared for himself.

Over the weeks that he was there, Jeremiah became quite friendly with Fred the decorator and was sad to see him go when the job was done, but the flat had been improved beyond measure, the sunlight bouncing around the light and airy rooms through the big south-facing windows, everything looking pristine and clean. Jeremiah then instructed an estate agent to put his flat on the market.

There was one thing that Jeremiah had to do that he had been somewhat dreading. He picked up the phone and rang Stephen.

"How are you feeling, Jerry?"

"Oh, I'm on the mend now, thanks. Look, Stephen, there's something I need to tell you and Jenny."

"Go on."

"I've decided to leave London. For good."

"Well, it's not like we couldn't see this coming."

"What do you mean?"

"Well… the mugging, and the business closing… You've got to do something with the rest of your life, so why not this. I'm pleased for you mate. I'll miss you, but I think it's a good thing."

Jeremiah let out a long slow whistle. "I don't know why, but I was dreading telling you."

"I only want what's best for you Jerry, and anyway, we can always come and visit you. Where are you thinking of moving to?"

"Well, the westcountry, possibly. I'm going to book into a hotel in Bude and have a look at what's for sale."

"You should call in and see Bernard whilst you're there. He might have some advice and ideas."

"I'm not sure he'll even remember me," said Jeremiah, though he certainly remembered Bernard.

"He will," Stephen chuckled. "You're more memorable than you think. And anyway, if you're serious about this 'moving to the country' lark, then you're going to need to make some friends."

In the first week of October, Jeremiah hired a car and drove from London to Cornwall via the A303 – a route that he preferred to the monotony of the motorways. He had planned to stop for lunch somewhere near Stonehenge, but the traffic was so heavy, he just carried on, instead stopping at a roadside café near Honiton for a very poor lasagne and a very good cup of tea.

He had booked himself into a rather lovely family-run hotel in Bude, quite near to the canal and the house he'd once stayed in with Stephen and Jenny. Although autumn was definitely in the air, the town was still busy with holiday makers. He remarked on this to the rather bored-looking woman who was the receptionist at his hotel, and she said, with a wry smile, "Oh well, sir, at this time of year, the kids are back at school and instead we've got what's known in the trade as the 'newly-weds and nearly-deads'."

She gave him his key, and Jeremiah supposed that he was a 'nearly dead'.

The following morning, he went to see several of the local estate agents who had premises in the town and came back to the hotel with a dozen sets of particulars. He settled down with a cup of coffee to read through them all, and one or two looked quite promising. Then, Jeremiah rang Bernard who did indeed recall their meeting some years ago and promptly invited him over for tea that afternoon.

Jeremiah began to feel good, lighter somehow, enjoying a sense of adventure as he drove across the border from Cornwall into Devon, and then through the narrow lanes to the village where Bernard lived. The countryside seemed to welcome him, with its burgeoning hedgerows full of blackberries and tall grasses, the fields dotted with black and white cows or sheep, and always a distant view of the sea glittering in the sunshine.

"How very nice to see you again," said Bernard, as he opened his front door. "Do come in." He ushered Jeremiah through the house into the warmth of the walled garden, where they'd sat for lunch once before. He had prepared a tray of tea and biscuits.

"So, you're thinking of moving this way?"

"Well, yes, I am," said Jeremiah. "I find I have become weary of London, and I want to move to somewhere in the countryside or beside the sea. I really liked it here last time I came, so I thought I'd come back and have a look around. I must say, it is a lovely part of the world."

"Yes, isn't it," Bernard beamed. "Though the winters can be quite brutal – constant westerly gales and horizontal rain. You have been warned. Anyway, have you decided what area might suit you? Are you drawn to Cornwall or Devon?"

"Both, really. I've got details of some places in Bude and inland a little, towards Holsworthy, and I also have some particulars of a rather nice place near Appledore, which is supposed to be a lovely little town. Do you know it?"

"I do, but the houses there are quite pricey."

"Yes, I noticed. I suppose that's the second home market for Londoners like me?"

"Yes, that and being on the coast, which always pushes the prices up. And the town gets very busy in high summer."

"Is that why you chose a little village like this?"

"In a way, but it was also by happenstance. When my late wife and I were looking for a place, a friend of ours who lived here heard about this house coming onto the market and arranged for us to see it. We saw it and fell in love with it. So that was that."

"Sounds like fate."

"Yes, I think it was. Talking of which, there is a cottage in a nearby village that is about to come onto the market. It belongs to a friend of mine, Geraldine Burton. She's moving to Plymouth to live with her sister, who has a nice place on the Barbican, apparently. Do you remember going to see that rather lovely church in Elmsford, last time you came?"

"I do, very much so."

'Well, it's right opposite that church."

"No! How extraordinary – that does sound like fate."

"Would you like to see it?"

"Yes, I would."

"Let me give Geraldine a ring. Two ticks."

Bernard went into his house to make the phone call,

then shortly after came back shaking his head.

"I'm sorry, there was no reply. But if you leave me your mobile number, I'll call her again later and then ring you back."

"Thank you so much."

Jeremiah felt a slight twinge of disappointment. He'd enjoyed his day so much and had dared to hope that fate would point him in the right direction too.

Later that afternoon back at the hotel, after restoring his spirits by taking a long walk along the shoreline, noting how the golden sand was flecked by the footprints of wading birds and roaming dogs, Jeremiah received a call from Bernard to say he had managed to speak to Geraldine.

"Excellent. What did she say?" Jeremiah sat upright, eager for the news.

"Well, I feel a bit awful really – I feel like I gave you false hope, because she's already accepted an offer from a young local couple who'd heard she was leaving to live with her sister. So, the house is off the market before it was even on the market. I do apologise, Jeremiah."

Jeremiah had not expected this. He was certain that things were beginning to fall into place for him, and this felt like a setback.

"Oh well," he replied, obviously rather deflated, "perhaps it wasn't meant to be. Please don't worry Bernard, I'm very grateful for your help."

"Well, good luck in finding the right place, Jeremiah, and do let me know when that happens. I very much hope you will come for lunch again once you've moved here."

"I'd like that, thank you. Goodbye Bernard."

Jeremiah put the phone down. The news had knocked the wind out of his sails.

He spent a few more days half-heartedly looking at houses and cottages, but none of them seemed quite right – there was a lovely house near Holsworthy, but it was right next to a huge farm with bellowing cows and tractors rumbling past the garden gate constantly, which Jeremiah thought would get on his nerves; then there was the place in Appledore which was quaint and had lovely glimpses of the estuary from the upstairs windows, but it was on the north side of the street, and so it was very dark inside. It was the middle of the day and the estate agent had to switch the light on for him to look around; and then there was a nice, detached house between Bude and Widemouth Bay, a rather lovely house actually, but it was so near the edge of the cliff that the garden had begun to crumble into the sea. Oh no, he didn't want the stress of wondering if he was next to go over the edge.

With his tail between his legs, Jeremiah returned to London, feeling defeated, as if his grand idea of moving to the countryside had been just a silly fantasy; that he'd been clutching at straws after the mugging.

One evening he broached the subject with Angel.

"Was I really so naïve as to think that I'd find a place in the country just like that?"

"My friend, when you set an intention, it takes some time for the molecules to align. Perhaps patience is all that is necessary?"

"I have no idea what you mean, Angel."

"Think of your intention to move to the countryside as similar to sowing a seed. Does a gardener expect to see a row of peas the day after sowing them? No, it takes weeks, sometimes months for them to grow. Your intention was powerful – I felt a strong energy emanating from you as you focused your trajectory westward. Now you must trust that energy to align and create your path."

Jeremiah sighed. Angel's words simply confused him all the more. And then there was the constant stream of phone calls from the estate agent, who wanted to arrange viewings of Jeremiah's flat. Jeremiah didn't know whether to take his flat off the market, or not.

"I thought I was getting better, Angel. After the mugging, I thought I could see my path ahead, but now that vision has disappeared, it's gone. I feel so downcast, as if I couldn't now muster the energy to start all over again in another part of the country."

"What is it that you humans are fond of saying… 'Do not stumble at the first hurdle' – have faith and trust that everything happens for a reason."

But despite Angel's words of reassurance, Jeremiah's hopes had been dashed, and a black mood like the one that had engulfed him when he'd first retired, slowly descended upon him once again.

In the following weeks Jeremiah returned to his routines but could not shake off the feeling of agitation that had been his companion since the mugging. He could not relax, nor concentrate on the books that he'd had delivered from Foyles, hoping they'd take his mind off his situation – and because he was now too afraid to go out for a walk, his restless legs seemed worse than ever. Estate agent particulars of properties in Devon and Cornwall plopped through his letterbox and onto the mat nearly every morning, but Jeremiah didn't open them and they had begun to pile up on his desk, taunting him, reminding him of his stupidity.

For that was how he'd begun to see himself; as impulsive and gullible for thinking he could reinvent his life, reinvent himself.

"Why not just open the letters and see what's new on the market?" Angel had suggested.

"What's the point?" Jeremiah sighed.

The mugging began to take its toll on him, subtly at first – he'd stopped going out for a walk after his return from hospital, but now he'd stopped going out at all, and had his groceries delivered from the little supermarket he'd frequented all his life in a white van; and then he had his front door fitted with a lock and chain and after a while he would not open the curtains that looked out over the street and London life below. He couldn't bear to see what was going on beyond the confines of his flat.

Angel observed what was happening but said nothing as Jeremiah turned in on himself.

THE PROFESSOR

Winter was not far away. Sarah loved the winter, and this year she was longing for its coming. She loved its darkness and coldness, the magical quality of the light and the transformations going on in Nature. For Sarah, winter was a time of contemplation and reflection. It promised the possibility of settling into the darkness, and her delight was only tempered by the fact that the Elmsford Elderberries were unable to swim so often because of the Atlantic storms that blew in.

In some ways, for Sarah it was the beginning of the year, not the end, as the season drew towards the shortest day. In that turning of the year, she always felt there was great hopefulness, much more so than the blousy brightness and overbearing heat of summer.

Sarah walked through the churchyard and along the road to The Sanctuary so that she could finalise preparations for the new winter visitor, Professor Husk. Alice had made the beds and ensured there was enough food in the cupboard and the fridge for her first few days, but she had asked Sarah just to give it a final look over. Sarah had brought with her a tin of shortbread, which she left in the kitchen with a note welcoming Professor Husk to the house and to the village, telling her she would be able to find all that she needed at the local shop. Then she walked through the house just to check that everything was in order.

When she came to James's study, she saw that one of the drawers under the worktop was very slightly open. She went to close it, but as she did so she saw James's journal lying there.

How odd, she thought. *I'm sure I cleared this drawer out before the very first visitors came to the house. In fact, I'm certain of it.*

Sarah took the journal from the drawer and sat at the desk, hesitant at first to look at it, but eager to see the familiar handwriting, his handwriting. The first page she read had been written on a winter's morning such as this one.

> I woke this morning, with Sarah beside me. Now she has gone, but she has left the faintest scent of lavender on her pillow. I like that. She stirs my thoughts and my memories, and I think how blessed I have been that she came into my life.

Tears came to Sarah's eyes and she wiped them away with her handkerchief. It smelt of lavender. She read on.

> It's a beautiful winter's morning and I have walked down to the sea, making my way along the base of the cliffs so that I can find a place to sit and write this. The wind is in the East, which

is unusual for this part of the world. It turns the waves into long rollers that stretch across the bay and blows 'white horses' from the crests of them. It is sunny today and occasionally the sun shines through the spray and creates a fleeting rainbow. I have come to sit here because I want to write down some thoughts that have been with me since I awoke.

I realise now that I have discovered something I was looking for. But what I have discovered is not something I was told, it's something I already knew, deep within myself; something I have always known and only needed to be reminded of. It is that I am whole; that all about me is an ordered and whole realm of being. I come from it, I have always been in it and one day, I will return to its deep bosom.

Sarah knows this. You only have to be with her to know this is so, and it is she who has helped me to remember. Love is the ordered whole. And Love is the way in which all becomes whole, the place in which we discover our true being. That's what Sarah and I have found – our true being.

Sarah put down the folder and looked out of the study window, towards the sea. How James had loved this view. And soon someone else would be sitting here, looking out of the window.

I just hope she loves it, too, thought Sarah to herself, closing the journal and putting it into her bag. She could not understand how it had got there – perhaps one of the previous guests had found it somewhere and put it in the drawer – but anyway, she knew it was meant for her.

"Thank you, my darling James," she said aloud, as if he were there beside her.

She was beginning to understand that however separate people might seem to be, they are all part of something, too – part of this 'whole' that James had written about.

It was Friday, at about eleven o'clock in the morning, when Sarah saw Katharine's little yellow car flash past her cottage. She was headed for The Sanctuary with her passenger, Professor Husk, whom she had collected from Exeter train station. After giving them half an hour or so to settle in, she put on a coat and walked through the churchyard and past the little row of fishermen's cottages to James's old house, to welcome them. She knocked on the door and Katharine greeted her.

"Come on in, Sarah. Miriam, this is Sarah, who I've told you about."

Standing behind Katharine was a tall elegant woman. She was dressed in a long grey cashmere cardigan over a white blouse and black trousers. She had close-cropped grey hair and sharp blue eyes, and Sarah guessed that she was sixty-something, a bit younger than herself, perhaps. She had no shoes on, which endeared her to Sarah immediately, and was wearing a long string of pearls, knotted halfway down. She was quite striking.

"Welcome to The Sanctuary," said Sarah.

"Thank you. It's such a beautiful house," said Professor Husk, smiling at Sarah. Her voice was soft but firm. "I'm so grateful to everyone for making it possible for me to stay here, and to you, Sarah, for helping to prepare it for me. Your shortbread was exactly the right gift."

"You're most welcome. I just thought I'd check that you have everything you need," Sarah said. "I've left my telephone number on the kitchen table in case you have any questions, and perhaps I'll see you another time, once you've settled in."

"I'd like that."

"Oh, and by the way, Professor, you may be visited by Willow, who was James's cat. She sometimes lives here and sometimes with me."

"Willow – what a lovely name. I look forward to meeting her. I'm very fond of cats. And I do hope you will call me Miriam."

"Thank you. I will."

Sarah hugged Katharine and went back to her cottage. A little later, Katharine returned too.

"Well, she seems very nice," said Sarah.

"She is, and we had such an interesting conversation in the car on the way here. She's asked if you would go and have tea with her one afternoon so that she can hear all about the village."

Later that week, Professor Husk phoned Sarah to invite her for afternoon tea. Sarah felt slightly hesitant as she knocked on the door of James's house, but that feeling soon lifted, as she noticed the wood stove had been lit, and a tray of tea, which included her shortbread was on the low table between the sofa and the armchairs. It felt cosy, inviting.

The two women sat opposite each other, and as if she knew where to be, the Professor had chosen to sit where James used to. She poured the tea. There was a steady quietness about her.

"Tell me," she said after a while, "did you know the man who lived here? James – wasn't that his name?"

"Yes, I did," Sarah replied. But not wishing to share James with Miriam she said no more.

"There's something here that he has left behind."

"Oh?" Sarah thought she was referring to yet more books or slippers, but it was something else.

"He has left his stillness here. It was waiting for me when I came through the door and it is just what I need. I know this will be a good place to work."

"I hope so," said Sarah.

Miriam became silent, as if she were contemplating something. Sarah liked that. It was oddly comforting and not at all awkward.

"Katharine has told me a bit about your work," Sarah said.

Miriam looked at her and smiled.

"My work? I sometimes wonder what that is."

"Well, she says you have written books, and that you teach."

"I have and I do."

"And you write about the voices of women."

"Yes, I do, and from what Katharine has told me, I think I may have written about a favourite of yours."

"Really?" said Sarah, wondering who Professor Husk was talking about.

"Yes, Mary Magdalene. She's a favourite of mine, too. I understand you have read her gospel."

"Well actually, James and I read it together before he died."

Miriam smiled, as if in those few words Sarah had told her all she needed to know.

"And she is such an important voice for us now," said Miriam. "Can you imagine what it must have been like for her when Jesus was taken from her? And when she was dismissed and denied?"

Sarah noticed that as Miriam spoke about Mary Magdalene there was a liveliness about her, almost as if she was tensing her muscles, leaning forward a little, her face bright and open.

"I remember James saying that we don't really know what happened to her once Jesus had gone." Sarah surprised herself at how easily she conversed with a Professor about these matters.

"You are right. We don't know for sure, but there is a story that after remaining for a while with the followers of Jesus, she was arrested and set adrift in a boat without a rudder – or possibly she just set sail of her own accord. Anyway, it is said that eventually she came to southern France where she spent the remaining years of her life in solitude. They say she taught of something called 'The Way', rather like the Buddhist 'Middle Way', a way of Love and Compassion."

"James left me his copy of her gospel," said Sarah.

"He must have loved you very much."

For a moment Sarah was shocked, wondering how this woman had so quickly seen that this was so, and shocked too, that she spoke so directly about it. But her voice carried no tone of judgement. Indeed, Sarah now felt that she would like to tell Miriam about it.

"He did love me, and I loved him."

A silence settled upon them, as if this confession had removed a boundary between them, and they could now be at ease.

"You must miss him," said Miriam.

"I do," said Sarah. "Very much."

Quietly, Miriam stood up and took the teapot into the kitchen to top it up. When she came back, it was as if that moment of intimacy had passed, and now Miriam wanted to talk more about her work.

"Of course," she said, settling back once more into James's chair, "Mary Magdalene is only one of many women teachers who have been ignored or dismissed. And still are. There is a long and ancient tradition: Sophia Goddess of Wisdom is one of them, and in this country in the legend of King Arthur, all the women were scorned – Guinevere, Nimue, Enid and, of course, the infamous hag, Kundry."

She leaned across the table and took from a pile, a book called *Invisible Women*. She offered it to Sarah.

"If you've read Mary Magdalene's gospel, you might like to read about some of the women in this book, too.

I wrote it some time ago and I'd be interested to know what you make of it."

Sarah took the book and saw her name – Miriam Husk – on the cover.

"Thank you, Miriam. I'll look forward to reading your book," she said, and put it in her bag.

"Elmsford is a beautiful village, isn't it?" Miriam was now looking out of the window, admiring the view, her attention taken by something else. "I couldn't quite believe it when Katharine pulled-up outside this house; I didn't expect it to be quite so remote from the outside world."

"Will that bother you, do you think? Winters can be quite hard here, with day after day of rain and gales."

"Do you know, I think I'll relish it," said Miriam, turning to smile at Sarah. "Not just the isolation, which is perfect for us writers – no distractions, you know – but I love to settle into a place, to stay put, come rain or shine, to dig in. And I love the rain too – most people long for sunny days and warm weather, but I love a grey day, when you can light the fire and snuggle up and not feel at all guilty for staying in all day just reading a book."

Sarah smiled. *It is by such small things that we come to know one another*, she thought.

During the course of the next few days, Sarah did indeed read Miriam's book. It was a collection of essays detailing the stories of the women whom Miriam had spoken of. Apparently, each story had originally been written down by men, and in every case, they had placed the woman in a submissive and subservient role. There were also stories where women had been accused of being witches, who were tortured, and in many cases killed. Miriam had reinterpreted these stories, bringing the women to life as teachers and goddesses, wise women and healers.

The one that Sarah liked most was a story called The Wheel of the Year. Placed in the centre of the book, this story, written by Miriam herself, told of the three aspects of the Feminine: Flower Maiden, Harvest Queen and Old Woman. The most important of the three was the Old Woman, for it was she who shaped the year, or rather, in her triple form, she expressed each part of the year. And at the end of the story it became clear that these three women were one woman, the Divine Feminine.

The book was easy to read, and Sarah loved it. It sent her mind whirling. Although she had never read such stories before, they were familiar to her – of course, these feminine role models had appeared in the fairy stories of her childhood, Sleeping Beauty and Cinderella – yet as each story progressed in Miriam's book, the images of the Maiden, the Queen and the Hag were utterly redefined. The women were presented as shaping events and making things happen in ways Sarah had never considered possible.

The stories affected her profoundly, and they stirred something in her. She wanted to know more. Somehow, Sarah knew that this was the beginning of an adventure and she felt excited, like she had done when she decided she would walk barefooted and paint her toenails, or when she took the plunge and became a wild swimmer with the Elderberries.

She sensed a rebelliousness in her soul, and she was eager to explore where it might lead. And when she returned Miriam's book and discussed her response to it, the Professor took her seriously, seeming genuinely pleased that Sarah had resonated with the stories.

Although, at first, she longed to share all of this with James – as it was he who had first awakened her to her divine feminine heritage – she was beginning to accept that he really wasn't with her in any tangible way anymore. She longed to hear his voice, and she still spoke aloud to him, but she knew he was slipping further and further away. She could not hold on to him much longer.

AND SO IT BEGINS

One evening, two months after his trip to the westcountry, Jeremiah was flipping disinterestedly through the latest cookery book he'd had delivered from Foyles, and Angel was lying on the sofa his arms behind his head, wings unseen, when the phone rang.

Jeremiah looked at Angel, apprehensively. The phone rang so rarely these days that its insistent tone alarmed him.

"Shall I answer it?"

"You hold the future in your own hands, my friend."

Tentatively, Jeremiah picked up the receiver.

"Hello?"

"Jeremiah? It's Bernard here. How are you?"

For a moment, Jeremiah couldn't think who Bernard was, but then the penny dropped, and an incredible fizz of energy stirred his body.

"Bernard! Hello. This is an unexpected pleasure. I'm… I'm…" and then, because he hadn't told anyone, not even Stephen, how devastated he was about his westcountry dreams being dashed, he decided to simply keep it to himself. "I'm fine, thank you. How are you?"

"Yes, all is good here. Now listen. Did you find what you were looking for? The right house, I mean?"

"Actually, I didn't, Bernard. Nothing was quite what I wanted. You know, too small, too large, too expensive, that sort of thing. You were right about some of the prices, too. I was quite surprised. And a wee bit downhearted, to be honest."

"Well, perhaps you've changed your mind about the whole thing, then?"

It was at that very moment that Jeremiah realised he had not changed his mind. Perhaps it was hearing Bernard's voice again, or the insistent ring of the telephone – or maybe it was what Angel had said about holding the future in his own hands – but something had shaken him out of his reverie; something had woken him up.

"No, no, I'm just taking a rest."

"Well, that sounds sensible. House hunting can be an exhausting business. So, do you remember the cottage in Elmsford that I told you about? The one opposite the church?"

"The one belonging to your friend, who'd sold it to a local couple?"

"Yes, that's right. Well, as it turns out the sale didn't go through. Geraldine rang me this morning and said that the mortgage company were querying the state of the thatched roof and there are a few other issues, I think. Anyway, this young couple decided to buy one of the new-builds on the edge of the village instead. Apparently, they could get a very good mortgage deal on a new house, so they couldn't really refuse. Anyway, if you're still interested, Geraldine asked me to mention it to you before it goes back on the market."

Jeremiah hesitated. He didn't want to get his hopes up again – he simply couldn't take the disappointment.

"Do you think I should come and see it, Bernard? Do you know the cottage?"

"I do. It's a traditional Devon thatch, and partly cob-built, which again the mortgage company queried, something to do with the insulation rating I think. Will you have to get a mortgage, Jeremiah, as you could have the same problems?"

"Well… depending on what I get for my flat here in London, probably not."

"Then come back and see it. It's in such a lovely little village. To tell you the truth, I've always felt there was something rather special about the place, but I can't quite put my finger on what it is. Perhaps it's the proximity to the sea, but it's more than that, it's the community. It's how villages used to be years ago, when I was a boy."

"Well, I need to have a think about this. Can I call you back in a day or two?"

"Of course, but don't leave it too long as Geraldine is putting it on the market at the end of the week."

Jeremiah said goodbye to Bernard and put the phone down. He began to pace around the room, but he couldn't order his thoughts. He felt a mixture of intense anxiety at the thought of leaving his flat, and extreme excitement at the thought of perhaps leaving his flat for good.

Angel rose from the sofa, his wings outstretched and shimmering, his robes iridescent.

"What do you think Angel? What should I do? I

feel so… frail, as if another disappointment could shatter me."

"What do you want to do?"

Jeremiah stood still his eyes fixed upon his angelic friend. After a long time, he sighed.

"I want to be done with this, Angel. This prison I have made for myself. Even if Geraldine's place doesn't work out, I have to somehow summon the energy to make a change in my life. I can't keep blaming everything else or everyone else for what happens. I'm so tired of all this…" He sank to his knees, his head bowed low. "I have to find a way home."

Angel knelt beside Jeremiah and enveloped him in his wings. "You may well have just taken the first step," he whispered.

Jeremiah awoke early the next morning and opened the curtains in his bedroom. The sunlight dazzled him. He waited impatiently for the clock to strike nine – a reasonable time to make a phone call, he thought – before he dialled Bernard's number.

"Bernard, it's me, Jeremiah."

"And…?"

"Can you tell Geraldine I'll be there tomorrow. I want to come and see the cottage."

"Oh, I am pleased. Now here's the thing. Geraldine has gone back to Plymouth to be with her sister who's rather unwell at the moment, but she told me that if you want to come and view the cottage, there's a spare key under a flowerpot by the back door. Apparently, she always leaves it there just in case she loses hers."

Jeremiah chuckled. "Do people still do that? A key under a flowerpot? We used to do exactly that in

Duncan Way where I lived as a child, but I wouldn't dream of doing it here."

"Well, yes, I suppose we do. It saves a lot of bother, really," said Bernard. "Now then, Geraldine is quite desperate to sell the house, and this whole thing with the young couple has been a bit exhausting for her. She'd be happy to keep the estate agents out of the equation and just go through the solicitors, and also she told me to tell you that as the survey has shown that the thatched roof is in need of repair, she'll come down a bit on the price."

Jeremiah still would not allow himself to get excited.

"Well, that's good to know. All I have to do now is hire a car and book a hotel in Bude, and I can get on the road. Thank you Bernard, for all your help."

"Well, what are friends for? Come and have a cup of tea with me, once you've looked around the place."

Later that day, having hired a car and booked into the same hotel in Bude where he'd stayed previously, Jeremiah set off for the westcountry. His nerves were jangling, set on edge by the busyness of London, and the sheer volume of traffic on the roads, but also because of all the thoughts in his head, not least that he had done something he'd not been able to do for many weeks; he'd stepped out of his comfort zone.

He turned the radio on to Classic FM to try and soothe his anxiety, but as the miles passed, the tension began to slip from his shoulders anyway. He looked in his rear-view mirror and saw Angel sitting in the back seat, serene, with his eyes closed. Thank god Angel was with him.

By the time he'd checked in to the hotel, it was too

dark to visit the cottage. Though he was eager to see it, he had to admit that he was very tired from the long drive and so he decided to wait until the morning. Instead, he ordered his supper from the Room Service menu, and sat at the table in the bay of his bedroom window, admiring the early Christmas lights that were glistening in the dark waters of the canal.

The next morning, he set off north on what was now becoming a familiar road, and then turned left onto the narrow country lanes towards the village of Elmsford. On the brow of each hill, he could see the church tower of Elmsford in the distance, reassuring him that he was on the right track.

Eventually, he pulled into the drive of Geraldine Burton's thatched cottage, which was down a steep little lane opposite the church. He could indeed see that the thatch was old and weatherworn, but it wasn't as bad as he'd imagined. The garden was quite overgrown, but he could see that it would be pretty in the spring, and the plastered and whitewashed walls were covered at the front by what he assumed was an ancient wisteria and a rambling rose. It felt as if the cottage was part of the garden in which it rested, and there was a deep quietness about it. Jeremiah was immediately attracted to it. He found the key, opened the front door and walked inside.

The cottage had low ceilings and Jeremiah was tall, but he didn't hit his head on the beams once, so he concluded the ceilings were not too low, and although the windows were quite small, with lots of square panes of glass, they had deep window seats in front of them on which Geraldine had placed colourful cushions, books and vases of flowers. The cottage felt welcoming somehow. He walked into an open-plan living room and kitchen, which was spacious and inviting with its wood stove at one end and Aga at the other; then there was a downstairs cloakroom, and a small sitting room that Geraldine seemed to be using as a workroom, with its tapestry frames, skeins of coloured wools and a sewing basket. But what really appealed to Jeremiah was a room at the rear, a garden room, which had probably been added on to the cottage quite recently. It was well built, with cream plastered walls and tall sash windows with wide windowsills. A pair of Velux windows in its sloping roof filled the room with light. Upstairs, within the slope of the thatched roof there were two bedrooms. The larger one had an ancient bathroom, with a loo, a large bath, but no shower; and the other smaller bedroom was beside a tiny bathroom with the most curious but delightful sit up bath in it. He walked back into the largest of the bedrooms and looked out of the window onto the front garden and across the road to the church.

Again, he felt his anxiety slipping away, and he knew at once and without doubt that this was where he needed to be.

"Are you here Angel?" Jeremiah was excited and wanted to ask Angel's opinion, but Angel didn't appear. Jeremiah knew it had to be his decision.

Hidden from view by a clump of hydrangeas, a slim black cat with a patch of white on her chest looked up at him, twitching her tail.

Later that afternoon, after calling in on Bernard for a swift cup of tea on the way back to the hotel, Jeremiah dialled the number he had been given for Geraldine's solicitor. Subject to the survey not finding anything structurally unsound, he made an offer that was not too far off Geraldine's revised asking price.

"Well, I'm pleased to tell you that I can accept that offer on behalf of Mrs Burton, but there is a condition," the solicitor said.

Jeremiah's heart sank, and fear enveloped him. Fear that he could still not have what his heart desired, fear that his hopes would be dashed again.

"Oh dear… what is it?"

"Well, Mrs. Burton is moving to Plymouth and she will not be able to take her cat with her, so she would like the new owner to agree to take care of her."

Jeremiah laughed. So, he was going to have a cat and an angel.

"Is everything alright, Mr Browne?"

"Oh yes, sorry. That'll be fine," he said.

"Her name is Jezebel."

"Sorry?"

"The cat. She's Jezebel. Now, Mrs. Burton would like to proceed as quickly as possible, if that suits you."

"That suits me very well," said Jeremiah, a sudden feeling of elation and excitement flooding through him. It was as if a great weight had been lifted from his shoulders – a weight he hadn't realised he was carrying – and at once he began to envisage living in his new home. He went over to the desk in his room and, taking the writing pad with the hotel's logo on it and the pencil also provided, he began to make a list of things to do. The first of which was to call in on Bernard on his way back to London, and give him a bottle of good malt whisky, for all his help. He was a true friend.

Angel appeared by the window, flooding the room with light..

"Good news?" he asked, preening his wings.

"Good news indeed. My offer on the cottage in Elmsford has been accepted! Oh, and by the way, I have also adopted a cat. Her name is Jezebel."

"And so it begins," said Angel, enigmatically.

"What do you mean by that?"

"Can't you feel it? The beginning?"

Jeremiah looked up from the writing pad.

"You know, you're right," he said. "That's what this is. A beginning. Just like when I left Ilford and moved in with Stephen all those years ago. That changed my life beyond anything I could have expected. And so will this. Living by the sea in the back of beyond. It feels wonderful. I wonder what kind of cat Jezebel is?"

"Well, if she is anything like her name-sake, she will be a handful."

"Why is that, then?"

"You know, Jezebel, the wanton, shameless woman who worshipped Mother Earth."

"Really?"

"Really."

"Well, it seems I'm going to have a wanton shameless woman in my life then. That'll make a change." They both laughed. And then a sudden thought came to Jeremiah.

"You are coming to Elmsford aren't you, Angel? You're not going to abandon me?"

"I have no choice," said Angel. "I'm always with you. And, actually, I have my own reasons for wanting to be in Elmsford."

"You do? Why?"

"All in good time, my friend."

Over the next few weeks, Jeremiah busied himself with his preparations. Once he had decided to buy the cottage in Elmsford, he instructed his estate agent to inform the cash buyer who had offered the asking price for his flat that he was now ready to sell. Jeremiah was surprised at how much his flat sold for. The estate agent had told him that Spitalfields was now the up-and-coming place to be, and the asking price would more than cover the purchase of the cottage and the work he was going to have done there.

As Christmas was soon to be upon them, all parties agreed to make an exchange date early in the new year, giving Jeremiah time to get a structural survey done.

Although Jeremiah was eager to leave and to start what he now thought of as the next step in the rest of his life, he also recognised that he wanted the ending of the previous chapter to be dignified and meaningful – not a catastrophe as the end of his relationship with

Angela had been. He wanted to begin his new life in Elmsford on a positive note. And so, for the first time ever, he invited Stephen and Jenny, Olivia, Johnny and their children to his house for Christmas dinner. He put up some minimal, but tasteful, decorations and bought and prepared all the food necessary for the most traditional of Christmas dinners.

Feeling flush, he went to Harrods and bought expensive presents for all his guests, and then on a whim, he ordered the most impressive Christmas hamper he'd ever seen and had it shipped to Angela and Francesca at great expense so that it would get there in time for Christmas.

He felt that he had turned over a new leaf, and these offerings of hospitality to his dearest friends – in fact, people he regarded as family – were his way of saying thank you – 'Thank you for standing by me whilst I found my way, even though it took a lifetime.' And they all knew it, without Jeremiah having to utter a single one of those words.

A KIND OF KNOWING

In the last week of November, Katharine had come to stay for the weekend with Sarah. They had finished their supper and were sitting together in the living room, warmed by the wood stove. That morning, Katharine had received confirmation that she had been accepted for her work experience in a secondary school close to the city centre in Truro, and she was telling Sarah all about it when there was a ping on her phone and Katharine checked to see who it was from.

"Oh wow – it's Tom. Oh my god, look Sarah," and she showed her the text.

> Guess what? Just had good news. I'm coming home for Christmas. I'll be back for three or possibly four weeks from the middle of December. I can't wait to see you. Love Tom xx

"Well, that's great," Sarah smiled. "Will he stay with you in Truro?"

"I don't know what his plans are. He still has a room in a house-share in London until the end of the year, and it's near his work HQ so he may need to be there."

"Well, you'd both be welcome here, you know that. Why don't you call him and make plans? Then you can get excited about your holiday together."

Katharine checked the time. It would be early afternoon in Washington. "Good idea," she said and went up to her room.

When she came down again, she looked very happy and gave Sarah a hug.

"Well, what did he say?"

"Oh, Sarah, he said he couldn't wait to come home. He said he's really missed me, and this time apart has made him realise that more than anything, he wants to be with me."

"Oh, darling, that's just what you needed to hear, isn't it?"

"It is, and I feel the same, Sarah. I know I want to be with him and that we'll find a way. He's got one or two meetings in London, but then he'll have three whole weeks off – can you believe it? Apparently, they're trying to make up for all the extra time he's had to put in over the last year. Three whole weeks!"

"That's so exciting for you. So, what are you going to do?" There was a part of Sarah that needed to know if she would be included in their plans; if they would come to Elmsford, if they wanted to be with her.

"Well, I'm going to go up to London to stay with him whilst he has his meetings, but Tom has agreed that we should catch up with our best friends from university, Izzy and Frank who live in Paris. They've already asked us to join them for Christmas, but I wasn't sure because of not knowing Tom's plans.

Christmas in Paris sounds good, doesn't it?"

"Yes, it does. Very good indeed. It will be so romantic!" Sarah hugged Katharine, who was quite obviously over the moon with her news. But deep down, Sarah felt a pang of sadness. She had been hoping that Katharine would stay with her for Christmas, like last year. How quickly plans change. She hid her disappointment.

"But what about you, Sarah?" Katharine perhaps picked up on Sarah's wistfulness. "Will you be alright?"

"I'll be fine. I'll probably go to Alice and Rachel's like last year. I'm happy for you, darling. Truly, I am."

That year, Sarah didn't go to Alice and Rachel's for Christmas, and on Christmas Day, she was alone. She didn't get up until about ten o'clock, and then she made herself some tea. The village was quiet. It was raining and everyone was indoors. Soon they would be tucking into roast turkey and Christmas pudding, neither of which Sarah wanted to eat. She had bought herself some turkey breast, but she hadn't cooked it, and she had made her own Christmas pudding, but she wasn't hungry. Both the turkey and the pudding remained in the fridge.

Everyone she loved and might have wanted to be with was somewhere else. Her neighbours, the sisters Linda and Felicity Downe were with their friends in Yorkshire. Alice and Rachel were staying with Rachel's sister and family in Exeter, and, of course, Katharine and Tom were in Paris. Her son and his wife had sent her a lovely present, a cashmere sweater, but had not invited her to join them in Dublin. Sarah wasn't sure where Miriam was. James was not there, but Sarah wished him Happy Christmas anyway.

As she did so, she felt a chill, and pulled her cardigan about her, kneeling to light the wood stove. To her surprise, in that moment she knew she had to let James go. She had accepted his death, had come to terms with no longer feeling his presence as she had when he first passed away, but in her heart, she was still holding on to him, clinging to the memory of him. Yet suddenly she knew that he needed to leave her. That he was leaving her. She became very still.

James had once told her, "For each of us who loses someone, there comes a time to let them go."

"But go where, James?" she asked, a tear falling from her cheek. "Where is this other place you want to go, without me?"

Of course, James didn't answer, and Sarah didn't know where he would go – all she knew was that he wanted to go. It was a kind of knowing she could no longer ignore. She sat in her armchair and took a deep breath.

"Perhaps this is why I am alone this Christmas, Willow?" She looked at the cat curled in front of the wood stove, without a care in the world. "Perhaps I have been given this time and space to let James go, and to go with my love? What do you think?"

Again, the cat didn't answer. She was asleep.

Without really thinking about it, Sarah got up and

fetched a candelabra from her sideboard. It was made by a local potter and was shaped like a branch of a tree, with two little nests in it that held the candles. It was glazed in a gorgeous deep turquoise-blue which had crackled in places giving it a frosted look. It was a work of art. She found two gold Christmas candles and placed them in the nests and set the candelabra on the coffee table. Then she poured herself a large glass of Cabalié Grenache, her favourite wine, and put on a CD of Leonard Cohen 'Live in London' which contained hers and James's favourite song, one they had often danced to in his house whilst waiting for supper to cook, or the sun to set over the sea… 'Dance Me to the End of Love'.

She began to cry as she lit the candles, but she found she had something to say.

"My dear James, I miss you so much. I miss your touch, your kindness, your wisdom. But I know you need to leave now. I know you need to go. These candles represent you and me. When they burn out you will be released, and whilst my flame for you in this lifetime will be extinguished my love for you is eternal."

She had no idea where those words came from.

She sat there in the warmth of her living room, with Leonard Cohen crooning in the background and Willow's body gently lifting and falling as she slept in front of the fire. She drank most of the bottle of wine and cried her final tears for James.

Now there was an ending. After two years of grieving, she could feel a bridge from her grief forming in her heart, leading to another place. It felt like unchartered territory, but she was ready for the adventure. She had already taken the first steps.

As evening fell, she warmed-up her Christmas pudding and ate it with her homemade brandy sauce. She knew she would always love him.

That evening, as she sat beside her fire watching the flames dancing and feeling at peace with the world, she became aware of a strange feeling. It was as if she was being embraced, as if someone was wrapping their arms around her.

The moment Sarah awoke the next day, she felt an overwhelming need to talk to Miriam. She picked up her phone and sent a brief text, asking if Miriam was free to meet that morning. The reply came promptly.

> Absolutely, I am. I was hoping that I'd see you at some point this Christmas but wasn't quite sure of your plans. xx

Sarah now knew why she hadn't made plans, nor reached out to connect with any of her friends, and when she met Miriam later that morning, she told her so, and of the ceremony she had created to honour her love for James and to relinquish him.

"I feel as if I've made a step into another world," Sarah said. "A world without James. Of course, I know I've been there for some time really, but saying goodbye in the way I did has given me a kind of closure, though

I never really knew what that meant until now. And I have a sense that this may be a beginning, not an ending – that this coming year may be very different from the last."

Miriam was silent, waiting for Sarah to continue.

"James has gone," she said, "and in a way I know that it will not be long before Katharine goes, too. I have so enjoyed being a mother to her. Perhaps you know that? But Tom is coming back into her life – I can feel it – and they will reclaim each other, as they should. And although you and I have become friends, I know that you'll be going soon, when the winter ends. What then is next for me?"

"Actually, as it happens," Miriam said with a smile, "I won't be leaving Elmsford."

Sarah looked at her newfound friend inquisitively. "You won't?"

"No. This is such a good place for me to work that I can't imagine not being here. In fact, I've already spoken to Julia, and we are working out a way for me stay until June."

Sarah was delighted, and then Miriam said something that caught her by surprise.

"Now that James has gone, would you mind if I slept in his study, on the campaign bed?"

Until now, the idea of someone sleeping in the study would have upset Sarah very much. This had been James's most hallowed place; the place where he worked, the place where he was most himself. But because it was Miriam, and because she was getting to like Miriam so much, Sarah heard herself agreeing to it and not minding at all.

"Thank you." Miriam smiled and reached for Sarah's hand, squeezing it gently. "I knew I needed to ask you first, but it will help me to deepen my work. Like James, I want to be living and sleeping in the same room. My hermit cell."

"Is that how it feels?"

"Yes, and now you and I will have plenty of time to talk about all the things we hold dear, because I'm planning on staying put."

"Excellent news," Sarah said, reaching into her bag to find the book that Miriam had lent to her. "I'd like to know more about this, then," she said, passing the book back to Miriam. "I'm interested in what you say about how the true nature of these women has been hidden from us. And I know how this happens, because it happened to me. I was expected to be submissive and to make sacrifices for the sake of my family, allowing myself to be taken for granted, not feeling like I could speak honestly about how I felt. That was my life experience as a younger woman. It didn't feel good then, and I'm now wondering why I didn't stand my ground like the women in your book?"

Miriam smiled. "I guess it was hard to find your voice when you were a wife and mother," she said. "You were expected to focus on the needs of others first, and you were living in a society that did not value the voices of women. But things have changed for the better over the last 50 years. Our voices are not as censored as they once were, though there's still a long way to go. I'm glad you like my stories."

"I do. The one I liked best was The Wheel of the Year, and I also liked the story of Guinevere and the

Grail Quest. The men in the stories would have got nowhere without the women."

"Well, if you liked those, there's another story I must tell you," said Miriam. "This is an old medieval story, the story of Eric and Enid, but what I shall tell you is my version of it."

They settled into their armchairs and Miriam began.

"Imagine yourself at the court of King Arthur, the sounds of jousting and the sight of flags flying; all those knights and maidens and, of course, the Queen, Guinevere. Eric, a young questing knight, is about to set off on an adventure to find the source of all that is True, the Holy Grail. Before he sets off, Guinevere asks that he take his young wife, Enid, with him on his journey. Reluctantly, he accepts, but insists that she keeps behind him and never interrupts him.

"Off they go and after a while Enid sees a band of robbers coming towards them out of a forest. She rides forward to warn Eric who chides her. He tells her, although of course, it's not true, that he has already seen them and that he is prepared to do battle with them, which he does, and they scatter and run away. This happens two or three times, and each time Enid warns Eric, whilst, each time, he scolds her as he cannot bear to admit that she has seen the danger before he did.

"Eventually they arrive at an apple orchard in the middle of which is a large bed strewn with flowers. On the bed lies a beautiful maiden asleep.

Realising that this must be the culmination of his search, Eric approaches the bed, and as he does so the maiden sits up and looks at him. At once, he recognises her, because of course, he sees that she is Enid. For all that time and through all those dangers, that which he was seeking was right there, riding with him. Eric and Enid embrace and set off together, back to Guinevere and the court of King Arthur."

"That is a wonderful story. Why have I never heard it before?"

"Because it is never told as I have told it. In all the books that record the story – please note, all written by men, probably scholarly and celibate monks – the role of Enid is ignored, and it is only the valour and bravery of Eric that is reported. But there is a clue that suggests that my way of telling it may be the right one."

Miriam walked into the kitchen to fetch a kettle of hot water to top up the teapot.

"Do you know what we are told in Chaucer's *Canterbury Tales*," she asked, as she poured water into the teapot, "in the tale of the Wife of Bath? We are told what it is that women want most. And what do you think it is?"

"I don't know," Sarah replied. "I've never read *The Canterbury Tales*."

"The answer is: 'Sovereignty'. Women require sovereignty, and that actually, it is the responsibility of men to serve women, not the other way around. We may love and take care of each other, but women must lead and men must follow. All my studies have taught me that this has been the great error of humankind. I know it may sound strange, but it's true. Men have sought to dominate instead of serve. That is the error. And, not surprisingly, and even if they have resented it, many women have come to accept that this is so. And look where it has brought us. To fear and submission."

Miriam poured the tea and Sarah fell silent. She had never heard such ideas before, but as she listened to Miriam speaking, she felt a strange exhilaration. She was someone who had cared for others and loved them, and although her relationship with her husband and her son had been shaped by a submissive deference, she had been able to love James completely. But even then, she had been happy to let him take the lead and to take her with him. Now though, now that he had gone, it seemed that something else was arising within her, something that she'd not experienced before. She tried to name it, and the closest she could come was 'a sense of adventure'.

"So much of this is new to me," Sarah said, "but I want to hear it, because I want to make some changes in my life; not just put up with what happens to me, but actively work towards what makes me happy." She looked at her friend, who nodded in agreement. "It's strange, but I can see now that this began to happen whilst James and I were lovers. I felt a kind of liberation with him. The way he looked at the world opened up new horizons for me. And now, I feel I'm ready to make my own way. I know there is a lot more for me to discover, but I'm ready."

"Sounds good," said Miriam. "That sounds very good indeed."

After Sarah left The Sanctuary, she went for a walk. The rain had petered out, and now instead of a lowering grey sky, beautifully shaped clouds had formed, the tops of which were tinged with apricot and pink hues as the low winter sun cast long golden rays all about.

Sarah was thinking of Miriam. Who was this woman who had come to live in James's house, and why was she so drawn to her? She was a scholar and had written lots of books, and she was also enthusiastic and spirited, prepared to share what she knew even if the subject matter was somewhat taboo. But more than that, she felt Miriam was searching for something. She had a restlessness about her that never seemed quite satisfied. She was always writing, thinking, researching, contemplating; it was as though she had a thirst that could not be slaked.

What had come as a surprise to Sarah was that often, she felt as if she already knew what Miriam was telling her, just that she had somehow forgotten it. Take the story of Eric and Enid: to Sarah, it was obvious from the outset that it was Enid who would save the day. Isn't that what women always do? Men are valorous, women are observant. She knew the ending before the story had begun, she just didn't know that anyone had written about it.

She'd also felt something like this in the silence of the Quaker Meeting. A sense of deepening into the wisdom of the silence and knowing she would find answers there; answers to things she didn't even know she was contemplating. It was like a kind of knowing. Yes, that's what it was. A kind of knowing.

Now another door was being opened for her, and Sarah wanted to walk through it, cross its threshold; and instinctively she knew that when she did so she would find herself in a land that was both strange and familiar. She might have never been there before, but she knew she would recognise it. Miriam had both disturbed her and guided her – and now she was going to be living in James's house until June. And sleeping in James's study. Whatever next.

Between Christmas and the New Year, Sarah and Miriam saw each other every day. Their conversation flowed like a river; Sarah asking questions about the suppressed voices of women, Miriam asking questions about the village and the people who lived in her new-found community, and where the footpath in Cuckoo Wood led. They were exploring each other's territory and it was fascinating.

But Sarah was left with a question, one that she could not shake: Why had her own spirit of enquiry not been nurtured like Miriam's had, and why was it that she had been content to let it be so? No-one was now going to stop her finding out.

On New Year's Eve the two women sat around Miriam's wood stove and ate a delicious dish of wild mushroom stroganoff, with a glass of red wine. Then, later, they donned coats, hats and boots and walked across the fields in the moonlight to the edge of the sheer and treacherous cliffs, then turned and walked down the steep hill to the little harbour at the bottom. At the water's edge, they saw in the New Year with hugs and a toast to all that was to come. They picked up little pebbles from the beach and threw them into the waves and made their wishes. For the first time she could ever remember, Sarah's wish was something for herself.

The next day, Sarah invited Miriam to join her for the New Year swim, determined to make it an annual ritual in her life.

"I don't swim," said Miriam, "but I'll certainly come and watch."

For Sarah, the New Year swim was as crazy and exhilarating as the year before. The mixture of excitement and fear she felt as she plunged into the icy water made her feel so alive, ecstatic almost – it was a feeling like no other. But this year, as she immersed herself in the water, another emotion washed over her. She felt a deep sense of love for herself, for all that she had experienced in her life; the loneliness of being an unloved wife, the grief of losing her lover so soon after finding him, the unexpected joy of finding a group of women who uplifted her... From somewhere deep in her soul, a warm pool of contentment began to fill her body, countering the frigidity of the water. The feeling stayed with her all day.

When she got home, her phone was ringing. It was Katharine.

"Happy New Year! Sorry we've not been in touch, Sarah. We're at the airport in Paris on our way back to London, but we'd both love to come and see you. Could we come down next weekend? Would that be okay?

There's lots to tell you."

Of course it was okay, and Sarah was delighted to know that all was well with Katharine and Tom, and that she would see them soon.

The following weekend, a little yellow car pulled up outside her cottage and Katharine came running through the door, flinging her arms around Sarah and hugging her. Tom, full of smiles, followed carrying their bags.

After they'd taken their luggage upstairs and settled in, Sarah made a pot of tea and they sat together in her living room, the happy couple talking excitedly about their holiday. They'd evidently had a wonderful trip to Paris and were very much in love; it was in their eyes and in their touch when they reached out for each other. Theirs was a story of renewed love and delight in being together again.

"So, what are your plans now?" asked Sarah.

"Well," said Katharine, beaming, "the good news is that Tom is coming back to London to work. Isn't that great? It means we can be together at weekends until I finish my course. The bad news is that he has nowhere to live."

"No, but I'll find somewhere," said Tom. "I've already put out feelers with a few friends in London. In November, I put in a request to relocate with the company, and I've just heard that they've agreed. I'm going to join a new team who are building some amazing instruments for deep sea research."

"You won't be leading the team this time, though," Katharine prompted.

"No, I won't, but it doesn't matter. I've taken a

different role so I can come home. I want to be with Katharine – that's the most important thing to me – to us." He smiled at her and reached for her hand. Katharine just beamed from ear to ear.

"That's absolutely wonderful news. I think it calls for a celebration. Do you fancy dinner at the Hare & Hound tonight? My treat."

"Awesome," said Tom, kicking off his shoes and settling into the armchair.

"By the way, how's Miriam?" Katharine asked. "Have you seen anything of her?"

"She seems fine. I saw her quite a lot over the Christmas holiday." Sarah was about to tell them all that had been happening but then, suddenly, her relationship with Miriam felt private, for, beyond their friendship, Sarah was beginning to find an intensity of feeling towards Miriam that she was not yet ready to share.

"So, she was here? She didn't go away?"

"No, she was here, but she keeps her solitude, as you know."

"Yes, I imagine she does. I'd like to pop by and say hello to her whilst I'm here. Do you think that would be okay?"

"I'm sure she'd love to see you. Just give her a ring first to make sure she's not busy."

As Tom and Katharine continued to speak animatedly about their trip to Paris and all the galleries and museums they'd been to, Sarah realised that she was beginning to let Katharine go, too. She felt genuinely happy for these two young people, but her own journey of discovery meant that this time, she did not feel so great a loss.

Sarah went into the kitchen to top up the teapot with boiling water. She had readied herself for the changes that were to come because she knew that letting go was one of the greatest lessons of getting older. Learning to let go. And to let go again and again. She wished it wasn't so, but it was. She wished she could just love and be loved for ever, but she knew that the dynamics of love were always fluid and changeable.

As she put the teapot back on the tray, she thought she heard a fluttering of wings behind her, as if there was a bird caught in the room. She looked around, startled, wondering if Willow had brought a poor creature in to despatch, but although she felt there was something there, she couldn't see it. Not then, and not for some time to come.

Before they departed the next day, Katharine asked Sarah if she fancied joining her and Tom for a walk. A cold easterly wind had set in, so they wrapped up warmly and set off towards Kingfisher Bridge. As they turned down into the little lane past the flight of stone steps that led up to the churchyard, Katharine noticed that the thatched cottage opposite had a 'Sold' sign pinned on the estate agent's board.

"Who's bought that place then?" she asked Sarah.

"I'm not sure. Alice and Rachel wanted to buy it, but their mortgage company turned it down. Something to do with the state of the thatched roof, I think."

"It looks alright to me," Katharine laughed, "but then, what do I know about thatched roofs?"

"Actually, they've just bought one of those new-build houses out towards the main road. They're part of an affordable housing scheme and they're very 'eco' which ticks a lot of boxes for Alice, so she's very happy, and it's much closer to the market garden too. They're having a housewarming party soon – I'll let you know when it is. It'd be lovely if you could come."

"Oh, that would be great. I'd love that."

"I went to the Post Office the other day, and Grace told me she'd heard that a gentleman from London has bought Coombe Cottage."

"Really? Did you enquire as to whether he's single?" Katherine nudged Sarah's arm playfully.

"Of course not!"

"Perhaps he's gay then?"

"Katherine!" Sarah laughed. "What are you like? I didn't enquire about his marital status, and neither am I interested. But from what I can gather, he'll be moving in any day now, because Frank Pegg has asked Connie's husband to help him with some of the renovations. Anyway, whoever he is, I hope he'll be very happy here in Elmsford."

They walked through the woods and down into the valley, turning south along the steep and winding coast path until they came to the L-shaped bench, where they stopped for a breather before heading home.

Sarah looked down at the harbour where she often swam with the Elmsford Elderberries and thought she saw two men standing on the sea wall, looking out across the ocean. It struck her as rather strange as one of them seemed to be dressed in a long brown robe with a hood, like a medieval monk, but from that distance, with the sun in her eyes, it was hard to tell. When she looked again, she saw only one man standing there, his hands deep in his jacket pockets, seeming lost in a world of his own.

FIFTY SHADES OF NORMAL

Jeremiah made a fleeting visit back to Elmsford soon after New Year, to meet the local thatcher, John Butters, whose work was highly recommended by Bernard, and also Frank Pegg, a local builder who was going to improve the chimney flue and remake the main bathroom to include a shower.

By the end of the month, all the searches and completions had taken place and he was the proud owner of Coombe Cottage, Elmsford. Jeremiah hired a removal firm to transport his belongings to his new Devon home, and could hardly believe how quickly the three strong young men and the older, very helpful driver, packed his lifetime of belongings into their lorry.

They set off on the M4 and then the M5 and across the North Devon Link Road which was rather treacherous and icy, with Jeremiah following in his car, and then just as quickly they unpacked all his goods and chattels into his new home and positioned them exactly where Jeremiah had envisaged they would go. Together with his Turkish rugs, it soon became a home from home and Jeremiah couldn't quite believe how smoothly it all went and how homely it felt. But it was more than that – it felt to Jeremiah that this was exactly the home he had always wanted.

Jeremiah turned the small sitting room overlooking the garden into a study. His new laptop now sat there on a beautiful plain table he'd recently bought. The table was made from beech planks and had rounded corners. He'd also treated himself to a modern adjustable desk chair. And now he sat there, trying it all out, adjusting the back and the height of the chair and arranging his laptop so that he could look out of the window into his garden and the fields beyond.

He had a wonderful feeling that living in Elmsford was going to be a lot more interesting than living in London, and that he might now begin to know all sorts of things he had never known before – starting with the legend of Jezebel. His new companion, was taking her time to become familiar, keeping a distance and watching him from beneath the hydrangeas.

Having settled in, Jeremiah thought he would try to find someone who could help him with some of the household chores, perhaps for a couple of mornings a week. As luck would have it, although Angel insisted there was no such thing as luck, one afternoon, whilst Jeremiah was sitting on the bench in his garden enjoying the weak winter sunshine, the vicar called by. She was a cheerful woman who introduced herself as

Carol, which Jeremiah thought was rather appropriate.

"Jeremiah Browne. Pleased to meet you."

"And are you a churchgoer, Mr Browne?"

Suddenly, Jeremiah felt guilty. As if he ought to be and was now going to be found out.

"Ah, no. I'm not what you would call religious."

"Oh well," she sighed, "not many of us are these days. Amateur dramatics?"

"Sorry?"

"Do you like to tread the boards? We have a great village hall with a fully functioning stage. Do you sing, Mr Browne?"

"Ummm – no. Sadly not."

"Oh." She looked at him with disappointment. He would obviously not be joining her ranks. "Well, is there anything I can do to help?"

"Well actually I am looking for a housekeeper. Just for a couple of mornings a week. Do you happen to know of anyone?"

"I do indeed," said Carol, pleased that her visit was not in vain. "Francis Higgins could be the ideal person for you. Shall I put you in touch?"

"Would you?" Jeremiah was pleased. "Thank you, vicar. I appreciate it."

The next morning, as Jeremiah was enjoying a cup of tea in the garden room, there was a knock at the front door. Taking a swift slurp, Jeremiah went to see who it was, straightening a picture in the hallway as he did so. Standing outside was a handsome young man of indeterminate age – anywhere between 25 and 35, Jeremiah thought.

"You must be Mr Browne? Pleased to meet you," the

young man said, extending his hand to shake Jeremiah's. "I'm Francis Higgins."

Jeremiah's mind went blank. *Francis Higgins... that name rings a bell...* He gathered his wits.

"Francis – pleased to meet you. Do come in."

"You were expecting a woman, weren't you? Probably older and wearing an apron? It's the vicar. She finds it amusing."

Jeremiah chuckled. "Well, that'll teach me not to be so... what do they call it these days – 'gender biased'?"

"Don't worry about it. I know it is quite unusual for a man to be a housekeeper, but I really enjoy it. I've got three other clients I work for in the village, and so if you and I hit it off, you'll be my fourth."

Jeremiah thought at once that they would hit it off. Francis had a light-heartedness about him that immediately put Jeremiah at ease.

"Come on through," he said. "Let's go into the garden room. Tea or coffee?"

"What are you drinking?"

"Tea."

"Okay. Tea."

Soon they were settled.

"To be honest, Francis," said Jeremiah, "I'm not at all sure what I need you to do."

Fortunately, Francis Higgins was very clear about it.

"I can come on Tuesdays and Thursdays," he said. "I'll be here at nine and leave around eleven-thirty, if that works for you. I can help you keep the place clean; hoover the floors, wash the windows, stack the dishwasher, make sure your bed is changed every week, launder and iron the linen – that kind of thing."

"That sounds just the ticket," said Jeremiah.

"Good. What about food shopping? Do you need any help with that? I go into Bideford a couple of times a week, so I can always pick stuff up for you, and in fact there's a wonderful shop in the village where you can get just about anything you'll ever need."

"Thank you, Francis, but actually, I like food shopping," said Jeremiah. "I've recently become interested in cooking, so I'm happy to sort that out."

Before leaving London, Jeremiah had bought himself a car, knowing that he'd probably need one in Elmsford. He'd learned to drive when he was a young man, but living in London, he'd never actually needed a car. But now he thought he would. And he was right – there was only one bus a week that went from Elmsford to Bude, and one that went to Bideford, and each journey took over an hour. So, Jeremiah had already been out and about, exploring the local farm shops and markets.

"Have you met Grace and Tim from the village shop yet? They've recently taken it over, and if they don't stock what you want, they'll order it in for you. They're always very helpful."

"Yes, I met them last week. I signed up for a local veg box that I can pick up from their shop every Friday They were so welcoming. And I've met a lovely woman called Sarah, who bought me some daffodils from her garden, and some of her homemade jam. I do hope I'll bump into her again sometime."

Jeremiah liked the sound of all the arrangements with Francis very much, and he liked the energy of this young man.

At that moment, Jezebel walked into the room. She stopped, looked at Francis and then turned and walked straight back out again, her tail swishing in irritation that her special morning place was occupied.

"That was Jezebel," said Jeremiah, "I hope you like cats, as this one is formidable."

"I love cats. Giles and I have two, although neither is called Jezebel – now, that is rather special. Why did you give her that name?"

"I didn't. She came with the cottage. The vendor made it a condition of the sale that I adopt her."

They both laughed.

"Actually," said Jeremiah, "I googled 'Jezebel' and discovered that her story is rather damning. She was a Phoenician princess who married King Ahab of Samaria. She was accused of bringing drought and famine to Israel before she was killed by being thrown out of a high window. Poor thing."

"Ah yes, such is the fate of those who dare to be different," said Francis.

"What do you mean?"

"Well, in the Jewish society of her time, strong independent women were not liked. Men wanted and expected their women to be submissive, and anyone who challenged the supremacy of their God, which she did, would've been called a heretic. Even today, women who dance to their own tune are called 'Jezebels'."

"Yes, indeed – but how do you know all this?" Jeremiah was intrigued.

"Well," Francis paused, weighing Jeremiah up, considering if he was a man to be honest with. "I'm interested in gender politics. I studied it at Exeter

University amongst other things, and I became fascinated by feminism and gay rights. Basically, anyone who isn't straight down the line 'normal' – male or female – has always been vilified: women are witches and men are queer, and both must be silenced at all costs. And this has happened since the dawn of time."

Jeremiah winced, knowing exactly what Francis was talking about. "That sounds like a lifetime's study," he said.

"It certainly is. What's amazing is that there's a woman who lives just over the other side of the village who is a Professor in this very subject."

"Really – in Elmsford? How extraordinary. I should like to meet her. What's her name?"

"She's called Miriam Husk. I'm her housekeeper too, and we have some excellent conversations whilst I'm scrubbing her floor."

They laughed again, and for a moment, Jeremiah wondered whether he should level with Francis about not being 'straight down the line' either, but decided it was much too soon for that. After all, they'd only just met.

While they were talking, Angel had appeared in the room with his wings spread wide. Jeremiah no longer panicked when Angel did this, for not one of his visitors over the years had ever seen Angel.

"By the way," said Jeremiah, "have you seen the angels that are painted on some of the panels on the church ceiling?"

"I have. I think they're beautiful."

"Me too. Do you believe in angels, Francis? You know, not the one's painted on ceilings, but guardian angels, angels who become a part of people's lives?"

Francis thought for a moment and then said, "No. I don't think I do. Why do you ask?"

"No reason," said Jeremiah.

So that was that, and before too long, Jeremiah could not imagine life without Francis. When he turned up on a Tuesday morning, they talked about what they'd done at the weekend, which in Jeremiah's case was usually a long walk and some experimental cooking or settling down to a new book that he was reading. At first, Francis didn't give much away, but as time went by, Jeremiah discovered that Francis and his partner Giles, had met at university in Exeter, and often spent their weekends there meeting up with old friends and enjoying the night life. Jeremiah felt his life must seem very dull in comparison to Francis' rather bohemian and colourful world, but his new friend always seemed to be interested in his news.

In these first few weeks of coming to Elmsford, still suffering from the after-effects of the mugging, Jeremiah's relationship with Francis had become important to him. He felt both safe and at ease with him, and through Francis, he began to find out about the local community and the newly opened organic farm shop in the village where Bernard lived. Jeremiah would occasionally drive there, and then call in for a cup of tea with his old friend.

In a way that Francis found endearing, Jeremiah often insisted on doing the hoovering while Francis cleaned the kitchen and bathrooms.

"But you're paying me to do that," Francis said.

"I just like hoovering," Jeremiah explained. "Always have done. It's one of those tasks that shows immediate results. It transforms a room; makes everything feel somehow pleasing, and in order, which I like."

Francis raised an eyebrow. "That's what Giles says about weeding," said Francis. Giles was a freelance gardener who also had a part-time job at Bude Golf Club, helping to keep the greens in pristine condition. "He says it gives him great satisfaction to weed a veg bed because it transforms the plot and reveals the beauty of each plant – something like that, anyway."

"I utterly get that," said Jeremiah. "You know, Francis, I could do with a bit of help in the garden. When I first came here, I didn't really grasp quite how big the garden is. It's not just the lawns and the flower borders, it's also the hedges, the shrubs and the trees that are overgrown and need pruning, not to mention the vegetable beds that are now completely wild. I didn't have a garden in London, so I don't really know what I'm doing. Do you think Giles would know someone who would be able to give me a hand every now and then?"

"Well, I can certainly ask him," said Francis, stacking the recycling in a cardboard box to be put in the boot of his car.

The next time Francis came to clean, Jeremiah asked him more about his gender studies course at university, admitting that such matters had never been discussed in his undergraduate study of history.

"It was a different time for us," said Jeremiah. "We were more focussed on marching to 'Ban the Bomb'," and he told Francis about the Aldermaston March that he'd been to, pleased that his newfound friend seemed impressed by his youthful antics.

As they sat together one morning, having a cup of coffee after all the hoovering and cleaning had been done, Jeremiah asked a question that had been troubling him all of his adult life.

"Tell me, Francis, why do you think it has always been so frowned upon not to fit in to what is perceived as 'normal' gender roles?" Jeremiah still had not admitted to Francis that he was one of these frowned-upon people, but he was beginning to think that his housekeeper may have guessed anyway.

Francis sipped his coffee, deep in thought and for some time didn't answer. But then he said, "That's a very good question, Jeremiah, a very important question and I think it has to do with control."

"In what way?"

"Well, established gender stereotypes create a trajectory for both men and women that is acceptable, normal – but woe betide any of us who step off that path and set out to discover who we really are. If we all act as our gender infers, if we all do as we are told, we are easier to control and boundaries are not broken. But if we don't, then we become a threat to society, which doesn't know how to manage us or categorise us."

"Right..." Jeremiah's head was in a spin as he was trying to take in all that Francis was saying.

"Do you know, Jeremiah, depending on which books you read, there are now between 15 and 50 different gender identities for society to get to grips with. 'Normal' no longer exists, and people of all ages are now questioning what gender means to them and that rocks the fragile edifice of society."

"Fascinating... and what is 'normal' anyway, if there are so many shades of it?" Jeremiah mused.

"Exactly. We are told that what is normal is dictated by our culture and our history, and that we must abide by these social constructs. But what if we don't? If the way I express my gender and sexuality differs from the norm, I don't see that as making the norm less possible; I see it as making the norm more interesting, more diverse and colourful. After all, isn't history about the art of the possible?"

"I suppose it is... That's another thing they didn't teach us in our history studies."

Francis laughed.

"The thing is, Jeremiah, I think this whole issue of gender is much bigger than any of us can imagine. I've been interested in it all my life and I've studied it and talked about it endlessly with my friends, but it seems to me that matters of gender are actually part of our evolution."

Jeremiah was absolutely intrigued by all this young man was saying. "I'm not quite sure I understand what you mean?"

"Well, think about it this way. There are over seven billion people on this planet – seven billion... and a population that vast is wreaking havoc. We are raping and pillaging the natural world, and climate change and species loss and so many other tipping points are the consequence. And yet, Nature, or God or Evolution – whatever you call this impetus of Life – keeps on mutating and changing to create balance. All things tend towards balance, don't you think, Jeremiah?"

Francis stopped for another sip of coffee, giving Jeremiah time to ponder what he was hearing.

"The thing is, we don't need any more people on this beautiful planet of ours; the imperative to reproduce is no longer as strong as it once was, but we do have to evolve. And here's the thing: I see our changing relationship to gender as a response to those evolutionary impulses and I think that in the not-too-distant future, androgyny and gender neutrality and all the myriad ways that people express who they truly are will be seen as God's way or Nature's way of fine-tuning and rebalancing the human species."

Jeremiah was speechless. He had never in his life thought of his own sexuality as part of an evolutionary impulse as Francis called it, but now he could see how that could be the case. And he was part of that change. Slowly but surely, an utterly new light was being cast upon his life, a light that softened the shadows, that felt somehow liberating.

And whilst he still felt unable to share his authentic self with Francis – not because he feared Francis' judgement of him, but simply because he was not yet standing on that threshold – this sense of liberation gave him the courage to slowly begin to accept who he was.

"I hope you are right, Francis," he said eventually, "I really do."

One evening a few days later, Jeremiah spoke to Angel about the changes he was feeling within himself.

"Have you been listening to my conversations with Francis, of late, Angel?"

"Yes, of course, and what Francis said about the changing nature of gender is absolutely true. You are part of these winds of change, Jeremiah, and yet it is just a small facet of a much bigger picture; not the whole picture. When you become an angel, you will be able to forget all about sex and sexuality."

Jeremiah laughed. "Oh yes, when I become an angel – I wonder how many lifetimes that will take? But seriously, what do you mean about it being only a small facet of a bigger picture?"

"Well among the myriad misconceptions that humanity labours under, at the moment you still perceive everything in opposites, or what some call duality: light and dark, good and bad, male and female, and so on. And this has caused so much suffering, so much deviation from the golden path. In truth, duality does not exist – only complementarity. Light can only exist in relation to dark; their complementarity allows them both to arise, and unity – by which I mean the glorious infinity of night and day – is their state of balance. Until we see all things as complementary to each other rather than as opposites, suffering will continue, but once humanity accepts this truth and unity awareness becomes established, then fulfilling your real purpose on Earth can begin."

Jeremiah was somewhat bemused, not really able to

comprehend all that Angel was saying to him.

"Right...okay, but until then, I have a question, a bit of a mundane question after all you've just said. Angel, do you think I rejected the relationship that Angela offered me because it wasn't normal enough? Because I was more concerned about what other people would think of us, rather than of our own happiness?"

"Well, from the beginning your relationship with Angela could have hardly been described as normal, could it? And yet for years you were both content."

"But here's the thing, Angel – I think that I was so brainwashed by my gender stereotyping, that I imprisoned myself in judgements about what is normal and what is not. Nobody else seemed to judge me as harshly as I judged myself."

"That may be true, but I saw what was unfolding slightly differently. You just couldn't accept how your relationship was changing, how it needed to become different. It needed to grow into something else, something that included who Angela was becoming."

"But that was selfish of me, wasn't it, Angel? I thought I'd never tried to control her like she said her father had, but maybe I did? Maybe I was trying to make her fit in too?"

For a moment, Jeremiah was filled with sadness as he recognised that what Angel said was true.

"Yes, that's it... I was trying to make her fit in so that from the outside, we looked like a normal couple. I wanted her to fit in to how I wanted our relationship to be, not how she wanted it to be. I can see it now, I feel great sorrow for not having the courage to grow into what could have been."

He sighed and gazed deeply into his angel's eyes.

"I really am truly sorry that I couldn't open my heart and grow with her. What a fool I was."

"Dear Jeremiah, we all have to be foolish to become wise, otherwise, how would we learn? Try to see all that happened as part of your journey, that has led you to be here, now. If you see the bigger picture, then everything becomes clearer. That is why angels have wings."

"Why? Why do angels have wings?"

"So that we can rise up and see the bigger picture."

"Oh..." But Jeremiah was lost in thought, wondering what might have been if he'd been able to accept things as they really were.

PIECES OF THE JIGSAW

As the winter deepened, and a cold February settled upon Elmsford, Sarah saw Miriam almost every day. Miriam had bought herself a car, a small Fiat, and sometimes they drove to Appledore, a beautiful town on the Torridge estuary that had an exceptional riverside restaurant. They would order lunch and a glass of white wine and sit by the huge windows overlooking the water, feeling almost as if they were in a boat. It was such a treat for them both.

It was during one of these lunchtime trips, sitting side by side in the car, that Sarah asked Miriam about her family.

"I hope you won't think me nosey," she said, "but ever since you first came to Elmsford, I have been wanting to ask where you grew up, and about your earlier life. Have you always lived in this part of England?"

"No, not at all. I'm a late-comer to the Wild West." Miriam chuckled at her own joke. "Okay then, do you want the complete story, warts and all, or the potted version?"

"The complete story," said Sarah, pleased to have elicited this response from Miriam.

"Well, though both of my parents were English, I was born in the Pyrenees, in southern France, in a small village called Arques. My parents moved there after they were married. I think my father had a job there as a construction engineer, though I'm not sure. I lived there until I was seven, when both of my parents passed away."

"Oh gosh, I'm so sorry."

"Thank you, Sarah. My mother died giving birth to my brother, when I was six. Actually, both she and the baby died, so I am an only-child – and then my father died of a broken heart a year later. Well, that's the story I tell myself, though apparently he had a car accident. Anyway, I was sent to England to be brought up by my mother's sister who had married a farmer and who lived near Stow-on-the-Wold, in the Cotswolds. My aunt and uncle were sent from heaven, I can tell you. I loved them so much. They've both passed away now, but they had no children of their own and so I was like a surrogate daughter to them.

"When I was sixteen, my aunt sent me to a private school in Oxford to study for my A' Levels. It was an all-girl's boarding school and I liked it there very much and fortunately, I did rather well in my exams. Then, when I was only just eighteen, I got a scholarship to St Hilda's College, in Oxford. I had such a great time there, Sarah, I really loved it. St Hilda's was also a women-only college until quite recently."

"Did you like that aspect of it especially?"

"I did, and I think it has to do with the degree of

compassion that is often shared between women who are in a similar situation. It felt like we were all in it together, and we were always ready to help each other out. We were a tight-knit little gang and, perhaps unusually, there was very little competitiveness between us, so we all thrived. I still have several longstanding friendships from that time, you know.

"Anyway, I took a degree in Divinity, and then, when I graduated, I was invited to stay on and study for a PhD."

A large lorry was coming towards them and because the road was so narrow, Miriam had to stop talking and concentrate on squeezing past.

Then Sarah asked, "Do you remember much about your childhood in France?"

"I have some memories of my mother, who always seemed to be surrounded by books, but I don't remember my father – though my aunt told me he was dashingly handsome."

"Of course he was," laughed Sarah. "That's where you get it from."

Miriam took her eyes off the road for a second and looked at the woman in the passenger seat. She was always full of surprises and that's what Miriam liked about her. Though her life could be considered quite traditional, quite ordinary, Sarah herself was far from it. Miriam found her fascinating.

"I have his eyes, according to my aunt." Miriam grinned. "Where was I? Oh yes – well, I've been back to visit that part of France on many occasions because it's closely connected to the legend of Mary Magdalene – I think maybe that's why I'm so intrigued by her, because my studies of her reconnect me to my past..."

"And did you marry?"

Miriam laughed.

"I knew you would ask me that question. No, I never married nor had children. It's funny, but that is the one thing I've always been quite certain of in my life: that I wouldn't have children. I used to joke that I must've been a Catholic mother in a past life and had eight children to contend with, but now as I get older, I wonder if it was a joke – perhaps it was some kind of past-life memory or something? Anyway, I am what used to be called a spinster."

"I hate that phrase," said Sarah vehemently. "It seems to belittle women somehow, don't you think? It's as if only by getting married do women have any kind of status."

Again, Sarah's response was a pleasant surprise to Miriam and she couldn't help but smile.

"I agree, Sarah. I never usually refer to myself as a spinster. I don't know why I did just then."

"But you must have been in love?" Sarah felt she could press the matter; felt she had connected on a deeper level with Miriam now.

Miriam sighed.

"Ah, love... Yes, of course, and I have been in love more than once. And actually, in case you're wondering, I have loved men and women, and still do, although these days my solitude has taken over almost entirely. I think that is perhaps why I've never settled down with anyone. When it came to it, I always chose my work and my solitude."

She paused and drifted off momentarily, recalling

times past when love seemed so urgent, so pressing.

"I've experienced all kinds of love, but if anything, I have preferred the love of women. For me, it's somehow more complete than being loved by a man."

Sarah closed her eyes and thought for a moment of her marriage to Alan and of how lonely she had been.

"I can understand that," she said. "I only found one man I could really love and be loved by. I wish James and I had met when we were younger. We had so few years together."

"But perhaps if you'd have met at another time, you may not have felt the same way about each other? Sometimes I feel that there's a kind of perfect timing in everything we do."

"I hadn't thought about it like that… And I think you're right. I think James had to lose his wife to really acknowledge the depth of his love for her, and perhaps the depth of his love for me. He said as much. And I loved him so much, Miriam. I loved him with all my heart. But recently, in my friendship with Alice and Rachel, in caring for Katharine and – dare I say it – getting to know you, I have come to know what it means to love a woman, but to love them in a platonic way, without the sex! I suppose, it's more like friendship, but with a love that is totally unconditional."

"Well, in case you're wondering, sex with another woman is an incredible experience, but of course, it's not for everybody," said Miriam, "although all that was quite a long time ago, now. And there was one time when I thought I might fall in love and live with someone. But then the relationship became angry and quarrelsome, and I decided that I couldn't manage it. I could cope with separation and loneliness, but not jealousy, not rage. So here I am, alone but not lonely."

Sarah was intrigued that Miriam 'thought she might fall in love'. It seemed that for her, love was cerebral – for Sarah, it came from the heart.

They arrived in Appledore and parked in the car park that overlooked the vast estuary that was the confluence of the Taw and Torridge rivers. The ebbtide was running, exposing muddy sandbanks rippled with undulating patterns created by the receding water. There were not many boats on the river, and even the little ferry from Instow did not seem to be running. Only one lone fishing boat was making its way seaward towards the infamous Bideford Bar sandbank at the mouth of the Torridge that was such an infamous hazard to shipping.

As they sat there watching the world go by, Miriam slipped into that stillness that Sarah recognised as being so much a part of her. Then she spoke.

"There is something I want to mention," she said. "Something I have learnt. There is a love that is shared between all of us, all of us, and it is sacred. It is the union of the feminine and the masculine. Each one of us has both of these qualities within us, and their union is necessary for the balance and wellbeing of all that is – us, the Earth and the Cosmos. It doesn't matter whether it is love between a woman and a man, or between a woman and a woman or a man and a man. In fact, it is present in all relationships where love is true and where the qualities of feminine and masculine are expressed equally."

"Oh, that is so beautiful, Miriam... Thank you for

sharing that with me," Sarah whispered.

When she heard the words 'where love is true' Sarah knew they were important, but she couldn't immediately work out why. She needed to let Miriam's words just float in the ether and then settle. She knew that if she prodded them and poked them there and then, tried to pull them apart too much, their meaning would disappear. She needed to let the words take their place in her, let their meaning open up and fill her.

After sitting for a while longer, looking out over the river, the two women got out of the car and walked along the quaint narrow street with its multicoloured houses, and on to the pub.

Many questions were still circling for Sarah.

"I'm sorry," she said as they took their glasses of wine to their table, "but I seem to be full of questions today. Do you mind?"

"No, not at all. I'm in the mood. What else would you like to know?"

"Well, I was wondering where you live. I mean, when you're not at The Sanctuary? I know you sometimes teach at the university in Truro, but where do you actually live?"

Miriam took a sip of her wine.

"I move around quite a lot," she said. "When I am in Truro, I rent a lovely room near the university, and I have good friends who I visit in south-west France – they have a farm at the edge of the village of Arques where I was born – but my base is a flat in London, in the Barbican. It's small but perfect for me, and I can come and go easily. And you, Sarah, have you always lived in Elmsford?"

"No. I was born in Exeter, and that's where I met and married my husband, Alan. I was only nineteen."

"That was young to be married."

"I know, but we all married young in those days, you know, before the pill. Then, Alan got a job at St Austell Brewery in Cornwall, and so for years, we lived there. It was a small town where nothing much happened, but we brought up our son Nicholas there, and when he left school, he worked at the brewery too, before he got his job working for the Guinness brewery in Dublin. He's done quite well for himself there.

"I only came to Elmsford after Alan died, which is nearly twenty years ago now – I can hardly believe it's been that long. Alan and I had a holiday in Elmsford when Nick was little, and I fell in love with the place, so when I found out that the shop was for sale, I knew it was the next phase of life for me – like it was meant to be.

"But my son was dead set against me moving to Elmsford, you know. He thought I should stay in St Austell so that I could tend Alan's grave. Can you believe it? He made such a fuss about that. For the first few years I lived here, once a month, I'd get the bus to St Austell – which takes forever, I can tell you – just to put some fresh flowers on Alan's grave, and the irony is that Alan hated flowers when he was alive. He thought they were a terrible waste of money. But Nick seemed to think this was my duty. Anyway, despite all that, I have never regretted moving here. I love Elmsford."

"I love Elmsford too. There's something about the village that makes it feel like a safe haven, isn't there? It seems to attract people who need to take refuge, or who just need to step to one side, out of the mainstream. Like James, perhaps?"

"Yes, like James. And like you?"

"Yes, like me."

The barman walked over with their lunch of locally-caught fish pie, and for a while they stopped their conversation to relish the food. As they were waiting for their coffees, Sarah told Miriam a bit more about what it had been like when she first came to the village.

"Sometimes, in those early years in the shop, I wondered whether I would ever get the hang of it. I had so much to learn, but somehow, I did. And as time went on, I came to love it more and more: opening up in the mornings before the village got going and closing after everyone had gone home. Being at the centre of things."

"You must have been very brave to take the village shop on, all on your own."

"Looking back, I think you're right. A friend of a friend told me that the shop was for sale, and at the time I just wanted to get out of St Austell. I wanted to leave my past behind. Luckily, Alan's wages were good enough for us to be able to buy our house, and after Alan died, it became mine. The house was quite big, and it was in the centre of town and so it was easy to sell. And then, all those years ago, Elmsford was a bit run down, which meant I could afford to buy the shop without having to get a mortgage or anything. I'd done some part time work in a local shop in St Austell, so I had a bit of an idea what it would be like. So, I did it. I bought the shop."

They talked for a long while, at ease, slowly drinking

their cups of coffee. By the time they arrived back in Elmsford, Sarah felt she and Miriam had become closer.

And then it became certain that this was so.

Sarah awoke early, and as the day had dawned fair, she decided to take a long walk through the woods and then headed south along the steep and twisting coast path. This brought her to the top of the cliffs overlooking the harbour where she met the Elderberries for her weekly swim.

There was an 'L' shaped bench by a grassy bank that looked north-west towards Lundy Island, and as usual, Sarah stopped there to catch her breath and admire the view. But then, by some intuition she couldn't explain, as she walked home past The Sanctuary, she felt a strong urge to go and see Miriam. It was still only eight o'clock, so she wouldn't usually consider it an acceptable time to call on a friend, yet on this morning, she didn't hesitate to knock on the door.

After a while, she heard the big brass key turn in the lock, and then there was Miriam standing in her nightdress, wearing one of her long grey cardigans over it, which she was holding close about her. Much to Sarah's consternation, she was sobbing.

"Whatever's the matter?"

Miriam threw her arms around Sarah and held her for a long while.

"Come in," she sniffed, eventually.

Sarah was taken aback. She had never imagined that Miriam could be overwhelmed with emotion like this; that she, the scholar, Professor Husk, could be weeping uncontrollably. But here she was.

"Let me make some tea," said Sarah.

"That would be good."

Soon they were sitting opposite each other in the living room, holding their mugs of tea. And then Willow appeared, rubbed herself against Miriam's legs, and jumped up onto the sofa and began washing herself. For a while, all three of them sat together in silence, punctuated by Miriam's diminishing sobs, until Sarah, feeling the need for comfort, offered to light the fire.

"Yes, please," said Miriam wiping her eyes, "that would be lovely. It's all laid and ready – it just needs a match."

Sarah knelt down and opened the door to the stove and lit the firelighter under the kindling. Soon the flames brought warmth and comfort to the room.

"That's better," said Sarah. She knew that for the moment nothing needed to be said, and that Miriam would talk to her when she was ready.

After a while, in the quietness, she collected their mugs and took them into the kitchen and washed them up, returning to the room to find Miriam quietly stroking Willow, seemingly wrapped in her thoughts.

"Are you okay, Miriam?"

"I'm fine. I'm just… I can't talk about it right now," said Miriam, a sob catching in her throat.

"That's okay. Not to worry. Why don't you have a

long soak in the bath – I find that helps any situation. And then you could come to me for lunch, if you would like that?"

"Oh yes, that would be lovely, Sarah. Thank you."

They hugged each other, and Sarah left and went back to her cottage.

So, here's something I've not seen before, she thought to herself. *A tenderness, a vulnerability. I wonder what it's all about?*

Later that morning, there was a knock on Sarah's front door, and there was Miriam, restored to her normal assured and elegant self. She smiled at Sarah and hugged her.

"Come on in," said Sarah, "everything is ready."

They sat together in Sarah's small but pretty kitchen and ate lunch. Sarah had laid a blue and white gingham cloth on the table which she thought looked cheerful and had picked some colourful tulips from the garden and put them in a little vase in the centre. She'd made a simple pasta dish with leeks and mushrooms, which they ate with pesto and parmesan cheese and a green salad to go with it. And then they had ice cream. It was one of those posh ones with bits of chocolate and caramel in it.

"This is really decadent," said Miriam.

"I know," said Sarah, "but I thought we needed something sweet and wicked."

After lunch, they sat in Sarah's living room, Miriam with her coffee and Sarah with a cup of mint tea.

"Thank you for rescuing me today," Miriam said. "You just caught me at a bad time."

"I'm sorry."

"No, I don't mean it like that – I was pleased to see you – what I mean is… well, I don't get upset like that very often now, and I don't find it easy to talk about either, but with you I want to be open."

"Go on," said Sarah gently.

"Twenty years ago today, on my 46th birthday, I found a lump in my breast."

"Oh my god…"

"Yes. It was a terrible shock. I kept it to myself for about a week, every morning in the shower tentatively feeling the lump, thinking it might have gone away, but it was still there. And I was in the midst of a very romantic relationship with a man at the time, someone I thought I could perhaps make a life with. He was the last man I ever loved…

"Anyway, after a while I could bear it no longer, so I made an appointment to see my local GP. He was a very brusque man, who always had food stains on his shirt. I didn't like him much." Miriam chuckled at the memory. "It's funny what you remember, isn't it?

"He felt my breast and said, 'I think you know what this is.' And I did. After that I was catapulted headlong into an endless nightmare of hospital appointments, scans, surgery, chemotherapy, radiotherapy, more surgery… check-ups and x-rays. All my hair fell out and I lost so much weight because I couldn't keep food down during the treatment. It was hellish, and all the time I thought I was going to die. All I could think about was death, my death. I didn't expect to recover, but I did."

Sarah wiped a tear from her eye.

"Happy 66th birthday, Miriam." She moved nearer

to her friend and put her arms around her. They embraced deeply, both women letting the tears flow.

Eventually Sarah stood up.

"So now I know it is your birthday today, I think we should celebrate. I have a fabulous bottle of wine in the pantry. I'll go and fetch it."

She returned from her kitchen with a bottle and two glasses with large bowls. She held one out to Miriam and began to pour.

"Hang on, is that Cabalié Grenache?" Miriam asked, reaching for the bottle to read the label.

"Yes, it's my favourite wine."

"Mine too – how extraordinary. It comes from the Languedoc, you know. Where I was born."

"Well then, it's most appropriate for your birthday," said Sarah. "Cheers! Here's to you Miriam, for surviving and thriving, against the odds."

"It's strange, because usually I sail through my birthdays without feeling emotional. It's twenty years ago now, and I refuse to think of myself as a victim. But… I don't know – maybe it was all that talk of love and lovers yesterday, it just hit me hard this morning. One of the reasons I prefer a platonic relationship now is because my body is so wounded from the illness. I had my left breast removed, and a small portion of my right breast that was found to have pre-cancerous cells.

"And then I was told that I would have a much better chance of survival if I had my ovaries removed too, to stop the production of oestrogen. So, I had an oophorectomy, which meant one day I was pre-menopausal and the next, post-menopausal, which as you can imagine was a massive trauma. And then for five years I had to take horrendous medication that made me feel terrible, just in case my body had the audacity to produce any more oestrogen." Miriam sighed at the weight of the memory.

"My relationship with the lovely Gregory fizzled out because I couldn't bear for him to see my scars, or touch my body… and for years after, I didn't feel comfortable about being physically close with anyone. I still don't. And usually, I'm fine with it all – I'm still alive, for heaven's sake. But just occasionally, I am overwhelmed with sadness for a life that might have been. Cancer takes everything from you, Sarah. Everything. You have to start again; you have to reinvent yourself. Otherwise, you cannot survive."

Sarah looked at her friend, a woman who seemed so confident, so worldly-wise, the consummate professional, and she realised that every day she lived with loss, as Sarah herself did. Whatever your path in life is, loss accompanies it. Sometimes it becomes a sweet sorrow, a cherished memory, but sometimes it has to be stowed away in the recesses of the mind, lest it rears its ugly head and fells you.

"Well, I don't know why I came to see you this morning, but I just knew I had to. Something urged me to knock on your door, even though it was so early."

"Women's intuition, I'd say," said Miriam, taking a sip of her wine. "I feel better for telling you this bit of my past though, Sarah. And you know, part of the reinvention of myself has been that I've become fascinated with the many aspects of Love – Platonic Love, gender-fluid Love, empathic Love – and how it is actually Love that is the most powerful force in the

Universe. It's led me down some fascinating paths, I can tell you.

"I've studied hundreds of texts and visited many holy places, but still, there's something missing, Sarah, and I don't know what it is… I know there's a part of the jigsaw that I am trying to complete that I can't yet see. I know it's close. I just know it. Ever since I came to Elmsford, I've sensed around me a feeling of 'possible completion', but it has not yet settled into place."

"I find myself thinking a lot about Love these days," Sarah replied. "It came to me late in my life and now it pervades my every thought. It interests me too, in all its aspects."

"You see – it was providential we should become friends," Miriam exclaimed. "I know you'll help me to complete my jigsaw."

"Well, I can but try," said Sarah, refilling their glasses, "but I'm not sure I shall be much use. You're a scholar and I have read very little. You've travelled the world and I ran a village shop. You have an enquiring mind and an amazing imagination, and I see only what is in my cup or on my plate."

"But that is it, Sarah – don't you see? You help me to see what is before my very eyes. That which I overlook. I'm so taken up with what is in my head, that I don't always see what is right before me."

"Well, perhaps we'll make a good team, then?" Sarah smiled and squeezed Miriam's hand.

Miriam stood up and went to the window. It had begun to rain. She turned, holding herself in her arms and letting out a deep sigh.

"I think I'll wander home now," she said. "I'm

suddenly very tired. But you've absolutely salvaged my birthday and I feel so much better. Bless you. Can I borrow your umbrella?"

"Yes, of course."

Sarah found her umbrella and gave it to Miriam. In that moment she would have given her anything she asked for.

Miriam turned and hugged Sarah.

"Will you have lunch with me tomorrow?" she asked. "I feel so much more settled and centred when you're around."

"That would be lovely. I'll see you tomorrow."

A HEART UNFURLS

Gradually, Jezebel had come to accept that she now shared her cottage with Jeremiah. In fact, she found him pleasant company and being a man of routine, he was easy to live with. At any time of the day, she knew more or less where he would be and was pleased that he seemed to respect her preferred places, which followed a regular pattern as the sun moved around the cottage bringing sunlight and therefore warmth to one room after the next in a circular order. And, just as her former companion had been, Jeremiah was quiet, which she liked.

At first, she kept a distance, but then as she grew more confident of his manners, she would sometimes come and sit beside Jeremiah when he was in the living room, especially if the wood stove had been lit. Or, if he was in his study and the sun was on that side of the house, she would curl up on the small armchair beside the table. This familiarity was then extended first to Angel and then to Francis.

Although Jeremiah could not know it, Jezebel had seen Angel from the very first time he appeared and, as she had seen many angels before, she was not at all surprised by his shape-shifting, preferring his quieter human-like form in the brown robe to the radiant light with wings outspread, which she regarded as nothing but showing off. And anyway, it detracted from her own evident beauty.

Most days Jeremiah went for a walk, through the surrounding woodlands and across the fields, keeping to the footpaths and then looping back through the village. He had begun to recognise people and occasionally stopped for a brief chat about nothing much: the return of the house martins, or the dreadful weather. At weekends, he'd venture out further for walks along the coast path, usually turning south towards Cornwall, and on a clear day, occasionally getting a glimpse of Trevose Head in the far distance. He was enjoying getting to know this unfamiliar landscape, which was ancient and well-trodden, but cared for.

As a way of life, it had almost everything that Jeremiah was seeking. It felt safe, he loved his cottage and now that Giles had agreed to help with the garden, nothing much disturbed his peace. Jenny or Stephen phoned occasionally, and his friendship with Angela continued to blossom by email. Every so often, he would receive a beautiful postcard of some exquisite painting, instantly recognisable as being from Angela because of her terrible handwriting. Jeremiah often wondered how the cards found their way to his door, such was the scrawl with which they were addressed.

Francesca was still struggling with her health, the after-effects of her treatment being quite severe, but on the whole, they were happy enough, enjoying their life in Italy.

Yet for Jeremiah, all of this wasn't enough, not quite, and he couldn't discern why. Once more, he found himself waiting for something to happen, a slight feeling of frustration – or perhaps, anxiety – welling in the pit of his stomach.

And then the nightmares started: the young mugger with the knife and the leer, his weight bearing down on Jeremiah's sprawled body. Jeremiah would wake in a sweat, his heart racing.

"Angel, Angel, are you there?"

"I'm here.

"I've had that dream again."

"I know."

In the dark silence of the night Jeremiah felt a deep loneliness. He wanted someone to put their arms around him, to comfort him, to hold him and care for him.

"Can you see how it was the values those young men had been taught that led them to do what they did to you?" said Angel, gently.

"Just like my own values led me to shut myself away from life, you mean?"

"It is always possible to tell yourself a new story of who you are. And Jeremiah, it would help you so much if you could forgive those young men."

"I don't know how to do that."

"Open your heart and let love guide you."

"I don't know how to do that," Jeremiah's voice broke and he let the tears flow.

"That is a good start," Angel whispered.

One Saturday morning as Angel was levitating in the kitchen, slowly whirling in small and obviously pleasing circles, Jeremiah remembered that he wanted to ask him a question.

"Angel, you know when Francis or Giles are here, they don't see you, do they?"

"Evidently not. As you know, they don't believe in angels."

"But, even so, they still have an angel, don't they? You once told me that everyone has an angel."

"That's right. They just can't see them yet, which is very frustrating for their angels."

"You mean their angels just have to wait until they are believed in?"

"Yes, that's it. Who'd be an angel, eh?"

"And can an angel be shared with someone else?"

"Yes, indeed. But it doesn't happen that often. People who are very close to each other can sometimes share an angel."

"And does Jezebel see you?"

"Of course."

"Well, that's something."

Jeremiah resumed flipping through a cookbook.

"Oh, by the way, I've invited Francis and Giles to supper."

Jeremiah opened the lid of the tagine and with a small spoon, tasted the spicy sauce that accompanied the slow-cooked lamb and apricots. It was delicious. Jeremiah rarely ate meat, but as the farm shop sold its own home-reared organic lamb, he felt it was a suitable treat for his guests. He emptied a tin of chickpeas into the stew and put the tagine back in the Aga. Then he opened a bottle of red wine and lit the candles on the dining table. Jeremiah did not entertain often. The last time he had cooked for guests was at Christmas with Stephen and Jenny and their family, and he had enjoyed that. Tonight, he felt slightly nervous – or was it excited? Both.

Angel was sitting upright on the sofa and although his large wings were folded back and his eyes were shut, Jeremiah knew he was very much present and aware of what was happening. Because this was a special occasion, Angel was wearing a rather magnificent white hooded gown trimmed with what looked like gold lace. Jezebel, her shiny black coat catching the candlelight, was perched on the arm of the sofa opposite him, watching Jeremiah's every move.

Suddenly, Jeremiah found the scene incredibly funny. He burst out laughing, pointing at the two of them.

"Look at you two – you look like statues from the British Museum's Egyptian department!"

Neither of them found the comparison amusing, and neither jumped when the doorbell rang, though Jeremiah did.

"They're here," he said, removing his spattered apron and taking one last look at the room. Satisfied, he opened the door to Giles and Francis.

"Would you look at this," Francis' eyes surveyed the room. "What a transformation. It looks like something out of that *Homes & Gardens* magazine."

"Well, I do have a wonderful housekeeper, you know." Jeremiah smiled and took their coats.

Giles handed Jeremiah an expensive-looking bottle of wine and made a beeline for Jezebel, who seemed intent on being unusually friendly, pushing her head into his hand as he stroked her. Jeremiah watched as he did so, aware that Angel was still there, now standing behind the sofa, wings unfurled. Giles did not see him.

"Well, you are very beautiful," cooed Giles, and as he continued to stroke Jezebel, her purr became audible. "Mmmm, supper smells good, Jeremiah. I'm ravenous. I've hardly eaten a thing all day."

"It's lamb and apricot tagine. Please, take a seat at the dining table. Let's eat."

Conversation between the three men was easy. Giles and Francis were relaxed in each other's company and knew Jeremiah well enough to tease him a little, but they also appreciated his refinements – his good taste, and his evident love of books and carpets.

"What's your connection to Persia, then?" Giles asked Jeremiah as he served the food.

"What do you mean?"

"Well, the Persian carpets, the Persian cat, the Kilim slippers – and the tagine, which I believe is also from Persia..."

"Oh... I hadn't thought of it like that. But I suppose I do feel quite drawn to that part of the world. Actually, the carpets are from Turkey, but I think Turkey was once part of Persia – bits of it, anyway. My partner and I used to import Turkish rugs and carpets, which is why I come to have so many. Maybe I had a past life in Persia?"

"You don't believe in all that past life stuff, do you?" asked Francis. "We have a friend who thinks he was once a Roman centurion stationed at Hadrian's Wall. He's done regression therapy and everything to try and find out more about it. Quite interesting really, but I don't know if I believe in it or not. In his case, I think it's just that he loves the uniforms. He always dresses up as a centurion at New Year's Eve parties."

"I don't know what I believe, not really," said Jeremiah, enjoying the conversation. "I think we are so varied that perhaps all of our experiences are valid. If your friend believes that he was once a Roman centurion, who are we to say he wasn't? Many people believe they have a guardian angel, don't they?"

"Oh well, my client Miriam would certainly agree with that – you remember the professor I told you about, Jeremiah? Actually, we should invite you to supper and introduce you properly to Miriam and her friend, Sarah. They're so lovely. I think you'd get on like a house on fire."

"Get you, Frank, with your 'clients'," chuckled Giles. "You're a housekeeper not an accountant."

And the moment had passed. Jeremiah didn't quite know how to steer the conversation back to angels. Instead, he said, "Supper would be lovely. I've met Sarah – she came to introduce herself and brought me some flowers when I first moved in. That would never have happened in London. And talking of accountants,

I've often wondered why you two choose to work as a housekeeper and a gardener. After all, I know that Francis studied gender politics and I think he told me that you studied music, Giles. So, have you left all that behind?"

Francis and Giles looked at each other. "Can you keep a secret?" Giles asked, conspiratorially.

"Yes, that is something I'm very good at."

And then for the next half hour or so, Giles and Francis regaled Jeremiah with their plans. They explained that after they'd graduated, both of them had gone on to take a diploma in Business Management and that is where they met each other. It turned out that Giles was also a saxophone player in a band that was doing quite well in the southwest. Their big dream was to open a recording studio. Francis would manage the studio and Giles would oversee the technical side. And today was especially exciting for them as they'd been to see a run-down old barn that looked like a perfect fit for their vision.

"So, whilst we're doing the day jobs – which we really enjoy, by the way – we're also devising our business plan, saving as much money as we can, seeing bank managers – ugghh – and generally getting excited about the whole thing," said Giles, looking over at Francis, his eyes animated and sparkling. "We just need some seed capital."

"How wonderful," said Jeremiah, opening the fridge to retrieve the pavlova. "To create a business together that you can enjoy and put your hearts into is so satisfying. I suppose that's what Stephen and I did all those years ago. It was all Stephen's idea and to begin with, I just went along with it. But after a while, I began to love it. In fact, I was obsessed with it. It became my life and looking back I can see how much I learned and how much I enjoyed it, how it deepened my relationship with Stephen."

"Is he… was he… were you 'together'?" Francis didn't quite know how to say it and did the inverted commas thing with his fingers.

"No," Jeremiah smiled. "He's married to Jenny and they have two children, my god-children. He was my business partner and is my best friend."

"And you, Jeremiah, did you marry?" asked Giles.

Jeremiah put down his spoon and fork, looking towards Angel who was now sitting in the corner of the room.

"No," said Jeremiah, quietly, "I never married. But I did live with a very lovely woman called Angela for more than ten years and we were happy. Then we had to part, but we're still in touch."

"What happened," said Giles, "if you don't mind me asking?"

Now it was Jeremiah who didn't quite know how to say what it was that needed to be said.

"She… she was a woman who loved women."

"That must've been hard for you, Jerry?" Francis squeezed his arm, then ate an enormous spoonful of pavlova, the strawberries falling back onto his plate.

It was the first time anyone apart from Stephen and Jenny had called him Jerry, and he liked it.

"It was, but we have forgiven each other, and as it happens since I left London our friendship has begun to blossom again. It's rather lovely, actually. I really value it. And talking of friendships blossoming, a little plan is forming in my mind."

The evening was not going to the plan Jeremiah had intended – to introduce Angel to his friends – but now an unexpected plan was taking shape and Jeremiah felt a tingle of excitement, like there was a possibility he could be part of something. Giles and Francis looked at him attentively.

"Look guys, my business with Stephen did rather well over the years – very well, in fact – and I had a flat in what is now a fashionable part of London, so when the business was sold, together with the proceeds from my flat, I could afford to buy this house and live comfortably here. But I miss being part of something, having an interest in something. So, I've had an idea. What if I could help you? What if I was able to offer you some financial support to set up your business?"

"Really…?" Giles looked wide-eyed at Francis.

"Well, subject to seeing your number-crunching and hearing more about how it's all going to work, what if I invested some money in your recording studio? I'd be a sleeping partner, or a shareholder or something like that. Seed capital, I think you called it. We could draw up an agreement that suited us all. I wouldn't want anything to do with the day to day running of it, nor would I interfere in any way – unless you wanted any support or advice, but I'd enjoy being part of something and seeing it flourish."

Jeremiah wondered if his guests could hear Angel fluttering his wings in approval, but they seemed not to notice.

For a moment, Giles and Francis were actually

speechless, seemingly unable to take in all that Jeremiah had said. And then...

"Oh my God. OH MY GOD!" Giles jumped up, wrapped his arms around Jeremiah and kissed him on the cheek.

"Sorry – I hope you don't mind me doing that?" he blushed, realising what he'd just done.

"I don't mind at all."

"Are you serious, Jeremiah?" Francis ventured. "Do you mean what you just said?"

"I mean it. I would love it."

Jeremiah smiled at the two young men in whom he recognised so much of himself – and something unfurled in his heart.

FINDING FAMILY

Sarah was pondering the deep connection she felt with Miriam, particularly now that they had shared their life stories about the painful losses they had both experienced. As she walked down the village street and through the churchyard, she wondered how Miriam would be feeling this morning, the day after her birthday, the day after she revealed her vulnerability. She knocked, and Miriam opened the door and they embraced like old friends, best friends.

As Sarah stepped into the house, she was greeted first by Willow, who miaowed and then disappeared along the veranda, and then by the evocative smell of incense, which was burning in a black cast iron vessel standing on top of the wood stove.

"Do you mind the incense?" asked Miriam.

"No, not at all, I like it. Can I do anything to help?"

"No, just make yourself comfortable." Miriam was once more her usual bright and confident self, as she came through from the kitchen with a bottle of rosé wine and two glasses.

"Shall we treat ourselves again?"

"Yes, lets. What a beautiful colour."

"It's another wine from the Pyrenees. It reminds me of being with my friends in southern France. It's the colour of sunshine and roses, don't you think?"

Sarah took a sip. "I do, and it's delicious too. Oh, by the way," she said, "did I mention that Katharine and Tom are coming to stay this weekend?"

"No, you didn't. That will be lovely for you."

"Yes, I think they want to tell me about a flat they've found in London which they're going to rent together."

"Well, that's good. She'll make a wonderful teacher you know."

"I'm sure she will, and I guess that will be in London now that Tom has come home. I knew our special time together was coming to an end, but I feel good about it now that I've got used to the idea; like it's a natural progression, not a parting. I'm sure we'll keep in touch."

"Of course you will. She needs your love, Sarah. You've given it to her unconditionally and that's allowed her to find her balance and confidence. That's a rare gift, my dear. Let's eat."

They sat at the dining table, where the view out towards the sea was obscured by a sudden heavy downpour of rain. Miriam had prepared basmati rice with roasted vegetables and raisins, and then one of Sarah's favourites, a custard tart with crème fraîche. She was a very good cook.

"When we went to the pub the other day," said Sarah, as they ate, "you were telling me your story, but you didn't finish it."

"Okay. Where did we get to?"

"You were telling me about your time in Oxford."

"Oh, yes, Oxford… full of earnest academics and clandestine love affairs. And when I was there, everything changed for me. New worlds opened up, worlds I knew nothing about. As I told you, I studied Divinity, and I was almost immediately taken up with Christian mysticism, and then, later, with exploring the mysteries of the Divine Feminine. I had the most wonderful supervisor, a woman called Jenny de Coeur. She was half French on her mother's side and, unusually in those days, she had taken her mother's maiden name. Together we explored heresy."

"Heresy?"

"Yes, week after week, term after term, I sat with Jenny de Coeur, surrounded by books, with papers strewn everywhere, listening to her speak of these brave dissenting voices, mostly of women who refused to be bowed by the prejudice of patriarchy, and I just loved it. I was in my element."

"I don't think I really know what heresy is," Sarah mused, stroking Willow who was now by her side.

"Well, it can be many things, but in this case, it was all about the gender of God."

Sarah's eyes widened. It had never occurred to her to question the gender of God.

"You see," said Miriam, her energy rising, "Jenny believed that God was both male and female, entangled and indistinguishable. And she believed that in each of the Abrahamic faiths, Judaism, Christianity and Islam, the voice of the feminine had been deliberately excluded from orthodox teachings so that we finished up not only with a church dominated by men, but with teachings that speak more of power and discipline than of love and compassion. Nevertheless, the evidence that supported Jenny's view, our view, is in the Bible."

Miriam stood up and brought to the table a copy of her Bible in which many slips of paper marked passages of text. She opened it at the beginning, her long fingers turning the pages until she found what she wanted.

"This is the text that Jenny showed me all those years ago. It comes from the first book of the Bible, *Genesis*. For in this very first chapter, God is spoken of as plural. Listen: 'Let us make man in our image, after our likeness.' And why would it not be so, since in the whole of creation the feminine and masculine are intertwined and interdependent. Neither one exists on its own, and all of life requires them both."

"But why was this excluded from the teachings of the Church? Why did men feel that they had to suppress it?" Sarah frowned as she took in all Miriam was saying. "What were they so frightened of? It doesn't make sense to me."

"Those are all good questions, Sarah." Miriam smiled. "You shall have a gold star!"

They laughed.

"Let's go and sit by the fire," said Miriam. "This might take a while to explain. Would you like your usual mint tea? I'm going to have coffee?"

"You know what," said Sarah, "I think for once I'll have a coffee – I feel like being rebellious after hearing all that."

"Two coffees coming up," smiled Miriam.

And so Miriam and Sarah made themselves comfortable, Miriam as usual sitting in what had always been James's armchair, and Sarah sitting on the sofa with Willow curled up beside her. Sarah had never really liked coffee much, but now she was enjoying its dark and bitter taste.

"You have to remember," began Miriam, "that Jesus, or as he was really called, Yeshua, was a Jew born into a culture with a dominant male ethos. Women were subservient then. Actually, there had been a time, hundreds of years before, when this was not so, when the God Yahweh had a consort, Asherah. But this had long since been denied, and the creation myth now came not from the womb of the Mother but from the mind of the Father.

"So, women had become subservient, and although Yeshua in his teachings and parables challenged this, once he was gone it was unacceptable to those who remained that women should be treated as disciples let alone apostles. Men were in charge, and those women who had been followers and companions of Yeshua were cast aside. That included Mary Magdalene."

Sarah was listening intently. Miriam's words seemed to put a spell on her; she felt as if she had travelled through time and was walking the streets of Galilee with Mary Magdalene. Miriam noticed that she had drifted away.

"Are you sure you want to know all this?"

"Oh yes, I'm sure. It's fascinating. I was miles away there, imagining what life was like in Biblical times… But you know, when I think how I was expected to be obedient – yes, obedient, not only to my father, but to my husband, too – it makes me want to scream. Why did I just accept all of that, Miriam? Why didn't I question it? Why did no-one tell me about any of this? Bloody hell!"

Sarah drained the rest of the coffee, a slight flush of alcohol and caffeine showing on her cheeks.

"I'm afraid the prejudice has run very deep," replied Miriam. "Somewhere in the Old Testament, I cannot remember where, but I remember the words because they are so frightful, it is said: 'Of the woman became the beginning of sin, and through her we all die'."

Sarah gasped. "That's so awful… but I do know that women didn't remain silent and subservient – having read your book, I do know that somehow, we found ways to be heard."

"That's the remarkable thing, isn't it? Women didn't just disappear, and if you look for them, they are there in the annals of history: Mary Magdalene as the companion to Jesus; Guinevere and Nimue in the Grail Quest and the stories of Merlin, the Christian women mystics like Hildegard of Bingen and Julian of Norwich, and in the lives of the Beguines who were lay religious women living in community eight hundred years ago. But we do remain at the edge, outside the core teachings of the Church and of history. And so, if we go back to my time at St. Hilda's, you can understand why it was considered heresy to study them. After all, the only woman to be revered in the New Testament is the Virgin Mother, and even she is hardly spoken of at all."

"Yes, of course, I can see that."

"But what excites me now is that there's a shift of energy. In all parts of the world, women are taking a stand and are speaking out, not just for themselves but for the hurt and injustice they see around them. People are beginning to recognise that the Divine Feminine, which is what I call this rising energy, is as much a part of Nature as the rise and fall of the tide, and whatever is done to hide Her cannot prevent Her from coming forth. Doorways are opening, Sarah, enabling the Divine Feminine to be heard, to be seen and to be felt once again. And what really fascinates me is why it is happening now."

Sarah felt an excitement swirling through her body. When Miriam got going, she had a magnetism that drew her attention completely. As she spoke, she gestured with her hands, drawing Sarah in and laying before her the richness of all that she knew. And her face lit up, and she held Sarah with her eyes.

For a while they sat in silence.

And then Sarah said, "I'm not a scholar like you, Miriam, but I do know that we need to care for each other. I know of the love between Katharine and Tom or the love that James and I shared. And I know about friendship, too and the love I feel for my friends. I think it is only where love is that we dwell aright."

Sarah was not sure where what she'd just said came from, but she knew it to be true. She just knew it.

Miriam smiled at her. "Yes, indeed you do know these things, dear Sarah."

As Sarah walked home some time later, she thought about her feelings of deep affection for Miriam. The more she got to know her, the more intriguing Miriam became. When she first came to the village, Sarah, had not expected that this would be so; she had assumed that this 'Professor' would remain remote from her and keep herself to herself, not that they would become close friends. But now she felt a growing intimacy between them, and she liked it. She liked all the stories about wise and brave women that Miriam spoke of. But it was more than this. The more time they spent together, the more she could see that despite her scholarship and her books, Miriam was still discovering herself, just as she was.

She almost bumped into Jeremiah as she rounded the corner of the church making her way toward the lychgate.

"I'm sorry, I didn't see you there. I was deep in thought." When she saw it was the gentleman from the thatched cottage, she smiled. "Oh, hello again. How are you getting on in your new home... sorry, I didn't catch your name before...?"

"Jeremiah Browne." He held out his hand to shake Sarah's then changed his mind, thinking it too formal, too old fashioned. But she caught it anyway and shook it warmly.

"Sarah Silver," she said. "It's good to be properly introduced at last.

"Yes, of course – Sarah – I remember your name. Hello again, and I must say I really enjoyed your homemade jam, which is all gone now. And things are very good with me, thank you. I'm enjoying finding my way around the lanes and footpaths and I seem to have settled into the rhythm of country life."

"I'm glad to hear it. There are some absolutely lovely walks around here."

"There certainly are. Well, I hope to bump into you again some time. Goodbye Sarah."

"Goodbye Jeremiah. Enjoy your walk."

As he walked away, Sarah heard him talking to someone. *Perhaps he talks to himself,* she thought, *like I do.*

Easter brought fine sunny weather and the Elmsford Elderberries were able to swim more regularly as the sea calmed from the winter storms. Sarah joined the Elderberries on nearly every occasion that they congregated for a dip. She had become one of the gang and was able to swim to Ship Rock with the others, without getting too exhausted. She loved the thrill of the cold water, how it took her breath away, and then how her body acclimatised and felt naturally buoyant. At these moments she felt a kind of freedom, free from day-to-day worries and free from the physicality of her body as it was held and caressed by the water. And she also enjoyed the amiable conversations as the women on the slipway dried-off and got changed. She felt blessed by this turn of events in her life.

On the morning of Maundy Thursday, just before midday, Katharine's car pulled up at Sarah's front door and Tom and Katharine jumped out, all energy and smiles.

"Come on in. How are you both?"

Tom took their bags upstairs and then bounded back down.

"It is so lovely to be here," he said. "I can't wait to go and check out the surf. I've borrowed a boogie board, so

I'm hoping to catch a few waves."

"Wow, Tom – good for you. It's still a bit chilly and there's not much of a wave today, but it's worth a try."

"Do you girls mind if I head straight off?"

"Not at all," said Sarah. "It'll give me and Katharine a chance to catch up."

Tom hurriedly got back in the car and disappeared along the street towards the sea.

"So, tell me what's happening." Sarah gestured for Katharine to sit beside her on the sofa.

"Well, we got that flat I told you about. Our tenancy begins on the first of May, so it's not long to wait now. We're so excited, Sarah. It's a bit small, but it'll be our first place together and it's in a really nice area, near Hampstead Heath, so we're very lucky. I'm feeling pretty exhausted though – it's been hectic since we saw you at New Year. I can't tell you how much I've been looking forward to these few days away. I have my final exams coming up and I am beginning to realise how important they are to me. It's a bit scary."

"But you're happy? You seem happy."

"Yes, I am happy."

"I'm so glad it's all worked out for you, darling." Sarah reached out for Katharine's hand. "When Tom was in America, I wondered if your relationship could survive the separation."

"Me too, Sarah, but we did survive and what it taught us is that we want to be together more than anything in the world. So that is our top priority now – to be together. I've started applying for teaching posts in the north London area. I've handed in my notice with the online teaching, and I hope to start a full-time job in September, which will give Tom and me some time to settle into the flat and perhaps have a holiday and see a few friends this summer."

Sarah thought how this news of Katharine looking for work in London and being away for the summer would once have deflated her; how she would have felt her absence keenly. But now Sarah felt she was forging her own future, just as Katharine was.

After a while, Tom came back, his wet hair proving he had indeed braved the elements.

"How was it?" Sarah asked.

"You were right, it was freezing – and there were hardly any waves, so I didn't get much of a surf. But I enjoyed myself. I met your friend Miriam while I was getting changed. She's something else!"

"What do you mean?" asked Katharine.

"Well, to begin with, she is unusually elegant for Elmsford."

"Thank you, Tom," chuckled Sarah.

"Present company excepted, of course," he said. "But I'm sure you know what I mean. She was an apparition in grey and white. And she has… what's the word…? Oh, I don't know – she has a kind of 'presence'."

Sarah nodded and smiled. That was Miriam.

"Anyway, she seemed to know who I was. She just said, 'Hello, Tom,' and sat on the harbour wall beside me."

"I hope you were nice to her," said Katharine.

"Of course I was!" said Tom, kicking playfully at her foot. "What do you make of her, Sarah?"

"Well, actually, we've become good friends. I've enjoyed spending time with her since the turn of the year. She is somewhat solitary, but then, so am I."

"She reminds me a bit of Grandpa," said Tom. "She has that same quality he had. Whenever I was with him, he seemed to be somewhere else."

They laughed. That was how James had been – sometimes. But at other times he would be absolutely there with you. And perhaps Tom had forgotten that he had been there for him more than once whilst he was struggling to find his way in the world.

"I would like to see Miriam this weekend, if it's possible," said Katharine. "Apart from anything else I'd like to introduce Tom to her properly.

And so Katharine rang Miriam who invited them all to her house later that afternoon.

As the sun was just beginning to drop into the western horizon Sarah, Tom and Katharine set off for Miriam's house, shading the glare from their eyes as they walked through the churchyard.

Suddenly, Sarah stopped in her tracks and turned towards the woodland.

"Can you hear it?"

"Hear what?" asked Tom.

"Listen... there!"

"A cuckoo – it's a cuckoo. I haven't heard one for years." A smile crept over Tom's face. "I haven't heard a cuckoo since I came to spend the summer holidays here with Grandpa when I was a kid."

Not for the first time, Sarah marvelled at how the song of a bird could weave memories in time.

Miriam was waiting for them and ushered them to the veranda. On the little table were four glasses and an opened bottle of wine, the condensation on the outside confirming it had just been taken from the fridge. It was her special rosé from the Pyrenees.

Conversation came easily and Tom was soon telling Miriam about his work. Sarah noticed how intently she listened to what he was saying.

"So, we're really at the forefront of scientific research on climate change," he was saying, "and some of the instruments I've helped to design are picking up strong signals of climate feedback loops that are very worrying. Actually, we no longer refer to it as climate change," Tom said, "we call it 'climate breakdown', because that's what's happening. The climate that we know and depend upon is breaking down before our eyes."

"Yes, I've read a lot about this in *the Guardian*" Miriam said, "and I wonder sometimes that no-one asks how all this has come about."

"What do you mean?"

"Well, with respect, it's all very well looking at the data on the latest warnings and forecasts, but it seems to me that we won't be able to make the changes that are necessary until we change the way we see things."

"What do you mean?" repeated Tom.

"Well, these disasters don't just come from nowhere. They are caused."

"Yes, they're caused by our way of life."

"But more importantly, they are caused by how we see the world and our relationship to each other and the Earth. If we saw the world as it really is, we would see it as whole and interconnected. And then we would understand that if we harm one part, we harm the whole, including ourselves. Nothing is separate, and what's more, everything is inclined towards balance and order, even if that balance and order is always shifting. It is foolhardy and dangerous to disrupt it."

"James told me once that everything has consciousness," said Sarah, "and that every being is intimately connected with every other being. That the whole planet is alive."

"Yes, that's exactly it." Miriam smiled warmly at Sarah. "And not only our world, but the Cosmos, too. What happens is never an accident, it is always a consequence, and in our case, a consequence of believing we could separate ourselves from the natural world. It is a kind of separation that has arisen over hundreds of years and it's coming to a head now, but its roots are very old."

"In what way?" asked Katharine, seemingly mesmerised as the professor in Miriam took charge.

"The roots of the climate crisis are entwined with the suppression of women's voices and the rise of patriarchy, which as Sarah and I have been exploring, has allowed the mind and the intellect to overrule all that our hearts and Love tell us. But the tide has turned and the great rebalancing has begun. The rise of the Feminine Principle will enable much healing to be done."

"Really? You think so?" Tom could hardly comprehend what this scholarly woman was telling him, but he had the good sense to listen carefully.

"I really think so, Tom. I'm not saying that we won't experience a great deal of upheaval – that always comes with change – but I think along with the collapse of old systems and ways of life will come a new sense of the miraculous potential in living harmoniously with all life on this glorious planet."

"Ah... If only my mate Tyler could hear you speak. He feels so crushed by our work sometimes, but what you've just said is quite hopeful. It's like..." he paused to order his thoughts. "It's like climate change is symptomatic of deeper change and we need to find a way to dialogue with what this change is telling us."

"We do indeed Tom. We do indeed." Miriam smiled at this young man who was looking so intently at her, a look she'd grown accustomed to. She saw in him the Divine Masculine uncorrupted, pure. She hoped he would always stay that way.

Katharine and Tom stayed until late on Monday afternoon, but then they had to head back to London. It had been a memorable weekend for Sarah, seeing these two young people beginning to make their way together. It was exactly what she wanted for them. And she felt sure that they would be back. She knew that Tom's new-found love of surfing was also now accompanied by a desire to hear more from Miriam and a philosophy that gave him hope.

More than this, though – the weekend had confirmed Sarah's own growing feelings of wholeness and connection. *I've found my family,* she said to herself as she made her way to bed.

On the first of June, Miriam signed the lease to extend her stay at The Sanctuary, and on the following day, to celebrate, she invited Sarah to have afternoon tea with her. Sarah took some of her fruit scones and flowers from her garden, roses and the first sprigs of honeysuckle. They sat on the veranda looking out towards the sea and celebrated Miriam's decision to remain in Elmsford.

"Yes, for the next three years," Miriam beamed.

"Three years?" exclaimed Sarah in surprise.

"Yes – I've agreed a long let. I'm here to stay."

Sarah threw her arms round Miriam.

"I'm so pleased! That's wonderful news."

Over the months, these two women had formed a deep bond of friendship, and to know that it was not going to be broken felt wonderfully reassuring. They were both filled with happiness. Sarah drew such sustenance from all she was learning from Miriam of the Divine Feminine and women's wisdom. Somehow, she was growing into herself. And Miriam was learning and growing too.

Since being in Elmsford and more specifically since meeting Sarah, with her uncomplicated love and generosity of heart, Miriam had begun to realise that part of her own healing journey was to find a way to express her innate femininity. After all the medical interventions she'd experienced, her coping mechanism was to forget her ruined body and the needs of her heart, and to dive into academia and the joy of study. But meeting Sarah, being in Sarah's presence, had begun to soften what had become a hardened carapace. Miriam was beginning to recognise what her heart needed. She recalled a book she'd been reading which was an Aramaic translation of Yeshua's teachings – so different from the King James' Bible. In the book, it stated that Yeshua's original teaching was not, 'Blessed are the meek, for they shall inherit the earth,' but 'Blessed are they who soften their hard edges for they shall receive from the Universal source.' She knew that softening her edges was part of her healing.

The two women were learning from each other, moving together in love, and gaining strength from each other, too. In their different ways, they affirmed each other and encouraged each other, and Sarah now thought of Miriam as her beloved friend.

As they sat together on the veranda one afternoon, enjoying the quietness, the sound of the breeze in the trees, Sarah had a question.

"What does Love mean to you, Miriam?"

For a moment, Miriam did not answer. And then she said, "I suppose I see it as something that is vast and eternal, something that holds the fabric of the Universe in place. What about you?"

"I think I see it as something that is very small," said Sarah. "Something that happens when people truly care for each other."

"That's beautiful," said Miriam. "And I think perhaps it's both."

"Yes, I think it could be."

DIVINE PROVIDENCE

Although Jeremiah did not know many people in Elmsford, his arrival had been noted, and he had received an invitation to a drinks party from Jonathan and Matilda Jackson, a rather grand couple who lived just outside the village. When Jeremiah asked Francis about the Jacksons, he said that Giles had done a bit of gardening for them once, that they had both been 'something in banking', and that Matilda's family had links to the area going back for generations.

"Actually," said Francis, "Giles didn't really get on with them. They wanted him to spray the veg beds with chemicals to get rid of the weeds, and when he refused, they 'let him go'. Giles prides himself on being an organic gardener, as you know. Anyway, you should go, Jerry – if only to see how the other half live."

Jeremiah laughed, and even though such parties were quite a long way outside his normal comfort zone, he decided he would go to this one.

The Saturday morning of the party was sunny and warm, and Jeremiah decided to set out and walk the short distance to the Jacksons. Their house was approached by a graceful driveway, through a kind of idealised parkland with wrought iron fencing and sheep grazing under ancient oak trees. This, Jeremiah supposed, was what you can buy if you have been 'something in banking'. Nonetheless, he was enjoying the walk and the scenery.

The house was not especially beautiful, but it was large. According to Francis, it had originally been a priory, but Jeremiah could see that it had been added on to, the older stone walls of the priory being overwhelmed by more modern plastered extensions on either side, and the huge oak doors, and heavy framed windows seemed a little out of place. Now it was rather dark and forbidding.

Jeremiah walked through an open front door into a hallway that led towards the garden at the rear of the house, where he could see that people were already gathered, glasses in hand, milling about.

Jeremiah had always found drinks parties intimidating. He thought it was the sheer number of unknown people, all glancing around to see who was there, and who they might want to speak to, and somehow making you feel that it was not you.

Somewhat in dread, he walked onto a garden terrace beyond which was a marquee, with many more people drinking and taking food from trays carried amongst them by young men and women dressed all in black.

Matilda spotted him and waded through the throng to greet him enthusiastically.

"Welcome! Welcome - you must be Jeremiah Browne? I'm Matilda Jackson and I am so glad you could come. Would you like a drink? Champagne?"

Jeremiah had never understood why everyone except him wanted to drink champagne.

"Actually, I'm not particularly fond of champagne."

Matilda winced. "A glass of wine then?"

"Yes, a glass of wine would be lovely. I'd prefer red, if possible."

"Wait here," she said, and set off into the marquee.

Something must have happened, because she didn't return, and for a while Jeremiah was left standing on the terrace. He looked around wondering if it would be best to find his way back into the house and head for home before it got any worse, but just as he decided to do so, two women came towards him. One he recognised as Sarah, the lady who had brought him flowers. The other was tall and elegant, dressed from top to toe in grey and white. Very striking. In each hand she was holding a glass of red wine.

"Jeremiah?" said the lady in grey. "Matilda asked me to bring you your wine. I understand you don't much like champagne."

"I'm afraid I don't."

"Nor do I – always gives me a terrible headache."

Jeremiah smiled. "Well, thank you," he said. "I rather thought I'd been abandoned."

"No, you haven't. My name is Miriam, and I believe you've already met Sarah."

"I have, and it's nice to meet you Miriam," Jeremiah smiled. "I have to say, I don't know anyone else here."

Jeremiah saw that Sarah was shorter than Miriam and a little older, with greyish-blonde hair cut straight at her shoulders. She was wearing a blue linen dress and smelt nice, even from a distance – lavender perhaps.

He smiled at them both. It seemed things were definitely improving.

And then it dawned on him.

"Hang on a minute – you don't happen to have a housekeeper called Francis, do you Miriam?"

"I do indeed. Why do you ask?"

"Well then, we have friends in common. Francis is my housekeeper too, and he's been mentioning for some time that he wants to have a supper party to introduce us. And now, here we are."

"Well, what good fortune that we've met today," said Miriam.

"Is there anywhere to sit?" said Jeremiah. "For some reason, I dislike drinking standing up."

Sarah looked around and pointed to some wooden garden chairs that had just been vacated, set off to one side of the terrace.

"We could sit there," she said. "I'm with you, Jeremiah, I'd much rather sit. I've only been here for about twenty minutes and I'm already feeling a bit exhausted by it all."

Jeremiah knew he was going to like Sarah.

The three of them sat down. Jeremiah was relieved to have moved away from the main throng of guests, and now took a sip of his wine. To his surprise – for he had expected something much better – it was thin and sour and, he thought, probably cheap. Hoping no-one was looking, he tipped the remains of the glass into a flower planter.

Miriam saw what he had done.

"You don't like wine either?" she asked.

"Not when it's sour."

She took a sip from her glass.

"You're right, it's horrid," she said, and tipped her glass into the planter, too.

They all giggled.

"So why are you here?" asked Miriam, her tone forthright, authoritative. "We only know the Jacksons because we've met them at one or two concerts in the church. Matilda is on the organising committee."

"I'm not quite sure why I'm here," said Jeremiah, "I think to be inspected; you know measured-up to ensure I'll fit in to the village."

More laughter.

"I moved to Elmsford about four months ago, from London. I'd lived in London all my life, but suddenly couldn't bear it any longer, and divine providence brought me here, to this beautiful, remote little village."

Was that right? Jeremiah thought to himself. *Was it divine providence?* He hardly knew what he meant in saying those words, but somehow, at that moment, sitting with these two interesting and attractive women, he knew he was meant to be here.

"And how do you find our remote little village, Jeremiah?" Miriam asked. "Are you settling in?"

"I love it. It's so… what is the word? It's so tranquil. And I'm enjoying exploring all the footpaths. There's a great circular walk from my house, through the woods and out onto the coast path, and then back via the churchyard. I'm sure you know it."

"We do. And you'll have walked past my house many times," said Miriam. "I live at The Sanctuary."

"I know it. You must have some stunning views to enjoy." Jeremiah turned to Sarah. "And when you're not at drinks parties, Sarah," he asked, "what do you do?"

"Not much," said Sarah effortlessly, as if doing nothing did not have to be explained, "but Miriam is very busy. She's a scholar and a writer and she spends all her time surrounded by books and papers. That's why she needs a housekeeper."

"That's not quite true," said Miriam.

"It is," said Sarah.

Again, Jeremiah smiled, this time at Sarah's direct honesty. She seemed to be marvellously uncomplicated and yet quietly self-confident. It was a long time since he'd found a woman quite so attractive.

He asked Miriam what she studied.

There was a brief moment before she replied, and Jeremiah sensed that she might be sizing him up to see whether he was worth engaging with. She apparently decided he was.

"I am interested in the history of what women have tried to say," she said, rather as if she was about to give a lecture.

"Tried to say?" he asked.

"Yes, tried to say, and have very often been prevented from saying."

"By whom?"

"By men."

"Ah, men."

Jeremiah could not imagine Miriam being prevented from saying anything by anyone.

"And I am especially interested in what it was that Mary Magdalene had to say," she said.

Now he was lost.

"About whom I know nothing at all," he said. "And

what did Mary Magdalene have to say?"

Jeremiah was intrigued by the way the conversation was going, and he could tell that Miriam knew all sorts of interesting things.

"She taught the Gospel of Love. She was a holy woman and a companion of Yeshua, who you would probably call Jesus."

"I'm afraid you are talking to a heathen," said Jeremiah. "I know very little about religion."

"I'm a bit of a heathen too," said Sarah.

Jeremiah beamed at her.

"And that's a very good place indeed to start," continued Miriam.

"What is?"

"Knowing how little you know."

"Not difficult in my case," he said, "although I do believe in angels."

Where did that come from? Why did he say that to two complete strangers? Thank goodness he'd tipped his wine away, or else he might say things to these women that he'd later regret.

"Really? We must talk about that," said Miriam, who was finding Jeremiah rather fascinating.

Jeremiah looked across the terrace towards the marquee and caught Matilda's eye. He knew that this conversation, which he was so enjoying, would soon be interrupted and that he would be obliged to go and speak to other people at the party. Now was the time to make his apologies and leave.

"Listen," he said, "I think I have to go home. I've been spotted by Matilda and interrogation is imminent." And then, without thinking, he said,

"Would you like to come with me?"

"Why not," said Miriam, quite unaffected by his sudden decision. "What do you think, Sarah?"

"Suits me," she said.

"Then let's go," said Miriam, already standing and walking towards the house.

"Should we say goodbye?" asked Sarah, evidently more thoughtful of others than Miriam or Jeremiah.

"I think not," said Jeremiah. "No-one will notice. Just follow me." He did not think he was going to receive another invitation from the Jacksons.

They made their way back through the hall and out of the front door.

"Oh, I walked here. Did you drive?"

"We did," said Miriam. "We were a little late."

"Shall I jump in with you then?"

"Good plan."

They set off and within minutes pulled into Jeremiah's drive. As Miriam got out of the car, she pointed towards the church.

"What do you think of our church? The wooden ceiling is rather lovely, isn't it?"

"Yes, it is," he said, looking under the flowerpot for the key to his front door.

Sarah commented on how beautiful the thatched roof looked now it had been repaired.

"Would you like something to eat?"

'Yes please," said Miriam.

"Just a little something, perhaps," said Sarah. "Can I help?"

"No, it won't take a moment, said Jeremiah, smiling as he spotted Angel by the window with his wings outstretched. “Please, make yourselves comfortable.”

He walked into his kitchen and arranged some cheeses, olives, hummus, butter and oatcakes on a beautiful platter that he’d recently bought in a tiny pottery in a neighbouring village, and rummaged in his pantry for a decent bottle of wine.

“I think it looks like rain, so let’s go into the garden room,” he said. “Then we can admire the garden without getting wet. Giles has transformed it – do you know Giles, Francis’ partner?”

“We do. Lovely chap.” Miriam was reading the label on the bottle of wine.

Although it had been Miriam who’d talked the most so far, Jeremiah was interested to hear more from Sarah, and after a bit of probing he discovered that she had once owned and run the shop in Elmsford.

“It’s now run by our friends Grace and Tim, a lovely couple who came to the village from Bristol to be nearer to Tim’s mother,” she said.

“Yes, I’ve met them. It’s a great little shop.”

“I help them out every now and then, when they’re short of staff, or to cover for holidays. I enjoy it – it’s like being back at my shop, but without any of the stress. And, of course, I hear all the village gossip.”

They smiled at each other. There was a gentle mischievousness in her which Jeremiah found amusing.

He discovered that Sarah lived almost opposite her old shop, and that Miriam had come to Elmsford much more recently. It was evident that she and Sarah had become close friends. But whilst he found Miriam fascinating, he was especially drawn to Sarah. There was something about her... what was it? She reminded him of someone, but he couldn't for the life of him think who it was.

"And you, Jeremiah, what about you?" Sarah asked.

So, Jeremiah told them about how he had been a schoolteacher for a short while and then set up in business with his friend Stephen, buying and selling Turkish carpets.

"But no wife or children?" asked Sarah, with a directness that caught Jeremiah off guard, and before he knew it, he had told them about Angela, about their life together and their life apart. He didn't tell them was about his own 'gender neutrality' as he'd recently come to define it. He'd found the phrase online. That was something that remained his secret.

See how easily I've opened up to these two women, he thought to himself. *I think they have bewitched me.*

And he might have said more, but Miriam looked at her watch and stood up.

"Goodness, I must go home."

Sarah smiled at him.

"You'll get used to Miriam," she said. "She doesn't mean to be abrupt, but she has probably thought of something that she needs to write about, immediately."

"The writer's curse," Miriam smiled.

"And I must go, too," said Sarah. "I'm meeting my friends Alice and Rachel, later. They've just moved into a house on the edge of the village, and they've invited me for supper."

"How lovely. Well, it has been a pleasure to meet you both properly," he said, and he meant it. "I'm sure I'll bump into you on the coast path, or in the shop or the café."

"Or we could keep those boys to their word and get them to invite us all for supper," said Miriam. "I do like being in the company of younger people – especially when they have that capacity for imagination that seems to diminish as one grows older."

"Do you really think it does?" asked Sarah, "I think I have much more imagination now than I did as a young woman."

Jeremiah smiled. *Me too,* he thought to himself.

He walked with them to their car and waved as they disappeared up the lane, realising that he had enjoyed their company very much.

Angel was now sitting on the arm of the sofa.

"So, you have new friends," he said.

"I think I may have."

"And what do you make of them?"

"They were guardian angels and rescued me from the drinks party."

"Angels, eh? Can they do this?" Angel opened his translucent wings, and with one elegant movement rose from the sofa into mid-air, his ankle-wings fluttering.

Jeremiah laughed and applauded.

"No, of course not," he said. "Only you can do that! Miriam is a scholar, you know; she's interested in Mary Magdalene."

"Now she was an angel."

"Really?"

"In a manner of speaking," said Angel, coming back to rest on the sofa. "She was a teacher and a companion to Jesus."

"So Miriam said, and his real name was Yeshua."

"That is the Hebrew version of his name, yes."

"She is also interested in what she called, 'the voices of women'."

"Given your conversations with Francis, that might be interesting for you."

"What do you mean?"

"I think you have some unanswered questions in your life that have to do with women and men and who they really are."

Jeremiah smiled at Angel.

"You know about these things?"

"Well, not really. For me they hardly matter. I am both and neither. But I do think they matter to you."

"Why do you think that?"

"Because you are more like me than you suppose. In fact, you have to be."

"What are you talking about, Angel?"

Angel fluttered open his wings again and stood in front of Jeremiah with his arms crossed over his chest.

"Sit down," he said, "this is important."

Jeremiah did as he was asked.

"As you know, angels are neither male nor female, and I only appear to you as a male because I know that this is comfortable for you. When you were a teenager and even when you were a young man, I was simply your friend, someone you could depend upon. And sometimes I am still that. But actually, I am more than that."

Jeremiah leant back against the cushions of his chair, unsure of what he was being told, unsure of how much he wanted to know.

"What do you mean by 'more than that'?" he asked.

Angel looked at him with deep kindness.

"I am who you may become," he said.

"I don't know what that means."

"I am no more and no less than who you may become. Your future self. For I am you and you are me."

"You're talking in riddles again."

"Just listen."

"Okay."

"I am who you may be when you come to know who you really are. I am the masculine you and the feminine you, and one day when these qualities are fully integrated in you, you may be able to accept that this is truly who you are. And if you do, you will become like me. Angels offer men and women the possibility of fulfilling themselves. That's what we do; we enable people to become complete, ethereal, made of stardust."

"Oh..." said Jeremiah, trying to understand what Angel was saying. "But if my feminine me and my masculine me are integrated, what happens to you?"

"We become one, subsumed, and you will no longer see me as you do now."

"I don't want that."

"Not yet."

Angel had hit a spot, and Jeremiah went silent.

Later, as he was getting into bed, Jeremiah thought about what Angel had said, and that night he had a dream, rather like the one he'd had many years before, but this time the ending was different.

In his dream Jeremiah found himself once more walking through meadows and woodland towards a river. When he came to the river, he could see a host of angels on the far bank, fluttering their wings and singing softly. He could not make out the tune or the words, but it was very soothing. He sat down on the bank of the river and, as before, a moorhen swam out from the reeds and then back into them, as if returning to a nest. Jeremiah lay down and closed his eyes. When he opened them, he found that he had crossed the river and was now standing amidst the angels, soothed by the fluttering of their wings. He looked back across the river and saw himself laying naked on the opposite bank. The figure he could see was certainly him, and evidently male. Then, peering at his reflection in the waters of the river, he saw himself amidst the angels, naked, but with the body of a woman. He peered closer and closer into the river until his face was under the water. He was struggling to breathe. He stood back from the water and felt Angel behind him. And then as he 'accepted' Angel and fell back into his embrace it was as if their bodies merged into one.

When he awoke, he felt at peace. He looked at his bedside clock. It was 3.33 am. He saw that Angel was standing at the end of his bed, so he sat up, but did not turn on his lamp because light was radiating from Angel's body. He truly was the most beautiful being.

"I have just had an extraordinary dream," said Jeremiah.

"I know," said Angel.

"You were there by the river, weren't you? I saw you. But what does it mean, Angel? The dream?"

"It was just telling you something about angels and about who you are."

"Why are angels sometimes behind me and sometimes in front?"

"It's just something we do, something that has arisen over time."

"Go on."

"Well, we have found that when we are giving comfort it is best to stand behind the person we are comforting, wrapping our wings about them. Whereas, when we are giving guidance, it is best to stand in front of them. As I am doing now."

"Okay."

"And then sometimes when we are bringing a very special message, we kneel, you know like in all those paintings of the Annunciation."

"Ah yes… those paintings – the ones that Angela loves so much."

"Yes, but it doesn't happen very often."

"But when you say, 'bringing a message', who are you bringing a message from?"

"There is no 'who'," said Angel. "I know you must find that difficult to understand, but the message doesn't come from some 'one', it comes through a realm you cannot know. But it is familiar to angels, and our task is to listen, to open ourselves to these messages, teachings if you like, and when necessary, bring them to people like you.

"Do you remember what I said about time? That it is not linear but more like a spiral or a loop? Well, the messages angels bring are stored energetically in this realm. Every thought or word that has ever been expressed or will ever be expressed is 'recorded' in ripples and waves of energy. Once they are thought or spoken, these words or teachings become like memories and are stored in the finest realms of the Cosmos. Some humans have begun to sense it and have called it the Akashic Field. You cannot interpret these messages, but angels can, and when we do, and when the time is right, we speak them to you."

"I don't really understand any of that," said Jeremiah.

"Everything you are looking for is inside you already, Jeremiah. You are the keeper of your own wisdom. All I do is mirror aspects of you – past, present and future – into the Now, for in reality there is only Now. I am your reflection."

"Ahhh," Jeremiah groaned. "Why is everything so complicated? So bound up in riddles and paradox?"

"Therein lies the truth. Human beings have an almost unique capacity in the Universe to make things overly complicated. Ultimately, there is only Love. Love transcends everything."

"That's it, Angel, that's what I felt in my dream: pure Love. But when I looked in the river the Love seemed to dissipate and my mind took over, wanting to know 'why' and 'how' and then I couldn't breathe… And then, at the end, for one moment I thought I could see."

"You must see," said Angel, "and you must go on seeing."

"I'll do my best," said Jeremiah.

"Yes, do your best," said Angel. "You should know that you came to a very special place in what you call your 'dream' – although it was just another aspect of your reality – a place where many angels gather, a place which is sacred. Just like I am you, Jeremiah, you are me. That is why I have always said that you are more like an angel than you think."

And with that, Angel shimmered and faded, leaving Jeremiah reeling both from the dream and from what Angel had said.

He could hardly comprehend the enormity of it. That Angel was a part of him, that Angel reflected him, and that the wisdom of which Angel spoke, and that had always been so soothing to him, actually came from within himself, even from his future, wiser self and that in coming full circle with that wisdom into the Here and Now, he could evolve and change his destiny.

No. It was all too much. All too much.

STORIES OF SISTERHOOD

Sarah awoke and felt the weight of the day looming. She did not often feel like this these days and it took her by surprise. It was a 'Missing James' day. She thought perhaps it was because of meeting Jeremiah yesterday; of being in the presence of a man who seemed warm and… somehow familiar. His masculinity, his energy, it just reminded her of James and the old yearning for him returned. She yawned, stretched and walked into her bathroom. When she looked in the mirror, she saw the face of her mother staring back at her.

"Hello Mum," she sighed. "Do you recognise me?" Sarah observed her reflection, then looked at her hands marked with brown spots. "I feel as if my age is wrapped around me like a cloak, Mum. And everyone can see it. An old woman, alone and weary of life."

She washed her face and looked out of the window. "But then," she added, "there are forget-me-nots and foxgloves in the garden."

Sarah walked down the street and knocked on Miriam's door. Miriam must have seen her because she called out for her to come in. As usual, she was in what Sarah still thought of as James's study, although, of course, it was Miriam's study now. She was in her dressing gown and slippers, a cup of tea beside her and Willow curled up on what was also now Miriam's bed. Sarah smiled and at once began to feel better.

"Help yourself to tea. The kettle's only just boiled."

Sarah made tea and went and sat on the bed beside Willow, who lifted her head and then rolled onto her back so that Sarah could stroke her tummy.

"It's not so difficult being a cat, is it?" said Miriam, her fingers moving easily across her keyboard.

"I just called in to tell you that Katharine rang me last night," said Sarah. "She got that job she was hoping for at South Hampstead High School."

"Oh, that is good news. She'll be a natural teacher."

"Like you are, Miriam. I think Katharine has learnt so much from you and has modelled herself on you."

Miriam turned her chair, looked at Sarah over the top of her glasses and smiled.

"Or me as I was," she said. "But not as I am now. Now I am a student, learning all over again. And I'm learning as much about myself as anything else. I have you to thank for that, Sarah."

It always astounded Sarah when Miriam acknowledged her friendship like that, but she often did, and Sarah had begun to accept that Miriam, the Professor, really did honour her in this way.

Miriam came over to sit beside Sarah. "We have a lovely relationship, don't you think? You know, since I told you about having had cancer, it unleashed something in me, something I'd kept bound and silent for years. I've begun unravelling something, Sarah, and it's one of the missing jigsaw pieces. I can't quite put it into words yet, but when I do, you'll be the first to know." She took Sarah's hand. "We're lucky to have each other."

Miriam went back to her laptop, and for some time, Sarah sat on the bed watching her friend who was now deep in thought, which was then transmuted into words emanating from the tips of her fingers as they tapped across her computer keyboard. She was in awe of this process, having never learned to type herself.

Eventually Miriam stood up and walked into the kitchen to refresh her tea.

Sarah and Willow followed her.

"It's funny you should say that about being lucky to have each other, because I awoke and felt quite alone this morning. Alone and old."

"Well, in a way, we are alone, in as much as we are the individual who inhabits this body of ours, and this body will age and die in its own unique way – but having a friend to share that experience with, having another being who understands us, makes us less alone, doesn't it? I think we feel less alone because we are in relationship to one another."

"You're right, Miriam. Don't mind me this morning. In my younger day I would've said I was premenstrual, but I can't blame that anymore."

Miriam burst out laughing. "Oh that! How quickly one forgets the vagaries of the female body when it ceases to function as it once did. You have to admit, there are some advantages to getting older. But as always, Sarah, you've hit the nail on the head. You seem to embody what I'm contemplating. Part of the jigsaw is my understanding of femininity. It was taken from me under the knife, and I lost my womanhood, or I thought I did, but now I am beginning to realise that the Divine Feminine isn't really to do with our physical bodies at all. It's beyond hormones."

"Well, I'm certainly beyond hormones," Sarah sighed, looking out of the kitchen window towards the distant sea. "And I'm not really sure I know what you mean, but I do know that as we age, we change, and we have to surrender to this metamorphosis, otherwise we end up judging ourselves and disliking who we have become."

Sarah looked back at Miriam, who was busy scribbling down something. She'd gone into that place in her mind where she worked everything out.

"Well, anyway it's cheered me up, coming to see you," said Sarah. "I've been nothing but gloomy since I woke up this morning."

"Sorry to hear that. Any reason?"

"No reason and every reason."

"That can be very tiresome. Have you tried a glass of vodka?"

"Miriam! You are a wicked woman. Actually, I think it was meeting Jeremiah, yesterday."

"Oh? I thought he was rather charming in a melancholy kind of way."

"Well, yes – he is charming, but he reminded me of James… not in looks or anything, just his maleness, his presence."

"Ah… that must've been hard for you."

"Not hard, not really, it just brought a kind of

sadness upon me. I call it a 'Missing James' day. I think I need something good to read to take my mind off it. Have you got any suggestions?"

"Let me think. What would be good for a gloomy person? Oh, I know. Try this."

She reached up to one of her bookshelves and took down a book.

"Close your eyes," she said.

"Really?"

"Yes, close your eyes and hold out your hands."

"This is silly."

"I know. But do it anyway."

Sarah closed her eyes and felt the book as it was placed on her upturned palms.

"Open..."

"*Winnie-The-Pooh*?"

"Yes, *Winnie-The-Pooh*. One of the most important books you will ever read."

Sarah turned the pages and before long she was laughing out loud.

"Listen, this is perfect:

> "Good morning, Eeyore," said Pooh.
> "Good morning, Pooh Bear," said Eeyore gloomily. "If it is a good morning," he said. "Which I doubt," said he."

Sarah laughed.

"You see," said Miriam. "I told you it was perfect for someone who was gloomy."

"Your stories always help me to see life differently, Miriam. I thank you for that."

And that was the way of it. Sarah and Miriam in relationship; enjoying each other's company. Before they knew it, the morning had been enveloped by stories.

"You remember all those stories we've shared about the voices of women?"

"You mean the stories in your book?"

"Yes, and others. In all of those stories, all of those legends, it was the men who were shown as being strong and the women as being weak. But if men are strong, we are too, don't you think?"

"Yes, I do," said Sarah, "and I think we strengthen each other, as well."

Miriam sat down beside Sarah. "It's a different kind of being strong, isn't it?" she said. "We endure, us women. We hold together."

There was a silence, and Sarah thought about this 'holding together' and what Tom and Miriam had said about climate breakdown and the dangers and difficulties that it would bring.

"Perhaps there's going to be a need for this kind of strength and holding together," she said.

"What do you mean?"

"Perhaps the difficulties we are going to have to face as a society require our kind of strength? You know, caring for families and communities when they are in danger, caring for the birds and the trees… caring for the small things. If what Tom says is true, if we are heading for climate catastrophe, small, isolated communities like Elmsford may have to find ways of surviving with not much more than what we've got. We will have to look after each other."

"Well, if we're facing imminent disaster, we'd better make the most of the here and now," said Miriam. "I was wondering whether you'd like to come to London with me? I have to go for a meeting which will only take an hour or so, but I thought we could stay in my flat and have a bit of a holiday. We could take the train from Exeter, so at least we don't have to worry about our carbon emissions."

Much to her surprise, for it was a long time since Sarah had ventured out of the westcountry, she heard herself say, "Well that would be fun, I could do with a change of scene."

"We could do a bit of sight-seeing if you like," said Miriam, "We could go and see Buckingham Palace or the Tower of London, or we could go to a gallery or to Harrods."

None of these were places Sarah wanted to visit, but there was one thing she had wanted to do for a very long time.

"Have you ever been on the London Eye?" she asked Miriam.

"No, I haven't. Shall we go?"

"I'd love to. I've often wondered how much of London you can see from the top of the wheel."

"I think it would be a great thing to do. Oh, and by the way, do you have a passport?"

"It expired just after Alan died and I never renewed it. Why do you ask?"

"Maybe one day we might decide to travel abroad, and so you'll need a passport. You can get the application form at the Post Office."

Sarah felt a sudden flush of excitement.

"Do you have anywhere in mind?"

"Well, I've mentioned my friends, Angelique and Max, in France" Miriam replied, "and I thought perhaps we could visit them at some point, if you'd like to?"

"Do you know, I'd like that very much," said Sarah, again surprising herself and feeling, not for the first time, a sense of adventure arising within her.

The next day, Sarah went to the village shop where Connie who used to help her when she ran the shop, was looking after the Post Office counter.

"Morning, Connie," she said. "Can I have a passport application form, please."

Connie raised her eyebrows.

"Where are you off to, then?" she asked.

"Miriam and I might be going to France."

"That sounds nice."

"Yes, it does, doesn't it. I'll take this home and fill it in later."

"Okay, but you'll need to go to Chopes in Bideford to get the photos they need."

"I'll do it tomorrow."

"Do you mind me saying something?" asked Connie.

"You can say anything you like, Connie," said Sarah. "We've known each other long enough."

Connie laughed. "Well, it's just that… I wondered whether you might want to stop wearing black, now? It's been quite a long time."

Sarah was a little taken aback.

"I suppose it has," she said. "Thank you, Connie. I'll have a think about it."

About three weeks later, Sarah received an envelope in the post, containing her passport. When she opened it and held her passport in her hands, again she felt a flush of excitement. She put it in her underwear drawer to keep it safe.

Sarah and Miriam took the train from Exeter to London Paddington. Then they took a taxi to Miriam's flat in the Barbican where they left their bags before heading off for the London Eye. They had reserved tickets for three o'clock. There were people everywhere, and although Sarah was utterly delighted to be in London, she was pleased that she was with Miriam because she knew where she was going and wasn't at all intimidated by any of it.

The London Eye was much larger than Sarah had imagined. She and Miriam went through the turnstile and were shown into their own capsule. Just the two of them. Slowly, very slowly, they began to rise up one side of the great wheel until they were almost at the top and could see all across London. Sarah gasped at the sight. As the wheel slowly turned, she followed the line of the Thames as it ran through the city and out towards the sea, and then, as Miriam pointed out Tower Bridge and the Tower of London, she was able to take in the vast spread of London, first the skyscraper offices of the City with the familiar outlines of the Shard and the Gherkin, and then houses upon houses as far as she could see. Then, looking the other way, she could see right out towards Heathrow Airport, with planes landing and taking off in what seemed to be an endless stream. She didn't know how long the whole rotation had taken, but it seemed to be over too quickly. She was breathless.

"Wow - that was such a treat!" she said as Miriam hailed a taxi.

"I'm glad you enjoyed it. I did too. But look at you, Sarah, you look radiant. Something's changed in you..."

"I'm not wearing black."

"That's it – you're not wearing black. That's what it is – I knew there was something different. A bit of colour really suits you."

At Miriam's request, they were driven back to her flat via the Houses of Parliament and Big Ben and through Trafalgar Square.

"Wait till I tell Alice about this," said Sarah, peering out of the windows of the taxi.

"Are you hungry?" asked Miriam as they pulled up at her flat. "We didn't really have lunch."

"Yes, although I'm not really sure what I am. All of that was so wonderful my mind is utterly blown away. What an incredible capital city we have."

"We really do. There's a fantastic Thai restaurant near here that I go to sometimes. It does really wonderful food. Shall we give it a try this evening? I have to dash off for my meeting now, but when I get back, we can go out for dinner. What do you say?"

"I say that is perfect."

Miriam settled Sarah into her flat and then left for her meeting and Sarah took the opportunity to take a little snooze – it had been a busy and exciting day. Before she knew it, Miriam had returned and was reapplying her lipstick ready for their evening out. She didn't seem tired by the day's events at all.

Sarah had never eaten Thai food before, so Miriam ordered. They ate a hot, sour soup for starters which made Sarah's eyes water, but which was delicious, and then they had a noodle and vegetable dish which Sarah decided was the most incredible food she'd ever tasted. She was literally swooning from the taste sensations, from all the day's sensations.

And Sarah felt so much at ease with this woman who was becoming part of her life. They chatted and laughed, and although she offered to share the bill, Miriam insisted that this was her treat: "To thank you for helping me see the magic in this city and rediscovering things I had forgotten about," she said.

When they arrived back at the flat, Miriam asked Sarah where she would like to sleep.

"There are two single beds in the bedroom downstairs," she said, "or I could pull out the divan bed here in the living room for me, and you could have the bedroom to yourself. Come and have a look."

They went down a spiral staircase to the lower floor of the flat where there was a bathroom a separate loo and a large bedroom with twin beds.

"Well, I don't see why you should have to sleep on the divan," said Sarah.

"I'd be fine. Unless we both sleep here, like sisters. Two grown up sisters. What do you think?"

"Why not? Let's do that."

And so they did, and Sarah was woken the next morning by Miriam in her dressing gown, carrying two mugs of hot water and lemon.

"I thought you might like this," she said. "I have it every morning."

They sat in their beds with their drinks, relishing the leisurely start to the day.

"So, are we sisters now?" asked Miriam.

"I think we are," replied Sarah. "I've always wanted a sister. Thank you for showing me this part of your life, Miriam. I've had such a fabulous time."

"One of the best things about becoming older is that it removes a lot of stuff that often prevents good friendships, loving friendships."

"Like sex you mean?" Sarah laughed.

"Well yes. I mean, would we have wanted to do this if we were half our age?"

"Well, I'm not sure I would've, but from what you've told me, I suspect you might."

They laughed again.

"Yes, I guess that's right," said Miriam, and yet we are becoming as close as can be, aren't we? I don't suppose either of us thought this would happen. But it is rather enjoyable, isn't it?"

"It is. Enjoyable and completely unexpected."

Sitting back in her cottage, Sarah was thinking about her trip to London. She couldn't quite believe it had all happened. At the time, one thing followed on from the other and it all just unfolded – like an adventure. But now, now that she was home, looking out of her window at the empty village street, she wondered what would happen next.

Then she realised that what happens next is simply what is already happening. It's no great drama, it's just meant to be, and all the pieces that led up to it had first to be put in place, so that it could happen: buying the shop, meeting James, James's death, Katharine finding her and then meeting Miriam at the conference, James's house being available to let, the legacy of silence left by James that so attracted Miriam, Christmas alone, and much else, too – it all had to happen before this friendship could come about. And now it had, and everything in Sarah's life had changed.

She decided to paint her toenails a shimmering shade of pink.

BELOVED FRIENDS

A few days after their return from London, Sarah phoned Jeremiah.

"It's been a while since we've seen you, Jeremiah. Would you like to join Miriam and me for coffee on Thursday morning at about eleven o'clock? We thought we could go to the café in the village square – they do fabulous cakes."

"That sounds lovely. I'll see you there."

When Miriam and Sarah arrived, Jeremiah was already seated at a table by the window overlooking the village street. He was greeted with hugs, which he liked.

"Sorry if we're a bit late," Sarah said.

"No, I'm a bit early," Jeremiah replied. "It's a habit of mine to be early. Anyway, I quite like to sit here and just watch the world go by – our little bit of it, anyway."

They ordered their coffees and cakes and then Miriam turned to Jeremiah.

"I've been wondering about you," she said.

"That sounds ominous."

"No, nothing like that, it's just that I've been

wondering what it was that made you leave London, after living there all your life. You said you couldn't bear it anymore, and I've been wondering why? Francis told me about your carpet business and that you've now retired, but that's hardly a reason to 'run away' is it? You did run away, I suppose – why else would you end up in the middle of nowhere, in Elmsford?"

"Oh, come on Miriam," said Sarah. "Give him a break! There's no need to interrogate the poor man."

"Oh, but there is," said Miriam looking across at Jeremiah. "I like this man and want to know all about him. Sorry, Jeremiah, please forgive me, but I'm pretty good at reading the signals and everything about you, not least your performance at the party, says 'taking refuge'."

"You're right," said Jeremiah, as Sarah poured his coffee from the cafetière. "I did run away, and one day I'll tell you about it, but although at first I was, as you put it, taking refuge, more recently I've discovered it wasn't that at all. I now think I was actually looking for something."

As seemed to be happening often these days, Jeremiah wondered why he had said that.

"Now, that does interest me," said Miriam, taking a sip of her coffee. "I'm always looking for something, as well."

For a moment, Jeremiah thought he might say no more, but then, remembering what Angel had said about the unanswered questions in his life, he decided to continue.

"As it happens, perhaps you can help me find what I'm looking for – or some part of it, anyway."

Miriam and Sarah waited for him to continue, and he decided to take the plunge.

"You see, I'm interested in what it is that makes us a man or a woman – apart from the obvious, that is."

There was a silence as both Miriam and Sarah took in what Jeremiah had said.

"Look, I'm a man, obviously, if somewhat blurred by age, and as far as I can tell, you are both women. But what if it isn't as simple as that? What if we are not merely one or the other? What if we are all a mixture, part feminine and part masculine?"

Sarah smiled. "You will be a friend of Miriam's forever," she said with that mischievous tone in her voice that Jeremiah had noticed before. "That is the sort of question she loves."

Miriam smiled at Sarah. "Your question does interest me," she said, "and let me add another question. How is it that the masculine principle with all its logic and intellect has come to so dominate and overshadow the feminine principle, which once kept the world in a state of harmony and grace, so that we have become dangerously out of balance? I, for one, would like to know the answer to that."

"Well… I hadn't thought of it in that way."

"Perhaps not, but it's something that has been intriguing me for years."

"But I thought your studies focused on Mary Magdalene?" said Jeremiah. "What has that to do with who men and women are?"

"Everything," replied Miriam. "Everything."

"I'd like to know more about that," he said.

"And I would like to discuss it with you, but not

here. Shall we meet up at my house?"

"You've done it now," said Sarah. "You've become another of Miriam's students. I do hope you like hard work."

Jeremiah chuckled. "Well, when I moved to Elmsford, one of the first things I did was set up my study. I wasn't quite sure why that was, but now I'm beginning to see..."

Two days later, on a beautifully bright Thursday morning, with not a cloud in the sky and only a gentle breeze off the sea, Jeremiah found himself sitting in a rattan armchair with a stripy blue cushion on the veranda of Miriam's house with its magnificent view down into the wooded valley with the sea beyond. Miriam was sitting opposite him in another rattan chair, one with a stripy yellow cushion, and between them was a low table on which Miriam had placed a cafetière of coffee and some chocolate biscuits.

"First of all," said Miriam, "I want to respond directly to your question in the café about what makes us man or woman, because there's a fundamental misconception that we have all been told and which we live our lives by, unwittingly, from the moment we are born – and, in my view it causes a huge amount of confusion and suffering.

"You see, we all think we are separately and undeniably male or female. It's the first thing the nurse says when the baby is born, isn't it? 'It's a boy!' or 'It's a girl!' – although nowadays it's probably the person operating the ultrasound scan – 'See, it's a girl,' or 'See, it's a boy.' Anyway, that does it. From there on, from the sight of one small part of our anatomy, we are either a boy or a girl, and then we have no choice; we become either a man or a woman with all that it implies.

"And yet, at the beginning, in the time before some of us develop the Y chromosome, we are all feminine. And the Y chromosome is tiny compared to the much larger X chromosome. The X chromosome carries nearly one thousand genes, whereas the Y chromosome is one third the size and carries less than sixty. There are physical differences, of course there are, but these differences are not what is most significant. What is most significant is not our chromosomes but something else: it's what academics, who use these kinds of words, call 'social construction'. Compared to our social construction, they say, our chromosomes, and certainly our most private parts, wither into insignificance."

Jeremiah chuckled at Miriam's choice of words.

"Go on," he said. "This is fascinating."

"Apparently, it's all about what happens to us from the very moment we are born, because we are constructed by the expectations and beliefs of the families, the classrooms, the workplaces and the societies we inhabit. And here's another thing: apparently, given the importance of social construction, differences between men and men, or between women and women, are much greater than differences between men and women as a whole. How about that?"

After all of his discussions with Francis, this had

become familiar ground to Jeremiah. What astounded him was that he had waited all his life for this kind of conversation, and now everyone was talking about it. And through these discussions, Jeremiah had come to understand that society had constructed him into what society thought he should be, and so, Jeremiah had believed that because he could not conform, he was not normal. Now he knew there is no such thing.

"Now, I want you to know a little bit about Mary Magdalene, because she's an important example of what happens when you do not fit the norm," said Miriam and she set about telling Jeremiah of how the figure of the Magdalene had been corrupted by the Church, which, frightened of her power and of who she was, had presented her as no more than a repentant prostitute.

"What were they so frightened of?" asked Jeremiah.

"You may remember from our conversation when we first met that I told you it was because she was a woman and because she was very close to Yeshua."

"I do remember."

"After Yeshua had gone, there were all sorts of different versions of his teachings, but the one that survived and became the established Christian Church, the Great Church of Rome, was dominated by men. Women were dismissed and even reviled, blamed for what was said to be humankind's innate or original sinfulness. Even though it was widely accepted that Mary Magdalene had been the first to see the risen Christ, and though it was she who had been asked to bring these special teachings of Yeshua to the apostles, it was quite impossible to acknowledge her as a holy woman and a teacher.

"But there's more to it than that, and I have a book you may like to read. It's called *Love and the Divine Feminine* and it traces the ways in which the Divine Feminine was overcome by a male God, and the ways in which the teachings of Yeshua on Love were overcome by teachings of crucifixion, resurrection and the redemption of sin. The two are connected. So, Jeremiah, before we get to your question about what it is to be a man or a woman, why don't you read this book and then we can talk further."

Miriam disappeared into the house and came back with the book and gave it to Jeremiah.

He looked at its cover with the image of a woman's belly, full and round, with a spiral of seeds upon it.

He got up to leave. Undoubtedly, Miriam was an inspiring tutor, but he couldn't help feeling as if he had just come to the end of one of his history tutorials at university, and he had been given some homework, too.

He thanked Miriam and walked home, past the row of fishermen's cottages, across the churchyard and down the steep steps to his cottage, deep in thought. Maybe, just maybe, he could begin to fill the gaps in his understanding of himself, and his desire to feel whole, complete, at one.

A stir of excitement rippled through him.

Back in his cottage, Jeremiah sat in his armchair, reading the book Miriam had given him. Jezebel, growing fond of this quiet and reliable man, came and curled up on the sofa, which she now regarded as her sofa, lying herself against a cushion that she also increasingly regarded as hers. She began to purr.

For several days Jeremiah continued to read, engrossed in the subject matter, jotting down interesting details in his notebook. He had never before read such ideas and although he was not a religious person, he did know enough of the Christian bible stories to realise that the author was challenging them, redefining them. The book was easy to read, and it placed Mary in the historic setting of all that was happening in Judah at that time: the Roman occupation and the disputes between the rabbinic Pharisees, the priestly Sadducees and the mystical and ascetic Essenes.

Both Yeshua and the Magdalene were considered a scourge by the priests of the Temple, as they were closely associated with the Essenes. The book claimed that Mary was to be the one who would carry forth Yeshua's teachings of Love after he was gone, but when many of the disciples fled, Mary found no favour amongst those who would go on to build the Great Church, especially Peter and, later, Paul. Instead, she was dismissed, and all but lost for two thousand years.

He was appalled by the story, by the evident power of men to shape and repress so many lives with their own prejudices, hidden agendas and fears.

One morning as Francis was cleaning the bathroom, Jeremiah, leaning against the doorframe, broached the subject of the book with him.

"Oh, yes. I've read it – Miriam lent it to me, too," said Francis. "Don't you think it's shocking that 2000 years later, these very same preconceptions are still impacting us? We're still shaped by these beliefs, and they've prevented so many of us from being able to accept who we are. Instead, we have lived in fear. Fear of being different, fear of not being a 'normal' person, fear of expressing ourselves, the shame of loving in the only way we know how."

"That's right," said Jeremiah. 'It's the fear that incapacitates so." This was something he knew of only too well, a feeling that somehow he was going to be 'found out'. "I hope you don't mind me asking, Francis, but have you always known you were gay?"

Francis squeezed his cloths dry and gave one last glance around the bathroom to check all was in order. "I've always known," he said, and I had loving parents who had no concerns about it, but it took Giles many years to come to terms with his sexuality, and to accept himself for who he really is."

The two men walked downstairs carrying the hoover and the wicker basket with all the cleaning cloths and sprays in it, and Jeremiah put the kettle on for what had become their ritual cup of morning coffee, and then rummaged in the pantry to find the tin of flapjack that he had made at the weekend.

"The wonderful thing to behold that just gets deeper and more beautiful is the happiness it brought to Giles when he finally 'came out'," said Francis, "because then, he could accept our relationship for what it truly is."

"That must have been such a relief for you both?"

"Oh, it was. It really was. Now Jerry, I can't come next week, as we're going away for a few days. Will you be able to manage the laundry?"

A few weeks later, and true to their word, Francis and Giles invited Jeremiah, Miriam and Sarah over to their house for supper, and unusually for Jeremiah, he found himself looking forward to it. Like drinks parties, he used to find dinner parties quite a trial: being seated next to someone you didn't know and had no interest in getting to know, and feeling conscious of silences and gaps in the conversation always set his nerves on edge. But this time, it was different, because he felt comfortable with Francis and Giles and, more to the point, he was beginning to feel comfortable in his own skin. Something imperceptible had shifted.

On the appointed evening, just before Jeremiah was about to leave, the phone rang. It was Sarah.

"Can I get a lift with you tonight Jeremiah? Miriam's got a migraine, poor thing, and I don't drive."

"Of course. No problem. I'll pick you up in ten minutes. Is Miriam okay?"

"Yes, she's just taken herself off to bed. It happens occasionally when she's been at her computer for too long, and she had an important paper to write with a tight deadline.

Sarah and Jeremiah drove the short distance to where Giles and Francis lived, just outside the village towards the main coast road, a bottle of red wine and small box of handmade organic chocolates in hand.

Giles opened the door.

"No Miriam?" he asked.

"She sends her apologies. She's got a migraine."

"Oh, bless her," said Giles. "That's horrible for her. Come on in, take off your coats."

Jeremiah had never been to Francis and Giles' house before, but he was pleasantly surprised when he arrived. Unusually for these parts where most houses are stone or cob, theirs was an ornate red brick cottage rented from the National Trust. It had been built by an eccentric gentleman in the late nineteenth century in the style of the Arts & Crafts movement. It had original William Morris wallpaper, and an incredible art-deco stained glass panel between the living room and dining room. Francis showed Sarah and Jeremiah around, pointing out the mullioned windows and the ceiling mouldings. It was a listed building and they couldn't paint or decorate any part of it without first consulting the Trust.

"We don't mind that one little bit," said Giles, as they returned to the large kitchen with a huge table at one end, placed under another beautifully ornate window that looked out onto the well-kept and pretty garden. "We love it just as it is. We thought we'd eat in the kitchen tonight – keep it informal. Is that okay with you?"

"Absolutely," Sarah said. "Informal is just how I like it."

Jeremiah looked at Sarah as she helped Francis to set the table. She had an incredible smile. But more than that, there was a serenity that seemed to exude from her, her very presence creating an atmosphere of calm. Jeremiah recalled the word 'aura' that he read about recently. *Yes*, he thought, *Sarah definitely has an aura.* He couldn't work out how old she might be: perhaps in her late sixties? Not that much younger than himself, and yet she seemed somehow younger than that, as if she was in her prime.

Perhaps, I'm in my prime too? he thought to himself, and it amazed him that after all these years, when many people would assume that he was 'past it', he felt as if life was just beginning.

As they sat down to eat, Jeremiah saw Giles nod to Francis, who proceeded to gently tap the side of his wine glass with a spoon. He cleared his throat.

"Ummm, "he began, "we do actually have a reason for asking you here tonight to celebrate with us, and that is because..."

"We've bought the barn!" interrupted Giles, unable to contain his excitement a moment longer. "We've done it! The bank manager has approved our business plan and given us the loan we asked for, our offer on the barn has been accepted, and we signed all the contracts today."

"And it's all thanks to you Jeremiah," said Francis. "If it wasn't for your faith in our project and your generous investment, we wouldn't be celebrating now. Your kindness really came just at the right time for us, and it's allowed us to launch 'Studio Harmonia'."

Jeremiah was momentarily lost for words. "Ah, well..." he huffed, then cleared his throat. He found he did have something to say. "It is one of the greatest pleasures of my life to be able to support you both in this way. What is a lifetime of work worth if not to be able to help others starting out on their journey? You have the energy and commitment that my partner Stephen and I had when we started our business, so I feel quite confident in my investment. And anyway, you have given me as much as I have given you: you've given me friendship, and well…" Jeremiah looked at the two young men who'd unexpectedly come into his life, "well, you have both helped me to recover my trust in other people.

"I haven't told any of you this, but just before I came to Devon, when I lived in London, I was beaten-up; mugged by a group of young men, and I really struggled to come to terms with what happened. I just wanted to run away."

Moved almost to tears by the relief of sharing his story, Jeremiah paused, and Sarah touched his arm. Giles refilled their glasses. Francis gazed at this older man, whom he'd come to love.

"Go on," Sarah smiled at him.

"And in that running away," he continued, "I now realise that I was running towards… It's interesting isn't it, that what we might at first perceive as a disaster can be the impetus for life to change for the better… I couldn't see it at the time, but now I realise that the mugging, painful as it was, was a much-needed catalyst for me to make some choices. If it hadn't happened, I wouldn't be here now and there's nowhere I'd rather be. I'm with people I… I'm with people I have come to love."

There, he'd said it.

"And we love you, too," said Sarah. "Though we haven't known you for long, there's something about you, Jeremiah… I think we all feel it. We love your tenderness."

"Here, here," said Francis, then raising his glass he

said, "Here's to Jeremiah, our beloved friend."

It was the beginning of a wonderful evening and when Jeremiah arrived home, just after midnight having dropped Sarah back at her house, he felt… what was it? He felt exhilarated. For a while he lay in bed, unable to sleep but deeply contented.

As often happened when Jeremiah could not sleep, Angel appeared, his wings outstretched and luminous.

"You enjoyed supper with your friends?"

"I did, although Miriam wasn't there. She had a migraine.

"I know."

Jeremiah smiled. Angel knew everything.

"You know, Angel, until I came to live here, and until I met Francis and Giles and then Miriam and Sarah, I think I was asleep. I feel like I have awakened to life. Does that sound daft?"

"Not at all, my friend. Life has a habit of awakening us, eventually."

"I had no idea about gender politics really, other than what I'd read in the newspapers and even then, it was so biased and misconstrued, and all this I'm reading about Mary Magdalene's life… It's fascinating. I didn't learn any of this at university. Why is that I wonder?"

"Well, in the period of history you were studying, all this would most certainly have been regarded as blasphemous, as heretical."

"Yes, I think Miriam would have been burnt at the stake."

"And now you, too."

Jeremiah chuckled. "I guess that's so," he said.

He looked at the resplendent being before him remembering all the times Angel had been there for him, always appearing when he was needed.

"Angel," said Jeremiah, "I have been meaning to say this to you for a while, but I want to thank you for standing by me all these years, for your patience and your wisdom. You are an angel."

They both laughed.

"Do you know what?" said Jeremiah. "I had this clear feeling today. I suddenly felt overcome with joy, and I realised that for the first time in a long, long time, I felt happy."

"You've opened your heart," said Angel smiling.

"Do you know, I think I have."

"And an open heart can never be wounded. Your heart can only be wounded when it is closed, shut down. By opening your heart, you may experience pain, but it will not wound you because what feels like pain becomes your liberation."

"That is exactly how I feel, Angel. For years, your words were like riddles to me, but now I am beginning to make sense of them."

Angel smiled again.

"It is because you are blossoming."

"Hmmm. I wouldn't go that far."

The next day, Jeremiah looked once more at the last page of *Love and the Divine Feminine*, which finished with a series of questions, at the end of which, was a paragraph that now spoke to Jeremiah profoundly. It spoke of his deepest, most secret conundrum. He read the passage again.

> You see, I am beginning to wonder whether it is any longer useful to work with notions of 'the feminine' and 'the masculine' or whether these notions simply create harmful divisions and cloud our understanding. What could we say about a discourse that was ungendered, but which speaks of qualities to be found in us all? I find this a particularly difficult question, and, of course, I do not have an answer. But I do wonder whether we are now coming to a time when the qualities of the feminine, which are not only qualities of nurturing, love and compassion, but also qualities of strength, wisdom and balance, might be qualities we could associate with both the feminine and the masculine. I am, therefore, interested in a new culture of 'androgyny', something that I think may be emerging in people much younger than me, people who are no longer prepared to be defined by gender and whose identity has nothing to do with gender. If we do this, we are left with a language of Love for us all.

Jeremiah put down the book. *A new culture of androgyny…* he pondered. *Is that what I am – androgynous? Neither masculine nor feminine, but both… or neither? Like Angel. Does that explain why my love is not sexual, why I am not attracted to others in a sexual way?* He remembered his dream. *Was that what my dream was about: being both man and woman?*

He was intrigued. He called Miriam.

"How are you feeling Miriam? You missed a lovely supper the other evening."

"So I've heard. Sarah thoroughly enjoyed herself. And I am feeling much better, thank you."

"I have just been looking again at the question at the end of *Love and the Divine Feminine*."

"Isn't that what you want to know?"

"Yes, and I was intrigued by what the author said about recognising that some of us feel ungendered or androgynous." Jeremiah had used the pronoun 'us' deliberately.

"It's so interesting isn't it – so timely."

"Why do you say timely?"

"Well, as I see it, we are facing a crisis – or perhaps an opportunity. And that opportunity is to embrace the whole: to move on from notions of separateness – I am a woman and you are a man, or I am gay and you are not – and recognise that we are one family. In fact, some would say that we are all part of the consciousness of Gaia, or Mother Earth, and that whilst we live in duality, we will never fulfil our evolutionary potential."

"Wow. You remind me of someone else who speaks in riddles."

"Do I? Who's that?"

"I'll tell you, one day."

"Well, why don't you come over and have lunch with Sarah and me? Then we can talk more."

"I'd like that very much."

"How about this Friday, then?"

Jeremiah noticed that Miriam had a tendency to strike whilst the iron was hot.

It rained heavily all night on Thursday and when Jeremiah awoke, there was a veritable river running down the lane in front of his house. Thank goodness Giles had recently cleaned out the ditches on either side of his drive, otherwise the water would have diverted into his house. He had to put his wellingtons on to walk the short distance to The Sanctuary, as the paths were pocked with puddles and the verges and lawns of the churchyard were sodden.

He walked along the veranda and knocked on the back door that led straight into the kitchen. Sarah opened the door and invited him in.

"We had quite a storm last night, didn't we?" she said, taking his coat.

"Come and sit down," said Miriam. "It's lovely to see you."

"Would you like a drink?" asked Sarah. "A cup of tea or shall we have a glass of wine, seeing as it's very nearly the weekend?"

It was then that a tabby cat walked into the room and after inspecting the company jumped up onto the sofa beside Jeremiah and began cleaning herself.

"You have a cat? I've not seen her here before."

"This," said Sarah, coming into the room with a bottle of wine and three glasses, "is Willow. She used to live here, with my friend James. Then after he died, she decided to split her time, sometimes staying with me, and sometimes coming back to stay here. When Miriam agreed to rent the house from James's family, it was a condition that she would allow Willow to remain. When she's with me, I talk to her all the time, and sometimes I think she understands me."

"What is it with cats and Elmsford?" exclaimed Jeremiah. "She's just like my cat, Jezebel, who also came with the house. And I think she can understand what is being said, too, although, so far, she hasn't spoken to me about it."

They laughed, and then they talked for some time about the weather, the village, Sarah's next-door neighbours Linda and Felicity and their new electric bicycles, and the party at Giles and Francis' house. It was as if they were old friends. Jeremiah felt very relaxed with Miriam and Sarah – and their cat.

As they were talking, Jeremiah looked across the room to where Sarah was sitting and to his surprise, saw Angel standing behind her, his wings extended and shimmering. He gasped – Angel didn't usually appear in other people's houses.

"Are you okay, Jeremiah?" asked Miriam. "You look as if you've seen a ghost!"

"No, just an angel," said Jeremiah without thinking.

Sarah smiled, "Why, thank you," she said.

"Oh, no Sarah – I wasn't referring to you," Jeremiah blushed deeply. "I didn't mean you – although you are an angel. Oh God…" he could feel he was digging himself into a hole. "I just… I just um, well, sometimes I…"

"Of course, you believe in angels, don't you?" said Miriam remembering what Jeremiah had said at the drinks party. Don't tell me you see them, too?" Miriam looked him straight in the eye.

"Well, actually, I do," sighed Jeremiah. If he was to be a friend to these two women, he might as well be an honest friend.

"I thought so. How fascinating!" Miriam beamed at Jeremiah, and he could tell he was about to be quizzed, but it was Sarah who spoke.

"I once thought I could hear my James speaking to me, after he had passed away," she said, "but it was just wishful thinking. I do still miss him though, and sometimes I'm sure I can feel his presence."

"I'm sorry if I embarrassed you just now," said Jeremiah.

"That's okay – you didn't. Would you like to go for a walk now the sun's come out? We could go to the bench at the top of the cliff and then come back in time for lunch. What about you Miriam?"

At that moment, Miriam's phone rang.

"You two go on and I'll catch you up," she said, and flapped her arms as if to shoo them out of the door.

They walked in amiable silence to the L-shaped bench at the clifftop, Sarah having linked arms with Jeremiah, which he liked. He was pleased to be alone for a while with her.

"Here we are," said Sarah, seating herself on the bench with enough room for Jeremiah to join her. "I love the view from here. Breathtaking, isn't it? James and I used to come here quite often before he died."

"I always stop and sit here if I'm walking this stretch of the coast path. It's a great place to catch your breath."

"I saw you standing down there on the Wharf, soon after you moved in. I thought you had a friend with you, but I think it must've been a trick of the light."

Jeremiah thought it best to leave all talk of angels until another day.

A watery sun peeped from behind some scudding dark clouds, casting a shimmering light on the sea, and the waves which were still quite large after the storm, pounded the harbour wall shooting great geysers of white sea spray into the air. They didn't speak, but sat there for a while, just listening to the waves and the gulls, and to what was unsaid.

When they returned to the house, Miriam had set lunch on the dining table, the sort of simple lunch that Jeremiah liked best: a soup of garden vegetables and some crusty bread. Perfect.

As they ate, Miriam raised the subject of the book Jeremiah had been reading.

"I hope you can see why I asked you to read it?" Miriam buttered her bread as she spoke. "The question you're asking has very deep roots, as you now know. It's fundamental, actually: what makes us who we are?"

Jeremiah nodded and thought for a moment.

"I really enjoyed the book, and it helped me to understand myself a bit better. I mean, I've had this question in my head since I was a teenager – not always in the same words, but the same question: why is it that I've never felt as if I fitted the definition of what a man is supposed to be like?"

"What do you mean?" asked Sarah.

Jeremiah hesitated. He hadn't meant to talk about this subject either, but he felt so completely at ease with these two women that he continued, and there and then he told Miriam and Sarah his 'secret', who he had always been and who he was now. They sat quietly and listened to him. And when he had finished, he looked at them and waited to see what they would say.

For a moment no-one spoke, but then Miriam said, "You're not alone, Jeremiah. If you have spent your life feeling like an outsider, so have I. I have never felt that I fitted the definition of what a woman was supposed to be like. I didn't play with dolls when I was a child, I didn't want to get married, I didn't want to have children... And then I had breast cancer and that really altered how I felt about myself and my femininity. But I am coming to realise that our true essence lies beyond all definitions of gender. In my experience gender becomes a very fluid concept once we're past our reproductive capacity. And even then, so many of us choose not to have children."

"I didn't choose one way or the other," said Sarah. "Having a child just happened to me; it was expected of me as was getting married. I think I'm the one who has been truly – what was it you called it the other day, Miriam? – socially constructed."

"Really, Sarah?" Jeremiah was not expecting that.

"But that's it, Jeremiah," Miriam said, leaning forward. "The dilemma lies not in how you or Sarah or I are, or were – but in what we we're *supposed* to be like, who we were *supposed* to be."

"Yes, I see that now. That's what I have learned from you, and from Francis. How we have been manipulated through the ages to think and behave in certain ways: men do this, and women do that; men are superior to women, women are more emotional than men… It's chronic, isn't it? And all I can say is that after reading about how the Divine Feminine was suppressed and vilified, I'm glad I don't identify with the masculine roles that society has defined for me."

"Do you know, I didn't think about any of this when I was a young woman," said Sarah. "In fact, I didn't think about any of it until I met James. He used to talk about these kinds of things; he used to tie himself in knots pondering why he was the way he was, and yet when we just sat together in silence, when we just loved one another for who we were without trying to analyse our feelings too much, that is when we were happiest."

"So, you didn't question your life and your choices at all?" asked Jeremiah.

"Not really..." replied Sarah. "I didn't know I could. I suppose I often wanted to be someone else, or somewhere else, especially in my marriage, but the truth is I didn't have these kinds of conversations with anyone, not even in my head. I think it's all down to education, or at least the people you meet who educate you. In my world, my limited world, we were told to just accept that things were as they were, so we didn't question them, or at least, I didn't. I expected that we would all grow up just like our mothers and fathers had done, with the same expectations as them. And that was the world I married into. My husband Alan would have thought I'd gone mad if I'd asked him the kind of questions you are asking. And he certainly wouldn't have wanted to discuss them. To the day he died, we never had what you might call a discussion. To say he was a man of few words was an understatement."

"I recognise all of that," Jeremiah said. "Duncan Way in Ilford, where I was brought up, was not famous for its deep conversations."

Sarah smiled. "You and I have much to share."

"The other day," said Miriam, "I was reading a fascinating book that traces the history of how we have become gendered."

"You mean beyond the physical attributes we are born with?" asked Jeremiah, remembering earlier conversations on this subject.

"That's it. What this book suggests is that whilst we are born with particular physical sexual attributes – you have a penis and I have a vagina – that is not what our gender is. Our gender arises not from our biology, but from our sociology; as I've said before, it arises from who we are supposed to be, from what society requires us to be."

Miriam gathered up the plates and dishes and took them into the kitchen.

"I am glad you are not intimidated by Miriam," said Sarah. "Some people find her a little intense."

"And when you met her, you weren't taken aback by all of that?"

"No, I fell in love with her."

The way she said it, the way she spoke as if it was the most natural thing in the world for her to love Miriam, touched him unexpectedly. His newfound tribe, the people with whom he felt most comfortable were all people who didn't 'fit in' and he'd only just seen it. He wasn't 'different' in their eyes. It was such a relief to him.

"She must have made quite a mark when she came to this Devon village," he said. "I don't imagine the people of Elmsford spend much time talking about their genitals."

"You'd be surprised," said Sarah, and they both laughed out loud.

"What are you laughing at?" called Miriam from the kitchen.

"Nothing," Sarah chuckled. "Just genitals."

"Oh, those things," grinned Miriam, putting a large platter on the table. "How about some apple strudel? I have clotted cream, too."

That evening sitting in his study, Jeremiah wondered about how much of who he was had been born in him, and how much was the consequence of all the things he had been told were true. He thought it was probably a bit of both. Clearly being brought up in Duncan Way in post-war Britain must have shaped his beliefs and attitudes, set by a generation that experienced war and rationing, fear and hatred – and deference. His parents' values still influenced him to this day, and yet the world he now inhabited bore little resemblance to the one they knew. No wonder he'd had such a difficult time trying to work out how to fit in.

For Jeremiah, the discovery that people were openly discussing androgyny, or gender neutrality, really resonated with him. This seemed to be something that was evolving as an issue, and it was one that, despite his age, he felt very much part of. And then something else occurred to him. The other thing that set him apart from everyone else – at least as far as he knew – was that no-one, at any time, ever talked about angels, let alone shared their life with one.

Angel appeared.

"You know, Angel," said Jeremiah, not in the least surprised by this sudden appearance, "I sometimes wonder if any of the clever people I've met – you know my professors at university and people who write books – have ever seen an angel?"

"Probably not," replied Angel. "Seeing angels requires a vulnerability that does not come easily to those who are experts in whatever it is they are expert in."

"I guess so."

"There was a time when it was different, when scholars often saw angels, although they could never agree on what to call us, or what we looked like. And that was their mistake: we appear to those who need us and believe in us in the form they expect us to take. I appear to you as winged or robed, because that is what you believe angels look like. In the angelic realms we do not have clothed bodies, we are more akin to energy and light. I come to you like this because this is how you believe me to be.

"Some scholars got close to seeing us as we are. In what you call the thirteenth century, Aquinas and Bonaventure – you must have heard of them – thought that it was necessary to speak with angels in order to understand the Cosmos, or what they would have called 'the mind of God', the fabric of reality."

"I didn't know that."

"And I thought you studied Medieval History?"

"Well I did, but as far as I remember, we didn't

study what people were saying about angels."

"Well, you should have done. How can you understand what was happening in those times without knowing how their scholars regarded angels?"

"Good point, Angel. And I must say, I do like how sometimes you appear fully winged and sometimes not. I remember when you said that this is because you are like a mirror to me. Perhaps when you are fully winged, you express a part of me that I don't really know yet – my spiritual being?"

"One day you will find how true that is. It all comes from you, Jeremiah. Once you open your heart and begin to make choices that express your deeper creativity, everything will begin to align for you. I am just a reflection of that."

"That's all well and good, but what were you doing at Miriam's house, standing behind Sarah? I've never seen you appear in someone's house before."

"The answer to that, my dear Jeremiah, is something that will unfold."

"Ooh, there you go with your riddles again."

At that moment, Jezebel walked into the room and took up her position on the sofa. She had been sitting in the Garden Room listening to the conversation. She couldn't really understand what all the fuss was about. Surely everyone knew about angels, and if they didn't know that everyone, especially cats, were made both feminine and masculine, they must have been walking around with their eyes closed.

CARING FOR SARAH

Jeremiah didn't see Miriam and Sarah for a week or so, but then early one morning his phone rang. It was Miriam, and she sounded distracted.

"Jeremiah, I need your help."

Sarah had fallen and badly fractured her arm. She had been to the hospital in Barnstaple and her arm had been put into plaster, but she was still in pain, and she had to go back for a further x-ray. She was now resting at home and just about coping. But there was a problem. Some time ago, Miriam had been invited to give a paper at a conference in America and was now in a dilemma, because she was set to leave at the end of the week. She wanted to go very much, for many of the people who would be there were her peers in her work on Mary Magdalene and the history of the Cathars, including her friend Angelique. But who was going to keep an eye on Sarah and take her to the hospital?

"Sarah's next-door neighbours could have helped, but they are away," said Miriam, "and our friends Alice and Rachel both work fulltime, so we don't feel we can ask them. Grace and Tim are..."

"It's okay, Miriam," said Jeremiah. "I'll be happy to look after Sarah. It will be an honour."

"Really? Oh, Jeremiah, I can't thank you enough. It would mean taking Sarah to the hospital next Tuesday morning, if that's okay?"

"That's okay. No problem, Miriam. I can wander up to see Sarah in the mornings and make her some lunch. And the same again in the evenings, if she needs me. I'll enjoy it. When are you leaving?"

"This coming Sunday."

"That's fine."

"Thank you, Jeremiah. It's so kind of you. And I know Sarah will be pleased. I told her I was going to phone you and she didn't make a fuss about it at all."

The thought that Sarah was happy for Jeremiah to look after her in Miriam's absence pleased Jeremiah immensely. He liked being needed and he liked being helpful.

"Well, that's settled then," he said.

Since that moment of epiphany at Giles and Francis' house, where he realised that something even as traumatic and painful as a mugging could become a strange kind of blessing, he had begun to trust his life a little more. He felt that if Miriam asked for his help, it would lead to new experiences for him. He was more at ease with his life than he had ever been, and he noticed that he'd stopped berating himself for not living up to other people's expectations; he'd started to say 'yes' to things where previously he'd baulk and make excuses and he felt more relaxed, as if – to use a phrase he'd begun to hear more often (well, Giles used it a lot) – he was 'going with the flow'.

He loved the life that was unfolding for him in Devon and his newfound friendships were extremely important to him. Caring for Sarah in this coming week was his way of saying thank you for the kindness she and Miriam had shown him.

Jeremiah also agreed to make sure Willow had enough food in her bowls at Miriam's house, and on the day she left for the conference, before he visited Sarah, he decided to go and check that Miriam had remembered to feed the cat.

Of course she had, and so Jeremiah took the opportunity to sit on her veranda and admire the view. It was such a beautiful vista; a huge sloping field that ran down one side of the valley had been 'set-aside' by the farmer and was now teeming with wildflowers, butterflies and insects. Jeremiah recalled Miriam telling him that she'd seen a hare as big as a small dog dart out of the undergrowth one morning, and the other side of the valley was flanked with woodland, which had a meandering footpath that ran through it, on which Jeremiah often walked.

He felt it could never be possible for him to have enough of this view, even if he'd lived here all his life. He'd heard of the term 'a sense of place' many times before, but had never really understood what it meant until he'd moved to Elmsford, but the sense of place here was palpable, as if all the trees and birds knew one another; as if the sea sang a lullaby to them on the fall and rise of the tides.

He didn't know how long he'd been sitting there in contemplation, but at some point, he became aware that he felt he was no longer on his own. He even looked about him to see if someone was with him, but he was alone. And yet he felt distinctly as if someone else was sitting next to him. Then, just as quickly as it had arisen, the feeling disappeared.

How strange, thought Jeremiah. He stood up and after gazing for a final moment towards the sea, he walked back through the churchyard and then on up the street until he came to Sarah's cottage. He knocked on her door and after a short while, she opened it. Jeremiah was rather disconcerted to see that she didn't look at all well, her face pale and drawn, her arm encased in plaster, which was held across her chest in a sling.

"Come in, Jeremiah. I do hope this isn't a nuisance for you? I'm sorry to be such a bother."

"It's no bother, Sarah," he said. "I'm pleased to be of some use. How are you?"

She smiled at him.

"How do I look?"

"Not so good. How did it happen?"

"It was so stupid," she said. "I was carrying a pile of laundry upstairs and I tripped and fell. My arm smashed against the wall and I fell to the bottom of the stairs. Fortunately, I was able to reach my phone and call Miriam. We spent the rest of the afternoon in the hospital, which was tough for Miriam as she absolutely loathes hospitals."

"Oh, you poor thing, that sounds dreadful. Miriam said you are in quite a lot of pain."

"I am, although I have painkillers, but I don't really like taking them."

"I guess you have to. At least for the while."

"I suppose so. But I'm also taking arnica which is a wonderful homeopathic remedy for bone fractures."

"Really? I didn't know that."

"Yes. You know I've got to go back to the hospital for another x-ray on Tuesday?"

"Yes, I'll take you."

"Are you sure?"

"Yes, I'm sure. And Sarah, I want you to know that I am happy to help out. So, let's say no more on that matter. Shall I make some tea?"

Sarah smiled a big smile.

"That would be lovely and thank you so much Jeremiah. Actually, despite my arm, I am having quite a good day."

"Really? Why is that then?" asked Jeremiah from the kitchen.

"Look at this."

Jeremiah came back into the living room and placed the tray of tea on the little pine table in the centre of the room. Then he took the mobile phone that Sarah was proffering and read the text, though he had to squint to read it and hold the phone at arm's length, as he did not have his reading glasses with him.

> dear gran I hope u r ok. I know its bin ages since we all came to your luvvely house by the sea, but I would luv to come and see you again if thats ok. If mum n dad agree, can I come and stay with you in the school hols? I will be 16 in Nov yay, so I'll be old enough to travel on my own then and I really miss you [heart] luv, Bryony, kiss, kiss, kiss

"Oh, that's lovely Sarah – obviously, Bryony is your granddaughter?"

"She is, and what's wonderful is that I thought perhaps Bryony and her sister Iris didn't care about me and that I might never see them again. But this has really made my day. I've texted her back to say yes, maybe after Christmas or next year after she's finished her exams. It feels like a little breakthrough."

"I'm so pleased for you Sarah. It's just the kind of news you need to cheer you up. By the way, have you ever felt the presence of your friend James when you're sitting on the veranda at The Sanctuary?" he asked.

"Occasionally I have, yes, but not as often as I'd like. I sometimes speak to him if I'm there on my own – but not so much these days. Why do you ask?"

"It's just that, when I was sitting there earlier, I felt distinctly as if someone was sitting next to me, but nobody was there."

"Really? Wouldn't it be wonderful if it was James coming to say hello to you and welcoming you to his house. I still think of it as his house, although Miriam has lived there for two years now."

They continued to talk about what was happening in the village, but after a while, Jeremiah could tell that Sarah was getting tired. He left her sitting comfortably with Willow and went across the road to the village shop to buy the things she needed for the next few days.

And this became their daily routine, Jeremiah checking on Sarah in the mornings and running errands, and then again if she needed a bit of help in the evenings. He could see that Sarah was able to relax and rest and, he felt sure, was enjoying being looked after. Sometimes, Alice would call in on her way home from work, and Sarah told him that Katharine had rung her every evening.

Tuesday came and Jeremiah drove Sarah to Barnstaple for her appointment, which went well. They cut off the plaster cast and the x-ray showed that everything was in the right place and that the break was beginning to heal.

"Must be the arnica," Sarah whispered to Jeremiah.

They made a new cast and gave Sarah a prescription both for the painkillers and another to counter their effects. The people at the hospital were kind and professional, and Jeremiah could see that Sarah was feeling reassured.

As they left, Jeremiah asked Sarah if she wanted to go straight home or take a detour to Appledore, where he knew there was a café that she liked which served exceptionally chocolatey hot chocolate. She opted for Appledore.

"Life takes some wonderful twists and turns, doesn't it?" she said as they drove along. "Not so many months ago we had never met, and now, here we are like two old friends on an outing."

"And one of us has a rather impressive plaster cast on her arm," said Jeremiah, and Sarah laughed.

"So, did I need to fall down the stairs to make this happen?"

"Like I had to get mugged to come here, you mean?"

"It's an interesting theory, but it would be better if it didn't hurt so much," Sarah replied.

"I've enjoyed wandering over to The Sanctuary to feed Willow though she's never there – she's always with you. I like the house, very much. It has a really wonderful stillness – a quietness that you can almost touch. I love how light and airy it is, and Miriam has a remarkable library of books. Do you think she's read them all?"

"I think she has. Miriam becomes so absorbed in her books, that sometimes I think she inhabits a different world to me altogether."

"Do you feel a bit excluded by that?"

"Not at all. Actually, it reminds me of how James used to be. He'd read a book, then we'd spend the evening discussing the finer points of it, so that I didn't have to read it at all."

"I like the sound of James."

"I think you would've got on well." Sarah's mind drifted briefly, remembering those shared moments with James. "But sometimes I worry that Miriam works too hard. She's always switched on, if you know what I mean, whereas I really like to switch off."

"Funny you should say that, Sarah. I think when I sat on the veranda and had a fleeting connection to James, I was 'switched off'. Maybe one has to be switched off to feel these things? I hope you don't mind me asking you about your friendship with Miriam?"

"No, not at all. I think that Miriam and I were brought together, somehow – that we are meant to be friends. When she first came to stay at The Sanctuary it was only going to be for a short while, but she loved it so much that she decided to stay for longer, and as we got to know each other I think we both found something that we needed. She spends so much time in her head that she needs someone like me who is more grounded. And, in her, I have discovered possibilities that I had never known before. So, we have become like sisters, and we love each other."

Sarah looked at this man, who was caring for her, driving her around and cooking her suppers. He was handsome in a tousled, rather eccentric way. He had a strong jawline, as if he could be stubborn, but she couldn't imagine him being stubborn. His corduroy jacket had been patched at the elbows, and his plaid shirt was worn at the collar. But she liked that he didn't seem to care about these things. And what she found most attractive about him – and it struck her that she did find him attractive – was his eyes: they were as blue as the sky on a summer's day and his lashes were long and dark. And, more than that, she felt he somehow communicated with his eyes things that could not be spoken.

How fanciful, she chuckled to herself. *I don't know what I even mean by that, except that I feel I know him much more deeply than seems possible after a few months of friendship.*

On the day Miriam was due home, Jeremiah called in on Sarah, to find her on the telephone. 'Hold on,' she gestured to him as she finished the call.

"That was my friend Katharine. She's coming down for the weekend to 'take care of me,' as she puts it. It'll be so lovely to see her. I'd like to introduce you to her, at some point. She really is a very special person."

"I'd like that very much," said Jeremiah.

"You have been really kind, Jeremiah," Sarah added. "I've so enjoyed having you around."

"And I've enjoyed being around. Maybe we can just keep calling in on each other, once you're back up and running?"

"I'd like that."

When he left, he kissed Sarah on each cheek.

As Jeremiah walked the short distance home, he was thinking about Sarah. The truth is, he had not been attracted to many people in his life – he'd never had that gene that drew him towards others – but Sarah drew him to her, and he couldn't work out why. Was it her light-heartedness, her calm aura, as he'd once called it? Yes, that was it, her light-heartedness… she somehow leavened any gathering with her presence; made it feel special, enjoyable, fun… Jeremiah liked her sense of humour and that little bit of wickedness, certainly. But it was more than that, much more than that. She was so familiar to him. He felt like he'd known her all his life, which was ridiculous.

"Angel?" Jeremiah looked around to see if he was home, but he did not appear, then the familiar sound of the cat-flap told him that Jezebel had noticed his return.

The weather had turned colder, so Jeremiah lit his wood stove, watching the flames dancing behind the glass panel and almost immediately felt the stove's warmth. In London he'd had gas-fired central heating, which now seemed so sterile and utilitarian in comparison to a wood fire. One of his favourite things was to collect fallen branches for his fire on his daily walks. He'd built up quite a pile of wood, and Giles had promised to come over one weekend and help him saw it up and stack it in the woodshed.

On his most recent walk, as Jeremiah had come through the village with several big wet branches slung over his shoulder, an old man from the row of cottages that lined the main street had called out, "Been wooding then, Mr. Browne?"

Jeremiah had smiled and waved. It made him feel as if he'd become part of this small community and he liked that feeling very much.

On Tuesday Francis came to work and busied himself emptying the bins ready for the next day's collection. He'd insisted on retaining his cleaning jobs with Jeremiah and Miriam but had resigned from his other jobs to oversee the building work at Studio Harmonia. In all honesty, Jeremiah was quite capable of looking after himself, but he enjoyed seeing Francis and sometimes they just sat and talked.

Francis popped his head around Jeremiah's study door. "I'm going to clean the bathroom next, so if you need to use it, do it now."

"You go ahead, Francis," said Jeremiah. "Come in when you're finished, and we'll have a cup of coffee."

"Okay, will do. Coffee will be nice."

Jeremiah prodded the woodstove in his study and

added a few more logs. When he looked up he saw Angel standing in front of him, hovering slightly above the ground, his ankle wings whirring silently.

"Angel, I've been thinking…"

"Go on."

"Well, I know you once told me that it is not possible to waste time and that everything happens for a reason, but I really can't help feeling that I have wasted a lot of my life. More has happened to me in the short time I've lived here than all those years in London. I remember saying to you once before that it's like I was asleep when I lived there..."

Angel fluttered his shimmering wings.

"Being asleep is one way of describing it – and sleep is wonderfully healing and so it cannot possibly be wasteful – but I see it more as a form of gestation." Angel felt rather pleased with the word 'gestation'.

"What do you mean?"

"Some seeds fall to the ground and germinate instantly. Some seeds take months to germinate, and some seeds can lay dormant for many years before they germinate and very often, in order to germinate, they have to be disturbed in some way, like the mugging disturbed you. However you awaken from your sleep, the timing is always right. Until that moment, you are … gestating."

"I wish I'd germinated earlier, Angel – I've got so much life to fit in now – and as you know, I'm not getting any younger."

Angel levitated slightly, his wings reflecting the light from the fire.

"Nature always knows when the time is right. Do

you see a blackbird building a nest in November? No. Trust in The Now, Jeremiah."

"You are right, Angel – you are always right. I am beginning to trust in The Now, and I like it."

"Who are you talking to?" Francis shoved the study door open with his foot, a cup of coffee in each hand.

"Myself, as usual," replied Jeremiah.

A HOST OF ANGELS

In early December, Jeremiah rang Sarah to invite her and Miriam to have lunch with him at a rather trendy restaurant in Bude that was gaining a good reputation for its fish cuisine.

"It can be my Christmas treat to both of you," he suggested.

"How lovely, said Sarah.

"I'll book a table and pick you up at eleven-thirty, on Friday."

When Jeremiah pulled up in front of Sarah's cottage, both women stepped out, dressed in their finery and evidently ready to go.

"I have been so looking forward to this," said Miriam. "It'll be the first time I've left the house for weeks."

They drove to Bude and parked near the canal that led onto the expansive golden beach. As they neared the bridge across the canal, Jeremiah pointed to a house on the left.

"That's where I stayed the very first time I came to Bude," he said.

"Thank goodness it's so nice, or else you might not have come back," said Miriam.

"And then we'd never have met you," added Sarah.

There were not many people about, as the weather was brisk, cold even, a north-westerly breeze off the sea chilling them even though the sun was shining. They put on a quick pace to keep warm and soon they had walked across the beach and up the steps near the sea pool to the restaurant, with its huge windows making the most of the incredible view. Before long they had glasses of wine and a serving of humus, olives and sourdough bread to share while they waited for their food. They had all ordered the restaurant's renowned battered cod and French fries.

"I wasn't sure you'd have the fish," said Sarah. "I thought you were vegetarian."

"I love vegetarian food," said Jeremiah. "I rarely eat meat, and hardly ever fish, but whenever I come here – which is not all that often – I always order fish and chips. I love the batter."

"Me, too," said Sarah, smiling at Jeremiah. "Perhaps we should have just ordered batter and chips?"

Miriam raised her wine glass.

"Happy days," she said.

"Happy days," Jeremiah and Sarah said in unison. And they all clinked glasses.

"So, Jeremiah," said Miriam, "Have you any plans for Christmas?"

"I've been invited to stay with my friends Stephen and Jenny and their family. They've booked a house on the banks of the Helford River in south Cornwall, and they have invited me to join them. I've never been to that part of Cornwall, so I thought I'd go. Also, I haven't seen them or their family since I moved from London, so it will be a real reunion. I'm looking forward to it. What are you two doing for Christmas?"

"We're going to the Pyrenees!" said Sarah, "Miriam and Angelique are writing a new book and they need to spend time together."

"How exciting. I've never been to that part of France either. What's the book about?"

"Oh, the usual stuff, the Magdalene and the Cathars," said Miriam. "Angelique has discovered some new material that we want to look at. We're both rather excited about it, actually. And Sarah will meet the gorgeous Max, at last."

"Yes, I'm looking forward to meeting Max," Sarah smiled. "I've heard so much about him."

"Will you be away for long?" Jeremiah felt a faint twinge of anxiety as Sarah mentioned Max. Or was it jealousy? He brushed the feeling to one side, determined to be happy for Sarah and whatever adventures awaited her.

"It all depends on Miriam and Angelique. Maybe three weeks? There's some talk of us all going to Pisa to visit an elderly woman who has a collection of early texts on the Cathars. I don't know if I'll go, but I shall be happy to stay with Max, if not."

"I'm sure you will," smiled Jeremiah. "I bet he's rather dishy!"

"He certainly is," said Miriam.

"Don't be silly," said Sarah prodding Jeremiah's arm with her fork. "I thought you understood these things."

"These things?"

"Yes, you know, how a man and a woman can be together without sex coming into the equation."

Jeremiah laughed. "I didn't say you were going to go to bed with Max!"

"Not quite."

They all laughed, enjoying their easy companionship.

On the day before Christmas Eve, Sarah and Miriam flew off to France and Jeremiah drove south towards the Helford estuary. For miles, he had the vast Atlantic ocean to his right, glittering dark blue in the distance, and then disappearing from view; then the tors of Bodmin Moor rose into view and the scenery changed as he turned inland, across the Cornish peninsular. He was shocked to see how the industrial slag heaps from the China clay industry had marred the landscape, creating unnatural white tors that to Jeremiah's eye looked like they could collapse at any moment, but even then, they had a kind of beauty. 'The Cornish Alps' he'd once heard them called.

Jeremiah enjoyed his Christmas week in Cornwall immensely. The house on the Helford estuary was large and comfortable, and overlooked the most gloriously green and sparkling river Jeremiah had ever seen. Both Jeremiah's god-children were able to join the throng, with their own toddlers in tow, so the house was full of noise and laughter, which Jeremiah might once have found irksome, but now he found endearing. He made friends with his great-god-children as he called them, whilst Stephen and Jenny produced copious amounts of food from the kitchen. There were walks and pub lunches and games of Scrabble in the evening, sitting around the fire. But most especially, Jeremiah was delighted to be in the company of Stephen, who he realised he had missed very much.

"Perhaps we can encourage you to come and visit us in our villa in Turkey one day?" suggested Stephen, who really didn't think that Jeremiah would even agree to come to Cornwall.

"Perhaps," said Jeremiah. "One step at a time, though, eh?"

"It's so good to see you, Jerry." Stephen looked at this dear man, his oldest friend. "You've changed. You seem… different, happy?"

"Do you know, I think I am. Country life suits me, and I've made more friends in the short time I've lived there than I ever did in London."

"Well, you were a bit of a recluse in London."

"I was, wasn't I? I was so immersed in the business, I hardly had time for anything else, but now I realise there's more to life than work."

"I'll drink to that," said Stephen, refilling their wine glasses. "We were lucky to set up the business when we did, and lucky to have hardly any competition, but I wouldn't want to do it now. It's a totally different ball game now, Jerry. Thank goodness we got out when we did."

On the last evening of his stay, Jeremiah and Stephen sat on the covered veranda of the house looking out towards the Christmas lights of the village on the opposite bank of the river, which shimmered in the tidal waters. The occasional call of a curlew cast a spell over them as they listened to the night sounds, not saying much, just enjoying the tranquillity.

Jeremiah looked at his friend, still rakishly handsome after all these years.

"Stephen," he said, "I want to thank you for always being there for me, even when I was… well, I think I was depressed, for quite a while – certainly after Angela left – and if not depressed, then quite melancholy. I don't know how you put up with me."

"It wasn't easy," Stephen chuckled. "No, seriously mate – I am so pleased that you've found happiness at long last. You've reconciled with Angela, you've made good friends, you're living somewhere you feel safe and secure. I'm pleased for you, Jerry."

It was the nearest the two men could come to speak of their love for one another.

Jeremiah returned to Devon on the day before New Year's Eve, and although this was a night he had never enjoyed, Giles and Francis insisted that he should come around to their house and spend it with them. They were throwing a small party and they wanted to introduce Jeremiah to some of their musician friends. They had even reserved one of their guest rooms for him, so that he didn't have to drive home and could have a drink or two and retire whenever he felt like it. Jeremiah had not been able to think of a good reason not to go.

Much to his surprise, Jeremiah enjoyed New Year's Eve, though he noted that the guy who liked to dress up as a Roman Centurion was not amongst the guests.

Giles and Francis' friends were young, vibrant and interesting, with tattoos and piercings and strange hair, and they didn't seem to mind an old man in their midst at all. But when they started to make music together, Jeremiah was thrilled. They played a kind of modern folk music, with great rhythm and wonderful harmonies, saxophones, flutes and acoustic guitars and one of the young men, sang with a voice like Leonard Cohen, who was one of Jeremiah's favourite artists. So, it was a real treat. And after the hullabaloo of seeing in the New Year, Jeremiah slipped off to bed, mindful that he didn't want to wake up with a hangover.

And so, the days of winter passed. Sarah sent a postcard from the Pyrenees of a stunning landscape of mountains covered in snow. She mentioned that they would be home on 22nd January, which seemed a long time to Jeremiah. He was reading a lot of fiction again, sometimes driving to Bideford which had a really good independent bookshop, taking recommendations of what was new and a 'must read' from *the Guardian*, and from Giles and Francis, though he found his taste differed somewhat from theirs.

One evening, as Jeremiah sat reading, warmed by his wood stove, Angel appeared and said, "I have something to tell you."

Jeremiah looked up from his book.

"You are always telling me things," he said.

"Yes, but this is important."

"Go on."

"We are going to church tomorrow."

"Really? Why tomorrow? It's a Saturday, not a Sunday."

"You'll see."

"Why the mystery?"

"You'll see."

Jeremiah shook his head. "Here I was," he said, "quietly enjoying my book, being no trouble to anyone, and then you have to go all mysterious on me."

"I needed to tell you before you went to bed. We have to be there quite early."

"How early?"

"Eight-thirty."

"Oh, come on – why so early? You know I don't get up until after nine these days. It'll hardly be light at eight-thirty."

"It will be light."

"You are impossible."

"No, not impossible, unbelievable, maybe."

"Ha ha. Very funny. But now that you have ruined my evening, I'm going to bed. Do we really have to go at eight-thirty?"

"Yes, we do."

Jeremiah had set his alarm clock for seven-forty-five, but when it rang the morning was cold and he felt very reluctant to get out of his warm bed. Yet there was Angel, standing by the window with his arms folded across his chest looking at him serenely.

"Come on," he said, "time to get up."

"But it's too cold..." Protesting, Jeremiah climbed out of bed and, taking his clothes with him, went to his bathroom. Then he insisted on having tea and toast before they left. By the time he was ready to go, it was well past eight-thirty, but Jeremiah was warm, fed and in a better mood. Angel noted with a wry smile that Jeremiah didn't seem to mind being late anymore.

As they walked through the churchyard in the dim morning light, Jeremiah noticed that the lights were on in the church. He supposed it must be an early morning service, but it wasn't.

When they opened the church door and went in, it seemed at first as if the church was empty, but then over by the rood screen Jeremiah saw the figure of a woman on her hands and knees, mopping the flagstone floor. Hearing them enter, she turned towards them. She was small, elderly, and wearing a floral housecoat. She picked up the bucket and the mop and came towards them.

"So, you came, Jeremiah," she said.

Jeremiah didn't know what to say.

"And you brought your angel with you."

Somewhat confused, Jeremiah sat down on a pew near the altar. Angel remained standing.

"Forgive me," said Jeremiah, to the woman, who was now standing before him her hands resting on the mop, "but how do you know my name? I don't think we've met, and no-one has ever seen my angel before."

The woman laughed. "Let me introduce myself. My name is Sheila. I clean this church, and I am here every Saturday morning from eight o'clock until I'm finished. So, unless you come to say your prayers early in the mornings, which you don't, there is no way we would have met. And as far as seeing your angel, here we are surrounded by angels, in the paintings and the stained glass and in the books of hymns, and you are surprised that I can see yours?"

At that moment, there appeared behind the woman a soft but radiant golden light which spread and spread until it filled the church and took the form of a host of angels.

"You see?" she said.

Jeremiah was transfixed.

"My dear Jeremiah, you live in a place of angels," she said. "All you have to do is open your heart to them and you will see them everywhere, both here in the church and in the countryside around us. Elmsford is a place of angels, and many of us who live here can see them. There's nothing odd about you, Jeremiah – nothing odd at all. Welcome home."

Tears filled Jeremiah's eyes and Angel came and sat beside him.

Then the light slowly dispersed, and Shelia picked up her bucket and mop and disappeared into the vestry.

"So, I'm not alone," said Jeremiah, "and nor are you."

Angel smiled.

"You were destined to discover this, my friend. Although you didn't know it, it is one of the reasons why you came to live here."

A week later, when Jeremiah opened his laptop, he saw there was an email from Angela, and it contained distressing news. Francesca had died. Suddenly and unexpectedly her cancer had spread and could not be contained. At the end of the email, Angela had added her new mobile number. He called her straight away.

"Oh, my dear Angela," he said, "I'm very sorry to hear about Francesca."

Angela was quiet but seemingly calm.

"Thank you so much for calling. You and Francesca are the two people I have loved most in my life, and now she has gone... I thought you should know. I wanted you to know."

"Thank you for telling me, Angela. Are you okay?"

"Not really. I'm… I'm feeling close to chaos, Jeremiah," and her voice caught in a sob. "It's all so… I can hardly believe what's happened." She hesitated. "Look, can I call you back, this evening?" she asked. "There's so much going on here that I need to attend to, and several of Francesca's friends are about to turn up."

"No problem. Call me tonight. I'll be here."

That evening, at about seven o'clock, the phone rang and it was Angela, sounding exhausted. As she told Jeremiah all that had happened and as he listened, not asking questions but just letting her speak, he realised how much he loved this woman, how he'd never stopped loving her. But now he knew, after all those years of struggling with his sense of self, that just loving her was enough. He did not need to possess her.

Angela became lost in thought, and for a while neither of them spoke. And then, somewhat to his surprise, Angela asked Jeremiah if he might come to visit her when things had settled down.

"I know you don't like to travel," she said, "but how about coming to Florence, just for a short while? I'd love to see you and I'm sure you'd enjoy being here."

"Well, I would like to see all those paintings and frescoes that have been such an important part of your life. All those angels..."

He stopped.

"But?" asked Angela feeling his hesitation.

"But I can't."

Angela was not surprised. "That's a shame," she said. "It would be good to show you around Florence and our friends would love to meet you."

"I'm sorry," Jeremiah said. "I know it sounds odd, but I just can't."

"Why not?" she asked gently.

Jeremiah gathered his thoughts.

"I know I have always been hopeless about travel, but now there's something else, too."

"Do you want to tell me?"

Jeremiah sighed. It was all so new to him that he almost couldn't put how he felt into words.

"I'm not entirely sure," he said, "but it has to do with understanding acceptance and the importance of being here – you know, being content with where I am. And that requires practice. Practice, every day. I guess that's what I'm now trying to do now. I am learning to accept who I am, accept where I am, and just give myself over to being here."

"That sounds good, Jeremiah. That sounds just right. And maybe I could come and see you instead? I do still love you, you know.".

"I would like that," he said. "It would be so good to see you again and thank you for understanding about my need to just settle into this landscape. It is becoming part of me, I think... And Angela, dear Angela, I love you, too. I have never stopped loving you, though sometimes it must have seemed to you as though I had forsaken you."

They were both in tears, and yet they were healing tears of love.

A WAY OF BEING

When Sarah told Alice why she'd asked her to look after Willow for the Christmas holidays, Alice was surprised.

"You're going to spend Christmas in France with Miriam?"

"Yes. It seems that I am. And for three weeks. That feels like forever." And then, as an after-thought, "You don't mind, do you Alice – that I've become close to Miriam? I know I don't see you as often as I used to, but it doesn't mean I love you any the less."

"Of course not. I just want you to be happy, Sarah – but Ruth and I did wonder if you're…" Alice hesitated, choosing her words carefully, "… if you and Miriam have become lovers?"

Sarah couldn't help but laugh, recalling her conversations with Miriam. "I expect we're the talk of the village," she said, smiling at Alice with great affection. "We do love each other, but not in that way. We've become more like sisters – the sisters we both longed for in our childhoods, but never had; the kind of sisters who can share secrets and adventures."

"Oh, that's lovely Sarah, I'm so pleased for you, I really am – especially after losing James... It's just wonderful to have someone special in your life. I hope you didn't mind me asking?"

"Not at all, darling. We're old friends – you can ask me anything," said Sarah, though when Alice mentioned 'someone special', it was Jeremiah who came to her mind. She dismissed the thought and focussed on what Alice was saying.

"I am a bit jealous that you're going to the Pyrenees, though. I'd love to go to there – I've heard it's rather magical. You'll have to come over for supper when you get back and tell us all about it."

It wasn't until they boarded the flight that Sarah began to feel slightly nervous and was glad to have Miriam beside her. As the plane sat on the runway waiting to take off, Miriam handed Sarah a gift.

"This is for you. An early Christmas present."

It felt heavy and was wrapped in gold tissue paper tied with string. She unwrapped it. It was a journal, bound in sky-blue satin, with a ribbon to mark her place amongst the pages, which were silver at the edges. "It's just like the ones James used to use… Oh, thank you, Miriam." Sarah was overcome with pleasure and leant across and kissed Miriam on the cheek. "You're very good to me," she said.

"And you are very good for me," she replied. "I just

know there will be such a lot for you to write about when we're in Arques."

For a while they said nothing while the plane taxied and then took off. Sarah was less frightened than she thought she would be, in fact, she was finding it exhilarating. And soon, there they were, above the clouds in bright sunshine.

"I suppose it's always like this up here..." she said to Miriam.

"Indeed it is. Isn't it beautiful?"

The seatbelt sign went off and one of the stewardesses began to walk down the aisle with a trolley of drinks and snacks. Miriam and Sarah bought bottles of water and some nuts to share between them. They were only going to be in the air for a couple of hours, and Sarah began to think about what being in France for Christmas would be like. She asked Miriam to tell her more about Angelique and Max.

"Angelique and I have known each other for something like twenty years," said Miriam. "She's about ten years younger than me, and we first met in London, at a supper party given by mutual friends. I had been invited because Angelique was staying with them and they knew of our common interest in Mary Magdalene. I was amazed to discover we had both lived in Arques, although Angelique and her parents had not come to the village until she was in her early teens, by which time I was, of course, in England.

"She told me she was writing stories about the Magdalene – fiction based on her study of early Christian literature, the Gnostic gospels and the legends of the heretical Cathars that were part of the history of that region of France. Of course, I told her about my own research and we had a wonderful conversation. I'm afraid we ignored everyone else at the table. She was going back home the next day, but we kept in touch, and I started to visit her and her family in the summer holidays. She and Max live in what was her parents' house."

"And 'the gorgeous Max', as you call him," Sarah said. "Tell me about Max."

"Max is quite unlike Angelique. She is a scholar and writer and lives in other worlds. Max is a carpenter and lives in this world. He has virtually rebuilt the house and converted the outbuildings to provide extra accommodation for visitors. It was his idea to become a B&B, and he does nearly all of the cooking. He is also a very keen gardener. He grows all their vegetables, and the chickens are his, too. But not the bees. The bees are Angelique's."

Before the knew it, they had landed and made their way through airport security, and there was Angelique looking like something out of a pre-Raphaelite painting: tall, though not as tall as Miriam, and very slender, with pale skin and long red hair. And beside her was Max. Sarah had not thought of him as being short, but he was, with a lot of dark curly hair and a beard. And he had a wide and radiant smile. There was a lot of hugging of Miriam and then an introduction to Sarah, followed by more hugs. She was nearly squashed by Max. There was something about his physicality that caught Sarah by surprise. She knew she was going to like him.

They all bundled into Angelique's not very big Citroën and left the airport, the town and the sea behind them, heading inland through what Max said were the foothills of the Pyrenees, already capped with snow. Miriam had been right. It was a very beautiful place. Not at all like the Devon countryside that Sarah knew, but equally delightful. The high hedge banks and little fields were replaced by mountains and forests.

There was so much to take in, and Sarah for a moment felt nervous again; that she was heading out beyond her comfort zone. But then the chatter in the car was full of laughter, and despite Angelique's driving being somewhat cavalier, as the journey passed Sarah relaxed and decided simply to open her heart to all that was to come.

That evening they had supper together. A chicken casserole with baked potatoes, and a dark red wine that Max said had come from a local vineyard. Sarah remembered accepting a second glass and then a third. Angelique and Miriam were talking, sometimes in English but mostly in French, about Angelique's latest novel, which as far as Sarah could tell seemed to be about the slaughter of the Cathars by the armies of the Pope but written from the perspective of the women who were raped, their fathers, husbands and sons murdered. She listened for a while, but then, as Miriam and Angelique became more and more engrossed with each other's work, she turned to Max and asked him about the house and, of course, his chickens.

He spoke slowly and softly in broken but careful English, as if he wanted to choose exactly the right words, and Sarah liked this. He told her about his dogs, the countryside and the nearby villages. Sarah noticed that every so often he would look towards Angelique, and she wondered how it was that he had come to be loved by such an exotic creature. He was so solid and grounded, whereas she seemed almost ethereal. Not only the colour and abundance of her red hair and her pale skin, but her darting green eyes seemed restless, as if she was here, but somewhere else in her head. Like Miriam often was. Angelique exuded an energy that was palpable, and Sarah thought that without Max, Angelique might shatter into pieces.

She went to bed tired but full of all that the day had brought to her.

The next morning was Christmas Eve and, Sarah awoke in her simple wooden bed with its headboard painted with flowers. She sat up against her pillows and pulled the duvet up under her arms, remembering all that happened the day before. It felt so good to be here. It was very quiet and out of her bedroom window she could see distant snow-capped mountains. Then she heard the sound of someone going downstairs, and in the distance a dog barking. A door opened and there was the scrunch of boots in the yard. She got up and looked out of the window. It was Max, encased in a huge sheepskin coat and hat. He was off to feed his chickens. The day had begun.

Sarah smiled at the prospect of a new day and her delight in being where she was. She went back to bed and picked up her journal, in which she had placed her boarding pass from the plane and a postcard that Max had given her showing the Pyrenees countryside in high summer. She began to write, but then felt a little self-conscious. It was Miriam who was the writer, not her…

But then an idea came to her. She would write as if it were a letter – to Jeremiah.

> My dear Jeremiah
>
> I cannot really believe I am here. A little while ago I could never have imagined that I would be befriended by a professor and taken to the Pyrenees! But this is what has happened. Since James passed away, I have been blessed with many things, with unexpected friendships and with love. Katharine, Miriam and you, dear Jeremiah, have come into my life so unexpectedly and at a time when I thought that I had lost everything. And now, here I am, making more friends and having unexpected adventures. Yes, that is what my life has become – an unexpected adventure.
>
> My love for Miriam feels so natural, as I imagine it does between sisters. She has brought so much into my life. And I know that I bring something to her, too. I think it may be the same thing that Max brings to Angelique – a grounding, of sorts. But then I feel this love with Katharine and Alice, and Rachel too. Perhaps if I continue to open my heart, I can experience this kind of sisterhood with all the women in my life?

And yet – and I can say this to you Jeremiah, in a letter that you may never receive – I feel a growing fondness for you, a sense of love towards you; and I feel this fondness for Max, already. Perhaps as well as sisterhood, I am experiencing the love of brotherhood?

I have never been aware of feeling so much love in my life before, but it is an easy love; not borne out of duty or lust. It feels like an expansiveness in my heart, or perhaps Miriam might say, my soul. My soul is immersed in loving awareness.

I am so enjoying this adventure.

Christmas in the Pyrennes was magical. Angelique kept candles lit from early morning until they retired to bed and would not allow anything electrical to be turned on, giving the whole house a feeling of being lost in time. They had all put their shoes in front of the fireplace, and on Christmas morning a little linen bag had been placed inside each one, filled with home-made chocolates. Then Max ushered everyone out of the kitchen, and within a few hours he had cooked a feast fit for a banquet, with oysters to start, then roast goose and chestnut stuffing and a chocolate log for dessert. They didn't finish their meal until it was dark outside, and all of them retired to bed early, feeling replete in every way possible.

In the days following Christmas, Sarah and Miriam established a pattern of getting up late and having very long and leisurely breakfasts, with bowls of Max's homemade granola, yoghurt and frozen raspberries from the garden. And of course, coffee. Despite having been brought up on tea, Sarah had begun to relish a cup of coffee for her elevenses and staying with Angelique and Max it seemed contrary not to drink it at breakfast too. So she did, and she drank it with hot milk from a large china cup decorated in patterns of blue and red. And there were croissants, of course, which came from a tiny local bakery. It was another of Max's tasks to get them each morning, along with the crusty white bread. No marmalade, but home-made apricot jam. Sarah was in heaven. The food was delicious, and Max was so attentive and quite different from any man she'd met before – earthy, practical, and open-hearted.

After breakfast everyone had time to themselves before a snack at lunchtime of cheese and bread, and then a walk in the wintry countryside, but often without Miriam and Angelique who were busy with their writing. And so Max, Sarah and the dogs set off for long walks together, and this then became the way of it – Miriam and Angelique writing and Sarah and Max walking.

She liked his company, liked the ease with which they could walk together in silence, and then he would suddenly grab her arm and point at something, and she would follow his gaze and see a fleeting glimpse of a deer or a brightly-coloured mushroom in the forest undergrowth.

They didn't talk much, but just enjoyed the scenery and the peacefulness that had descended, as it often does in winter, Sarah's favourite time of the year. For Sarah, there was something in sharing silence with another person that said more than any words could ever say. She realised it was like the Quaker silence – full and fertile. Often Max would produce from his jacket pocket two delicious custard tarts or frangipanes, wrapped in a white linen napkin. It felt so special to be with him.

"This must seem very different from where you live," he said.

"Completely different," said Sarah. "When I walk out of my house, I can immediately hear the sea and I get glimpses of it between the trees as I walk through the wooded valley to the coast path. And when I get there, I see the Atlantic ocean before me, sometimes grey and turbulent and at other times, calm and a sparkling turquoise-blue."

"I'd like to see that," said Max.

"Then you must come," she said, and for a moment she wondered whether that had sounded too familiar. But it hadn't. For, although Sarah did not know this, Max was enjoying being with her.

He smiled. "Yes, I should like that. I've never been to England."

"But you speak very good English."

"I've always had a good ear for language," said Max, "and over the years, with our visitors and with scholars who have come to spend time with Angelique, I've spoken it a lot."

"Would you mind if I ask a question?"

"No, of course not. What is it?"

"I'd like to know how you first met, Angelique."

And so, Max began to tell her about his life.

"Although I've not always lived in Arques," he said, "I have always lived in this part of France. My parents were farmers and I grew up less than twenty miles from here. I was one of two sons, the youngest, and because I knew that my older brother was going to inherit the farm, I became a carpenter, first as an apprentice, then, after a while, a master carpenter."

Max stopped and for a while looked out across the pastures towards the distant mountains. Sarah waited for him to continue.

"I first came to Arques to help repair part of the roof of the church, and that is when I met Angelique. She was twenty, just a year younger than me, and she visited the church often while I was working, always sitting in the Magdalene chapel, with its high beamed roof and plain white walls. I was captured by her, and she seemed to be drawn to me. When I took a break from my work, she would bring me wine and food and, of course," and with this, he smiled, "she told me stories of the Cathars."

"Was she studying and writing even then?"

"Well, she always had her notebook with her, jotting down thoughts," he said. "I had never met anyone like her before and I found her utterly captivating. During the three months that I was working on the church roof, we spent lots of time together, and I think she liked me because I was so unlike her. She once told me that the only place she could rest was sitting beside me or watching me at work, cutting and planing smooth the wooden planks to make the rafters."

"But then you had to go home?"

"Yes, but not for long. My reputation as a carpenter had spread through the village and so I was asked to come back for other work, including work to her parents' house. And that was that. I've never left. She was an only child with no brothers or sisters, and when her parents became ill, I was there to help out. And then one day she asked me to marry her. She said she wanted to marry me, to know that I would always be there for her."

"And so you married and set up home here?"

"Yes. And because of her work, all the research she was doing, and then meetings with publishers and other scholars, she knew she had to travel, but she needed someone to come back to – she wanted me to be here. And that has always been fine because this is where I want to be."

He smiled his big smile. How good that must have felt, thought Sarah, to know that he was exactly where he wanted to be.

"And then her parents died, one quite soon after the other, and we decided we would use the house to help us make our living. We opened it as a B&B. Angelique has a talent for making places look good, and I do the things I love to do – undertake the renovations, keep the chickens and cook."

"And the bees?"

"The bees were always hers, or rather they were her mother's and then they were hers. They don't need constant attention and I can do what's needed when she is away. In fact, more recently, I have been doing most of the work with them. She is very caught up in her latest novel. When she is writing, nothing else matters as much as that book."

Sarah looked at this gentle, lovely man. He was wearing his big sheepskin coat again, and a red woollen scarf. His workman's boots reminded her a little of her father, who always wore similar ones. She found Max very attractive, though she was probably old enough to be his mother.

"When you tell me about all that you and Angelique do, it reminds me of that story in the Bible, the one about Mary and Martha."

Max raised an eyebrow. "What do you mean?"

"Well, as I remember it, Mary sits at the feet of Jesus, listening to his teachings whilst Martha works away in the kitchen, preparing the food and making sure that everyone has all that they need. Anyway, in the story as it has been written down, Mary is honoured as the one who is a disciple, the one who loves Jesus, but I have always wondered whether it isn't Martha who shows the greater love. Just like you."

Max laughed.

"I guess it might look like that," he said, "but the truth is I get to do what I want to do all the time, while Angelique is always under pressure from someone – her publisher and the people who want her to speak at conferences. Isn't the story just about love – about the different ways we love and are loved? And I am blessed with being loved."

That night, Sarah was once again moved to write in her journal.

Dearest Jeremiah

Being here, in a country where I do not speak the language, I have been engulfed in a kind of silence that I have rarely experienced; a kind of silence where I can hear who I really am. And when I listen deeply, I find that I am my true self when I allow my heart to open to this simplicity, by which I mean the simplicity of a lunch of bread and cheese, the simplicity of a walk in the countryside in the silence of companionship, simplicity in the love I feel for my newfound friends, which is not tainted by jealousy or competitiveness or ego, but is merely an acceptance of the other and who they are – who we are. I have come to realise that in the simplicity of acceptance lies the biggest adventure. Does that make sense to you?

As I have come to know you dear Jeremiah, I feel that you too are in a process of acceptance – accepting all that you are without judgment of what you are not. Am I right? And Max teaches me of acceptance which is not a passive thing. He has chosen his life with Angelique and he accepts their different but convergent paths. Isn't that wonderful? Simplicity and acceptance – these things are now shaping my own story.

It was their last evening in Arques, and Max was serving supper – coq au vin, a dish Max said Sarah must have before she left France. As usual, Miriam and Angelique were already deep in conversation about a long-lost text which they referred to as *The Book of Love*.

Sarah was intrigued. "Where do you think it is?" she asked.

"No-one really knows," Angelique replied. "At one time it was thought to be in Avignon, buried beneath the cathedral, but then others have said that it is in Tuscany, and others that it is still in the Holy Land."

"And do you think it is true that is was written by Mary Magdalene?"

"Well, the legend is that she created the book to record Jesus' teachings on Love, although some say it was written by him. It is a mystery, but perhaps it is fitting that this was to be his lasting testimony: not the crucifixion, not the resurrection, but Love."

Miriam was looking straight at Angelique as if she wanted to make sure she caught every word. She took out her notebook and wrote something down. Then, once more, the two of them were engrossed in a discussion about this *Book of Love*.

Sarah turned to Max. "This is a truly delicious meal," she said, and she meant it. And just as Angelique and Miriam deepened into their conversation, Sarah and Max deepened into theirs. It seemed to be what the four of them did: a beautiful ebb and flow of thoughts and ideas. Max told her what he was planning to do in the coming springtime, his schedule of repairs and maintenance, and his vision for the garden, too.

"You must come back next summer and see what I have done," he said.

"I'll try," said Sarah.

"No, you must return," he said.

"Okay, I will," she replied, smiling, "and I hope that you and Angelique will come and visit Miriam and me in Elmsford. I would love to show you the sights, just as you have shown me, here in Arques."

That was such a wonderful evening, and Sarah was as happy as she had ever been. Miriam had been right: now she was here she could have stayed for ever. And she felt a new confidence. She had left what she'd always known, had literally taken flight, and come to this foreign place and found it to be wonderful. She'd made new friends and enjoyed conversations about all sorts of things she hadn't known before – plumbing, repairing rafters, cooking with red wine, what chickens like to eat – to say nothing of all the stories that Angelique had told her about the Magdalene and the Cathars, people who until then she had only read about in books. And now, even when she got back to Elmsford, she would know that this place existed; that it was always there. She would be able to remember it and hopefully return to it. What was it that Max had said? "...you must return."

Sarah felt liberated, and as she went to bed that night, she was eager to write in her journal, to tell Jeremiah all about it.

My dear Jeremiah

It is our last night here in Arques, and it has been a wonderful experience. Tonight, I realised that for the first time in my life I have spent three weeks simply doing only the things I wanted to do. Never before in my life have I had such a luxury. And I have chosen to spend time with Max – who as Miriam said, is indeed gorgeous – and I have chosen to go for walks or simply sit and read. It has been as if I have stepped across a threshold and found on the other side nothing to be frightened of. Any fears I had of adventuring into the big wide world are entirely constructed in my imagination, for on the other side of the threshold is love, in all its many languages.

So now I have given myself permission to do exactly those things that feel right for me when I get home – just like when I decided to join the Elmsford Elderberries, which has become such a joy and a form of meditation for me.

When I return to Elmsford, I wonder if you will notice a difference in me, for I feel different. I feel like the real me for the first time in my life – as if nothing will ever be the same again.

On the flight back to Bristol, Miriam was preoccupied, busily writing in her notebook. She was so taken up with it that Sarah didn't want to disturb her, and anyway she was tired and closed her eyes. She must have fallen asleep, because before she knew it, they were preparing to land, and Miriam was packing her notebook into her bag.

As they drove back to Elmsford, they talked about their visit and Sarah asked Miriam what she had been writing on the plane.

"I just wanted to make sure I had made a note of that last conversation we had at supper – you know, when we talked about *The Book of Love*. It's all so fascinating. As you know, ever since my illness I've been interested in what Love really is, and now, having shared my ideas with Angelique, I want to look even deeper."

She stopped speaking so that she could concentrate on turning off the busy motorway, taking the roundabout that led towards Tiverton. It was a relief to be on the quieter country roads.

"You see, what I really want to do is to take Love seriously," she said. "Does that make sense?"

Sarah wasn't sure, but she knew that in a way, Miriam was talking as much to herself as to her. Sarah had come across this before with James. When he was focused on some particular aspect of his work, he would talk to her just as Miriam was doing, turning the matters over in his mind and talking about them aloud, in order to find what he was looking for. Now it seemed to Sarah as if Miriam was doing the same thing. She didn't mind.

Miriam and Angelique thought about Love in quite a different way than she did. It seemed to be an idea to them, whereas for her it was a way of being. And her time in France had made her realise that she could trust what she felt. She always enjoyed listening to Miriam and reading the books she'd given her, but something had changed. Sarah did not want to rely on books. She was deeply rooted and grounded, and this meant that she wanted to know Love in her heart and not her head. That was what Max knew. That was what she had learned from him.

They arrived back in Elmsford late in the afternoon. By then, both of them were very tired. Their time in France had been exhilarating but leaving it behind and the usual weariness of travelling had drained them. And so, when Miriam dropped her off at her cottage, Sarah was pleased to be alone.

"I'm going to be busy for the next day or so," said Miriam as they hugged each other goodbye. "I have so much buzzing around my head I need to find a space to sort myself out. I'll see you later in the week?"

"That sounds good," said Sarah.

That evening, sitting up in bed, Sarah was thinking about all that had happened in France, and what it now felt like to be back in Elmsford.

She opened her journal and once more, began to write.

My dear Jeremiah

I am home now, and I will see you soon, but part of me is still in France, revelling in all that I experienced, which is almost nothing and absolutely everything. Being there with Angelique and Max was very special, for it gave me a sense of self, and a sense of trust in myself. I am beginning to see that I understand love in ways that are different from Miriam and Angelique – but that is not to say better, just different. She has studied love and written about it, but it always seems to me that she looks at it from somewhere else, a little way away. Whereas, I have lived without love and with it, and whether it is there or not, I can't separate myself from it in the way Miriam does. I just can't.

For much of my life I had so little love that perhaps I came not to expect it. But when I fell in love with James, my dear James, I felt his love as if it held me, as if it had been waiting for me. And now, I feel it in such a variety of ways – my love for Alice, my sweet and gentle friend, my love for Katharine (I must call her tomorrow), and now my love for Miriam and for being in France and waking to each new day and the adventures it would bring.

There have been so many changes in my life recently. Some things I have lost – I've had to let go of James, and Katharine has gone to London

– but some things I've gained. My friendship with Miriam, and also, my friendship with you. It is all part of the language of love, which is so multifaceted, sparkling like the sunset on the sea.

Tonight, I am alone, and that is okay. I'm happy in my little cottage with Willow beside me, and dear friends so close at hand. I know that some people cannot bear to be alone, but I can; I need it. It is in solitude I find myself.

On a shelf in my kitchen is a cup and saucer, the cup painted with flowers, the saucer with a blue rim. Max gave it to me in case I wanted to drink coffee instead of tea. I shall do that and remember France and the understanding of loving awareness that deepened within me there.

ENCOUNTER WITH AN ANGEL

Jeremiah had invited Sarah and Miriam to join him for lunch in Appledore to celebrate their return from France, but Miriam declined for she was in writing mode, unable to turn her gaze from her computer screen and her mind from pondering what *The Book of Love* was really all about.

It was an unusually warm morning for early February, full of the promise of spring, with hazel catkins dancing jauntily in the breeze and the first few daffodils coming into flower to complement the snowdrops which were now in full bloom, whole swathes of them carpeting the roadside verges and dotted in the hedgerows. Sarah loved snowdrops. They seemed so hopeful, so brave.

Before heading to the café for lunch they decided to take a saunter along the busy harbour quay, Jeremiah noting that Sarah was in good spirits.

They stopped and sat on one of the many benches conveniently set for admiring the view across the estuary towards Instow. The little ferry boat had already begun to carry visitors from one shore to the other, and there was a line of small children sitting on the harbour wall, dangling fishing lines into the water, hoping to catch crabs. For a while they just sat there and watched the world go by.

Then they walked along the quaint street of colourful houses and out into the sandy bay where the lifeboat lay at anchor. It was almost low tide and the lifeboat had settled on the sand at a peculiar angle. Sarah bent down and picked up a shell that had washed up on the beach.

"I wrote letters to you when I was in France," she said, offering him the shell with a smile.

"Did you? I didn't get any," he replied, turning over the shell in his hand, admiring its lustre.

"I didn't send them! I wrote them in a journal that Miriam gave me as a Christmas present. But writing about my adventures to a dear friend really helped me to immerse myself in the experience of being in France. Does that make any sense to you?"

"It makes perfect sense, Sarah. I email my friend Angela on a regular basis, and I tell her about things that have been happening in my life – just the little things – but having written about them, I see them for what they are. Perhaps the focus of writing helps us to become more aware of how things really are– of what is changing and of what needs to change? That's how it seems to me anyway."

Was it because she called him her dear friend, or was it the serenity he always experienced being in her presence? He wasn't sure, but as they stood there,

Jeremiah decided that there was something important he wanted to share with her.

"Sarah," he said, "I want to tell you something that I've only ever mentioned to one other person."

"I'm honoured. What is it?"

Jeremiah hesitated, unsure of whether this was really a wise decision, but then, because he had begun to trust his heart, to listen to his heart, he came out with it.

"I have an angel," he said, looking straight into her eyes, "named Angel."

Sarah looked inquisitively at Jeremiah.

"You mean, like a guardian angel?"

"Yes, I suppose so. Ever since I was seventeen, I've had an angel who I can see and talk to."

"How wonderful! I don't think I've ever actually seen an angel," she said. "You are blessed, Jeremiah."

"Angel told me once that everyone has an angel."

Sarah stopped and looked out across the waves, deep in thought.

"Do you remember I told you that when my beloved James died, I wanted so much to be able to see him, but I never did? I certainly talked to him, and although he never spoke to me, I'm sure I felt his presence, like you did, that time you sat on his veranda at The Sanctuary. And I knew when he left this world, I knew the very moment he left. So, if it's possible to feel connected to someone when they die, then perhaps it's not such a leap of imagination to believe in angels? And I hope that if I do have an angel, one day, I'll see him – or her."

"Or both," said Jeremiah looking at the shell Sarah had given him. "Or neither."

"Did you see your angel that day at Miriam's when

we'd only just met, and she said you looked like you'd seen a ghost?"

"I did, but I didn't want to say so, in case you thought I was a bit strange."

As soon as he said that Angel appeared and stood beside them in his brown hooded robe, the small wings at his feet enabling him to hover an inch or so above the sand. He called her name.

"Sarah."

Sarah turned and at once, saw Angel, her eyebrows knitting quizzically.

"I'm sorry, I don't think I know you?"

"I'm Angel."

Sarah gasped, and reached out towards Jeremiah, taking his arm to steady herself.

"Don't worry," Jeremiah said. "The first time I saw Angel, I fainted."

"Are you really an angel?" she whispered.

"I am," Angel replied. And using his ankle wings, he lifted himself a few more inches off the sand.

For a moment, Sarah just watched in wonder, but then a memory came to her.

"I saw you one day, standing with Jeremiah, on the harbour wall at Elmsford Wharf. I thought you were a trick of the light, as one moment you were there, and the next you were gone."

"Yes, Angel is like that," Jeremiah chuckled.

Sarah looked at Angel for a long time, savouring this moment, hardly able to believe her eyes. Then a question began forming in her mind.

"Tell me Angel, have you ever seen someone after they have died?" she asked.

Angel slowly descended and looked at Sarah with deep kindness.

"You mean James."

"Yes..."

"I'm an angel, and what you think of as death does not exist in the angelic realm. You see, James's physical body returned to the earth and the sea when his ashes were scattered, but his spirit remained for a while before re-entering the realms of the Cosmos. That is why you felt his presence and why, from time to time, when he is close, you still feel him, particularly in places he loved."

"You mean, like on his veranda?"

"Exactly."

"But why did Jeremiah feel his presence?"

"Because Jeremiah has always been closer to our realm than most people. It's why he is as he is."

Sarah frowned.

"Sometimes it seems as if Angel speaks in riddles," said Jeremiah, "but eventually, everything settles and becomes clear."

At that moment Angel's whole being became shimmering and translucent, and with wings outstretched and magnificent, he said, "I shall leave you now, but I will be with you again, Sarah."

And with that, Angel disappeared from view.

"I wonder what she meant by that?" asked Sarah, a strange excitement causing her to feel breathless.

Jeremiah frowned. "What do you mean 'she'?"

"Angel – she's a 'she' isn't she?"

"Not to me."

"Really?"

"Well... Angel once told me that angels appear to humans in the form we expect to see," said Jeremiah, "so perhaps to you, angels are mostly female?"

"Yes, they are, now you come to mention it. I hadn't thought of it that way before, but when I see angels in stained glass windows or paintings, I always see them as feminine."

"Do you? How interesting – I always think of angels as masculine, but Angel tells me they are neither and both. It's all very confusing."

"But what do you think Angel meant when she said, 'I'll be with you again'."

"I'm not always sure what he means," said Jeremiah, "but there must be some connection between you and Angel. He'll tell you about it when the time is right. This is so wonderful for me, Sarah, because actually you are the only person apart from me who has ever seen him."

"Or her! Why me though, I wonder?"

"I don't know, but I'm really pleased it is you. And Angel will guide you when the time comes. That seems to be the way with angels."

"I think we need to go and have our lunch now," said Sarah, suddenly feeling cold. "All this excitement has given me an appetite."

"And let's keep what happened just now between the two of us, shall we?" said Jeremiah. "I think that would be wise, for now."

"I agree. If I told my son that I'd met an angel, I think he would try to have me locked-up."

They walked back to the café and found a table upstairs in a little window nook, looking out across the estuary. Jeremiah noticed that the tide was coming in at quite a rate now, covering the mudbanks and widening the river considerably. He loved high tide, and had begun to make a note of its various depths, which in the Bristol Channel with the second highest tidal range in the world, were extremely variable. A 9.4 metre high tide was a spectacular sight.

"It was lovely for me to be able to talk about James again," said Sarah, "and it's good to know that you're in touch with Angela. Our loved ones stay with us, somehow, don't they?"

"You are right, they do – if we let them – but there was a long time when I completely shut Angela out of my life. I blamed her for bringing our relationship to an end, but in fact, I did that. I wanted her to be someone she wasn't, and I couldn't accept that, not for a long, long time. But then, after we sold the business, I had what I now think of as a 'breakdown', although Angel calls it my 'breakthrough'. I had to hit rock bottom before I could pick up the pieces and recreate the puzzle of my life. And eventually, I felt strong enough to reach out to Angela, and she welcomed me with open arms. Now we keep in fairly regular contact by email, and sometimes letter, and it means so much to me. She often invites me to visit her in Italy, but I've never been a great one for travelling."

"Nor me, until I met Miriam. But now, I love it. You must come with us to France this summer, Jeremiah."

"That's so kind of you. I'd like that – I think! Perhaps the time has come?"

"The walrus said..."

They giggled.

Jeremiah drank some of the hot chocolate that they'd both ordered after their main course of fish chowder – it really was exceptional and deserved of the reputation it gave the café. Not too sweet, with bitter undertones and a velvety texture.

"You must think my story an odd one, Sarah?"

'Well, it is a bit… out of the ordinary," said Sarah, smiling at him and resting her hand on his arm, "but then, who wants 'ordinary'? I think people thought my relationship with James was odd, too. It doesn't matter really, does it?"

"No, it doesn't. And anyway, what makes complete sense to one person, may be gobbledygook to another."

"Quite."

"By the way Jeremiah, my friend Katharine's coming to see me this weekend. I'm sorry you didn't get to meet her last time she was here, so could we pop down to Coombe Cottage on Saturday to say hello?"

"Yes, please do. I'd like that very much."

It was dark by the time Jeremiah arrived home that evening, and he lit his wood stove. Thoughts were coursing around in his head. He poured himself a glass of wine and for quite some while just sat in his armchair, contemplating all that had happened.

Apart from Angela, he had never before spoken about his relationship with Angel to anyone, not even Stephen and Jenny, and yet it seemed Sarah did not think it odd at all. She accepted the whole thing. She did not judge. A sense of relief flooded over him. It was always so easy to talk to Sarah, and it felt so natural to introduce her to Angel, so… normal. And she saw Angel! She beheld Angel and spoke with him. Or her.

For Jeremiah that was such a validation of his whole life because here was someone else who could see his angel. It was like a miracle.

I really love my new life here in Devon, he thought to himself. *I feel more 'me' than I have ever done before.*

Angel appeared and stood beside him.

"Thank you for coming to Sarah, on the beach."

"She came to me, Jeremiah."

"What? You mean because she believed in you?"

"Well, that too, but her story has yet to unfold."

"In what way?"

"That is for Sarah to decide."

"And she saw you as a woman..."

"She did. And yet, we are not what you see."

Jeremiah smiled.

"Over the years, Angel," he said, "I have learned not to over-think what you say to me, because I know it will always, eventually, become clear. Quite when is another matter, but I now know that at some point I will understand what it is you are talking about. I have learnt to trust in your riddles."

"The wise fool always speaks in riddles."

"There you go – you've just proved that what I said is true."

Jeremiah began to laugh. Suddenly, he saw how utterly wonderful it was to have had Angel as his companion all these years and how everything Angel had brought to him was meaningful, although it sometimes took him forever to work out why.

"You know," he said, "this is another of those moments when I feel something shifting, something that allows me to see and delight in the wonderful absurdity of our lives together." And he laughed again.

"It's good to hear you laugh Jeremiah," said Angel. "Sometimes I think you take everything far too seriously."

"I do, don't I," smiled Jeremiah, "but I know I have been very fortunate. Moving here and all that has happened... I feel like I lived in a desert before I came to this oasis. Everything is starting to make some sense to me, now. I can see that we are born as we are, but with the potential to become ourselves.

"You once told me that I was blessed, Angel, and now I've come to realise that it is true. I am truly blessed. Sarah said it today, and I can see it now. I don't know why it took me so long to see it, but it took as long as it took."

"You are beginning to sound like me now," said Angel. "You are speaking in riddles."

"Perhaps you are rubbing off on me at last? You have helped me to be at peace with who I am. And now you are helping me be at peace with who you are. I am now at peace with my angel."

"Jeremiah, if you were not as you are, you wouldn't be asking the questions you are asking. And by asking your questions you are becoming who you are."

"That's a good one."

"It is not a riddle. It is your truth."

"I know. I'm starting to see it, or perhaps as you said the other day, I'm starting to see the possibility of it. I'm coming into bloom! There's nothing like a late bloomer is there?"

"It's not possible to be late. As I've told you, the timing is always perfect."

Jeremiah stood up and went into his kitchen to pour himself another glass of wine. Once upon a time, these conversations with Angel would have confused him, frustrated him somewhat. Now, every time Angel spoke it seemed like the fog was beginning to clear. A burst of happiness flooded his being. He found he could not stop smiling.

Angel smiled too.

"You always know what I am thinking, don't you?" said Jeremiah admiring his friend's beatific face.

"Well, of course I do," replied Angel, "but something else is beginning to happen, Jeremiah. You are coming closer to me. Our wavelengths are converging. Or perhaps yours are becoming more refined, although, of course, you may not have noticed it. It's very difficult for you humans because you are surrounded with things. Dense matter. So that is what you notice. It's what your senses notice, but it is not the whole story. Humans always assume there is a 'thing' out there – a god or a creator who makes the world the way it is, but that is only a glimpse of the reality; a rather clumsy way to grasp the magnitude of what is.

"But, my dear Jeremiah, you have begun to accept the no-thingness of reality. You are learning to accept presence, and beingness, the way everything is. That is a huge leap of imagination and you have been able to tune-in to it, and that brings you closer to me."

"I think I'm too old for all of this."

"Then stop thinking."

"And do what?"

"You don't need to do anything you just need to surrender. You just need to let yourself become at one with all that is, and then you will hear the voice of the Cosmos answering your questions."

Now Jeremiah was quiet.

"Try it," said Angel, "just try it. Take a deep breath in, and then let it out slowly. Feel the space that it creates inside you. A space between all the words that are swirling around inside your head. Just try it."

Jeremiah took in a deep breath and then let it out, and another, and another. Slowly, he felt a space opening within him and all around him. And as he did so he remembered his dream where he was sitting on the riverbank. That is how he had felt then and that is how he felt now. A deep, all-pervading peacefulness.

Angel disappeared, his work done for the day.

On Saturday morning, as had been arranged, Sarah and Katharine called in to Coombe Cottage to see Jeremiah. He opened the door to them, kissing Sarah's cheek and shaking Katharine's hand.

"I forgot to mention that there's an art exhibition over in the church this weekend, and they're serving teas and coffees. Shall we wander over and take a look?" he asked.

"Why not? That would be lovely," said Sarah, and Katharine smiled in agreement.

They walked through the churchyard and exchanged a few friendly hellos to the dozen or so people who were milling around by the tea tent, which was pitched near the south entrance. They entered the church where about thirty paintings and a couple of sculptures, all by local artists, had been arranged on easels or leaned against walls and balanced on pews. There was nobody else in the church.

Unseen by Jeremiah, Sarah had walked up to the rood screen where, to one side, she saw an elderly woman in an apron washing the flagstone floor. Sarah watched her as she worked and, as if she knew she was being scrutinised, the woman raised her head and smiled at Sarah. Her eyes were penetrating, discerning, unnerving.

Sarah turned briefly to see Jeremiah and Katharine walking towards her, but when she looked back to the woman she had gone.

"It's a rather good exhibition," said Katharine. "There's some real artistic talent in Elmsford."

The day had turned chilly, so they decided to walk back to Jeremiah's house for a cup of tea in the warm rather than stand in the windy tea tent.

Jeremiah lifted the plant-pot to retrieve his front door key, and then took their coats and hung them on the pegs in his hallway They were all cold and grateful to be back in the warmth of his house, Katherine noticing how tasteful the paintings and soft furnishing were. After moving into her flat with Tom, she'd come to realise that she loved making a house into a home and it seemed that Jeremiah did too.

Katharine and Sarah sat on Jeremiah's comfortable sofa to drink their tea whilst Jeremiah busied himself lighting the wood stove. Katharine was full of stories about her new job at the school in London and she swapped anecdotes with Jeremiah about teaching children, not all of whom wanted to be there. She also talked about Tom's work and how well thought of he was by his colleagues.

"His grandfather would be so proud of him," she said, turning to Sarah.

"He certainly would," said Sarah smiling. She put down her cup of tea to give Katharine a big hug, and as she did so she saw Angel standing behind Jeremiah, wearing a shimmering white gown, her wings outstretched with a soft light around her. She placed her right hand over her heart and bowed towards Sarah.

"I have something to tell you, Sarah," Katharine said unexpectedly. "Tom and I went to visit my mother last weekend."

"Oh, darling. I'm so pleased for you. How did it go?"

"It was good, actually. She seemed… different, happy even. And you'll never guess what? She's doing an Open University degree in English Literature. You could've knocked me down with a feather when she told me that, but she loves it. I'm so pleased for her – and she loved Tom too – but then, who wouldn't?"

As they prepared to leave, and whilst Katharine had gone to the bathroom, Sarah told Jeremiah that she had seen Angel surrounded by light and that she had bowed towards her as if to acknowledge her.

Jeremiah thought for a moment. "I think Angel is beginning to say something to you," he said.

"And when I was in the church, and you were talking to Katharine," she said, "I thought I saw an elderly woman washing the floor beside the altar, but then, when I looked again, she'd disappeared. It was almost as if I had imagined it. Have you ever seen her?"

"I have," said Jeremiah. "Angel introduced me to her, and I think that she is an angel too. I think she appears to those of us who need to be reassured about the presence of angels."

Sarah turned to Jeremiah and embraced him.

"Thank you for introducing me to the angels," she whispered.

RECONCILIATION

One morning in May after driving to the neighbouring village with Sarah to see Bernard for morning coffee in his walled garden, Jeremiah arrived home to find the post had been delivered and there was a letter from Italy on his doormat. He recognised Angela's inimitable handwriting. He walked into his study and sat at his desk.

My Dear Jeremiah

I hope all is well with you, though as you know for me, this has been such a sad time, getting used to life without Francesca. At first, all the legal stuff and the decisions that had to be made about the school kept my mind occupied, but now I find myself with time to think.

And I have been thinking how strange it is that we are both old and have lived most of our lives apart, and yet we still love one another. And then, I remembered what I said about coming to see you, and I remembered you telling me about the lovely village you live in now, with its wonderful church and glorious sea views... Well, I have decided that I would like to see the church and the views – and of course, I would like to see you. What do you think?

I am coming to London in June, and I was wondering if I could then come to see you? Stephen and Jenny have said they would drive me to Devon, and we could find a nice local B&B to stay the night in.

What do you think? Might we see each other again?

With much love

Angela x

Jeremiah set down the letter, looking at it as it lay there on his desk. Then he picked it up, read it again and smelled the paper to see if it carried a trace of Angela's perfume. It didn't.

Angel appeared and stood by the window.

"I have a letter from Angela," said Jeremiah. "She wants to come and visit. What do you make of that?"

"It is rather wonderful, isn't it?"

"You know, I think it is. After all these years we are now very tender towards each other."

"So, will you invite her to come?"

Jeremiah looked out of his study window, across his

garden and toward the church, which was caught in the sunlight.

"Yes," he said. "I want her to come."

It was a Friday morning in mid-June. Jeremiah looked out of his cottage window and saw coming up his garden path, three rather elderly-looking friends: the familiar forms of Stephen, Jenny and a short woman, with grey hair plaited and neatly coiled on the top of her head, and wide, piercingly blue eyes. It was Angela. After all the years, his heart now beat faster, and he could not help himself from smiling. He was very pleased to see her.

He opened his front door and welcomed everyone in, hugging first Stephen and Jenny and then Angela, who beamed up at him. She took his arm as they came into the cottage, looking around, admiring his home.

"How was your B&B?" he asked.

"Just perfect. And we arrived last night in time to call in and say hello to Bernard. What a nice man. Then he suggested that we all stay and have a bite of supper with him. It was so nice of him as we were all quite ravenous after the long drive from London," said Angela, wandering over to the window to take in the view of the back garden and out across the fields.

"It certainly was good to see him again," said Jenny, "and it's wonderful to see you too Jeremiah. You look so well. I do believe the country life suits you."

"I am well. And I'm so glad you had time to spend with Bernard. He has been such a wonderful friend to me over the years, and it's thanks to him that I found this house, you know."

It was Bernard who had recommended the B&B in his village, and so Jeremiah arranged for his friends to stay there, having only one tiny spare bedroom himself.

"I've made some coffee and Grace from the village shop makes fabulous cakes, so I've bought a selection. Shall we go through to the garden room? It looks like we might have a shower of rain, otherwise we could sit in the garden."

There was laughter and endless conversation; of Italy and Istanbul, carpets and frescoes, children, grandchildren, gardens and the joys of westcountry life.

"You seem very happy here, Jeremiah," Angela said, smiling at him. "You look so well, and you seem at ease, somehow."

"Do you know, I am at ease. That is the very quality I feel living here. I am at ease with myself – at long last!"

They all laughed and their smiles were imbued with great love for each other.

"Shall we go for a little walk before lunch?" asked Angela. "The rain shower seems to have passed and I'd like to stretch my legs and see this famous village of yours."

"You two go," said Jenny, "and Stephen and I will prepare the lunch. Take your time."

Jeremiah smiled at Jenny. She knew these two old friends needed a bit of time together.

Arm in arm, they set off up the lane overhung with

trees that led to the village, and then they took a roundabout route, out towards the cliff. They came to the L-shaped bench that had become one of Jeremiah's favourite places in the world.

"Wow," Angela exclaimed. "Shall we sit here for a bit? The view is incredible."

For a while they just sat in peaceable silence. Then Angela said, "This is such a beautiful place, Jeremiah. Not just here, but the village, your house… It reminds me of all that I have missed, living in a foreign country – you know, living away from that which is familiar. Living away from home."

"Is that how you feel about living in Florence, that you are not at home?"

"Well, sometimes it is, yes. Not all the time, of course, but I don't think I've ever felt fully settled in Florence. Not quite. What you said to me on the telephone that day about acceptance of where you are – it really resonated with me. Florence is undoubtedly a beautiful place, and for someone like me who has devoted her life to its history and art, it's been like attending a feast, but – I don't know… I think I'm full, Jeremiah. In the end one can have too much of a good thing. Sometimes I wonder if it is time for me to come home, but I know that now, so soon after Francesca's death, is not the right time for me to be making life-changing decisions."

Jeremiah looked at this woman sitting beside him, so familiar and yet in many ways, a stranger.

"I know exactly what you mean, Angela. Looking back, I spent most of my 'three-score years and ten' in Spitalfields and yet, it wasn't really home. It was just where I lived. But now, I've found my way home," he said. "It has only taken me a lifetime."

"It was home when we lived there together, though, wasn't it?" ventured Angela, unsure as to whether this turn in the conversation was still forbidden territory.

"Yes, it was home when we were there together. Maybe home is as much about the people as the place?"

"I think you're right Jeremiah, and I think that's why I'm feeling like this – because Francesca isn't there any more."

Jeremiah found her hand and squeezed it reassuringly. "Yes, perhaps it is."

By the time Jeremiah and Angela arrived back at the cottage, Stephen and Jenny had prepared a picnic lunch and laid it out on Jeremiah's garden table. Jeremiah had bought all the foods he knew they liked – cheeses, good bread, leafy salad, olives and quiches, and two bottles of Valpolicella.

It was a wonderful lunch and they talked and talked and talked.

Later that afternoon, as Jenny and Stephen were resting under the shade of the apple tree before the long drive home, Angela asked Jeremiah if she could see the rest of his garden.

He was delighted to show her all the work he and Giles had done to make the garden beautiful and productive, an organic haven. Eventually, they came to the summerhouse shaded by trees and shrubs. Jeremiah opened the door and fetched two deck chairs and set them side by side, so they could sit together in the dappled sunshine.

Jezebel walked up to them, her tail raised high and

Jeremiah introduced her to Angela, who stroked the cat's head. Jezebel, enjoying the attention, jumped up on her lap, padded her paws rhythmically a few times and then curled into a ball to sleep.

"You should be honoured," said Jeremiah. "She usually disappears when visitors arrive."

"So, are you happy, then Jeremiah – living by yourself in this beautiful countryside?"

"You know, I think I am. And I don't feel as if I am living by myself. I have made a few really wonderful new friends, which is enough for me. And I always have Angel."

"Of course – you still have your angel. That must be such a comfort."

"Oh yes."

"I never found mine… my angel. I suppose I've never really looked."

Angela stopped speaking and looked at the man beside her, taking in all the changes in his demeanour, not least the serenity he now seemed to exude.

"I'm so glad we were able to do this, Jeremiah. To put our past behind us and to acknowledge our love for one another. I'm so glad to see you again. Those sporadic lunches in London helped, but today I feel we have properly reconnected. Do you feel it too?"

Jeremiah smiled at his friend. "I feel it too," he said, and he took her hand in his.

"I know there were all sorts of reasons that separated us," said Angela, "and I know how painful that was – for both of us – but I am forever grateful that we met when we did and had those years together. They were some of the happiest of my life. And even though we may not see each other for a while, I know where you are now, and I can think of you being here. I can picture you in this beautiful garden, knowing you are happy, that you are content, at last."

"I am content, and I think you are wise to stay in Florence, at least for a while, Angela. Rebuilding a life takes a lot of energy."

"Yes, and I certainly don't have much of that at the moment. Losing Francesca has taken it out of me on so many levels, and Florence is where I have made a life for myself. Despite the fact that sometimes I really miss England I have many good friends there. My life is there, for now."

"Yes, of course. And who knows, perhaps one day I will be ready to come and see you. My friend Sarah and I have talked about doing a bit of travelling." It was the first time he had mentioned Sarah by name.

"Well, she is obviously a good influence on you. And if you did come to visit, you would both be made very welcome. I know my friends would love you, Jeremiah. As I do." She looked at him, tears in her eyes.

Jeremiah lifted her hand to his lips, kissing her fingers.

"Let us keep in touch, then," he said. "I do love those postcards you send me, with your crazy spidery handwriting."

She laughed. "That's a deal."

Angela gently lifted Jezebel and laid her in the long grass. They stood up and walked back into the house where Stephen and Jenny were packing things away.

"I guess we had better be going," said Stephen. "It's a long drive home." Then turning to Jeremiah, he said,

"It's been so good to catch up, mate. It's a lovely place you have here."

"Then come and see me any time – now we know there's a good B&B close by, you have no excuse."

The two men hugged, a lifetime of friendship connecting them.

Jeremiah waved as the car disappeared up the lane towards the village.

He wasn't sure when he would see Angela again, but he realised that the deep sense of loss he'd harboured for all those years had gone. She was part of his life, no matter how small a part. Loss was replaced with the recovery of love.

Jezebel brushed against his leg and he picked her up and held her, feeling her purring against his chest.

A SACRED MARRIAGE

Two weeks later, Jeremiah was putting the finishing touches to supper. A macaroni cheese was warming in the bottom oven of the Aga and a green salad was ready in its bowl under a cloth, waiting to be dressed. He had opened a bottle of wine and put out a bowl of crisps. At any moment he was expecting Sarah, who he had invited to join him for supper. Miriam was in France at a conference in Chartres, and Sarah and Jeremiah chose more and more often to be in each other's company.

She arrived at the appointed time, looking radiant, or so Jeremiah thought. Her long straight hair was held back with hair slides to keep it out of her eyes, and she was wearing a cream shirt and dark blue wide and elegant linen trousers. She had taken off her sandals at the front door and Jeremiah noticed that she had painted her toenails pink. She was holding a book.

"I thought you might like this," she said. "I saw it in the bookshop in Bideford and thought of you. It looks fascinating."

Jeremiah took the book and looked at the front cover: *Angels: A Visible and Invisible History* by Peter

Sanford. He flicked through the pages.

"It does look as if it might be rather 'me', doesn't it? I must show it to Angel."

And as if on cue, Angel appeared and glanced over Jeremiah's shoulder at the book.

"It's extraordinary how mistaken everyone is about angels," he said. "They always like to show us as being so far away, when actually we are ever present. No wonder people don't see us."

"Well," said Sarah, "ever since Jeremiah introduced me to you, I've wished I had my own angel to keep me company."

"But you do have," said Angel.

"What do you mean?"

"I mean you have an angel who has always been with you, waiting for you."

"Is that really true?" Sarah looked at Jeremiah for reassurance, and he nodded.

"It is true, my dear Sarah," Angel replied gently.

"But I've never seen my angel..."

Angel smiled.

"Do you want to see your angel?" she asked.

"Yes, I do, please."

"Come with me then. We are going to the church."

And Angel stood up and beckoned to Sarah and Jeremiah to follow.

Sarah again looked at Jeremiah, who smiled reassuringly and shrugged his shoulders. He wasn't sure what was happening but he knew it was important.

"We'd better go," he said. "It's not every day you meet your angel. Just remember what happened to me when I first met mine."

Jeremiah fetched Sarah's shawl and his jacket, and they followed Angel across the road and up the steep steps to the church, then went inside.

"Please come and stand here between the front pews and look towards the altar," Angel said, and Sarah and Jeremiah did as they were asked.

Angel stood in front of them in a long flowing white robe that shimmered like a pearl, wings spread wide. At once, all around them, there was a wondrous light, white and yellow and gold. Angel took both of their hands and knelt before them.

Then Angel spoke. "I am your angel Jeremiah, and I am your angel too, Sarah."

This time neither Jeremiah nor Sarah fainted, for they were transfixed by the golden light and by the enormity of what Angel had just said.

For some time they just stood there, gazing at this incredible being kneeling before them, who had uttered such momentous words.

Jeremiah and Sarah shared an angel…

Slowly, the light around them dispersed though Angel was still kneeling before them.

"There is something else," said Angel producing a square leather pouch, the size of a small book. Angel opened the pouch and took from it what at first looked like a wooden box with a beautiful painted lid. But then Sarah and Jeremiah could see that it wasn't a box at all, it was a triptych, an icon in three panels, the two outer panels folding on top of each other into the centre. It was very beautiful, painted in reds and greens and blues on a gold background. Angel stood and placed it on the altar, and then turned and spoke to them.

"This panel on the right is Mary Magdalene washing the feet of Yeshua, and this one on the left is Yeshua washing the feet of Mary Magdalene after the Last Supper, when he washed the feet of all his disciples. And this one in the centre is Mary and Yeshua sitting beside each other on a throne. It depicts the sacred marriage between them."

Angel beheld Sarah and Jeremiah, their faces rapt in attention.

"A sacred marriage has nothing to do with a physical relationship. It is an expression of divine tenderness, and it arises when two people come together in a spiritual union. Their souls become intertwined, and together they express both the feminine and the masculine qualities of the Divine. Sometimes when two souls are destined to come together in this way, a single angel will become their guardian. As I am yours."

The church was quiet and for a while neither Sarah nor Jeremiah said anything. Then Sarah lifted her eyes and looked at Angel.

"You mean that Jeremiah and I are souls entwined?"

"I do," said Angel.

A deep silence fell upon them and eventually Angel disappeared from view.

Jeremiah shivered and took Sarah's arm.

"Come on, let's go and have supper," he whispered, pulling his jacket closer around him.

Sarah sat at the dining table, deep in thought, whilst Jeremiah finished off the supper preparations.

They were both still trying to make sense of what had just happened, when Angel reappeared.

"What was that all about, Angel?" Sarah asked.

"Well, you did ask to see your angel."

"So… you are both Jeremiah's angel and my angel?"

"I am. It has always been so."

"But why haven't I seen you before?"

"You have noticed my presence in what you thought was the fluttering of birds' wings or the nearness of James, and being close to Jeremiah has helped, but also, you've never asked to see your angel before now."

"No, that is true… So, what happens now?"

"I have no idea, Sarah. I'm an angel, not a prophet!"

And with that, Angel disappeared again, leaving Sarah and Jeremiah contemplating all they had heard.

When Angel uttered the word 'prophet' Jeremiah suddenly recalled a day in London, not long after he had retired and was experiencing his 'breakthrough', and Angel had told him that he would one day fulfil his name, that he would have something to say. And this was that moment, Jeremiah felt sure. He knew what he had to say to Sarah. A feeling of everything falling into place settled upon him, bringing with it such a deep sense of surrender that it brought tears to his eyes.

"I think that this is what was always going to be, my dear, dear Sarah. I think that both of us had to experience deep love and loss in order to open our hearts to Divine Tenderness. I think that although we did not know it, we were destined to meet each other at some point in our lives and that Angel always knew this and led me to you. And now it has happened and there is something special between us – we are who we are, and we accept each other and love each other for being true to ourselves. I think we have lived a prophecy. And perhaps we have found something that we didn't know we were looking for – the divine tenderness that makes us whole?"

"Oh, Jeremiah – that is so beautiful. Divine tenderness is what my heart opened to after the death of James. Now I understand why I met him and how it led me to you. It was always going to happen."

They sat in deep silence for a long time before Sarah said, "You know, now I come to think about it, I have often felt a presence in my life; I have heard the flutter of wings and thought it a bird or felt the presence of another being and thought it was James, but since meeting Angel, I now know it was Angel. She has been by my side all my life, but it was you who opened me to her. It is you who has led me to this place of such tenderness. From the first moment we met, you have always felt very familiar to me – as if, somehow, I've known you all my life, or perhaps even in a past life."

She got up and stood behind him, putting her arms around his shoulders and kissing him gently on the top of his head. "I am so happy to be with you tonight. This is where I want to be."

"And I feel such gratitude that you are here," replied Jeremiah, "and it is so good to finally understand what Angel meant when, some while ago, he spoke to me of divine tenderness. Now I know what it is, what it feels like. Souls entwined."

"Souls entwined… Yes, I feel it's true."

They sat together in Jeremiah's kitchen eating and talking for a very long time. Eventually, Sarah looked at her watch.

"Goodness me! It's the early hours of the morning. I must go home."

"Why don't you stay?" said Jeremiah, surprising himself. "I have a lovely spare room upstairs, tiny but cosy. And I'm sure I can find a spare toothbrush."

"That's very kind of you, Jeremiah. I'd like that very much. I feel I want to be here tonight, with you and with Angel."

"And with Jezebel."

'Of course – how could I forget?"

Jeremiah showed Sarah to her room, pointing out the tiny guest bathroom with the sit-up bath, which she found enchanting. Then he kissed her tenderly on both cheeks and bade her goodnight.

As he lay in his own bed, contemplating all that had happened since the mugging and his flight from London, he realised that he had arrived at the very place he wanted to be. A place of tenderness and companionship, in a realm that was somehow set apart; here in Elmsford, at the edge of the world.

REMEMBRANCE

Sarah stayed with Jeremiah that night and after going home to get some fresh clothes, she stayed the following night and the one after that. They wanted to be together and together they explored the puzzle of their lives. Yet, in truth there was almost nothing to be said. Overwhelming acceptance was what they both felt. Acceptance of the way things were.

As Sarah and Jeremiah were having their lunch on the third day of her stay, the phone rang.

"Hello Jeremiah – it's Miriam. I've just got back from France. Sarah sent me a message to say she's staying with you. How are you both?"

"We're fine. How was the conference?"

"It was interesting, to say the least. I was wondering, would the two of you like to join me for afternoon tea? We've got lots of catching up to do."

"That would be lovely. Thank you. See you in a bit."

Later that day, Jeremiah and Sarah walked hand in hand through the churchyard, past the fishermen's cottages and along the little wooded footpath to The Sanctuary. The front door opened, and Miriam came out to welcome them, warmly hugging them both. They went into her house, and made themselves comfortable, Jeremiah and Sarah sitting together on the sofa.

"So, tell us about the conference," Jeremiah said, reaching for a piece of fruitcake from the plate Miriam was proffering.

"Are you sure you want to know? I don't want to bore you – it's just my work, after all."

"Miriam – we want to know," said Sarah vehemently. "You have brought so much to our lives with your wisdom – please don't stop now."

"Oh, alright then," Miriam beamed, obviously delighted that they were interested. "Most of it was what you might expect: all sorts of stuff about Mary Magdalene and whether or not she really did die in France. There was a lot of argument and disagreement, and the truth seems to be that no-one really knows what happened. There was even an argument about whether she was the first to come to Yeshua's tomb. Yes, she was. No, she wasn't. She was the first to have seen the risen Christ. No, she wasn't…

"But there was one rather remarkable moment when a woman who described herself as a 'Dreamer' shared a dream in which she was sitting at the foot of a crucifixion cross. Not quite at the foot, a little distance away. Nearby, she said, there were two men, who she thought were soldiers, because they carried spears. There were three women there, too, sitting together in front of her. They were looking up at the figure of a man who was being crucified. His feet were nailed and resting on a small platform. There were also nails, horrid big nails, through his hands, pinning him to the cross beam, and his head had fallen forward onto his chest. He was having difficulty breathing. The women were not wailing. It was as if they were concentrating too much to cry. Then one of them, said, 'Give it to him now,' and the woman to whom she had spoken took a sponge, having first soaked it in what looked like water from a bowl beside her and offered it up to the man on the cross on the end of a long pole. He drank from the sponge. She did it again, and he drank again. This happened once more, and then the first woman said to the third woman, 'Go, tell Joseph that it is done.' The woman ran off leaving the two other women, still looking up at the man on the cross, who seemed to have fallen into a state of unconsciousness. The Dreamer woman said she thought there must have been some kind of drug in the water that was carried to the man via the sponge."

Miriam paused, the scene vivid in her mind's eye.

"As you can imagine, by now everyone at the conference was listening intently, and you could have heard a pin drop in the auditorium. The woman continued and said she didn't know how long it took, quite some time she thought, but the man who was called Joseph came with two others carrying a ladder. They showed the soldiers guarding the cross a scroll of paper. The soldiers read the scroll, looked at each other and then nodded. The man called Joseph and the two other men put the ladder against the cross. One of the men climbed up the ladder and pulled out the nails with some kind of iron tool that he carried in the belt of his tunic. He climbed a little way down the ladder and took out the nail holding the man's feet. Then, she said, with great care they lifted his body off the cross. Cradling him in their arms, they walked away, and she heard the man called Joseph whisper to the women, 'He is still alive.' At this, the women wept for joy. All of their fears seemed to be washed away with their tears, and they stood up and ran away from the place where the empty cross now stood.

"That's when the Dreamer said she woke up, and when she did, she realised she was crying, too.

"For some while no-one in the conference room spoke. The silence was complete, as if all were in shock."

Neither Jeremiah nor Sarah could quite understand what Miriam had just told them. She'd said it was a dream, but it was clear from the way she had told the story that she thought it was more than that.

"What did you make of it all?" asked Jeremiah.

"I'm not sure," said Miriam. "I've read all sorts of accounts of the crucifixion, but not one like this. I'm going to do some research, though. I want to see if anyone else has suggested such a possibility."

"How fascinating," Jeremiah said. "It could certainly add a new dimension to your work."

"It will. Anyway, Sarah tells me you've been spending a lot of time together?"

"We have," said Sarah. "We've been totally lazy, going for long walks and having leisurely lunches, and just enjoying each other's company. It's been lovely."

"I'm so pleased," said Miriam, who had got up and was now searching for something in one of her bookcases. "Do excuse me, I just need to look something up."

And so it was that Miriam was home, but her mind was elsewhere.

After they'd had their tea and talked a little more, Jeremiah and Sarah took their leave of Miriam and walked back to her cottage on the main village street. Sarah felt she should at least check to see if Willow had been visiting and whether she needed more food.

As they walked in the door they saw Angel standing by the window.

Sarah greeted her, surprised yet delighted by this unexpected presence in her cottage.

"So, are you always going to be with me now?" she asked.

"Yes, of course."

"Did you hear Miriam describe the dream about the crucifixion?"

"Yes."

"What did it mean?" asked Sarah, sitting on her sofa with bits and pieces of unopened post in her lap. Angel came and sat on the sofa beside her while Jeremiah flopped down into an armchair. For a moment they thought Sarah's question would not be answered. But then Angel began.

"What the woman spoke of was not a dream – it's what is called a 'remembrance'. It was the memory of something that happened long ago, over two thousand years ago. A memory that has lain hidden, waiting for someone to recall it. It's not that she was there in the dream, but rather that the memory, which was always there, came to her in her dream."

"So, what did she remember?"

"She remembered the crucifixion of Yeshua, the man

you call Jesus. And the women were the three Marys: Mary of Clopas who ran to give Joseph of Arimathea the message, Mary the mother of Yeshua and Mary Magdalene who remained behind."

"But Joseph said that Yeshua was not dead."

"He wasn't. He was unconscious, but he wasn't dead. He had to look as if he was dead, otherwise the soldiers would not have let him be taken away."

"And what was on the scroll?"

"It was signed by Pontius Pilate, the Roman governor, and it gave Joseph of Arimathea consent to remove the 'dead' body from the cross and take it away for burial."

"So… Yeshua didn't die?" asked Sarah, bemused.

"No, he didn't."

Jeremiah was frowning.

"But I thought that was the whole point of the Christian faith? His death and his resurrection… All those paintings and frescoes Angela studied were there to show Jesus dying for our sins?" he said. "That's the point, isn't it? If he didn't die, why did they say he did?"

"Everyone had to say so. Think about it. The Romans and the temple priests had to, otherwise they would have looked weak or foolish. And Mary Magdalene and the disciples had to, because otherwise Yeshua would have been pursued and killed. No-one could admit that he survived, although we knew."

"What do you mean 'we knew'?"

"The angels – we knew and we made quite a fuss about it, singing and coming as a great light to where he was."

"And where was he?"

"He was taken in an ox-cart by Joseph and two other men to a nearby Essene community. He stayed there for the night, and the community cared for him. But then, once he had regained consciousness, he was taken to a place where he could be safely hidden away, just for a few days. The Essenes were great healers and herbalists and it was they who had provided the drugged water in the sponge. In time, and for a short while Yeshua went to Galilee, where he met his disciples, but then he fled north to Antioch, now known as the city of Antakya in Turkey, and then, further still, well beyond the reach of the Romans, well beyond the reach of the priests of the temple."

"What happened to him?" asked Sarah.

"I cannot tell you that."

"Why not?"

"I may not speak of it."

Sarah and Jeremiah could hardly take it all in.

It was getting late, and Angel disappeared from view. Sarah was still getting used to this phenomenon. Eventually, Jeremiah stood up, saying that he too needed to get home. He'd suddenly become very tired.

"Well," he said, "It's not every day that you discover that a huge part of our cultural heritage is not true, but then, as you'll find out Sarah, Angel does have a habit of saying things that are incredulous."

"I'm still trying to come to terms with finding my angel and taking part in a sacred marriage," chuckled Sarah, "let alone a complete rewriting of Christianity! I can still hardly take it all in."

"Me neither," said Jeremiah, "but we must let Miriam know what Angel has said about the Dreamer's dream being a remembrance. I think she will find it fascinating, don't you?"

"Yes, of course we must. I'll tell her when I see her tomorrow. And what shall I tell her about us?"

"Let us tell her together. We will know when the time is right."

Jeremiah and Sarah continued to spend more and more time together, just enjoying being in each other's company, and what had been a quiet, gentle companionship began to blossom into great love – not one that they felt the need to shout about from the rafters, nor one that needed anyone else's validation, more a deepening of joy in each other, a deepening of respect and gratitude.

Nonetheless, Sarah wanted to tell her son Nicholas that she had met someone and fallen in love, and with Jeremiah's agreement she was about to phone him and tell him. They had agreed she would not mention the sacred marriage that Angel had bestowed upon them, nor Angel either – Sarah could just imagine the raised eyebrows and rolling of the eyes – but, in a desire to be truthful and honest with her son in a way that perhaps she'd not been before, it was important to Sarah that Nick should know of her love for Jeremiah.

She picked up the phone and dialled his number in Dublin. Chloe answered.

"Hello Chloe How lovely to hear your voice – it's

Sarah here. How are you all doing?"

"Oh, Sarah, hang on, I'll get Nick."

"No rush – how are you?" Sarah repeated.

"Oh, you know, coping."

"How are your parents?" Sarah hoped that they were still alive and that she hadn't put her foot in it.

"They're as well as can be expected, thank you. How are you, Sarah? Are you still living in the back of beyond?"

"I'm well, thank you for asking, and yes I'm…"

"Here's Nick," and she could hear Chloe muttering something and handing the phone over to her husband.

Why has she always been so short with me? thought Sarah. *Why has she never once shown any interest in her husband's mother, her daughters' grandmother…?*

"Hello, Mum – what's the matter?"

"Nothing, love – nothing at all. I just phoned for a chat. How are you all?"

"Oh, you know, surviving," said Nick with a sigh.

It doesn't sound like it to me, thought Sarah. *It sounds as if you're all as miserable as sin* – but she didn't say that aloud.

"What about you Mum? How are you doing?"

"I'm very good, Nick. That's what I'm ringing for, actually. I want you to know that I've met someone."

There was silence on the other end of the phone, and despite the distance between them, Sarah could feel her son tense up.

"What do you mean, 'met someone'?"

"I've met a man, called Jeremiah. He lives in the village and over the last few months, we have become very close. I just wanted you to know, and I'd love you all to come over to Elmsford and meet him one day."

"I don't know about that... What about Dad?"

"What about Dad? Nick, darling, your father passed away more than 20 years ago. I'm not being disrespectful to his memory, if that's what you mean?"

"You are to me. It's not right, it's not fair on Dad."

"Nicholas! Honestly, are you telling me that if anything happened to Chloe – God forbid – that you would never seek another partner, another lover?"

"Bloody hell, Mother, spare me the details! And to answer your question, no, I wouldn't."

"You say that Nick, but you don't know what it's like to be left alone, to be bereft." Sarah was thinking of James, not her husband.

"Look, Mum, I suppose what you do with your life is your affair. It's none of my business, but don't expect me to approve."

"I've come to expect nothing of you Nicholas, and you've given me absolutely nothing in return. Now, what about Bryony coming for a visit? Will you at least allow that?"

"Certainly not. Not now I know you're shacked-up with some bloke in the village."

"I'm not shacked..."

"I have to go, Mum. I can't speak now. I'll ring you another time."

And he put the phone down.

Sarah slipped to the floor, tears welling in her eyes.

Is it like this for all mothers and sons? she asked herself. She remembered the little boy who used to look up and smile at her so adoringly. Where had he gone? Was it her fault he had become so aloof?

Sarah put on her coat and walked down the road to Jeremiah's house. She found him in the back garden attempting to prune the wisteria.

"Just in time," he laughed as he saw her. "You've saved me from sacrificing this beauty in my ignorance." He put down his secateurs and embraced Sarah, but at once felt her pain. "What's wrong?"

Bursting into tears, Sarah told him all about the phone call with her son. "He won't even let me see my granddaughter," she sobbed.

"Oh darling, I'm so sorry. It sounds like it was all a bit of a shock for him?"

"But why can't he be happy for me? Why do I always feel like I'm a failure in his eyes?"

"It is because he can't see you for who you really are. To him, you're 'Mum', not a woman in your own right. And look, there's really nothing stopping you and I from having a holiday in Dublin and taking Bryony and Iris out for lunch, is there?"

That made her sob even louder.

At that moment, Angel appeared, her wings outstretched and shimmering. She knelt before Sarah and gazed up into her eyes and held them.

"Your son is stuck, Sarah, and he has been for quite some time. He is stuck in the mud of his relationship, and he is wallowing in his self-pity. One day he may find that the mud is the most fertile place to be. If the lotus were not anchored in the mud of the lily pond, it would not be able to reach for the sun and come into bloom. Your son's trajectory is his own, his lessons are his own. Do not berate yourself, for these are the lessons he was born into this world to experience. His angel will guide him when he opens his eyes to see."

Sarah dried her eyes on her handkerchief and reached out again for Jeremiah, who embraced her and held her for a long while.

Eventually, she said, "Oh Angel, how did I ever survive without you?"

One morning a few weeks later, Sarah rang Jeremiah to ask if he would like to go for a walk with her and Miriam.

"I've noticed she's been closeted in her house for a couple of weeks, working on something, and I haven't been able to get her to take a break. If I tell her you're coming for a walk, she might come with us. How about we meet up at her house?"

The autumnal morning was warm and cloudless with only a gentle breeze as Jeremiah climbed the steep steps up to the churchyard and then across the short-mown grass to the wooded footpath that led to The Sanctuary, where he found Sarah and Miriam sitting on the veranda of Miriam's house ready for the walk. They'd both put on their walking shoes and waved as they saw him.

"Right, where shall we go?" said Miriam, in her usual forthright manner.

"Let's walk up the coast to the north," said Sarah.

"Okay, and then we can circle back to the house through the woodland," said Miriam.

They set off, Miriam walking ahead, apparently deep in thought, Sarah and Jeremiah following behind, hand in hand, as they'd become accustomed to. After a while, they came to a small rocky cove surrounded by sheer cliffs tufted here and there with grasses and lichens. On the pebble beach was a weathered tree trunk, horizontal and a silver grey in colour, which must have been washed up by a high tide. Miriam arrived first and sat on the trunk, waiting for Jeremiah and Sarah to catch up.

"I love this beach," she said. "I can see it from my bedroom window. And when the wind is in the west, I can hear the waves crashing on the shore."

"I have come to love it too," said Jeremiah. "It's so rugged, so wild. It takes my breath away," and he walked down to the water's edge and stood there for a while, picking up pebbles and examining the lines of white quartz that ran through them. He did indeed love this dramatic landscape, the pebbled beach, the open expanse of bay embraced to the north and south by rugged cliffs, and the vast dome of the sky. He breathed in deeply, feeling immense gratitude for being where he was. Eventually, he turned to see Miriam, and Sarah talking easily between themselves.

"Come on Jeremiah, we're heading back," Miriam called to him.

They turned inland down a lane and back through woodland, now walking one behind the other.

At The Sanctuary, Miriam brought out a bottle of rosé wine, a reminder of the Languedoc, and a plate of cheese, oatcakes and sliced tomatoes. They sat on the veranda, Miriam, taking one of the rattan armchairs and Jeremiah and Sarah sitting on cushions on the steps, their backs leaning against the veranda posts. A breeze was now coming off the sea, with the distant sound of seagulls and the turning of waves.

"So, what have you been working on, Miriam?" asked Jeremiah. "Sarah says you've been busy."

Miriam smiled.

"I have, and she has been very patient with me. It's just that sometimes, when I'm trying to work something out, I become obsessed with it; I can't let it go. I stay up day and night, scared that if I stop, I'll lose the thread altogether."

"And what might you lose this time?"

Miriam gave a deep sigh.

"I'm completely taken up by the idea of *The Book of Love.* It started when Sarah and I first went to France together last Christmas, but it came up again while I was in Chartres. The book has never been found. Some say that it was lost, and others say that it never existed and that the Magdalene herself embodied the 'book' as she continued to teach Yeshua's gospel of Love. They say that when she died the teachings fell silent, but that they were brought back to life by the Cathars twelve hundred years later, before being violently suppressed as heresy by the Catholic Church. Some have even suggested that secret texts were buried in the cellars and crypts of Chartres cathedral. Whatever happened, the written teachings in the form of a book have never been found, but I have this idea that nonetheless, the Magdalene's teachings have remained hidden deep within our subconscious, waiting to be recovered. It is an idea that has all but consumed me."

"So, let me get this right," Jeremiah scratched his head. "You're saying that there wasn't an actual book, but that in a way, Mary was the book?"

"Sort of. Angelique and I don't agree on this," said Miriam. "She believes there was a book, and so she is trying to uncover where it might have been taken to, where it might be found. Whereas I don't think she will find it, because I don't believe it ever existed.

"The story the Dreamer told at the conference in Chartres was like a revelation to me, and it helped me to realise how misguided I have been with all my research and studies. How it is simply 'Love', the practice of Love, the embodiment of Love, that lays at the heart of the teachings of Yeshua. That Love is all there is.

"What excites me now is how the application of Love, practically and at the very heart of our culture is not only relevant but essential to resolving the problems we face today – you know, climate change, racial and ethnic intolerance, poverty and all forms of violence. I want to encourage people to take Love seriously."

"Phew. So, are you going to write a new *Book of Love*?" Sarah felt slightly alarmed at the enormity of such a project.

"That's just it – I'm not sure. I'm thinking that perhaps it will not be a book, but a place where people can come to find Love, to learn about the true meaning of Love, a School of Love, perhaps."

"But how on earth will you do that?" asked Jeremiah, bemused.

"I don't know. That's my problem. That's why I have been hiding away for the past few weeks."

"Where do you even start with a project like that?" asked Sarah.

"That's what I am trying to figure out. I want to know as much as I can about the teachings of Love from all cultures and all spiritual traditions, and I want to share that exploration with as many people as possible. I want to see what people are doing in practice, which means the application of Love as the foundation of all that we do. And there is something else I want to explore, too."

"And that is?"

"The world of virtual space and time, but not the digitised version humanity has created... I am interested in the information that is stored in the Akashic Records, the original internet."

"Ah, the Akashic realm…" Jeremiah mused.

"You know of it?" Miriam was obviously surprised.

"A friend once spoke to me of it."

But Miriam's imagination was sparking, and she was not open to hearing more from Jeremiah on the subject, not at that moment. Instead, she said, "Well, just think about it. If Mary Magdalene didn't have a book, what did she have? She had memories. Memories of the teachings she heard Yeshua speak. She had to rely on her memory, and then she had to share that memory with everyone she met, and they too had to remember it. If I am right, and if Mary's teachings are held within memory, within our deepest consciousness, I'm wondering if we can, with concerted effort, bring the teachings back to life and share them once again. Whether, somehow, we can hear them for ourselves. That is what I am going to try and do. But I need to find people who can remember, like the woman at the Conference."

"Oh Miriam," said Sarah, "that is such a huge task. I'm worried you may burn yourself out with it all."

"Yes, I know. I certainly do set myself a challenge, don't I? I think I may need the help of the angels."

Jeremiah and Sarah looked at each other. For now, neither said anything.

They finished their tea and Jeremiah walked through the house to the bathroom, pausing on the way back to look at three icons that were placed on the bookcase in the hall. As he was standing there, Miriam walked in on her way to the kitchen.

"These are lovely – I've not seen them before."

Miriam stood beside him. "I've had them for some time," she said, "but they have always been placed separately. I've only just put them together like this. You see, I woke early yesterday and could not go back to sleep. I got up and went into the kitchen to make myself a cup of tea and as I was walking back to my bed, I looked at the icon of Yeshua and I knew that something was missing. He was on his own, and he should not have been on his own. It was almost as if something was guiding me to move him to the bookcase, so I did, and then I put the icon of the Madonna and the icon of Mary Magdalene either side of him, Yeshua between two Marys – to his left his mother and to his right his companion. One Mary who gave birth to him so that he could teach, and the other Mary who continued his teaching after he had gone."

"After he had gone?"

"Well, I say that because since hearing what the

woman in Chartres said, I am not sure what really did happen to him."

"You mean you think he didn't die on the cross?"

"Who knows? Will we ever know… unless we learn how to remember? But I do think she could have remembered something held in the Akashic Field."

"Ah yes, a remembrance – that is how my angel also described it."

In that precise moment, Jeremiah realised it was the perfect time to tell Miriam about Angel.

"I beg your pardon?"

"As it happens, the friend who spoke to me of the Akashic realm is an angel, called Angel."

Miriam smiled. "You too?"

"What do you mean?" Jeremiah was confused.

"My professor at Oxford, Jenny de Coeur, once told me that she had a guardian angel who she could see and talk to and who helped her. Is it like that for you?"

"Yes, that's how it is. Angel has always been with me, and he appears to me when I am most in need of guidance."

"Well lucky you. And had it not been Jenny de Coeur who first told me of the existence of angels, I would've dismissed it out of hand, but because it was Jenny and I trusted her completely, I began to consider the possibility of angels being present in our lives. But, try as I might – and I did, Jeremiah, I did try – I have never once seen an angel, and then over the years, I forgot all about the possibility of them, until now."

"And now?"

"Well, I've always known there was something different about you, Jeremiah – since the first day we met, I've known that there is a hidden side to you. And now I know what it is. You are blessed by the angels.

"Well, one at least."

"And your angel believes that the Dreamer at the conference was remembering, not dreaming. It's fascinating, isn't it? You know, for some time now the Akashic Field has been coming into my consciousness, through synchronicity and through my own research. I feel as if I'm being led towards it. As if it is the Great Cosmic Memory Bank, here long before the invention of the Internet. And now I know that your angel says the dream was a 'remembrance', my hunch is beginning to make sense; that if we can discipline this unruly mind of ours, we can remember deep into our past. We each have our own virtual memory."

"I think Angel would agree."

"Well, that would be an honour. I'm not used to receiving messages from the angels. And although as I said, I would like very much like to, I've never seen one. I've only ever been able to work with books and texts. All my work has been in my head, and I've had to dig hard for everything I've discovered. I've never had dreams or visions or angelic messages. Why do you think that is?"

Jeremiah hesitated before replying. Miriam was evidently sincere in all she did, it was just that she was… what was it…? She was unable to let go of her mind.

"Well, you knew that you had to move the icons, didn't you."

"Yes, I did..."

"And perhaps you knew you had to move them without really thinking about it?"

"Yes, that's true, too."

"So, although you say you are always governed by your head, it seems that sometimes you just 'know'. It's a bit like that with angels."

"What do you mean?"

"Well, before you can see angels, you have to believe in them, not by rational deduction, but simply because you do. It has to happen to you. Actually, it has to become you."

Miriam was listening intently. Although she could hardly imagine what Jeremiah was talking about, she somehow knew it was true. It was as if his words were rekindling a memory deep within her.

"I am so glad you have come into our lives, Jeremiah," she said. "Perhaps you can help me to meet my angel one day?"

"Perhaps," said Jeremiah. "All you really have to do is to open your heart to them."

They walked back out onto the veranda, where Sarah was still sitting.

"Jeremiah has been telling me about seeing angels," said Miriam. "It seems almost as if I would have to become a new person. Another Miriam."

"That doesn't sound so easy," said Sarah.

"No, it doesn't, but maybe it would be worth it?"

Jeremiah looked at Sarah and she nodded.

"Actually, he said, "there is something else that Sarah and I want to share with you."

"I do hope it has to do with angels," said Miriam.

"Well, there were certainly angels involved," said Sarah. "Do you remember that while you were at the conference in Chartres, I stayed with Jeremiah?"

'I do. I hope you two haven't been misbehaving?"

"No, of course not, but something did happen. And it explains why Jeremiah and I have become so close."

Miriam had noticed this and wondered about it.

And so Sarah told her about meeting Angel in Appledore and then what had happened in the church, about the host of angels, and about their sacred marriage and what it meant to them; that it was based upon divine tenderness and souls entwined; how it felt like a kind of fulfilment, a completion, and how it had changed their lives.

As the story unfolded, Miriam became quiet and deeply contemplative. She wondered if Sarah and Jeremiah's story was, in fact, the embodiment of everything she had been searching for; if it was this that was at the heart of the Magdalene's *Book of Love*. Was this the love that Yeshua had spoken of, the love that entwined him with the Magdalene – was this Divine Tenderness?

When Sarah had finished speaking, she took Miriam's hand in hers and held it there.

That evening, the three friends had supper together. Sitting around the table in Miriam's house, they spoke with a new kind of intimacy of the things they held most dear – of their love for one another and the adventures that they were now embarked upon.

"Like Mary Magdalene in her rudderless boat," said Miriam, "trusting the Divine to take us where she will. Acceptance. Surrender."

"So be it," said Jeremiah.

"So be it," said Sarah.

EPILOGUE

Winter came, and in the half-light weeks leading up to Christmas, Miriam and Sarah saw each other nearly every day, and Jeremiah was often with them, for he and Sarah were seldom apart now. It was during this time that Sarah noticed how Miriam had set her books aside. When they visited, instead of finding Miriam working in her study, there would often be a scrap of paper pinned to her door saying: 'Gone for a walk!' Or when she and Jeremiah went for a walk themselves, they would find her down at the little beach beside the harbour, looking for interesting pebbles along the tide line. Miriam's 'small madness', the turning in on herself when she returned from the conference in Chartres had gone and she seemed to be at ease.

On Christmas morning, Sarah and Jeremiah visited her with a basket of presents and some good wine. They found her sitting on her veranda wrapped in a huge shawl, gazing out over the sea to the horizon.

"Happy Christmas," said Jeremiah, placing his hands on her shoulders and bending to kiss her cheek.

"Happy Christmas, you two. Isn't it a beautiful day

– it's unusual for Christmas Day to be so bright, so clear. Come and join me, won't you?"

Jeremiah and Sarah pulled up the rattan chairs and sat beside her, wrapping themselves in the blankets that Miriam had put on each seat.

"Over the last week or two, I've been reflecting on what has been happening to me." Miriam turned towards them. "You see," she said, her voice quiet but firm, "one of the things I have learnt again and again from being here in Elmsford but particularly from you both, from what you have taught me, is that what I am trying to understand and write about cannot be found in books, it cannot be found in schools, nor conferences, in things that other people have said, nor in the places where other people live. It can only be found where we are – where 'I Am'."

Sarah began to smile, her whole body relaxing.

"For all my studying, I now know that Love isn't something you discover in the Akashic realms, or even remember or dream of. Love is what is present in your life; it is what you create. Love is who I am, and I am enough."

Sarah smiled. *At last*, she said to herself, *you're here. At last.*

"And let me tell you something," said Miriam, "in all my scholarship and reading, all I find is words. But when I am with you two, none of that matters. Your lives are full of love. I was beginning to come to this conclusion some time ago, but then I was distracted by our visit to Arques and by all those exciting conversations with Angelique. You see, she has the same problem. She supposes, as I did, that *The Book of*

Love is a book. And when you believe this, you are trapped by trying to find out where it is, where it is hidden, or whether it has been destroyed and what is in it. But, *The Book of Love* was not written down, it was spoken. There is such a book, but we have all been looking for it in the wrong place."

"Where is it, then?"

"Everywhere – it is everywhere! It is in the worm that sacrifices itself to the blackbird, it is in the way a mother feeds her children before herself, it is in the laughter and friendship of Christmas mornings… And that is why the Catholic Church were so frightened by it, and why the Protestants couldn't abide it. After all, if it had just been a book, they could have found it and burnt it. But they knew that it wasn't. Although they dared not admit it, when they looked about them, they knew Love was there in the meadows and the forests, along the beaches and in the flowing tides. And, fortunately, poets, prophets and wise women knew this too. Only they were able to keep these teachings alive, but they did.

"If God is Love and Love is everywhere, then why do we need priests and confession and the forgiveness of our sins? Why do we need them to intercede for us? And, of course, the fact that this truth had been spoken by a woman made it worse for them. It had to be stopped. So, they burnt the 'witches' and slaughtered the 'heretics.'"

"But it wouldn't go away, would it?" said Sarah.

"No, it wouldn't go away. And it still remains."

"And here it is," said Jeremiah. "Here, with us."

"Yes, that's right, that's exactly it – Love has been

waiting for me all these years. And that is what you, my dear Sarah, and you my dear Jeremiah, have awakened me to. That is how you have helped me."

"And we had the help of the angels," said Sarah. "Let us not forget the angels."

"Here's to the angels," said Miriam, raising her glass of brandy. "And to one day meeting mine."

Sarah smiled at Miriam, knowing that at last she'd found the missing piece of the puzzle. She reached out for Miriam's hand and kissed it.

"Welcome home," she said.

On a warm and calm afternoon in late April, Sarah and Jeremiah decided to go for a swim at high tide. It was the first swim of the year for Jeremiah, though Sarah had taken the plunge a couple of times with the Elderberries, earlier in the month.

Sarah was sitting on the harbour wall in the sunshine, having changed out of her wet costume, whilst Jeremiah was searching in his rucksack for the thermos of tea. There was not another soul in sight, apart from the oystercatchers.

"Isn't it wonderful that we both love to swim?" said Sarah.

"It's a passion I rediscovered late in life," Jeremiah replied, pouring them each a cup of tea, "but to swim with you, here in this beautiful bay... well it is like a dream come true for me. I feel... I feel at one with life, at last. I can still hardly comprehend how my life has transformed. I feel like a totally different man to the Jeremiah who lived in London and didn't know what to do with himself."

As they sat there, Angel appeared before them and then, behind Angel a whole host of angels gathered, golden white and shimmering as if suspended on sunbeams.

The appearance of angels no longer shocked Sarah. She turned and smiled at Jeremiah remembering the time when Angel had led them both to the church to proclaim their sacred marriage.

"So, here we are again," said Sarah, "together in the presence of angels."

"We feel the entwining of your souls, the Twin Flame," said Angel. "It draws us near you."

Sarah looked at Jeremiah.

"So, this who we are, Jeremiah," she said. "Entwined souls. I think it's rather wonderful."

"I think so, too."

"I wonder why it took us so long to find each other?"

Jeremiah pondered for a moment.

"Perhaps it was to do with the way I was, or rather who I was before I came here. I was so fearful of being true to myself, so fearful of the judgement of others and that made me frustrated and resentful. And though I have always had Angel to help me, it took me a long time to accept the truth of who I am."

"Well, I spent a long time being someone else, too – being 'the good wife' – and it was only when I came here, and got to know James, then Miriam and now you, that I have become who I am. The truth of it is that I couldn't have done this until now."

"Perhaps as Angel once said to me, the timing is always perfect?" Jeremiah looked at Angel who had become strangely transparent.

"Indeed the timing is always perfect my dear ones," Angel said. "All is now perfect."

Jeremiah got up and helped Sarah to her feet. They embraced and as they did so, the golden angelic light enveloped them, and time stood still.

"We will always be together now." Sarah stood on tiptoe and kissed Jeremiah tenderly.

"We will."

"And we have dear Angel to take care of us," she added.

"Or perhaps," said Jeremiah, taking Sarah's hand, "we can now take care of ourselves?"

They looked about them, but Angel was nowhere to be seen. They did not know it then, but Angel's work was done.

Printed in Great Britain
by Amazon

75103343R00300